Rachel Lee was hooked on writing by the age of twelve and practised her craft as she moved from place to place all over the United States. This *New York Times* bestselling author now resides in Florida and has the joy of writing full-time.

Lena Diaz was born in Kentucky and has also lived in California, Louisiana and Florida, where she now resides with her husband and two children. Before becoming a Heroes author, she was a computer programmer. A Romance Writers of America Golden Heart® Award finalist, she has also won the prestigious Daphne du Maurier Award for Excellence in Mystery/Suspense. To get the latest news about Lena, please visit her website, lenadiaz.com

Also by Rachel Lee

Also by Lena Diaz

Discover more at millsandboon.co.uk

CONARD COUNTY: TRACES OF MURDER

RACHEL LEE

DEADLY DOUBLE-CROSS

LENA DIAZ

MILLS & BOON

First Published in Great Britain 2021
by Mills & Boon, an imprint of HarperCollins*Publishers* Ltd
1 London Bridge Street, London, SE1 9GF

www.harpercollins.co.uk

HarperCollins*Publishers*
1st Floor, Watermarque Building,
Ringsend Road, Dublin 4, Ireland

Conard County: Traces of Murder © 2021 Susan Civil-Brown
Deadly Double-Cross © 2021 Lena Diaz

ISBN: 978-0-263-28337-2

0521

MIX
Paper from
responsible sources
FSC™ C007454

This book is produced from independently certified FSC™ paper to ensure responsible forest management.

For more information visit: www.harpercollins.co.uk/green

Printed and bound in Spain
by CPI, Barcelona

CONARD COUNTY: TRACES OF MURDER

RACHEL LEE

To my daughter who deserves angel's wings.

Chapter One

On a gray day, Hillary Kristiansen stood on a windswept hill in Conard County, Wyoming. She faced a gravestone, holding yellow roses in her hand.

Brigid L. Mannerly, United States Army
Bravely served
Bravely died for her country.

"Brigid," she murmured, grief welling up in her. She hadn't known Brigid for all that long, but from the moment Hillary had met her, they had bonded like sisters. Brigid's death had carved a deep, dark hole in Hillary's heart.

It seemed like a lifetime ago that they'd made promises to visit one another at home when they both got leave at the same time. Now this was the only way Hillary could keep her promise. Standing beside a cold grave.

Blinking back salty tears, Hillary squatted and laid the roses on Brigid's grave. A small token of a friendship that should have spanned decades.

The chilly autumn wind bit her cheeks, a harbinger of the coming winter, but Hillary scarcely noticed. She was accustomed to a far frostier climate.

Closing her eyes, she thought of Norwegian mountains, covered with snow, tipped with glaciers. Thought of how she had promised that she would take Brigid cross-country skiing, teasing her about how slowly she would move at first, how she wouldn't be able to keep up. How Brigid had gamely replied that she'd give Hillary a run for her money. They'd both known that wouldn't be possible, but it had stolen none of the fun from their teasing.

So many possibilities buried beneath a blanket of dirt sodded over with brown grass. It wasn't the first time Hillary had suffered such a loss, but this one was somehow worse. Her friend, her sister.

A small American flag tipped near the gravestone, and Hillary reached out to straighten it and plant it more firmly. Brigid had earned every bit of that respect.

KIA. Killed in action. Every soldier knew it was possible, but few thought about it until those left behind faced the reality of each new empty place in a unit. Gone. Never to return. Then necessity required them to shrug it off. To believe they were somehow immune.

Until the nightmares began.

Gradually Hillary became aware of someone standing at the next gravesite. She wanted to ignore the stranger, didn't want his intrusion into her private grief.

Then he spoke. "You knew Brigid?"

That brought her to her feet, and she pivoted to see a tall man, his build bespeaking steel, his face bearing the scar of a single knife slash. Recognition awoke deep within. He was a soldier, too.

"Yes," she answered. "Afghanistan." She looked at Brigid's grave again. Some rose petals had loosened and wafted away on the wind. Apropos. *Fly away, Brigid.*

She spoke again. "Do you know her husband? I was thinking about calling, if he wouldn't mind."

A pause. Then a gut punch in the form of taut words. "Allan is dead, too."

He pointed to the gravestone next to Brigid's. "Two months ago. They say it was suicide."

Hillary's heart clenched as she absorbed the shock, as she sensed that this man didn't believe it was suicide at all.

"Herregud," she whispered. "Good God."

His face hardened. "I came here to visit them both. We were friends since childhood."

She met his gaze, seeing eyes as gray as the sky overhead. "That is a shame."

He gave a sharp nod. "Definitely." Then he paused. "You sound British."

"My mother."

He looked down at the stones again. "Let me buy you a coffee. We're going to freeze out here."

She doubted she'd freeze, but the invitation was welcome. They could talk about Brigid, about Allan. About all that had happened. She needed that, and she suspected he did, too.

He held out his hand. "Apologies. I'm Trace Mullen."

"Hillary Kristiansen," she answered as she returned his shake.

They walked side by side to the parking lot, she in her dark wool slack suit and a light jacket, he in jeans with an open peacoat. His bare head displayed short dark hair, almost black. Around here, she thought, her own tightly cropped, pale blond hair probably stood out, flying in the face of her training. She wished for a watch cap.

In her rental, Hillary followed him into town, a small, quaint place she liked instantly. Brigid had spoken warmly of Conard City, of Conard County. Her heart had been here, and not just because of Allan.

Trace led the way to a small diner labeled the City Café. Inside, the booths and tables announced their age, red vinyl seats repaired in places with matching tape. A few older men had ensconced themselves in a far corner, having drawn tables together.

The two of them chose a table as far away as they could get. Some semblance of privacy.

A heavyset woman with a grumpy attitude took their coffee orders. "You'll be wanting some pie or cobbler," she said before stalking away.

Trace spoke. "That's Maude. She's a fixture, and I don't think I've ever seen her smile."

"If the coffee is good…" Hillary tried to summon a smile.

"Oh, it is. So is everything she cooks and bakes here. She's still giving Melinda's bakery a run for her money."

Casual conversation about nothing, a slow feeling out of one another.

"So," Trace said after the coffee arrived with a thud, "you're half British? You're in the British Army?"

"No. My father is Norwegian. I am Jegertroppen." The all-female unit of Special Operations.

He stared at her, raising his brows. "The Hunters. The Valkyries."

"So we are called."

"Good God. The BBC called you the toughest women in the world."

She didn't know how to answer that, especially since she wasn't feeling all that tough right then. She switched tack. "And you? Army?" It seemed a likely conclusion, given that Brigid and her husband had both been in the Army.

"One hundred and first Airborne."

She wasn't surprised. She'd sensed something about him at the cemetery, something more than *soldier*. And Brigid had mentioned her husband's unit. She spoke, using a phrase she had heard applied to the Airborne. "Death from the skies."

At that he smiled faintly. "I never had the pleasure of working with anyone from Jegertroppen."

"Just as well. I doubt it would have been an enjoyable situation." She waved generally toward the window. "Brigid talked about the mountains here."

"Probably not what you're used to."

"Depends on where you are. We have some flatlands, too. However, we did have a reason to invent the cambered ski. Long winters and a need to get around in those mountains." Surprising them both, pieces of fruit pie landed in front of them. Before they could express their gratitude, Maude had stormed off.

Trace spoke. "I guess we were offending her natural order of things."

They were also avoiding their primary concern. Hillary wondered how to divert them back to it but couldn't see a polite way. She decided to eat some berry pie and wait. Not that she felt very hungry. Her usual strenuous life had given her a healthy appetite, but grief changed everything. She pecked at the pie.

Trace didn't seem much more interested. "I heard you train with the US Navy SEALs?"

"Sometimes." Hillary shrugged it off. "For certain kinds of operations. I don't want to talk about me. Right now I'd prefer to leave that part behind. I'm here for Brigid."

"I know." He frowned slightly. "You'd better eat at least half that pie, or Maude will be insulted. Life with an insulted Maude could become complicated when you're hungry."

Then he turned his attention back. "Brigid. And Allan. Like I said, I knew them all my life. We grew up here. I won't say we never had our disagreements or that we occasionally didn't have different groups of friends. Youngsters are like that."

He looked straight at her. "But there was no one in this town less surprised than I when they decided to get married. There was an unbreakable bond between them despite the inevitable ups and downs. It always felt like destiny."

Hillary nodded, forcing herself to eat another forkful of pie, mindful of not upsetting the locals. "Did you all enlist at the same time?"

He gave a crooked smile. "Never hesitated. We talked about it for years, then did it. The Army was the first thing that separated us."

"It has a way of doing that. Physically, at any rate."

"It does. We had different paths to follow for a while. But the closeness remained. What about you and Brigid?"

"We met at an operating base. It was instant friendship." She paused. "Brigid talked a lot about Allan. She missed him every minute of every day."

"He felt the same. If they regretted anything about their choices, that was it."

Hillary put her fork down, refusing to force any more pie down her throat.

"I miss her," she said quietly. "So much." The Norwegian words came first to her tongue. *"Det er som om hjertet mitt har blitt revet ut."* Then remembering him, she translated, "I feel as if my heart has been torn out."

"Pretty much the same here."

He'd lost *two* friends, she reminded herself. Did that double the grief or just make it a hell of a lot worse? Could grief even be measured?

His somber expression matched her mood. So much pain between the two of them. Maybe she should just end this visit now. She had no comfort to offer. She doubted he did, either.

Off to their separate worlds to deal with the gaping abyss in their lives.

When he spoke again, it was another diversion. "Was it hard to make it into the Valkyries?"

"It is never easy."

"Like the women being admitted to the Rangers. No slack."

"Slack would make us useless." Undeniable. Special operations allowed no weakness. "Brigid was talking about training into spec ops."

"Allan mentioned it. She wasn't entirely happy with guarding convoys."

"Dangerous enough. Obviously." Too obviously. "Allan?"

"He wasn't exactly thrilled with the idea, but he never would have interfered." Trace paused a few beats. "Did Brigid tell you? Allan was invalided out, discharged for medical reasons. Too much shrapnel in dangerous places, and they couldn't remove it. Near his heart. Threatening his spine. He hated it."

"I can imagine."

"But he felt the greatest pride in Brigid. He wouldn't have dishonored her."

Then Trace leaned forward and lowered his voice. "Someone killed him."

Chapter Two

The words tasted like ashes as they left Trace's mouth. He could see the shock ripple through Hillary and waited for her to argue with him. To turn away and go back to her life. How could she possibly believe him? How could he possibly explain?

Outwardly, she remained impassive. "Why do they think he committed suicide?"

"Post-traumatic stress compounded by grief."

She nodded. "Makes sense."

"Of course it makes sense. It fits right in with the easy explanation. The too-obvious one."

"Okay. But why don't you believe it?"

"Because he wasn't one to give up. Because he told me he'd get through it. Because he and Brigid had promised each other not to do it. I've known Allan my entire life. He never broke a promise."

She looked away, staring out the window, absorbing, evaluating. As difficult as it had been to speak the words out loud, it must be equally difficult for her to accept them. Plus, she hadn't known Allan. How could she judge?

She sighed after a bit and returned her gaze to him. The pale blue eyes so often found in Nordic people. The pale, pale blond hair. High cheekbones, an athletic body trimmed by constant training. A very attractive woman.

He brushed the thought aside. Not the time. He had more important matters on his mind. Allan. His friend for over thirty years. A man who had never bent to anything. Who'd never been broken. Not even his wife's death could have made him give up the fight. *I'll get through this.* The words were stamped in Trace's mind. He'd never doubted them, even though Allan had begun to drink heavily.

Hillary drew a deep breath, searching his face. "You're saying he was murdered."

The ugly word hung on the air, a word he'd never allowed himself to say. *Killed*, yes. But murdered? No. Though it was the same thing.

"Do you have any ideas?" Hillary asked. "Enemies he might have had?"

"None that I'm aware of."

She shook her head slightly. "Then who? Why?"

"I'm going to figure that out. I swear. I owe it to him. To Brigid. This is a stain on my friend's memory, and if there's any way I can prove it, I will."

She appeared to understand that. Now she nodded slightly.

"Let's get out of here," he said abruptly. "I don't know about you, but I can't sit still for too long. My body requires activity."

SHE FULLY UNDERSTOOD THAT. Muscles so finely honed needed to move. Sitting on a plane for a long flight could be a form of torture, causing her to twitch, tightening every muscle until it could relax again. People who sat next to her must often be annoyed.

He tossed money on the table and led the way outside. Standing in the endless wind, concentrated by the narrow street, she once again felt the bite of cold.

"Are you going to stay in town for a while?"

"I had thought a few days."

"You gonna be warm enough?" he asked. "I'm thinking about taking a long walk, maybe do some running, if you'd like to."

She'd have liked to say she was fine but faced reality. There was nothing to be gained by toughing this out, even for a few days. "Yes, a jacket would be nice. I didn't bring one." Because she hadn't expected to be here long enough to care. Because she was on her way to warmer climates.

"Let's go to the Mercantile. We'll find something you like well enough."

She looked down at her feet, glad she'd at least worn her boots. Pretty shoes didn't usually fit in her wardrobe, although she had a pair of sandals in her suitcase back at the airport for her impending trip to the South of France. No good here.

He led her around a corner and down a street to a large, old building. Surprisingly few people were about on the streets, but to everyone they met Trace gave a nod.

The Mercantile held the musty smell of an old building. Wooden floors creaked beneath their feet. Trace led her to a section of women's clothing. Part of her resented that, because she often bought men's clothing, and part of her recognized that she needed something to fit her smaller frame. None of the frilly stuff, though, and she hated pink.

Her first choice was the watch cap she'd thought of earlier. Then she found a white and navy down vest that fit well enough, followed by a dark blue windproof winter jacket. Layers.

Insulated gloves as well. She paid with a credit card, asked the clerk to remove all the tags then pulled on her new acquisitions. "Ready."

He nodded. They strode out of the store with purpose,

nearly a march, and took a turn toward the nearer mountains. Their pace was brisk, determined. This was necessary exercise, not a casual stroll.

Unconsciously they fell in step, their strides matching perfectly. Training. Practice. Custom.

As the ground began to rise a mile or so beyond town, Hillary felt ready to run. Rising land beneath her feet was always a cue. But her run wasn't all-out. It was measured for maximum endurance. Long runs couldn't be taken at top speed.

She felt light as a feather without her full complement of combat gear. This was easy, maybe too easy. Trace trotted alongside her. Before long, their breathing became as synchronized as their footfalls.

The slope continued to steepen, but not so much it was a serious challenge. The road became dirt, easier on the knees than pavement, but harder on the ankles because it was uneven. Pine scents filled the air. A few late wildflowers dotted the roadside.

When at last they reached the top of a rise, Trace called a halt. "Stretched out?" he asked.

"For now." Turning, she looked back down toward the valley and saw the town, resembling a model that could have fit in a display case. Then she looked at Trace. He was no more out of breath than she.

"How," she asked, "do you intend to find this killer?"

"I haven't the foggiest idea. Allan and Brigid left me their house. I haven't wanted to go in there yet, but it's crossed my mind I might find a clue. A direction. Or maybe the grapevine will whisper in my ear."

He sighed heavily and paced, bending occasionally to stretch. Hillary followed suit. Her jacket was plenty warm, as was her vest beneath it, and the run had heated her legs.

His plan was amorphous. Clutching at straws. Not that she blamed him, not when he thought Allan had been murdered.

No one could leave that alone.

But it didn't seem like there was any good starting point. A quixotic quest?

He spoke again. "How did your parents meet?"

The question surprised her, coming out of the blue. Another diversion from the impossible?

"My mother's father was the British ambassador to Norway. They met at an official function and married rather quickly. I was born quickly, too."

He stared out over the valley. "This doesn't sound like a happy ending."

"It wasn't," she admitted. "They separated when I was eight. Mother went back to England, and I chose to stay with my father. Of course, I visited my mother every summer and some holidays, but I was Norwegian in my own mind. In my heart."

"Not a bad thing to be. What does your father do?"

"Army special operations," she answered simply.

"So it runs in the family?"

"It does now."

That brought a smile to his face, and she was glad to see it. Grieving didn't preclude moments of amusement or even happiness. Not that she was feeling either right then.

"What are you going to do?" she asked again.

"Damned if I know. When we get back, let's go to their house. I can't think of anywhere else to start looking for clues. Especially since the whole damned town believes Allan offed himself."

She was agreeable, if only to help him over the emotional bump he was likely to face when he entered that house. He'd already said he was avoiding it. Memories must swarm there, ready to sting him like wasps.

Jogging uphill hadn't been difficult, but running back down was easier and brought them both to a quickened pace. The sound of their thudding feet, perfectly in time, felt so familiar to Hillary that tension unwound in her and deep relaxation followed. When they reached the town again, Trace suggested dropping by Maude's, as he called the City Café, to recover their parked cars and pick up some food.

"We're going to need it after that run. Any preferences?"

"Fish, but I didn't see that on the menu. You choose."

The town was a bit busier now, and Hillary noticed the stares she received. She tried to return them all with a smile but figured by nightfall everyone was going to be wondering who she was.

Well, let them wonder. She just didn't want them to know the extent of her military background. That would probably raise a whole lot of questions. Not that she cared about the questions. She'd be gone tomorrow or the next day, and they could all enjoy speculating.

Except that her desire to go back to her original plans was fading in the face of Trace's concerns. What if Allan *hadn't* died by suicide? What if there was still something she needed to do for Brigid?

The question hung over her now, darker than the sky overhead.

MAUDE RAISED AN eyebrow over the size of Trace's order, but she was probably wondering if he meant to eat it all himself. He didn't bother explaining that two people who had just finished fifteen road miles needed to fuel up.

Jegertroppen, huh? A truly elite group. Trace hadn't let himself really think about that before, but he was impressed. He knew the kind of training he'd undergone to become Airborne, and he suspected hers had been as extreme. Up and down those Norwegian mountains in full battle kit, running or skiing. And that was just the beginning. They might well have taught the SEALs a thing or two.

Hillary waited in her rental outside, and he supposed her eyebrows were raising like Maude's as he stepped out with four plastic bags filled to the brim and a tray of four hot coffees.

He manhandled them into his vehicle and drove slowly with her right behind him. Allan and Brigid had had a tidy little house at the western end of town, where most of the houses began to spread away from each other, leaving a nice-size lawn. Looking at it, he decided he really needed to get out the lawn mower. Thus far he'd paid a couple of guys to do the job, but it appeared they hadn't been here in a few weeks. Not that there was much left to do. The grasses were turning brown and yellow in the face of the approaching winter. Still, a few green blades poked up bravely, reaching for sunlight that was getting too thin and watery.

Or maybe he'd just let it go. Before long even the bravest greenery would give up the fight.

Hillary was quick to help him carry the bags as he approached the front door with the tray of coffees. His steps grew heavier as he drew closer. The last time he'd entered, Allan had been there. That damn house was going to feel so very empty.

Not only were his steps heavier, but so was his heart. The ache in his chest grew tighter, like a band that wanted to suffocate him. This wasn't his first loss, but this one was closer. Much closer.

He fumbled the key from his pocket and pushed it into

the lock. A bit rusty, it resisted slightly but then turned. He pushed open the door.

The house smelled stale now. Even the cleaning fluids from the people he'd hired to remove the stains of Allan's death had evaporated into nothing. Empty. Every sense in his body noticed.

Hillary followed him, her watch cap shoved into a pocket. Her steps sounded gentler, as if she felt she trod upon holy ground. He turned. "Let's put these bags in the kitchen."

She followed him. The counters had gathered some dust, but not enough that he felt inclined to wipe it away. Everything was familiar. Too familiar. He didn't think he could bear to go into the living room, where he, Allan and Brigid had spent so many hours. The kitchen was bad enough.

Beers at that table. Brigid or Allan sometimes pulling something sweet and tasty out of the fridge. But mostly it had been pretzels and nuts. Their own private little bar.

He sighed, heard the break in his breath. He'd seen and felt plenty of sorrow over the years, but Allan was different.

"We can go somewhere else," Hillary said.

He shook his head. "Time to face up to it all."

They ate out of foam containers because Trace didn't want to see the familiar dishes. A bit at a time, he told himself. Just one step at a time.

When Hillary sat across from him at the table, the air seemed to clear a bit. As if her mere presence were changing a mood, an aura. Relief eased the iron band around his chest.

She asked, "This is your house now?"

"Yes. I don't know that I'd ever want to live here, though."

She reached for an onion ring. "I'm not sure I would, either."

Food, he reminded himself. Eat. That run had felt good,

but it required fuel. He'd eaten in the worst conditions. He could manage it now.

Food helped, bringing him back from the precipice. As his stomach filled and his cells responded, his mind responded, too, lifting his mood somewhat. He realized that Hillary's presence was not only changing the aura in here, but it was recreating his mental image of this room. Earlier memories gave way a bit to this new one.

He watched her look around the kitchen, as if she were trying to imagine Brigid in the room. He wondered if he should tell her that none of the three of them had been into cooking. When they gathered, it was almost always with takeout. Subs or frozen pizza from the grocery, baked goods from Melinda's, big meals from Maude's. Time spent down at Mahoney's Bar, eating fried chicken over tall, icy glasses of draft beer.

"Ah, hell," he said quietly.

Hillary looked up from the onion rings she was working on. "Memories?"

"Of course. Good ones, but now they'll be only memories."

She shoved food his way. "As you said, we need food after that run. And there'll be another run before this day is over. Eat up, soldier."

That dragged a smile from him. "Feeling antsy?"

"Antsy?" She frowned at the word.

"As in restless. Fidgety."

She nodded. "All that training. I'm not exhausted yet."

"We'll work on that." But he also knew that while she might feel antsy right then, her training had taught her to remain as still as an ice statue when necessary. A different kind of tension.

He reached for half a club sandwich. Time to answer necessity.

OUTSIDE, STAN WITHERSPOON stood wondering. Who was that woman Trace Mullen had taken into the house with him?

Hanging around Conard City for the last couple of months had given him a familiarity with the local people. That woman wasn't local. He'd never have missed that tousled blond hair. There wasn't much of it since it was cut so short, but that color was remarkable.

And here he'd begun to think that he would be safe if he left this county.

He watched her carry the four big bags while Mullen carried a tray of coffees. He watched the man fish in his pocket for keys, watched him open the door, watched the woman follow.

And now they were inside, beyond his ability to see what they were doing.

Uneasiness stalked him, but that was nothing new. He'd stayed here, using up a sizable chunk of his stateside rotation from his job working for a major contractor in the Middle East, because he'd been told to. The work with the contractor was tough, so the company insisted that every employee spend six months at home every few years. They didn't want any of them to "go native."

Crap. He hadn't gone native. He'd merely found a way to make money on the situation. And that money stream had been threatened. Worse, his own life was in danger because his boss in this operation would kill him if the truth got out.

He'd come to this godforsaken place explicitly to kill Allan Mannerly. For cover he used the community college as his reason for being here.

He'd been afraid of leaving before matters calmed down after Allan Mannerly's death. It hadn't taken long for the authorities to declare the death to be suicide.

Stan should have been happy with that. After all, he'd done a good enough job to mislead the authorities. As long as nothing else was suspected, Stan was in the clear. Right?

He'd decided to stay in this place because he didn't want to bug out too soon. Didn't want to draw any kind of attention, even after the verdict. Careful. He had to be careful. As he'd so often been warned.

Or maybe that was his conscience keeping him here, not the order. Regardless, he'd begun to hear that the Mullen guy didn't believe the death to be suicide. Everyone shook their heads sadly when the subject arose, Stan among them, but they thought Mullen was being affected by his grief.

"Out of his mind," some said.

God, Stan thought, walking away from the house. God. Would he have to kill that Mullen guy, too? He didn't exactly have a taste for murder, but self-protection was a higher priority.

And who the hell was that woman?

Chapter Three

After they finished eating, Hillary helped Trace store the large quantity of leftovers. Another meal at least.

"You were too generous," she told Trace.

"I guess so, but I don't do cooking, so it's all good."

"I'm not going to volunteer to cook," she said. "I have done so little in so many years that I can't guarantee edibility." Then she added a touch of humor. "I'm also unsure if I still know how to use a pot when it's not on a campfire."

He shrugged. "Being a bachelor, I was fond of the chow hall and local restaurants when I was stateside."

She imagined that Trace, like she, had spent quite a bit of time eating with friends when they weren't training or on a mission. She had a lot of good memories from such times.

But what now? she wondered as she dried her hands on a towel. There were still two cups of coffee in foam containers, and it would be rude of her to just leave it. Making a decision, she sat down once again and reached for one of the coffees.

Trace settled across from her and took the remaining beverage.

"This is awful," Trace said eventually. "You came here to visit Brigid's grave and maybe speak to Allan. Instead you find out he's dead and you meet me, a guy who is just making you sadder."

"Stop," she said mildly. "It is what it is, I believe the saying goes. I don't regret meeting you. I'm glad you told me about Allan—well, not glad, but I think you know what I mean. I needed to know, and all I can believe is that at least he's not suffering."

"Which is better than I can say for the two of us." Again that crooked, mirthless half smile. "We make a sorry pair."

"Sorry pair," she repeated. "I may have a British mother, but I'm not familiar with all colloquialisms. My mother had a proper education in all the best schools. I suspect I may have missed quite a bit of common English."

His smile widened a shade. "I bet you know more Norwegian colloquialisms than *I* ever will. *Sorry pair* means sad pair."

"Der er ugler i mosen." She looked almost impish. "There are owls in the bog."

He raised his brows. "Meaning?"

"I believe you would say something is not quite right."

That at last drew a chuckle from him. "I'd never have guessed, but that's a good description." His face tightened. "Also quite true right now."

"You sincerely believe this about Allan." It felt uncomfortable to ask, but she needed to know this conviction wasn't momentary, born from grief.

"I do," he replied. "I absolutely do. I realize you never had a chance to know him, Hillary, but I knew him all my life. Even in the midst of this, he wouldn't have quit. Drink himself into oblivion most nights? Sure. But he would have kept going. Allan didn't have quit in him."

But Allan, perhaps, had never met a grief quite this big. On the other hand, looking at Trace, she knew *he* believed it.

"Want to go for another run?" he asked abruptly.

Part of her wanted to, but part of her had to recognize her need for rest or she'd be useless to anyone tomorrow. "Jet lag," she told him. "I flew directly from Norway. I think I need a hotel."

"You might feel a little like you're on a mission if you stay in our motel. Listen, you should stay here in the guest room. That's where Allan and Brigid would have put you. If you won't be bothered by sleeping here."

"No, it won't bother me. Are you sure?"

He rose. "Absolutely. Brigid would want it. I believe there are sheets on the bed, but I'll go check, then I'll be on my way."

A short time later, after she brought in her duffel, she watched from the window as he drove away. Was he going on another run? She wished she didn't feel as if the world was beginning to spin, because she would have liked that, too.

He'd said he'd be back in the morning, and then maybe she'd discuss the kernel of an idea that was growing within her. After some time to think it over. She did very little on impulse.

Being alone gave her an opportunity, though. Hillary could wander through rooms and imagine what this house had been like when the Mannerlys had lived here. She had no clear image of Allan, except for some photos Brigid had shared, but she had a pretty good idea.

They would have laughed a lot. Brigid was usually cheerful and ready to laugh. She couldn't imagine that Allan could have been much different, at least when he was around her.

The house itself was from more than half a century ago, she guessed. The furnishings all appeared to be secondhand, in keeping with a military income. In keeping with the fact that they wouldn't be here most of the year. A sofa, a recliner, some occasional tables. There was, however, a gaping hole in the living room, which, judging by the rug and clean wall behind, had been the place where Allan had died. Unfortunately, she had seen too much to even have to imagine it.

The chair was gone, probably a match for the one that sat at an angle. Brigid's chair, she guessed, an older plaid recliner.

The TV was relatively new, however, a big flat screen on the wall over a covered fireplace. On the mantel were a DVD player, a stereo receiver and some other pieces. Unlike everything else in this house, they appeared to be relatively new. A splurge?

Heavy insulating curtains, navy blue, covered the windows. A cozy room except for the empty spot.

The master bedroom boasted a queen-size four-poster bed covered by a cheerful comforter in a splash of colors. Brigid had picked that out, she was sure. The same navy blue curtains covered the window beside the bed. All the usual furnishings.

Then she came upon an office. Battered wood desk, two office chairs, top-of-the-line computer. Naturally, the best for video calls between the two of them. Stacks of papers, filing cabinets… This was not going to be fun to look through.

The single bathroom boasted a claw-foot tub that had probably been in the house since its first day. A showerhead at the top of a long plumbing pipe. A plastic shower curtain decorated with fish swimming in the water. Matching towels.

A guest room, as large as the master bedroom, but showing less attention to detail. A double bed without a headboard against a wall. A wooden dresser, one straight-backed wooden chair. The same navy blue curtains. A polka-dot comforter in dark blue and white. Two plump pillows.

A second guest room, hardly larger than the office, with a single bed, a small cabinet and one hardwood chair. This bed had a black throw on it.

It was a house that said very little about the people who had lived here. Perhaps because they were home so rarely? Or because they didn't have time for kitsch? Or the taste for it?

Hillary swiftly unpacked the little she thought she'd need but didn't bother to take out more. She had a flight to catch the day after tomorrow.

After a hot shower, she climbed into the bed, beneath the comforter, and stared into the dark.

The kernel of her idea was beginning to crack open, to put forth tendrils. As she was drifting into sleep, those tendrils took root.

Maybe she wouldn't leave as soon as she'd anticipated.

Chapter Four

Hillary slept deeply but awoke more in keeping with Norway time. When she pulled back the curtain, she saw that night still blanketed the land.

She shrugged and went to take a shower. She expected cold water, that Trace must have shut down nearly everything, but the water was hot and welcome. She might be used to cold showers, but she still appreciated a hot one. Such a luxury.

Afterward, wrapped in the heavy fleece robe she'd brought with her, she found her way to the kitchen and started a rich, dark pot of coffee. There were some leftovers from Maude's, but the food was heavy and Norwegians preferred to eat later in the morning.

Sitting at the kitchen table, she at last felt the emptiness of this house. Her throat tightened, but she held back tears.

She spoke aloud. "You want me to do this, Brigid. I know. I know how much you loved Allan. He won't rest until the truth is known." *You won't rest.*

The last part grabbed her. Maybe visiting a grave didn't have to be her final act for a friend.

Even so, this seemed like a hopeless cause. How did Trace expect to learn anything the police hadn't? Or maybe he thought that the police simply hadn't looked because it would be so obvious to them.

He might be right about that. *Veteran with PTSD loses wife.* That could overwhelm anyone. And it would be the apparent conclusion.

Her heart was breaking for Trace, however. He'd lost so much in such a short period of time. As bad as the loss of Brigid had been for her, for Trace it had to be so much worse. Two lifelong friends in the space of less than a year.

Night still smothered the land when a rap on the door drew her attention. She never doubted it was Trace. Who else would show up at this hour?

When she opened the door, she found him standing there with two shopping bags.

"I thought you'd be awake," he remarked. "Can I come in?"

"Of course. There's coffee."

"Sounds great." He joined her in the kitchen. "I'm assuming you don't want to eat before a run?"

He was right about that. The coffee would be enough for now. "Where are we going?"

"Pretty much the same as yesterday. I like that hill. Or the side of that mountain." He flashed a short smile. "I hope you don't think I'm out of bounds, but these bags are for you."

Startled, she looked at them then at him. "What for?"

"You need some decent running clothes. So last evening I stopped by the department store, spoke to the very nice lady who helped you yesterday and asked her to judge your sizes. I hope she was right. Go ahead and look."

She felt a little embarrassed, as if she'd had to be rescued. "You shouldn't have."

"But I did. I like to have a companion to eat up the miles with me. Anyway, it's colder than yesterday, and I'm sure running in your dress slacks isn't the most comfortable way to go."

Hillary couldn't argue, so she began pulling items out of the bag. Fleece-lined pants in gray. A fleece shirt in the same. And at the bottom a silky thermal undergarment in dark blue that would cover her from neck to foot. There were also six pairs of new thermal socks.

"Good choices," she admitted. "Thank you."

"My experience counts for something, and I figured you hadn't come prepared for this. Do you want to run this morning?"

Her muscles ached for the activity. "Absolutely." She picked up the bags and headed for the bedroom. Everything fit well. No folds in the undergarment to irritate her. At least she'd brought her own boots. Breaking in a new pair meant blisters.

When she emerged, ready to go, he said, "You might want to bring your vest and watch cap. Wind's blowing down from the mountains."

She took his advice, and ten minutes later they were out the door. The first steel gray had begun to lighten the sky, but there was no promise the clouds would vanish. A bit of sun would have been welcome, but not necessary.

They left town behind them before there was much traffic and soon reached the point where the ground began to rise.

Hillary spoke, far from breathless. "Anything steeper?"

"Oh, yeah. A little farther ahead, we'll take a turn and test that mountain."

It sounded good to her. Her muscles stretched, loosening completely, ready for more. She loved the feeling of her legs devouring the miles. Her father had remarked that she was built for this. And for more, apparently, since she'd qualified for the Jegertroppen.

When they turned, they were no longer on the dirt road.

It became a treacherous track, probably carved by off-road vehicles. By people out for some fun.

It didn't faze her. She'd run over much more dangerous ground. Being something of a mountain goat was required.

Trace ran smoothly beside her as they climbed. Her breaths became measured, deeply in, then deeply out. She heard Trace begin the same rhythm. A thought occurred to her.

"Your legs are longer," she remarked. "Am I slowing you?"

"Hardly. You've trained. We all adjust our strides."

It was true, so she cast aside the concern. They continued upward. The air became colder. Gradually she felt the air beginning to thin. Not very much.

Trace spoke. "You been training much at altitude?"

"Not lately," she admitted. "Too many low-altitude missions."

"Then we turn around. No altitude sickness, please."

She thought he was being overly cautious. Gauging that they were at about twenty-five hundred meters, that wasn't enough to make most people sick. But most people weren't running, either.

Nor did she want a round of altitude sickness. If it became bad enough, she might need a hospital.

"We can go higher if you want," he offered. "This trail goes to about thirteen thousand feet."

She did a quick mental conversion. About four thousand meters. "I guess we should shorten it. At least for a day or two."

"A day or two?" He stopped running and began jogging in place. "I thought you intended to leave tomorrow."

"I'm reconsidering. I'll be ready for your four thousand meters in a couple of days. It doesn't take long for me to acclimate."

"Probably not since you do it so often." He surprised her with a smile. "This mountain doesn't go much higher than that. Maybe after a few days we can hit the peak and run down the other side."

They began their descent at a fast clip. "Does this mountain have a name?"

"Thunder Mountain. Lots of great stories about it if you want to hear them later. Such as wolves."

She dared a glance his way. "Wolves? I thought your country had exterminated them."

"We might still. There's been an effort to restore them to the wild, with all the attendant fury among ranchers. Norway?"

"We share a small number with Sweden. About four hundred. I suspect the disagreements are the same you have here."

"Yeah. Sometimes I see them when I run high enough."

"They seem shy, mostly. When we ski through hundreds of miles, they sometimes show up in small numbers. Never aggressive."

"Mostly curious," he agreed.

Thousands of meters disappeared beneath their feet until they reached the edge of town and the Mannerly house and passed it. An occasional car rolled by, the occupants waving.

"Friendly," she said.

"Mostly. And now I *really* want that coffee. Let's go get breakfast."

First they passed a dilapidated train depot. Next a truck stop full of grumbling trucks with a diner to one side. He led them toward the diner.

"Best breakfast around."

Well, she wasn't sure about that as she scanned the menu. While her mother had introduced her to the English fry-up, she was more accustomed to not eating at all until lunch. Anyway…

The foods she was used to were not on the menu, of course. Salmon mixed with scrambled eggs would have been nice, as would thin slices of meat on dense bread. In the end she chose the scrambled eggs, toast and a side of ham.

"Still looking for fish?" Trace asked.

She shrugged. "I eat what's available."

"I'll find you some fish at the grocery today."

"You don't have to."

"I know I don't. But I will anyway."

A very nice man, she decided. Brigid had chosen her friends well.

As they ate, he asked the inevitable question. "Why are you planning to stay longer? Not that I mind."

She thought it over, trying to decide what she could say without seeming to patronize him. This was such an important issue to him that she felt as if she needed to walk carefully.

"Brigid," she said finally. "She would want me to."

"Why?" His face appeared to have stiffened.

"Because you have questions," she answered. "Serious questions. Brigid wouldn't like them to remain unanswered if it's possible to find what happened. She wouldn't want me to walk away without trying. She wouldn't want me to walk away from her friend."

He resumed eating, appearing to ruminate. At least in Trondheim, or Afghanistan, the hour was later, and her appetite hadn't yet adjusted to the new time. She made a hearty meal once she reminded herself that this wasn't *really* breakfast.

Besides, after the run they had just taken, it wouldn't be long before hunger found her. Not long at all.

TRACE TRIED TO decide how to take her decision to stay here. It was obviously well-intentioned, but to do this because of Brigid? While *she* might be certain, he was sure that Brigid wouldn't have wanted Hillary to upend her life.

"What were you planning to do when you go home?" he asked as they finished up. He insisted on paying the bill.

"Oh, I was thinking I would go visit some friends." One corner of her mouth lifted. "It's a good time of year to look for the sun in the South of France. January would be better, but I don't know where I'll be then."

Outside, as they began to walk the short distance to the Mannerly house, he said, "You really should keep your plans. Brigid wouldn't want you to give up your holiday."

"Maybe not. Should we argue?"

He snorted. "Not without Brigid to referee."

For the first time, he saw a genuine smile light her face. It shone almost like an internal light. God, she was beautiful.

"Well, it seems we are at a stand," she replied.

Indeed they were. He gave up. For now.

When they reached the house, he suggested she go change into something less sweaty. "I'm going to the market."

"To look for fish? Then I'll come as well."

Seemed like the safest thing, he decided. He had no idea what kind of fish she would like. Or what she might need to prepare it.

He studied her quizzically. "I thought you didn't cook. I was going to look for something prepared."

"I exaggerated. I can cook, I just don't do it very often, which keeps me out of form."

As they drove across town to the grocery, he said, "If you can't find what you want here, there's another store just up the street, a chain that's trying to move in. But people tend to be loyal to Hampstead's because it's been here for nearly a century, and because it buys most foods locally."

"Then I will try to find everything I can there."

Inside, the store was busy and everyone was friendly. Trace expected the friendliness, of course, but he was surprised at how many people paused to talk. He'd begun to feel like a pariah after the ruckus he'd raised over Allan. But Hillary was an attention-getter, all right. He introduced her only as Brigid's friend. He had no idea if she wanted him to say more.

But apparently not. She spoke with a smile, shook hands, said only that she'd be staying for a while. Her slightly British accent made her more exotic, and Trace figured the whole town would hear about her by nightfall.

The conversations were limited, however. Most shoppers had their minds on tasks at hand. Funny, he thought, how many people developed blinders when shopping for groceries. Complete oblivion.

A few offered kind words about Allan but avoided the subject of his death. It was soon certain, however, that it was Hillary who had snagged their attention, not him.

How long did she plan to stay in town? Where was she from?

Casual, mildly probing questions. She *did* let it be known she was from Norway and answered a few questions about the cold. Making conversation–type questions. Not intrusive.

Hillary hovered over the fish, most of which was frozen, given how far they were from the sea. She didn't seem to have a problem with that, but she finally asked, "Salmon fillets? With the skin on?"

She had already chosen frozen cod, but this seemed important to her.

"I don't think we have any fresh salmon around here."

She laughed. "We have salmon farms in Norway, but the fish is becoming harder to find because there's such a market in other EU countries. Higher prices, too."

"I suggest we ask the butcher. He might have some ideas."

The butcher, Ralph by name, was jovial and slightly plump. He eyed Hillary with favor.

"Don't get many requests for that around here. I think I know where to get some, but it might take a day or two. And it might be frozen."

"I'm agreeable with that."

Ralph nodded and beamed. "How much?"

"Since I'm going to teach Trace to like it, too, maybe two pounds? And thin-sliced salami and other drier sausage slices?"

Ralph took out his notebook. "Now that I can find. I take it you don't like the package stuff?"

"Not if I'm going to teach this man about Norwegian breakfast."

"Gotcha. Anything else?"

"I doubt you have a dense bread. Sort of like a baguette, but much heavier."

He shook his head. "The place to go would be the bakery if you want it soon. Melinda can probably make you some." He winked. "But I can also try my sources."

"Thank you!"

"My pleasure. Should I call Trace when I have everything?"

"Of course," Trace answered. "Anything else?"

"I need to take a look at the cheeses. I imagine they're suited to American tastes?"

He half smiled. "I'm sure of it."

"It will do."

After a half hour, apparently satisfied with what she

could find and what she had ordered, they left the market behind.

"Now is it time for a shower?" he asked.

"Oh, yes. Hot and long."

"Then I'll run home to clean up. Back later. And oh, by the way? I doubt you packed for a long stay, so feel free to use the washer and dryer."

HILLARY WAVED AS he drove away, then carried her small bag of groceries inside. Not what she had hoped for, but it would do for now.

But after she'd put everything away and had showered, time hung heavy on her hands. She wasn't used to days with nothing to do, and Trace still hadn't told her how he intended to look for Allan's killer.

A glance at the clock told her it was nowhere near local suppertime. She thought about wandering over to Melinda's bakery, wherever that was, then decided against it. After noon, bakeries had usually shut down their kitchens.

Maybe bright and early tomorrow. Besides, she didn't have the meats she wanted yet. Not that she was accustomed to having familiar meals while she was training. She'd often wondered who had invented those rations. Dried everything.

She'd also picked up some black bread that would do with the butter she'd bought. And a bag of frozen broccoli.

Some things remained the same.

She wished Trace had pointed her in some direction that she could follow, but he hadn't. She was reluctant to dive into all those papers in the office. It would feel like a trespass, an invasion. Not that there was probably much to find, other than personal stuff that was none of her business.

The solitude wasn't good for her, however. There were

enough nightmare images engraved in her mind to haunt her. Hillary needed no photo to tell her what had happened to Brigid. She tried not to think about it, but silencing her brain was difficult.

She tried meditating but couldn't focus. She attempted some yoga, but that didn't help, either. Finally, she pulled on her favorite sweater, a natural-colored wool cable stitch, and waited for whatever Trace might bring.

IT WASN'T LONG before Stan Witherspoon heard that the woman was staying for a while. A friend of Brigid's.

Uneasiness crawled along his nerve endings until it became a full-blown anxiety attack. Had Brigid told her something? Mentioned it to her? Might he have as much to worry about from her as from Trace Mullen?

He felt as if a vise were closing around him. Almost suffocating him. What was he going to do about this? Wait and see?

Maybe that was the only thing he could do right now. Wait and see if the two of them started to act in some way other than as friends.

God. Sitting in Mahoney's Bar, he ordered a third boilermaker. Maybe it would settle his nerves.

He had to hope that nothing would come from this. But hope was a slender thread, and a sword hung over his head.

Chapter Five

Trace returned to Hillary as soon as he could. He had a feeling that leaving her alone in that house with all the unfamiliar ghosts it contained might not be comfortable for her.

Inevitably she had to be thinking of Brigid, and the kind of life she had lived there with Allan. Few enough answers for her in that house, in her friendship.

Sighing heavily, he wondered if he was haring off in some mad hunt to make himself feel better about Allan. Maybe Allan's despair had overwhelmed him after all.

But every fiber of Trace's being rejected that idea. What was bothering him as well now was Hillary's decision to stay. Was she just feeling sorry for him? Joining his crazy quest for Brigid's sake and not from any real belief that Allan had been killed?

Why should she believe him, anyway? She didn't know Allan well enough to feel one way or another. He almost wished he hadn't shared his suspicion with her. She had a life to get on with, people she had wanted to visit. Sun in the South of France.

He'd interrupted all that. No one else to blame for it. Maybe he needed to attempt more forcefully to persuade her to return to her plans.

His cell rang just as he pulled up in front of the Mannerly house. It was the butcher from the supermarket.

"Tell the lady most of what she wants will be here by noon tomorrow," Ralph said. "And you might want to add the salmon is fresh with skin on."

Trace blinked. "How'd you manage that?"

"Connections."

Trace was half laughing when he approached the door and knocked. Hillary answered quickly, her face a study in sorrow.

His first thought was to divert her, possibly make her feel a bit happier. "I think you like salmon with the skin on?"

She appeared startled as she stepped back to invite him inside. "Why do you ask?"

"Because I just had a call from the butcher. Most of what you want should be here tomorrow by midday. The salmon will be fresh and have the skin."

That drew a smile from her. "That's the best way. All the good vitamins are in the fat between the skin and the flesh. But that shouldn't be a question, should it?"

"Some people don't like the taste."

She closed the door. "Then some people don't know how to cook it."

"A distinct possibility."

She led the way straight to the kitchen, and inevitably he thought of all the times Brigid or Allan had led him in the same direction, often for a bottle of beer and something salty to go with it.

He didn't find beer, but he found a fresh pot of coffee waiting. "So you're a heavy coffee drinker?"

"Any time of the day. My mother preferred tea, but I never liked it. I want a stronger, bitterer brew."

He agreed with her. Running around on a mission where

you had to keep your mind clear in order to keep your head, you developed a passion for caffeine, even when the coffee was the instant kind and mixed with cold water.

And they still needed to eat. Damn, it was becoming a constant refrain for him, a desire to keep her fed because he understood her conditioning.

"You want a sub sandwich later?" he asked, wondering if they even had them in Norway.

She tilted her head. "We call them big bite sandwiches. You have them in this town?"

"Of course. The butcher makes them to order. But that's later."

Much later. The chasm still lay between them, a gulf about what they would do for Allan and whether she really wanted to join this hunt. Accustomed to walking through life with a great deal of confidence, Trace wondered why he felt such uncertainty with Hillary.

"You know," he said slowly as he filled two coffee mugs and brought them to the table, "you really should go back to your travel plans. I shouldn't have mentioned my suspicions, especially since they're probably lunacy."

Her tone took on a slight edge. "Do you think me incapable of making my own decisions?"

Trace realized he'd put his foot in it. He couldn't blame her if she got angry. Paternalism, he'd heard someone call it.

"No, I don't think that." And why the hell was he worried about it? He shouldn't even feel guilty. It *was* her decision.

She met his gaze straightly across the table. "Do you believe your suspicion?"

"Yes."

"Then we will look together. You for Allan, me for Brigid."

Sensible enough. "Then you don't think I'm crazy?"

That pulled another half smile from her. "Time will answer that, I believe."

Bingo. "I never saw myself as Don Quixote."

"Most of us don't see ourselves as tilting at windmills, even when we are. That book may have been a comedy, but it carried a core truth—that we have to try."

He liked that. "You're right."

Again that small smile. "We tilt at windmills all the time. Even at war. *The continuation of politics by different means.*"

"Clausewitz was right," he acknowledged. "We'd like to believe otherwise, though."

"It rarely makes one feel better to look through that lens. Dealing with it is difficult enough."

She paused and he took the opportunity to speak. "The human race is political all the time."

"Hence the jobs we have. We fight because it's the only way left to settle matters. And sometimes there are good reasons for it."

He liked her clear-sightedness, her willingness to stare at reality. "I don't think much about the reasons."

She answered firmly, "Nor should we. Our countries ask, and we answer."

He sipped more of his cooling coffee. They were growing philosophical, and that would take them nowhere useful. They both wore uniforms with pride. That was the beginning and end of it.

She spoke again. "When do you have to return to duty?"

"Not for a while. I'm on medical leave. Knee injuries."

"Not good for jumping from planes." She didn't wait for a response but moved on. "Where do you want to begin this quest?"

He'd thought about it, and the truth was that he wasn't

sure. He'd considered finding his way through Brigid and Allan's emails. Maybe some of the papers in their office.

"Emails," he said. "First thing that occurred to me. I'm reluctant, though. That's so personal, I hate to trespass."

"If there's a mystery behind Allan's death, I'm sure Brigid wouldn't mind. In fact, she would suggest it."

"No doubt. Still." The intimate peek into the Mannerlys' love life seemed an invasion of the worst sort. "After that, the papers and other computer files. If Allan killed himself, there had to be a reason. If someone else killed him, there was an even bigger reason."

"Then we'll start there. Do you have the passwords?"

He leaned forward. "It struck me as weird, but Allan left them to me in his will."

Her eyes widened a bit. "Then there was a reason. He wanted you to find it."

Also the beginning and end of it. Trespass he would.

THE OFFICE HAD collected some dust since Allan's death. Maybe it had started collecting even earlier. Nonetheless, even as they shook things off or wiped them down, he could still detect the faint scent of his friends.

Their journey through this world had been cut way too short. His chest tightened as memories began to rise within him. So much happiness and love simply erased.

"Before we really start," he said, "let's go for a run. I need to work off some agitation."

"I'm not surprised. Let's go." She cocked her head. "You run quite a bit for a man with bad knees."

"Two knee replacements. I'll keep working them until they stop hurting."

"Is this allowed?"

"Absolutely."

Choosing not to run in his jeans, he hurried back to his

house to get his workout gear. He hated leaving Hillary alone, then gave himself a mental kick in the butt. *Valkyrie.* She could damn well handle just about anything, including the emotional turmoil that might arise. The last thing she needed, or would want, was protection.

When he returned to the house, Hillary was doing pushups in the living room. He had to smile. Fine tuning. Answering her body's demands. Her expression appeared lighter, as if she looked forward to this run as much as he did.

Procrastination, he supposed, but both of them were engaging in it. Nor was the period they spent on a run going to deprive Allan, or Brigid, of anything. No time sensitivity there.

The day had brightened, a clear blue sky overhead. The air carried a chill that reminded him of a crisp apple. Perfect days were few and far between, but this was one of them.

He just wished his friends were here to enjoy it with him.

When they reached the top of the climb, silent agreement caused them to start down again. No running over the ridge today. The task awaiting them had begun to pressure them.

He just hoped that Hillary had been right when she said Allan had left him those passwords for a reason. Otherwise he was going to feel like a voyeur.

HILLARY COULD HAVE kept running for hours, but she was plagued by the feeling that she was running away. While she was sure Brigid would want her to look at private things, especially in light of Allan's death, that didn't make her feel any better about it.

Thinking of her own emails over the years, she was

sure she wouldn't want anyone reading them. They told the story of boyfriends past, stories that got more than a bit steamy when she was away training or on a mission. A sop to loneliness that might well reveal more about herself than she'd like anyone else to know.

Painting an emotional picture of her over the years, if someone cared to piece them all together. Emails to her father, private in the way only two soldiers could share. Some things she would never want her mother to read. Tears over death in her unit. Complaints about a particularly tough training schedule, most of them in her earliest days with the Jegertroppen. She'd gotten over herself pretty quickly. One had to or would never survive.

She survived her transformation into a well-oiled cog in the machinery that served a greater cause. A growth from girl to woman to Valkyrie. A steady toughening into an elite warrior.

No, she wouldn't want anyone to read those emails. Except in this case, she, Brigid, Allan and Trace were cut from the same cloth. If anyone could approach with understanding, it would be her and Trace.

But the fact that Allan had left Trace all those passwords… The idea had left a cold feeling in her heart, a presentiment of something awful around the next corner. It was a feeling she knew well, but familiarity didn't help.

Whatever they found might shift the world off its axis.

When she and Trace got back to the house, they took turns in the shower. He'd had the foresight to bring a change of clothing with him. She had one final change in her duffel, so she decided to do a load of washing. It would keep her busy in a different way.

She was down to her camouflage, the most comfortable clothing for travel. She hoped she didn't have to wear it outside, because it would give Trace more questions to answer about her, and she'd appreciated the brevity of his introductions to people they met.

Then it could no longer be postponed. No reason to put off the inevitable. Except Trace found one.

"I'll run out and get those subs now. We can eat them whenever."

"Are you reading my mind?"

His expression remained grave. "Possibly. Shamefully, I've reached the point of being a coward."

"So have I."

She watched him take off in his car, then started another pot of coffee. Once they began, she suspected they'd keep going late into the night. Well past bedtime for her Norwegian clock.

Her days and nights had begun to sift together, though. A familiar feeling and not a bad one. At least jet lag hadn't laid her low again.

Tough it out. Across thousands of miles came her father's voice. He was a loving and kind man, but he'd never accepted half measures. *Tøff det.*

She needed to right now.

Searching the cupboard, she found steel insulated mugs with covers. Pleased, she washed two and poured the rich black coffee just as Trace returned.

"I smell the good stuff," he remarked. He placed a large paper bag on the table, a bag that appeared to be holding four long sandwiches. Beside it he placed a six-pack of beer.

"Lager, I'm afraid. I didn't know if you'd want something else."

"Lager is good."

He put it in the refrigerator along with the sandwiches. Then, with full mugs in hand, they headed toward the dreaded task.

Hillary could almost feel Brigid right behind her, urging her onward. God, she missed her friend.

HILLARY SPOKE. "Jet lag may be catching up with me once again. I'm feeling a bit chilled." She stretched and yawned. In front of her stood a stack of papers on the corner of the desk. Beside her Trace stared at computer files.

He answered, "Eight hours' time difference, right? I'd be feeling a bit chilled, too, at four thirty in the morning."

"Yes. And I'm staring at my watch and trying to believe it's eight thirty in the evening."

He chuckled quietly. "Let's give it a break. Then I'll put on my food-pusher hat and mention that we haven't eaten anything in hours."

"Food pusher?" She raised her brow.

"Well, I keep noticing how often I talk to you about food. How often I suggest that we should eat. It's starting to become weird."

She laughed. "And when you're on active duty, how much do you eat? More, I would guess, than we've been eating. Anyway, food becomes an obsession for soldiers."

That was true, he thought as they went to the kitchen. The subs still awaited them, and he brought them out. She didn't object when he placed two bottles of beer on the table.

"I'm sorry I couldn't get fish on the sandwiches," he said.

She laughed again, a light, pleasant sound. "My obsession."

As they unwrapped sandwiches, she remarked, "We have a national dish in Norway."

"Really?"

"Really. Well loved. At the moment, there's a big argument about whether it should be changed."

"Why would anyone want to change it?"

She shrugged. "Ask the politician who started the argument. It's not like anyone has to eat it or will eat differently."

He nodded, lifting half his sandwich. He'd ordered just about everything on these subs, hoping it would tickle her fancy. "What exactly is it?"

"Boiled lamb and cabbage."

He was startled. "For real?"

"Actually quite tasty. Apart from fish, we consume a lot of lamb in Norway. Mainly because we raise a lot of it."

Boiled lamb didn't sound tasty to Trace, even with cabbage. He let it go, returning to matters at hand. "We haven't found anything."

"Not yet."

"Are you always so positive?"

She shrugged. "How negative are *you*?"

Not very, he decided. He couldn't jump into dangerous terrain without a lot of optimism. Look at his knees. He'd trashed them during a night jump on some very rough terrain overseas. And still he wanted to go back to full duty, although that didn't seem likely now.

"You get into the mountains in Afghanistan very much?" he asked, although he didn't expect an answer.

She shook her head. "You know I can't answer that."

Which told him all he needed to know. How had he not heard of the Valkyries operating in Afghanistan? He'd known Norwegian troops had participated as part of the allied operation since the beginning, but no word about a unit this unusual? Secrecy was common, but the novelty of the Valkyries must have been burning in someone, trying to burst out.

Sitting there with Hillary, he was impressed by the deep

cover that had apparently shrouded the Valkyries. "You have any problem with keeping secrets in the Jegertroppen?"

She cocked an eye at him. "Last time I looked, we were human."

He laughed. And once again he was avoiding the issue of Allan. God, he needed to stiffen his spine. The grief of this task was going to tear him apart. "I don't want to do this." As sorry a statement as he'd made in his entire adult life.

Hillary didn't ask what he'd meant. "I don't, either. Brigid. What if all this somehow had to do with her?"

Trace felt her words like a jolt. She had thrown it on the table. He'd been trying to avoid thinking about that possibility. Something untoward might have happened involving Brigid, but even so, why would it have reached around the world to Allan? Why would anyone come after him?

Maybe that was the question that needed answering.

He spoke. "Allan put their emails in encrypted files. Unfortunately, he created those files all on the same date, which makes searching them difficult."

"I've found a few written letters from her. Maybe the answer is there, if I can recognize it."

"They might have communicated elliptically. Not saying it straight out."

Her sandwich done, she reached for her beer and swallowed nearly half the bottle. "That worries me."

It worried Trace, too, but they had to keep trying. Or at least he did. "If their deaths are linked, then it's a helluva problem."

AFTER THEY FINISHED their dinner, Hillary stepped outside to clear her head in the fresh, chilly air. She had a feeling that Trace wasn't going to stop for hours yet, and, despite her internal clock, she wanted to help.

She needed the time in the fresh air, though. Just a bit.

Looking up at the stars overhead, she noticed she didn't see as many or as clearly as she did while skiing and marching through mountainous terrain. Too much ambient light from streetlamps, and maybe dust.

But she clearly recalled traveling over snow, across glaciers. At night she could see many more stars than here, like a sparkling diamond coat thrown over the world.

But never had she stood under such stars thinking about a man. Trace kept slipping into her mind, bringing warm syrup to her veins. She'd felt strong attractions before, but this was powerful. And pointless. She would be going home to her *real* life before long, job done or not. Trace would be left far behind to become only part of her memories.

Thoughts of Brigid were not far away, either. Her throat tightened, and her chest ached. So much loss. So much waste.

Determined to answer the questions Brigid would have asked about Allan's death and maybe her own, Hillary turned and walked back into the house. Sleep and fatigue had become irrelevant.

So the woman was moving in, Witherspoon saw as he watched. Brigid's friend, the grapevine said. Why was she staying? Hadn't her visit to the cemetery been enough? Or was she getting sweet on Mullen? It was possible. Women were often drawn like moths when it came to men like him. Strong, hardened, dangerous.

Or maybe it was something worse. Because Mullen had been quite convinced that Allan's death wasn't suicide and had made no secret of his belief. Damn him. Mullen should have accepted the decision of the cops and the inquest. Despite his protests, they had listened to him and then ignored him.

After the determination of suicide, Stan had hung around to make sure it was over. He *had* to make sure, because a mistake could cost him his life.

But since this woman's arrival, he couldn't stop sweating it. No matter how many times he told himself it was too late, that nothing further would be done, he couldn't escape the sense of threat, no matter how many boilermakers he put away.

Brigid had seen him twice. He'd had her killed. When the hammer didn't fall on him, Witherspoon had decided she hadn't reported up the chain of command. Hadn't caused trouble for his boss. Until the man told him to take care of Brigid's husband. The boss must have heard something.

Stan had been all over this ground so many times his head ached from the unending spiral of his worries. Sometimes he wondered if he wasn't going a bit mad over all this.

Then had come Brigid's friend. A friend close enough that she'd come all the way to visit a grave.

Well, he'd worried constantly that the boss was right about the husband. He'd taken care of that. Now he was worried that Brigid had mentioned the matter to her friend.

God! His worries just kept getting stronger. They were beginning to overwhelm him. Mad or not, he wondered if he'd be able to think through this clearly, to figure it all out to his advantage. His brain seemed to have escaped him.

He felt like a rat in a maze, unsure which way to turn. He didn't want to kill again. That seemed like hanging his butt out too far into the breeze.

He kept telling himself that if Brigid had talked to anyone, he himself might be dead by now. But no one would consider her report important enough for her to be killed. Except him. Hell, if she'd reported it, who would really listen? One woman, a couple of sightings of something she knew nothing about.

He'd made that argument to himself countless times.

But he was getting lost in the maze, unsure how much he was lying to himself. He'd been afraid enough to kill two people. Now a third?

Were money and a hazy threat really that important?

Well, it had gone past money. It was racing toward jail or possibly his own death. He *had* to tie up loose ends. He couldn't risk any ends to unraveling.

He had become a man wandering in a warren, hiding in bushes, losing his marbles. He had come to that.

Hell.

TRACE TRIED TO shut it down for the night. He knew what an eight-hour jump in time zones could feel like. But Hillary refused to go to bed.

She was determined to glue herself to his side and help him. He figured, given who she was, that she had at least as much determination as he did. No backing down. An argument was pointless.

Besides, he didn't want to argue with her. After her shower, the aromas of shampoo and soap had clung to her, and the enticing scent kept distracting him.

Trouble there, he reminded himself. Big trouble. Plus, she was Brigid's friend, and he didn't want to do the least little thing to offend her.

His own shower had disturbed him. Allan's shampoo. Allan's bar soap. Familiar scents. At least Hillary must have brought her own things. He might have gone nuts if he'd smelled Brigid as well as Allan.

There was nothing more evocative than smells, as he knew from shooting at the gun range outside town. The smell of burned powder could sometimes throw him back into battlefields he'd left behind. Bring a resurgence of memories that should be erasable.

He sighed, rubbing his forehead. Maybe he needed some glasses for this job. His eyes were growing tired.

He glanced at the time and saw it was nearly midnight. Nearly 8:00 a.m. in Norway. Her body must already have awoken to a new day.

"Are you going to bed?" he asked. "You need some sleep."

"I'm wide-awake."

"I was afraid you'd say that."

"You can go sleep if you want to. I can continue here, and for you it is late."

He smiled. "It's rumored. I'm fine. Maybe a little caffeine to help."

"Sounds good," she answered, her eyes on the papers she was sorting through. "I'm making a pile of Brigid's handwritten letters to go through when I'm finished. Odd that she wrote letters as well as emails."

"Good idea." He paused, studying her, with an unending curiosity about her that seemed to be growing. Little things. Maybe later some big things. "Do you ever get worried about avalanches? Or blocks breaking off glaciers and falling on you?"

She shook her head a little and glanced at him. "We are well trained to look out for the dangers. If we make a mistake—well, we get what we deserve." She shrugged.

He shared the same kind of training, although not about glaciers. It had been a dopey question, he supposed, but it had probably sprung from his fogged brain. Time to make that coffee or give up and go to bed. Since she'd already worked her way through her own fatigue to help him, he wasn't going to leave her working on her own. Besides, it wouldn't be the first time he'd sacrificed sleep to a mission.

And this had become a mission in the truest sense.

Chapter Six

In the morning, although worn out from the long night, Hillary and Trace took off for a run. Each strike of her foot invigorated Hillary, as did the fresh morning air. The rhythmic movement was also soothing, calming. A lot of tension began to drain from her.

Thinking about their search for a clue, she wondered if it would yield anything truly useful. Yes, she believed Allan had left his passwords to Trace for a reason, but that didn't mean the documents would have anything at all to do with his death. Or Brigid's, which was probably an even crazier thought. A rocket-propelled grenade had killed Brigid during a mission in dangerous territory. Easy enough to understand in the circumstances.

Even if they found anything useful, it wouldn't change the inquest verdict. Trace must be doing this for his own peace of mind, niggled by the concern that maybe Allan *had* died by suicide. Or maybe to find a killer. Allan's killer.

Of course he would want that. She fully understood. But with only emails and handwritten letters, they probably wouldn't find any kind of description of the murderer, even if he existed.

Hell! And now this situation had made her worry about Brigid's death. Now she couldn't stop, couldn't just say she needed to get back. Now *she* had a powerful need to know when before she hadn't even wondered about it.

She wished she hadn't thought of the linkage between the two deaths, at least not in the way she had. Were the deaths related? Probably, but most likely only because Allan had despaired after losing Brigid. That *was* the most sensible explanation.

When they reached the top of the ridge, she wanted to stay there. To continue this brief rest away from their self-imposed task. To maybe think very seriously about returning to Europe and resuming her interrupted plans.

Not that she would. She'd made a commitment here and she honestly didn't regret it, even if it turned out to be a waste of time. There was something to be said for paying full attention to the death of a friend, to settling with one-self before returning to daily life. Even finding nothing at all could bring a measure of peace.

Or maybe they would tumble into some information that recorded the details of Allan's descent into despair. The part of him he'd probably kept to himself even while expressing it through alcohol. Trace wouldn't like to discover that. He'd hate it. But at least then he wouldn't have to wonder.

As they approached the outskirts of town, she saw a man standing beside the road. Young and slender, maybe thirty or so. With an unshaven face, as was so popular. Dark hair.

He stared at them as they approached and passed, and she felt a tremor of unease. When they had left him behind, with the Mannerly house just ahead, she wondered aloud, "Why was he staring at us?"

"Maybe because he's never seen two lunatics running like this without being chased by an angry bull."

Amused, she chuckled. But the sense of uneasiness had

taken hold and she couldn't help looking back. In the distance, the man was walking away. He'd probably decided he'd had his entertainment for the day.

"Let's grab some breakfast," Trace suggested.

She didn't argue. It had been twelve hours or more since that sandwich had filled her, and right now she could do with a bit of sweet pastry, or whatever passed for it at the truck stop.

She needn't have wondered. She hadn't looked closely at the menu before, but now she turned to the back side of the four pages. The sweets were clustered on the back of the menu, a good selection. And down at the bottom was oatmeal, nearly invisible.

At the top, beside a stack of doughnuts, was something labeled Danish pastry, although it looked to her like Viennese bread. Whatever the name, she liked the pastry.

Now she had a breakfast that would do. A double order of oatmeal and two pastries. Plenty of carbohydrates.

When their food arrived, Trace spoke. "You looked a little troubled when we were up top."

"Just thinking about what we're doing. If we'll get any satisfaction." She didn't mention she'd thought about going home. He might try to send her on her way again, and there was no point growing irritated with him.

He grew serious, putting his fork down. "I know we might be wasting time. We might find out that there was no murder. That I was wrong."

She ached for him. He had been plowing alone through a painful emotional abyss. "But you need to know anyway. At this point, so do I." She reached for a piece of the so-called Danish. The delicious, sweet, flaky pastry pleased her.

"I admit," she said presently, "that it was easier to accept Brigid's death when I thought it was the result of ordinary combat. A common attack from insurgents. Now I feel unable to accept it."

He finished a bite of toast. "Exactly."

They shared a look of understanding, and Hillary experienced the first real camaraderie with him.

A while later he asked, "What are you going to do with that salmon you wanted?"

"Try to remember how to cook it."

That caused him to laugh. She liked the crinkles around his stormy gray eyes when he did so.

"You're invited," she said. "You might even enjoy it."

He nodded. "Thanks. Anything you need me to bring?"

"Yourself. I'll have to think about anything in addition."

"Think away." But as they approached the house once again, he said, "That man we passed really bothered you, didn't he?"

"Yes," she admitted. "Battle sense, I suppose. It can get overactive at times."

"Maybe."

At least he hadn't tried to dismiss the observer again. Uneasiness still clung to her like cold, wet leaves. Somehow that just hadn't been right.

She dreaded spending another day in those mountains of paper. Hours of inactivity looking through items, including utility bills, that probably had no relevance at all. Her friend hadn't spent a lot of time making files.

She might have sighed, but she didn't want Trace to hear it. It was difficult to appear impassive all the time so that he wouldn't feel guilty about her decision to stay.

Commitment. It meant as much to her as duty and loyalty. She *had* committed herself of her own free will.

THAT MAN HAD bothered Trace, too. A small thing. Maybe the guy had been gawking only because it was rare to see a man and a woman running in step around here. Different leg lengths usually would have made that difficult, especially about being in step, but as he had remarked, in a unit not every leg length was the same. They had all learned to adjust their strides to the same length.

Hillary was tall. How many times had she adjusted her stride when the soldiers ran as a unit? She had a hell of a lot of experience doing it.

After their showers, Trace began to feel angry. "What the hell happened, Allan? What is this all about? Another reason to drive me mad?"

Hillary looked at him, clearly a bit astonished, then said quietly, "I share your frustration."

"I bet you do. Neither of us is inclined to sit on our butts for endless hours. We need activity. Action. But I'm not going to get truths out there running my behind off. Left to my own devices, I'd probably be doing that run twice or more a day. Do you people ever run such distances twice a day?"

"Depends. For conditioning, yes, sometimes."

"Then we start feeling the lack of all the rest of it." He wiped a hand over his face. "I'm going to buy more beer, or something else. Any preferences?"

"Pilsner, if your stores carry it. It's what I drink mostly at home."

"I'm sure I can find it. Anything else?"

She tilted her head, as if considering. "Aquavit is excellent."

"I'll get some if it's available. We might need a few shots before this day is over."

She hesitated then stood. "If you can wait a moment or two, I'll go with you." She didn't want to make any kind of splash in this town, to get noticed too often. It went against her training and instincts. But he was right about needing activity.

"I'll wait. I'd really like the company."

Teamwork. They were both used to it. And being covert in strange places.

This time she allowed her sigh to escape. He was right about the inactivity. Before long they were going to feel like prisoners in this house.

TRACE RENTED A room by the week at a gracious house on Front Street. He ran in to get a change of clothing but didn't take long. He'd never tried to rent a place long term because he was so rarely in town. A room was plenty, and Brigid and Allan had often made their tiny guest room available to him.

For nights when they'd drunk a little too much at the kitchen table. For nights when they'd been having so much fun that it had startled them to realize it was nearing dawn.

God, he missed them both. Brigid's death had nearly gutted him. Allan's had finished the job. So he'd sit on his butt to make sure that neither of them had come afoul of someone or something.

It was nice, however, to come back to his SUV with Hillary. A comrade. A companion. Another soldier. Someone who understood.

But the more he dug into his suspicions, the emptier the horizon appeared.

Man, he was sick of spinning his wheels. Allan's death hung over him like a dark cloud, almost suffocating. Crying out for a resolution. Any kind of resolution that convinced Trace more than the inquest had.

Yeah, Allan *could* have died by suicide. He'd faced that much even if it had flown in the face of Allan's nature and his words. Allan would never surrender, even though Trace had been worried about his drinking. But what if he had?

Then Trace would have to learn to live with it.

The liquor store sold both pilsner and aquavit, the latter surprising him in such a small store. He'd often wanted to try it, but just in case he didn't like it, he bought a bottle of bourbon for himself.

When they exited with their paper bags, the breeze had escalated into a cold wind. Winter's breath forced itself down his neck like sharp needles. Not long and the snow would start falling.

As they strode toward his vehicle, he nearly paused. Wasn't that the man who had been watching them from the road earlier? Some instinct warned him not to make a misstep or to look with more than a casual glance.

Who the hell was it? Over the years he'd gotten to know nearly all the longtime residents around here, but there were still new people he'd never met, mostly from the community college.

He slid into his truck next to Hillary, and she said, "Did you see him?"

"The guy? I did. I also couldn't be sure it was the same man. I didn't look hard enough."

"Me either, but he troubles me."

Situational awareness. Drilled into him bone-deep by training and experience. Sometimes it just paid to be on high alert.

"Damn it, Allan," Trace grumbled several hours later. "My butt is killing me from sitting in this chair. I *have* to move around."

Hillary apparently agreed. She rose and bent over to stretch her glutes and hamstrings. Next were her shoulders, then she shook her arms as if to release the last tension. His moves weren't very different.

"You'd think," Trace groused, "that he could have labeled the folders somehow. But worse, the emails inside them aren't in chronological order. Like he took a mixer to them."

Hillary nodded as they strode toward the kitchen.

"I used to love this room," he remarked. "Good times in here. Now it feels... I dunno. Annoying? Like a prison? Confining. God!"

When he'd thought about starting this search, he hadn't thought about turning into a library rat. Stuck in a chair for hours on end. Those two had emailed each other at least once a day, sometimes more, and the emails went back for years.

"I tried a search," he told Hillary as he made yet another pot of coffee. Then, changing his mind, he got a couple of beers out of the fridge, giving her a pilsner. "The damn search algorithm won't go by dates on the emails."

"Frustrating," she agreed. She began pacing through the house, evidently as tired of sitting as he was.

Much as he had avoided the living room, he could avoid it no longer. The empty space where Allan had once sat wrenched him. The rest of the room was familiar, now feeling too familiar. Stuffed with good memories, now drowned by ugliness beyond words. But hell, he'd deal with it.

Maybe he was crazy now, but he'd been crazy for the last two months with the conviction Allan hadn't killed himself. He was going at the problem the only way he could think to do.

And it was nuts. They could spend a week going through all this and find nothing. There had to be a better way.

Hillary stopped pacing when they returned to the

kitchen, and she sipped more of her beer. "Allan mixed them up for a reason."

"I already figured that out. But if he was so damn worried about something in there, why didn't he share with me? With anyone? And then leave me all his passwords in a *will*?"

"We agreed it was some kind of message."

"Yeah, but what kind?"

Her lips quirked. "Did you expect to parachute in and conduct a quick reconnaissance?"

At last he relaxed enough to laugh. "Too impatient, huh?"

Hillary shrugged. "Perhaps. And perhaps you haven't considered how dangerous this could be."

"I have, actually." He waved a hand. "If Brigid and Allan are linked, if both were murdered, then we've got a huge problem by the tail. Especially if word gets out what we're doing here."

She half smiled. "So maybe it's best you haven't told anyone I'm a soldier, too. Just being Brigid's friend may bring enough attention."

True. Once again he thought of that guy in the parking lot and alongside the road. Had he been watching? Or was it coincidence?

She spoke, reaching beyond the anger that drove him. "Brigid was killed by an RPG. At least according to the after-action report."

Trace looked at her. "And so it ends?"

"If anything was going on, yes."

His spine stiffened. "Do you know what you're suggesting?"

"Oh yes." He watched as her face hardened. "It's impossible anymore to know who fired a shot. Too many US weapons out there among insurgents. Too many Soviet weapons out there. The RPG was probably US." Her face darkened even more.

"Are you thinking friendly fire?" he asked.

"I cannot ignore any possibility. Not now."

That was one thought that hadn't occurred to him, mainly because Brigid's death out there shouldn't be linked with Allan's here. *Shouldn't*. But maybe it was. They'd both realized that possibility yesterday.

"God, I'm starting to feel stupid," he remarked. "Maybe it's time to start thinking like the warriors we are and throw emotion out the window. At least me. I've been letting it govern me too much."

"That's understandable. I have had longer to get used to Brigid's death. To grieve her."

AT THREE THAT AFTERNOON, before they could discuss only the barest bones of new ideas, a knock at the door surprised Trace.

"Nobody's stopping by here anymore," he remarked as he went to answer it.

It proved to be Deputy Guy Redwing, an acquaintance of Trace's. A man in his early thirties, his face carried a hint of Native American heritage. "Hey, man," Trace said. "What can I do you for?"

Redwing smiled. "Just a check. This house hasn't stirred since Allan died, and now it's busy. And no one recognizes the woman who's here. Put it down to nosy neighbors, but I gotta answer the call."

"Yeah, I know. Come on in. You might as well meet Hillary and put everyone's mind to rest."

Hillary had come to the kitchen door and was smiling. "Coffee?"

"Yes, ma'am."

"Then come along. I'll make some."

Redwing made the same comment Trace had made upon meeting Hillary. "You sound kinda English."

"Kind of," Hillary agreed, offering no more. "I was Brigid's friend."

"It's all a sad, sad story," Redwing said. "I'm Guy Redwing, by the way."

"Hillary Kristiansen. Nice to meet you."

Guy settled at the table while the coffeepot burbled and steamed. "Neighbors around here are nosy. You'll have to get used to it, I'm afraid. Everyone's looking after everyone else most of the time. And then there's times like this when it's none of their business but they still want to know."

Hillary laughed. "I lived in a town like that."

"Then you understand."

Trace poured coffee for Guy and brought it to the table. "Is it still getting colder out there?"

"Enough that I can see my breath." Guy turned his cup around a few times before taking a sip. "I'm not trying to stir anything up, but Trace knows I grew up here."

Trace replied, "Just a couple of years behind me."

Redwing chuckled. "You guys were always my heroes back then."

"Why the hell?" Trace asked. "We were just like everyone else."

"Except the three of you always knew what you were going to do. Wear a uniform. I guess I got mine."

"A good one, too." Trace grinned. "So how's it going?"

"Sometimes busy, sometimes not. That Grace Hall investigation was something else. Imagine someone trying to drive her off her land and killing to do it."

Then Redwing eyed Trace. "I don't think it was suicide, either."

A pin drop would have been deafening. Breaths grew

louder in the quiet that seemed to fill the room. Not one muscle twitched among any of them.

Trace eventually cleared his throat. "You don't?"

Redwing shook his head. "Never could stomach it, despite the inquest. I knew Allan. I talked to him more than once after Brigid was killed. Messed up? Yeah. But determined as hell to get through it. A matter of honor, I thought. And maybe for Brigid."

Trace nodded then drummed his fingers. "But nothing specific, I suppose."

"If there had been, the inquest wouldn't have ruled it a suicide. But I've never believed that."

Trace unleashed a pent-up breath. "Everyone else does."

"I doubt it," Guy answered, "but what's the point of saying anything? The inquest settled it, and not many people want to argue with their neighbors or look like fools, either."

Trace and Hillary exchanged glances.

"Then," Guy continued. It was his turn to sigh. "Seems like Allan thought there was something fishy about Brigid's death. But what the hell was he going to do about it? That happened thousands of miles away. Enemy fire. Why didn't that ever sit quite right with him?"

"I don't know," Trace answered slowly.

"Anyway, it was just a feeling I got." Guy smiled faintly. "I wasn't going to shout about it the way you did. Not without decent evidence."

"I was freaking mad. Angry."

Guy sipped his coffee again. "It sucks," he said frankly.

Trace leaned forward, forgotten beer bottle in front of him. "Did you notice anything at all? Maybe some stranger acting oddly?"

Guy's expression turned wry. "Maybe you haven't noticed because you're away so much, but every summer and fall we get a new wave of students. Even faculty can change. No one sticks out, not with that college here. Besides, a whole lot of them act odd."

Trace smiled. God, he needed the humor, and his smile broadened when he heard Hillary laugh quietly. "I acted oddly at that age, too."

"Didn't we all?" Guy asked. "I suspect marijuana causes some of it, but so far we haven't detected signs of stronger drugs. The sheriff isn't exactly worried about personal quantities of marijuana, though."

"What's the point? He'd probably have to arrest half the students at the college. And maybe a bunch of high schoolers."

Guy chuckled. "It's becoming legal through use."

Once again silence fell. Hillary went to get the pot to heat up Guy's coffee. "Thanks," he said. "I can tell you, Trace, I'll keep my ear to the ground. Or the vine. Whatever."

She put the pot back and returned to the table. Guy looked at her.

"You're pretty quiet," he remarked. "You knew Brigid, though?"

Trace felt her tense beside him. He couldn't blame her for not wanting everyone to know she was a soldier, too. But maybe some things had to be revealed to put a lid on speculation.

"They met in the war," he said, leaving it at that.

Guy pressed no further. "Then I'm doubly sorry," was all he said.

But Hillary was evidently prepared to share some things. "We grew close very fast. Brigid showed me a locket she never took off. Inside it was a photo of Allan."

Trace hadn't heard that before. In fact, he hadn't known

about it at all. Apparently the Mannerlys had had a few secrets, even from their best friend.

"That's sad," Guy said. "I mean now. Not at the time."

Hillary nodded. "At the time, I was touched that she shared it with me."

"Did it survive?" Guy asked.

"No," she answered. Very little of Brigid had survived, but she wasn't going to tell these men that she'd been identified only by DNA. No one wanted to hear that.

After a bit, Guy stirred. "Back to duty, I suppose. I'll tell the neighbors there's nothing going on here, that Hillary is just Brigid's friend. Maybe that'll shut down the gossip."

Maybe, thought Trace as he watched Guy drive away. But then they'd find something else to speculate about. Like why Trace was practically living here with Hillary.

The curse of small towns.

WITHERSPOON WATCHED GUY REDWING drive away. The tension in his neck was beginning to strangle him. Law enforcement? What had those two found out?

Maybe it was time to just pack up and go. Get out of here in case those two *did* discover something. Pretend he'd never found evidence of it. Would the boss believe him?

But how could it lead to *him*? He'd been banging his head on that wall ever since this had begun. Had Brigid discovered his name somehow? If so, had she repeated it to anyone?

Damn. But if she had, the rock fall of her revelation would surely have landed on his head. Stan Witherspoon would even now be facing a trial. Or would have been murdered at the hands of the man who had hatched the scheme. As far as Witherspoon knew, however, the big guy hadn't discovered Stan's fears.

It wasn't that Witherspoon was alone in his misdeeds.

Plenty of contractor equipment got diverted, stolen or just never shipped at all. A military contract meant money, and more money if the company could find a way to cheat.

Stan was only a small part of the problem, a man they would leave alone unless someone raised a ruckus. Then the higher echelons, having known this was going on all the time, would want to make an example.

Either way, Witherspoon would find himself in a vise that might be fatal.

No, he had to make sure he was never discovered, that no one linked to him was discovered. Especially now that he'd committed two murders.

He probably should never have done it. Never let fear and threats guide his actions. All he had now were more serious problems.

But fear drove him, and fear didn't yield to reason.

Chapter Seven

Trace looked at Hillary. "What did you think?"

"Guy seems like a nice man."

He snorted. "You know what I mean."

"I could use a shot of the aquavit, if you don't mind."

He glanced at his watch. "Late enough for me."

"And I need to try to cook a supper for us. I don't want that salmon to spoil."

"Hillary…"

She smiled. "I know. I'm being difficult."

Difficult didn't begin to cover it.

"I found dried dill in the cupboard," she remarked. "Fresh dill wasn't available at the market, but dry will do. There are bread crumbs here, too. In this house, someone cooked."

Trace had to smile. "Maybe I just wasn't here when it happened."

"It's likely. You were more fun."

He shook his head once. "I haven't been fun lately."

She didn't answer, just brought the aquavit to the table. "Do you want your bourbon?"

"I'll try yours first." He rose and went to the cabinet where Brigid and Allan had kept the shot glasses. He rinsed and dried two of them, then placed them on the table while she peeled off the seal and opened the bottle.

Then she poured two shots of clear liquid, saying, "I believe this label is infused with caraway. Others may have a dill undertone, or possibly other herbs."

"Do you like this one?"

"I like caraway. It's just a hint, but you will probably taste it. No surprises."

He had to smile as she joined him. "So it's not vodka."

"It may look like it, but it is made mostly from grain and isn't as strong as some vodkas."

She regarded him over the shot glass. "In the summer many of us drink beer. In the winter, more aquavit. Maybe it helps with the long, dark nights."

He laughed. "Makes sense."

"We are a sensible people," she answered wryly.

He thought more about her home country and what little he knew about it. "You have a border with Russia?"

She nodded. "It is a difficult border. Mountainous, of course, but also too porous. We share part of the North Atlantic oil field with Russia, mostly in the North Sea but not entirely. That means we must patrol with our navy also." Then she downed her shot of aquavit.

It appeared to go down easily, so he tried his. It surprised him with its viscosity. "That's good."

"As to the border, we train to defend it, although we judge the likelihood of Russian invasion to be small. But it makes our NATO neighbors feel more comfortable."

"Do *you* train for defending the border as well?"

"We train in the mountains," was her only answer.

Good enough, he supposed. He drained another shot. "I like this."

"Have another."

He was agreeable. Other than running, having a drink was the most pleasant thing he'd done recently. Too focused on Allan. It was a wonder he had any friends left, and he wasn't too sure about that.

She turned the conversation back. "As to Guy Redwing, well, he surprised me."

"Me too. I've been feeling pretty much alone since the inquest. I had no idea that anyone didn't think I'd gone nuts."

"I don't think you are nuts. You have legitimate questions about what happened."

"And no evidence."

He poured himself another drink. He liked the caraway undertone to it. And a hint of something else he couldn't identify. "I wonder if he'll learn anything."

"I don't know. He hasn't learned it yet. But perhaps he'll look harder now."

Trace wondered about that, then his mind wandered back to that man they'd seen twice. It might be odd; it might be nothing at all. Now he wished he'd taken a closer look.

"That man," he said.

"Yes. It seemed strange, but this is a small town. No reason to think it wasn't just coincidence."

No reason at all except that uneasy crawling along his neck that often warned him he was being watched.

She spoke. "We might find something in those papers and emails. Allan seemed to think them important."

"He must have known I'd be reluctant to go through them, though." But the passwords. He kept coming back to them. "Hell. Spending all our time in that office is uncomfortable."

"We will just keep running."

That almost made him laugh. Running from what? A boring and endless task?

"Is it your dinnertime?" she asked after a while.

"I'm flexible."

"We have to be, don't we? But I need something to do."

He could sure understand that. "I suggest a walk around town tonight. Maybe folks will talk with us."

"At least out of curiosity."

"That much, anyway." He watched as she preheated the oven and spread a large piece of foil on a baking pan. Then she took the fish from the fridge and placed it skin side down on the foil. Next came quite a bit of dried dill and some fresh lemon juice. Over the top she sprinkled bread crumbs. At last she wrapped it all in the foil.

"Looks good," he said.

"Even the dill?" she teased.

"Even the dill."

"Now I need something to go with this. The fish won't take long, maybe eighteen to twenty minutes, but anything else might take longer."

"I thought you didn't know how to cook."

She laughed. "This I think I can remember."

Her laugh was such a pleasant sound, filling the kitchen in a way he very much liked. Some kind of cheer needed to return to this house. To his heart.

"This house needs two ovens."

That startled him. "Why?"

"Because I bought frozen french fries. I didn't want to peel and slice potatoes. And the frozen fries take a different temperature than the fish."

"Oh, the problems."

She laughed again. Activity seemed to make her happier. He watched as she brought broccoli from the freezer. "This will do in the microwave. I hope you like buttered dark bread."

Hillary was making his mouth water. "Now I'm starving."

That pleased her. From out of nowhere, a desire to

please her *all* the time struck him. *No go*, he reminded himself. Soon she'd be thousands of miles away again.

HILLARY HADN'T COOKED dinner in a while, although she'd misled Trace a bit. When she and her father were home at the same time, she often cooked, and she enjoyed doing it now. Scents wafting from the oven made her homesick and brought back good memories.

The wooden cabin where they lived together, by no means small, with a steeply sloped roof so snow would fall off. The nearby village, brightly lit in the long, dark nights. Welcoming.

The nights that lasted three months were among her favorite things about her home. Even having lived there all their lives, some grew irritable before the end of the darkness. Not Hillary. Those days were a time for gathering with friends when she wasn't on duty. For sitting beside a dancing fire on the hearth.

After supper, they headed out for their walk, bundled up against the icy night.

Trace spoke. "That was the most delicious dinner I've had in a while."

"I'm not surprised," she answered drily.

He laughed. "Where do you live in relation to the Arctic Circle?"

"North of it."

"Kinda cold and dark. I'm not sure I'd like it."

"I do."

"Why doesn't that surprise me?" he joked.

"Because I haven't moved south?"

"How would I know? I have no idea where you started."

The weather hadn't grown cold enough yet to drive the evening crowds indoors. Freitag's Mercantile was still open with plenty of customers. She had liked shopping in there.

People greeted Trace as they walked, and he seemed surprised. "I guess I've been too obsessive about Allan to think anyone wanted to speak to me anymore."

Curious looks came Hillary's way, but only a handful paused to talk to them. To them, Trace introduced her as Brigid's friend.

Everyone expressed their sorrow at Brigid's passing, often with a nice memory of her. Hillary got the feeling they had truly liked her.

But some also mentioned Allan. Those that did seemed reluctant to bring him up, as if they knew that Trace still wasn't convinced it was suicide. And among them were people who said they didn't believe it was suicide, either.

"Damn shame," said one man. "A blot on his memory, and I don't think Allan deserves that. He was tough enough to get through anything, including the death of his wife."

Trace nodded, refraining from reiterating his opinion. Hillary imagined he thought they already knew it. He must have made quite the uproar.

Apparently the instant the seeds of suspicion had been planted in Trace, they'd grown fast and sturdy. Suspicions always did. But she had begun to believe he was right. The only difficulty was solving the problem.

Trace spoke to a few more people, and more than one said they thought he was right. It appeared both Allan and Trace had some good friends in this town. They'd stand by Trace no matter what.

Hillary spoke, thinking of good friends as they turned back in the direction of the Mannerly house. "My father was often away, so I had a nanny." The memory came with easy grief. "She has been gone for years, but she was good to me and became my friend. I always wondered why my father did not marry her. Then as I got older, I realized Pa didn't spend enough time at home to grow another love inside himself."

"Our lives are much the same."

She scanned the street continuously, a habit learned from being in the military. Always know your surroundings, where people are, where buildings are, what's the best cover or escape route. Even here in this quiet town it wasn't something she could quit doing.

And with her awareness came a subtle tension.

Then she saw the man again. He might be trying to be invisible, but the way he held his head... It was him.

She kept walking but said quietly, "You see him?"

"Yes."

Matters were rapidly growing more interesting. And making her just a bit concerned.

"OKAY," TRACE SAID when they got back to the house. "I've got to find out who he is. Twice could be coincidence, but three times?" Tension coiled him tight as a spring.

He looked at Hillary and saw her nod. She said, "It's not likely even in a small town."

"You feeling hunted?"

"Yes."

"Damn it!" He didn't bother to moderate his voice. Along with the tension came anger, a lot of anger. "But if he's trouble, I have to be careful about how I poke around."

"Are you trained to gather intelligence of this kind?"

"Like this? Not exactly."

"Neither am I. My training focused on urban interface and gathering intelligence from women."

He lifted a brow. "Why women?"

"Because they will talk more freely with another woman."

"I can see that," he admitted. "Especially in some regions of the world where a woman can be killed for talking with a strange male."

"Yes." Then she shook her head again. "I feel this could get bad."

So did he. That feeling of being hunted was all too real to ignore. He'd felt that way more than once when on a mission, but never before in this town.

"Hell," he said, expressing his anger once again. When he looked at Hillary, he saw a spark in her gaze. Anger? Maybe. She'd lost Brigid, after all. And he didn't think a Valkyrie was feeling nervous. Nope.

They spent a long night going through files and papers. Trace kept feeling he was on the cusp of a discovery, but it eluded him. Once again he felt seriously annoyed by the way Allan had mixed all this up. No question but that he'd been trying to conceal something.

A small stack of handwritten letters grew beside Hillary. All the envelopes had been opened, but she didn't pull out the letters. Not yet.

She *did* say, as she had thought already, "It's odd that they handwrote so many letters. In these days, email has replaced that."

"Yeah. Let's leave them, though, until you finish sorting. If the letters contain something, it might be easier to fit all the pieces when we look at them in sequence. Which is more than I can do with these files."

He sighed and got back to work, convinced all over again that Allan had wanted him to find something. But what?

Chapter Eight

The next afternoon, after some sleep, they were interrupted several times. Trace was surprised as relationships that he'd ignored began to knit themselves back together. Evidently he was being welcomed back into the fold.

But where had these people been during the inquest, or right after? Had they been hoping for a different decision? Or maybe Guy had been right. They didn't want to look like fools in front of their neighbors.

Among the flow of people who stopped by, claiming they wanted to see how Trace was doing, came one who surprised him because they'd been acquaintances but never close.

Edith Jasper, a woman who might have been in her late sixties or early seventies, stopped by with her harlequin Great Dane, Bailey. A frail-looking woman, everyone wondered how she handled that dog. She managed, considering that she and the dog could not be parted. Nor had Edith ever suffered an injury.

Bailey's huge head reached above Edith's waist, and Trace was sure the dog would totally dwarf her if he stood on his hind legs, but Bailey was also polite. He had what Edith called *house manners*. He leaped on no one, but when he sat and grinned, he still looked gigantic.

Trace invited them both in, and after introductions he

watched Hillary fall in love with the dog. She knelt on the floor, Bailey sat down and the two of them immediately began to cuddle.

"Well, that's the seal of approval," Edith remarked.

Trace smiled. "Can I get you something, Edith?"

"It's cold out there, but Bailey needs his walks. Anything hot or warm will do, thank you."

Hillary looked up. "There's an unopened bottle of cider in the kitchen closet. Warm it up with a cinnamon stick."

Trace went to follow orders. Behind him he heard Hillary laugh and Edith chuckle.

Later, as they settled in the living room with hot cider, the subject of Allan and Brigid came up.

"I liked them both, have since I taught them in seventh grade," Edith said. "A very pleasant young couple, and they seemed truly happy together. At least when they *were* together." Then she frowned at Trace. "Do you know that I wanted to see you ever since Allan died? Only you were too busy chasing your own tail. When I was out and about, you'd always vanished somewhere."

Trace nodded. "I guess so. I did a lot of running."

"Eating those miles up. Like I do with Bailey. Dog keeps me young and healthy."

"And he doesn't give you any trouble?" Hillary asked.

"Not a bit. Folks used to worry that he'd pull me off my feet, but he's never tugged once. It's like he senses I'd wind up on the pavement."

"He is an angel," Hillary replied.

On the floor, Bailey lay with his head between his front paws, but it was clear neither his nose nor his eyes were missing a thing.

"When angels start visiting me," Edith answered, "I'll begin to worry."

She turned again to Trace. "About Allan."

Trace felt his shoulders begin to tighten. His stomach started feeling like a hollow pit. Again. "Yeah?"

"He was a good man. One of the best. But I was concerned about him after Brigid died."

"He was drinking a lot," Trace remarked, his voice heavy.

"But not that much. Too much, but not enough to make him stagger."

"You think he was depressed?"

"Of course he was depressed," Edith said sharply. "Who wouldn't be? But it wasn't his drinking that bothered me. That's just a man's way of dealing with too much emotion." She cocked a brow at Trace. "Men need to learn how to cry."

He smiled faintly. "Maybe so. But about Allan?"

"Yes, Allan. He was ripped up, but he'd have come through it. And you insisting it couldn't be suicide. Unless I'm sorely mistaken, that man didn't have quit in him."

Trace tensed even more. "I don't think he did."

"A lot of people heard you. Made everybody a little nervous about what you might do."

"As in?"

"Ripping this town apart from end to end."

Hillary smiled faintly but said nothing.

Edith continued. "Then you went into that shell and didn't seem to see anyone. Folks stepped back. Didn't want to disturb you."

Trace frowned. "Not a pretty picture, Edith. Did I make you feel that way?"

"Not about ripping the town apart. I've known you since I taught you math. I figured you wouldn't even put your fist through a window. Too sensible."

"I hope so."

Edith nodded, appearing satisfied. "I was right. Seventy-odd years have taught me a few things about human nature. Anyway, I wondered if you were right about Allan."

Trace drummed his fingers on the arm of the chair. He was growing impatient, feeling as if Edith might know something. If so, she had a roundabout way of getting to it.

Edith sipped more cider. "Regardless, my old brain began to rattle around in my head. It does that every so often, and when it does things pop out, useful or not. I suspect Allan wasn't just grieving Brigid. He was bothered by something."

Jolted, Trace leaned forward, resting his elbows on his knees, thinking about those passwords. "By what?"

"I wish I knew. He never said, and I guess he never told you. It was just a feeling I got. I can't be sure, Trace. Just a sense."

Edith set her cup aside and rose. "I've got to get Bailey back to his walk before he starts whining like a baby."

She started toward the door, Trace accompanying her. Before she stepped out, she looked up at him. "I really am inclined to believe he didn't commit suicide. Period."

After Trace closed the door, he discovered Hillary right behind him. She looked uneasy.

"What do you think?" she asked.

"That Edith might be right. But we already considered the possibility."

"I know. But she validated it."

Trace closed his eyes briefly, thinking over what Edith had said. She had only a sense that Allan had been troubled by something other than grief. But her sense was good enough for him.

"Let's go for a run," he suggested. "I need to work out all this tension. You?"

"I'm always ready. Then we'll dive in again."

Hillary was clearly hooked.

THE MOUNTAINTOP WAS PEACEFUL. After stretching, Hillary sat on a boulder and looked down at the town below. Brigid's death had been bad enough, but this growing belief that it might have been murder was twisting her insides into knots.

That someone might have plotted to kill Brigid seemed impossible, but the impossible now stared her in the face, growing more possible by the minute.

Her sorrow deepened. What had always felt like a waste now grew into something bigger. She looked at Trace and thought about his fight against the idea that Allan had died by suicide. About the intensity of his drive for months.

Now she felt the same intensity. Edith's words had stamped the need into her heart. If it was murder, Brigid must be avenged. Anger twisted around her grief, stronger than it had been in the immediate aftermath.

She noticed the shadows were deepening, warning of the approach of early night. She rose, stretching a few times, then said, "Let's go before we stiffen."

Not that Trace had been likely to do that. While she'd been sitting morosely on a rock, he'd kept moving.

She ran faster than before on the downslope, taking a big risk on the rutted track. She needed that risk, needed to feel her head clear, needed the adrenaline rush that came from danger.

Trace, on the parallel rut, kept pace with her. Not a word about this being hazardous on such uneven ground. The dirt before her was pitted, full of rocks, utterly uneven. She knew she was foolish to do this without a threat chasing her, but she didn't care, relying on her boots to protect her ankles.

The pounding of her feet on the ground felt almost like the rage pounding inside her. A Pandora's box had opened inside her, unleashing the Valkyrie, the hunter.

She wanted a battle.

TRACE SENSED THE shift in Hillary. He couldn't glance at her until they reached level road, but then he did. It was a wonder she hadn't bared her teeth.

In that instant he saw the warrior inside her, the one she kept beneath a carefully controlled exterior. As they all had to do, but this was his first true introduction to the woman within. The Valkyrie.

He'd seen that expression on the face of other soldiers going into battle. During battle.

As they approached the end of their rapid run, they both breathed heavily. He still managed to ask, "Are you going to start a war?"

Her blue eyes looked icy. "Against who?"

That was the problem for them both. No idea where to direct all this rage, all this angry sorrow. They were shadowboxing.

They went home without seeing that guy, leaving Trace to consider the possibility that they'd both overreacted. He had mixed feelings about that. He wanted a person to focus on but doubted that would be likely. Not after all this time, unless the killer lived in this town. Which, given what Edith had said, seemed extremely unlikely.

Rage, like a banked fire, burned within him.

What the hell, Allan?

LATER, HILLARY INTRODUCED Trace to a "Norwegian breakfast" that felt more like a supper to Trace. It had consisted of slices of the hard sausage the butcher had ordered for her, small cubes of Jarlsberg cheese and thick, crunchy crackers.

"That's breakfast, huh?" he asked as they headed back to the office.

She shrugged one shoulder. "Most of us prefer not to eat breakfast at all. You will have a hard time finding any café or restaurant that is open to serve breakfast. We tend to have what you call brunch."

"I liked it."

She smiled. "You should consider yourself special. That was a buffet style, which is found in hotels."

"I'm honored."

Her smile turned into a laugh as she took her seat at her side of the desk. When she looked at the stacks of paper, her smile faded, however, and her face turned grim. "Trace?"

"Yeah?"

"I may go mad if we don't find something soon."

"Me too." He had begun to drag the scattered emails into folders by date, most recent first. Initially, it had made him squirm to peek into the love that had flowed electronically between them. Made him feel like a voyeur. Anger had burned out that concern.

He understood why Allan had opened all this to his scrutiny, however. He doubted that Allan had trusted anyone else to read this intimacy.

"Damn it, Allan, give me a clue!" He only realized he had spoken aloud when Hillary made a sound. He turned to look directly at her. "Sorry."

"Go ahead, Trace. I feel the same way, and I may soon be cursing Brigid."

"Maybe it would do us some good to have a minor temper tantrum, stomping our feet and yelling."

She laughed outright, her face clearing. "I didn't think of that. I was wishing for a punching bag."

"Better idea. Maybe we can get over to the high school gym and pound them."

"Make it a date."

Date? Trace wondered how she had meant that. A flicker of hope sprouted inside him, but he tried to stomp it out. He didn't want to disrespect her with a one-night stand kind of thing.

He glanced at her from the corner of his eye. Unless that was her style?

Ah, hell, he thought. His mind and body usually bent to his will better than this. But with her so close, her feminine scents enticing him, it was difficult. He'd have liked to escape into her for a few hours. To discover once again one of life's greatest beauties. To drag himself, and her, out of this ugly swamp they'd walked into.

After he felt he'd moved all the recent emails into one file and was once again on the edge of going stir-crazy, he found something. His heart sped up.

"Hillary?"

"Mmm?"

"Take a look at this. It's not much."

She scooted her chair over and peered over his shoulder. "Where?"

Stuck in the middle of some graphic prose, Allan had written, *Let it go, sweetheart. Just let it go.*

Hillary read the email twice before saying, "That doesn't fit. It is out of place."

"It might mean almost anything. Maybe a small squabble."

"But it doesn't belong there."

He passed his hand over his face. "No, it doesn't." Allan was worrying about something. But Trace felt it like a sharp prod. His determination revived, he leaned over the computer again. "Let's keep going. Whatever it is, Allan tried to bury it."

He checked the date again on the email. He'd been out of town. Maybe Allan hadn't wanted to share the issue, or maybe he'd forgotten all about it.

Or maybe he'd been too worried to speak about it.

"When was that email sent?" Hillary asked.

"Mid-January."

"Brigid died in late January." Her frown deepened. "Too close."

"I agree."

Something had been going on. Something bad enough to get Brigid killed? Out there that wasn't impossible. Life began to feel cheap.

Hillary spoke. "It wouldn't be the first time someone out there has been killed for no reason."

He knew exactly what she meant. "When you pull the cork out of that bottle, it can splash anywhere."

"Good analogy."

"But this time it sounds like there might have been a reason."

"It does." Her face impassive, she turned back to the stack of letters she'd been compiling. "Maybe it's time to actually read some of this."

HOURS LATER, THEY called it quits. The night had grown deep, settling into silence except for the sound of a cold wind whistling around corners and through tiny cracks.

"Banshee," Hillary remarked.

"Are you trying to give me chills?"

A smile leavened her face. "I doubt you ever get chills."

"Neither do you, except possibly when it's forty below."

Her smile became a laugh. "I would like aquavit. You?"

"It might help get us some sleep."

If nothing else, weariness lessened the pressure. There was just so long a person could stay wound up. As Hillary walked to the kitchen, she rotated her shoulders, trying to ease the tightness in them. She was definitely unaccustomed to spending so many hours at a desk.

The laugh had felt good. Brief as it was, it had unknotted her stomach a bit. She was on the hunt now, deeply involved. That one line in Allan's email seemed heavy with portent. Dark. She'd known Brigid well, and her friend wasn't one who needed to be told to *forget it* over a disagreement.

Brigid had had a good soul, part of what had drawn Hillary to her. How that soul had survived combat operations, survived risking her neck to escort convoys, survived having to fight, Hillary didn't know.

Her own soul had suffered cracks. She knew she wasn't as forgiving as Brigid had been. Hillary was less ready. She was quick to dismiss someone as an idiot. Or even as evil in an extreme case. She was also quicker to remember, to not forget.

Her feeling was that when a snake bit you, you shouldn't go back to playing with the snake.

Brigid had walked this earth lightly.

As she sat across from Trace with aquavit, she said, "Brigid was a bright soul. Was she always like that?"

One corner of his mouth lifted. "Frustratingly sometimes. She wouldn't let you get a good mad on. *Forget it* was one of her favorite phrases. The other was, *Is it important enough to waste your energy on?*"

Hillary nodded, remembering Brigid saying just that. "I admired that in her. I am not so good."

"Me neither."

Hillary slipped briefly into memory, then returned. "Allan. He was like her?"

"They were kind of yin and yang. He was… I don't know how to describe it. He was a lot more reserved. He was harder. You know what I mean."

She did. Then a stark thought occurred to her. "That phrase that leaped out of Allan's email?"

His gaze grew intent.

"Allan was harder, you said, but he tossed those words back at her. Maybe it wasn't a reminder. Maybe it was a warning."

Trace tossed back the last of his aquavit. "Hell. I'm awake now. I'm going back to work."

Hillary waited just long enough to brew another pot of coffee. Then she followed him with two insulated mugs.

The hunter inside her had fully roused, and she was on the trail. She would not be deterred.

As MORNING BEGAN to creep into the cold world, Trace looked at Hillary. She looked back. Fatigue was written on her face, a slight draining of color, but she sat upright, her posture firm. This woman would keep going until she dropped into a coma.

So would he, probably, but they would quickly become useless. "Operational readiness requires at least some sleep. We both know that." They both parted to go to their separate rooms. Hillary found it difficult to sleep and wondered if she had just grown too tired. A paradox she had faced before.

Closing her eyes, she wandered her memories of Brigid. They hadn't spent a whole lot of time together, as their missions were different and Hillary didn't spend long periods at the rear base, although for a while she had visited frequently.

Regardless, their friendship had happened almost explosively. Hillary might never understand how it had happened so fast. It just had.

Brigid was a dark-haired woman with sherry-colored eyes that seemed to glow from within. She smiled most of the time and appeared to be surrounded by good buddies of all genders.

But somehow Hillary had leaped into the inner circle.

To become someone in whom she could confide, who could confide in her. Even about the locket Brigid kept concealed inside her uniform. A secret.

For the first time, Hillary wondered just how many secrets Brigid had guarded.

Hillary rolled over and hugged the other pillow.

She hadn't done that since before she joined the Jegertroppen, partly because there was never an extra pillow, and partly because it might be interpreted as softness. Or childishness.

She didn't know who she was angrier at—Brigid, because she might have involved herself in a matter that had gotten her killed, or the person who might have arranged it.

As she hugged the pillow, other thoughts trailed in, mostly thoughts about Trace. He appealed to her on so many levels. Men outside the special forces never really understood, and there was much she couldn't share.

Trace crossed those boundaries. She didn't have to explain, because he knew.

He was sexy as hell. She wasn't immune. She'd seen the glint of attraction on his face, but something kept pulling him back, maybe the same thing that kept pulling *her* back. The distance that would soon lie between them. Half a world.

She liked him, too. Her practiced impassivity wasn't too deep for that. Inside her there was also a woman like any other.

And she wasn't afraid of fleeting sexual relationships. She'd had a few before. She was the one, usually, who ensured they were fleeting. Giving her heart might be a very stupid thing to do, so she kept it, clinging tightly to it.

But this would be different. She wouldn't have to fight her way out or think of a million reasons for leaving. Trace already knew that was coming.

Maybe, she thought. Warmth filled her just by thinking about it. A warmth full of desire. Of heat.

She drifted away to sleep at last, thinking about Trace. OUTSIDE, IN THE frigid wee hours, through slight slits in a couple of curtains, Witherspoon watched the lights turn out at last.

Bundled up against the cold, he thought he resembled one of those puffy cartoon characters found in an ad. Given the temperature out here, he doubted anyone would notice his gear, but they might notice him standing in the yard behind bushes.

Yet he needed to move on before he froze to death. He'd been out here too long, giving serious thought to breaking into that house while the two of them slept and taking them out.

Except that taking out two people was a lot more difficult than taking out one. Whoever he shot first, the other was going to come after him. They were both soldiers. He'd heard that late last night in the bar. He knew all about Trace Mullen, about his Airborne background. That man could be serious trouble.

But a female soldier, according to gossip about her being in the war? He'd never seen them as a serious threat.

Maybe, just maybe, he could take out Mullen first, then the woman. Hell, she might have been nothing but a glorified paper pusher.

But still. He had enough sense left to consider two murders to be a dangerous proposition. Enough sense to turn away and walk back to the student apartment he rented. Enough sense to get home before he turned into an icicle.

If the woman went back to wherever she came from, the problem would be halved. He needed to add that to his planning before he did something he'd truly regret.

He regretted killing Allan Mannerly. Still, the whispers

around town suggested that Mullen still didn't believe it was suicide. And now the whispers suggested that a whole lot of people in this town were questioning it, too.

They might have zipped their lips for a while, but they were not zipping them anymore.

That frightened Witherspoon as well. Too many people were shifting positions for reasons he didn't know.

What the hell was going on?

Once again he thought of moving out, but the mess he might be leaving behind could come back to kill him.

He was getting to the point of wanting to tear his own hair out. He'd bitten his fingernails to bloody nubs, and now he was chewing his lower lip raw. Making his teeth hurt from grinding them constantly.

Brigid Mannerly and her husband had gotten the easy part of all this, he decided. An easy, fast death.

Witherspoon feared he would not be as lucky.

Chapter Nine

Two days later, Hillary glanced to her right as she headed for the bathroom. Trace sat on the edge of his narrow bed, a towel wrapped around his waist, displaying a rather respectable six-pack as he pulled a shirt over his head.

But what she most noticed were the black neoprene knee stabilizers. Given that he never complained about his new knees, she was a little surprised to see those stabilizers. Regardless, he put a lot of tough miles on his legs. He should have been reaching for paracetamol or ibuprofen, but she had never seen him reach for a thing. Tough guy. Not giving an inch.

Without a word, she grabbed a large blue knapsack she'd found in the bedroom closet. So he wouldn't wonder, she left a brief note.

Then she headed to the grocery, determined to remember how to cook well enough that they didn't need to go out again. She'd never really liked dining out except with a group of friends. Besides, she wanted some different flavors.

She filled her cart with vegetables and fruit. She was unable to resist the bananas, which must have traveled a very long way, and six fresh, crunchy apples fell into her cart. Amazing, she thought with amusement. As if they might have jumped right in.

She wasn't a heavy beef eater, but a really impressive steak looked back at her from the cold case. She bet Trace would like that. In fact, he might even have a preferred way of preparing it. That joined the stack in her cart.

Her shopping list got longer as she went, until she nearly laughed at herself. She must have been craving some things without realizing it.

She was, however, happy to see Trace come through the door just as she was ready to check out. She knew she had chosen too much to fit in the knapsack and decided it would be easier to carry the rest with help. Grocery bags could have a mind of their own, even with handles. She wished for the net bags she'd used at home.

He smiled when he saw her. "Looks like you picked up a lot. Hungry?"

"For something different."

"Mind?" He looked through her cart. "Well, I have to confess I can read a recipe. If we can get some potatoes, I'll brown them in the oven. Do you like rice?"

"Brown rice."

"Coming up." He also brought a few mixes that looked like they'd provide some muffins or loaves. "We need our carbs."

Very true.

"Are these real bratwursts?" she asked as they passed down the meat aisle again.

"They're American bratwurst. I don't know how that compares to what you're used to."

"I'll find out." She watched him put two gallons of milk into the cart, along with chocolate syrup.

When they left the store, Hillary realized the break had refreshed her. Surprisingly, she looked forward to getting into the kitchen.

Something besides poring over the files and letters. Two days and they'd found nothing more. She suspected they might already have gone too far back in time. "We need to run through those emails and letters again."

"Start to finish," he agreed. "Man, how elliptical can you get?"

"Quite a bit, it seems."

"Or worse, that whatever it was, they may have Skyped it."

She sighed. "That's a possibility. So now we have to find if there are copies."

"Probably in one of those damn random files I haven't gotten to yet. If Allan saved them." Then he shook his head. "I have to keep reminding myself that Allan wanted me to find something."

"Maybe he hid it too well."

Trace snorted. "He may have. Some idea of what I'm looking for would be a great help."

"You didn't see him before he died?"

"I didn't get here for Brigid's funeral. I was on a mission. Then I was in the hospital and rehabilitation, under medical control until they decided I'd recovered enough to be turned loose. By then I only had a month with him before…" He shook his head as they pulled into the driveway.

She mulled that over as they carried the groceries inside. Only a month with Allan before he died and no secrets shared.

At times she faced the sacrifices demanded by her career, but she preferred not to think about them. It did her no good to focus on selfish desires.

Putting the groceries away, which had originally seemed like a distraction, now felt like another delay. They had to find something so they could really get started on their search.

She took an apple back to the office with her. Trace followed with a banana. There was a chance they had missed something.

Because if Allan had become aware of a problem, it must have happened before Brigid died. Before he'd written that telltale *Forget about it*.

She and Trace exchanged looks before they dived back in. In Trace's eyes she saw a steel she felt within herself. He'd spend years on this if he had to. She didn't have that much time. It didn't help that English was more of a second language to her, despite her mother, despite English being spoken by so many the world over. It remained a second language.

Trace spoke. "It occurs to me, dunce that I am, that when I was here, Allan may not have shared the secret because he didn't want to put me in danger."

Hillary drew a breath. "I would believe it."

Then she reached for a letter and slipped it out of the envelope for a second reading. She hoped she would find something she had missed.

An hour later she felt a small bubble of excitement. "Trace?"

"Hmm?"

"She writes of there being too many American weapons in the hands of insurgents. *Too many* is underlined."

He swiveled his chair and leaned toward her. "Show me."

He scanned Brigid's writing. Then he looked at Hillary. "You're right. It has something to do with weapons."

"That could well be dangerous information."

"Depends on why she said it. But the way she underlined…" His voice trailed off. Then he said, "I think we may have found a clue."

TRACE WAS AWARE that there was a black market in weapons. A lot of money could be made on a single M4 carbine and some ammo. Or either model M203 grenade launchers, again, if the grenades could be sold with them. The M4 was particularly versatile, as it could be mounted on the grenade launchers for added firepower.

"Hell!" He knew it happened, but rarely did anyone get caught diverting the weapons. However, if Brigid had obtained specific information about a person or organization, she might have become expendable.

Another look at Hillary told him she shared his thoughts. Trace felt sickened. Bad enough to redirect arms for money, but worse to consider a woman disposable if she learned about it.

This is what had worried Allan. No question.

He stood up. "Time for a run."

He didn't ask, and Hillary simply stood up.

Run it off, man. Run it off.

THEY PUSHED HARD on their way up the mountainside and they went farther this time, following the ATV tracks over the ridge. A bit of snow had settled up there overnight, a light dusting like confectioners' sugar.

"Winter's close," he remarked.

"Too close."

He wondered what she had meant by that. Her words hadn't sounded casual, but instead freighted with meaning.

They turned to run back down, but this time followed a slower pace, one that allowed them to talk as they ran.

"She had to have found out more," Trace said.

"I feel the same. Now we need to find out what it was. Someone must have been afraid of her."

"Maybe." Or maybe just a dyed-in-the-wool psychopath who shoved any obstacle aside without remorse.

It didn't matter what kind of enemy Brigid and Allan had faced. Trace was determined to put an end to whoever they were.

THE STEADY HAMMER of their feet relaxed them physically, but Hillary felt no easing of the stress that had grown in her after finding those words in Brigid's letter. Nothing more than that, but a strong hint. Now she was truly eager to get back to work.

She suspected Trace felt the same. Her desire to find the person or persons who might be involved in this not only brought out the hunter in her. It brought out the soldier who would never give up, never surrender.

When they got back to the house, they ransacked the refrigerator and cupboards for something quick to eat while they worked. Another pot of coffee brewed.

"Later," Trace said, "I want to make some of those brownies I bought. I don't know about you, but chocolate is practically a medicine."

Trace had bought some thinly sliced ham that morning, and they built thick sandwiches with ham and Jarlsberg cheese.

"This is a Norwegian cheese," she remarked.

"Better in Norway, I bet."

She gave him only the attempt of a smile she wasn't feeling. "Depends on what you're used to."

"Very generous of you."

Plates and cups in hand, they headed back to the office.

Neither of them could have stopped now unless dragged away by wild horses.

They began their search again, looking for some further

indication of what had happened. A name. A description of what she had seen. Somehow Allan had known.

But when you were in a combat zone, you couldn't bring your personal cell phone or computer. Everything went through protected military equipment. No truly private email or phone call or Skype.

Hence the great caution the two had displayed.

A COUPLE OF hours later, they took a break. Muscles had knotted bent over keyboards and letters, exacerbated by the pressure of finding an answer.

They sat in the kitchen over beers talking in spurts, mostly generalities. After a bit, they grew serious again.

"This whole thing doesn't make sense," Trace remarked. "One person couldn't have enough evidence to threaten any corporation. God, they've got enough lawyers to tie up the matter in court for years. What could Brigid have discovered that would be enough to threaten them, anyway?"

"It had to have been something important," Hillary agreed. The cold beer bottle sweat, making her fingertips wet. "It's a long way to go to come this far to kill Allan."

"Exactly. Silencing Brigid might make perverse sense, given she was probably an eyewitness, but Allan? I doubt much in her letters would constitute any kind of real evidence. Hearsay, probably."

"He had told her to forget it. He wasn't inclined to pursue the matter."

"But who would know that? If he decided her death was a direct result of her knowledge, then he might have been pursuing the matter on his own."

She nodded. "This problem is growing bigger. If we are right, what can we do about it?"

His gaze grew steely again. "I need to know for *me*. Even if I can't do damn all about it."

Hillary understood, but she also understood that the clue had drawn him in deeper. He wasn't stopping. He wanted much more than knowing.

She tapped her bottle with her fingertips, considering the entire situation from another perspective.

Then she spoke, a chill trickling down her spine. "We haven't considered the army itself."

"How so?" He stared at her.

"If someone up her chain of command was involved, he'd have a lot more to lose than a corporation would."

He closed his eyes briefly. "Yeah. And some officer or NCO would have a much longer reach. A lot of friends here and abroad. Hell."

"It could be like tumbling dominoes, revealing people higher in the command."

"And with each step upward, the danger would grow." Trace swore again.

THE HOURS HAD bled together. Neither of them thought of the clock, or the time difference that had affected Hillary at first. Their awareness of time was only that they wouldn't run at night. Either of them could be injured by a stumble or fall, Trace's knees especially.

But because the hours had flowed together, it was no surprise when Trace suddenly announced, "It's time to cook something. My banana has long since vanished."

In response, Hillary's stomach growled, making them both laugh.

First they spent some time in the living room working out kinks. Stretching, push-ups, sit-ups, lunges, twists… everything to loosen up and quiet muscles that needed to work.

Trace enjoyed having someone alongside him as they did calisthenics. Even more, he enjoyed the view of Hillary in a T-shirt and exercise shorts. Such long, perfectly shaped, athletic legs. A guy would like to have those legs wrapped around him.

When they got to jumping jacks, they faced each other with an added benefit. Hillary had enough breasts to bounce a little. He figured she wouldn't like his repeated glances at all, but she *was* sexy.

But he thought she looked faintly amused, as if she knew.

A couple of times he suspected she might be regarding him the same way, but he couldn't be sure.

They traded on quick showers and a change into warmer clothes before returning to the kitchen, where beer sounded better to them both than another pot of coffee.

Hillary studied him, looking less impassive than usual. "That scar on your cheek? Do you mind telling me?"

He shrugged. "A knife."

She didn't ask how, which was fine by him. Thinking about the war wasn't going to give either of them the break they needed.

"Dinner," she said, changing the topic. "Any preferences? You helped put it all away, so you can't claim ignorance."

He smiled. "No excuses. Well, I was eyeing that steak. I can't cook it on the grill in this weather, but I *do* remember how to cook a steak in a frying pan. What else?"

She considered. "Vegetables. And perhaps those frozen fried potatoes?"

"Oh yeah. And maybe I'll make some of those dang brownies." He wiggled his brows at her. "I'm pretty sure I can follow the directions on the box."

"I think you would be very good at following directions."

"Oh, I like the sound of that."

She laughed. "You would."

She had flirted with him. Unmistakably. He liked it, but it ratcheted his desire for her to a whole new level. Looking at her now, he wondered if her reserve was cracking.

Not that he'd been opening up very much. He'd been taking his private trips down memory lane, but he hadn't shared them. Keeping an emotional distance. Why should he expect anything else from her?

The war. It hovered over everything. The endless war that was steadily becoming the modern version of the Hundred Years' War.

He got out the thick steak, nicely marbled. Hillary pulled out the frozen veggies and fries. Together they calculated cooking times.

"As best we can," Hillary laughed. "Two rusty cooks. What do you think we'll make of this?"

"If I ruin that steak, I'll never forgive myself." He flashed a grin, surprised that it was coming so easily. Some of the somberness and anger had faded, at least for now.

"You brighten this place up," he said as he stabbed the steak repeatedly with a knife and spread butter all over it.

"What are you doing?" she asked.

"My dad always made them this way. Good browning and some buttery flavor throughout."

She poured vegetables into a glass bowl. "French fries in the oven first, I think." She pointed at the package. "I can follow directions as well."

Again. Damn, his groin was beginning to feel heavy with hunger. He forced his attention back to the steak.

"What did you mean, I'm brightening this place?" she asked.

"This house. It's so full of memories of Allan and Brigid that at first I could barely stand to be in here. Now, well, you're changing that. This house was never intended to be a mausoleum."

Her voice softened. "I think it was intended to be a haven for wounded hearts."

"And a happy one. They made the most out of every moment they were together. Made the most of our friendship, too." Forgetting the steak for a moment, he stared into space, remembering all the laughter, all the joy. When those two had been here, they'd shed everything that might have haunted them.

"Haven," he said, returning his attention to finding a frying pan while Hillary spread the fries on a baking sheet and popped them into the oven. "That's a good word for it, Hillary. A truly good word. It was a healing place."

"Maybe that was the reason they wanted you to have this house."

He hadn't thought of it that way. Instead he'd seen it as a dark place full of grief. As a place haunted by people he had loved who were now gone. A repository of good memories that could only bring pain.

"Maybe so. I sure couldn't imagine why they wanted to give it to me."

"Perhaps because they weren't the only ones who were happy here." Having closed the oven and set a timer, she said, "Flip in eight minutes. I can manage that."

That drew a laugh from him. "Like there's very much you can't manage. Should we go out back and build a fire with twigs?"

She joined his laughter. "That's easy."

"I was afraid you'd say that. I'll have to think of something more difficult."

Later, as he was frying the steak, she asked, "Do you have family here?"

"None. Mom died giving birth to me. My dad raised

me, then skipped out right after I left for the Army. I have
no idea where he is."

She fell briefly silent. "That's sad. Maybe he felt he
couldn't risk losing you, too."

"I don't know. I didn't see him that way, but I could be
wrong. He was always taciturn and strict. No-nonsense. I
turned to my friends. He steadily turned away." He paused.
"Sometimes I wondered if he blamed me. If he looked at
me and got angry or something."

She didn't answer. *What answer could there be?* he
wondered. No one could know.

But then she offered, "It's awful you felt that way."

He shrugged. "It was what it was. A fact of life. I didn't
concentrate on it—I just built my own life. What about
you?"

"What about me?" The timer dinged, and she pulled
the fries out, beginning to turn them over.

"Your mom, your dad. That couldn't have been easy
for you."

"It wasn't especially difficult. I didn't have to wonder
if they both loved me."

"And your dad?"

She smiled as she placed the fries back in the oven.
"My best friend. We talk about everything." Her smile
grew softer. "I have so many images of him, sometimes
stern, but mostly with his eyes crinkled in a smile for me."

"It would be easy to smile at you."

She glanced at him, seeming to hold her breath, but only
for a second. "That is a very nice thing to say."

"It's just true. How did you grow up?"

"When my father was home, we did nearly everything
together. Long ski trips in the mountains, some camping,
some traveling, sometimes just sitting by the fire and talking with friends. Many good times."

He had never known that himself, but the image she painted was warm and inviting. He could almost picture it.

He pulled the steak out of the frying pan. "We're doing pretty good," he remarked as the microwave beeped that the vegetables were done. A minute later, the oven timer went off.

She tossed him a glance over her shoulder. "Just the way a military operation *should* go."

"But never does."

"Never," she agreed.

Trace had grown more comfortable with the dishes in the cupboard, so he pulled them out and set the table for them. Icy bottles of beer accompanied the settings, and then the food.

"Damn, it smells good," he said.

They sat facing each other. Trace had cut the steak in half as best he could and put a portion on her plate. After that it was every man or woman for him or herself.

"I forgot to make those brownies," he said.

"Thus failing to prove you can follow directions."

Damn, she made him laugh. At long last when he sensed Brigid and Allan in this house, he felt as if they were smiling at him.

Chapter Ten

Stan Witherspoon's fears continued to grow. The longer that blonde woman stayed in town, the more worried he became. A soldier. One who had been Brigid's friend.

On the one hand, he was glad of this town's busy grapevine. On the other, he worried that it might expose *him* in some way.

There was no way to shut the gossip down. None. He just had to continue trying to remain unremarkable.

Although unremarkable was his general description. He blended better than a potted plant.

Sometimes he liked his inherent invisibility. Sometimes he hated it. He sure hadn't been invisible those two times Brigid Mannerly had spied him at his avocation. He preferred that term, *avocation*, to the real one: arms merchant.

Hell, he'd been moving weapons for years, a cog in the chain between manufacturers and the battlefield. What he'd begun to do for money really wasn't that different. Or so he told himself.

He knew it could get him in some serious trouble, especially with the man who had been running the operation and maybe others.

A lot could happen between leaving manufacturing plants and arriving at destinations. Even shipments of socks turned up missing, and the security on weapons didn't seem to be much more stringent. At least not when you knew what to do.

He even had heard of weapons and ammo disappearing from stateside military bases. Amazing the power of a soldier working in such a place. A little here, a little there, and a small cover-up and no one would notice.

For a while, at any rate. Didn't anyone do inventory?

A stupid question. When the guy diverting the stuff was the same one who was doing the inventory, the cover-up was easy.

As well he knew. That's why he'd been selected for this operation.

Which had brought him here. The only place that was more back of the beyond than Conard City was the place he had come from. Now he'd committed a murder in both places and was thinking about another one or two.

Had anyone asked him five years ago if he would do any of this, he'd have sworn he never would.

Until the money was offered. Until the fear took over.

He was a changed man.

He hated to think about it.

LAST NIGHT, TRACE BELIEVED, something had almost happened between him and Hillary. A look, an atmosphere, something. There had been a huge ground shift between them. Like an earthquake.

But nothing had come from it, probably because they were both cautious. Any kind of relationship would be fraught with problems.

He felt almost guilty for entertaining such ideas, given all that had happened. Well, guilt never did a damn bit of good. His mind was going to rove wherever it chose, and maybe it needed a serious break.

"We've got a lot to think about," he said to Hillary as they finished up their run. "A few threads to weave together."

"We certainly need more information to act on. Are you growing satisfied, though?"

He thought about it. "I'm growing even more convinced that Allan didn't die by suicide."

"I thought you were already convinced."

He shook his head. "There's always a doubt when you have little but belief. Now I feel justification ahead. Maybe."

The lack of answers aggravated the hell out of him. "Brigid had to have known something important. Allan wouldn't worry over nothing."

"She must have told him somehow."

"Which is why we're on this quest. And I'm sick of jawing over the same ground."

Hillary remained quiet as they slowed into a cooldown walk. Then she spoke the obvious.

"It's already clear something was being concealed."

The endless hamster wheel, Trace thought. *Totally endless at this point.* But Allan had evidently felt that Trace could figure it out.

"Hell," he said aloud. "I was never good at puzzles. Allan knew that."

"I imagine he believed otherwise. At any point after Brigid died, he could have written it all down for you to find."

"So what was he afraid of at that point?"

"Dragging you into danger."

Trace looked up at the sky. It was darkening again, pregnant with clouds. As they were.

HILLARY STEERED THEM to Maude's diner. Trace needed another break whether he knew it or not. Something to divert him a bit longer from his search. Obsession was rarely a good thing and could become blinding.

"You know," she remarked, "I have no idea what time of day it is anymore."

That drew a laugh from him. "Did we ever have? After a while in the military, you need a watch just to tell you the time wherever we are."

"Very true."

Trace glanced at *his* watch. "It's past noon and well before dinner hour. Maude's shouldn't be too packed."

Nor was it, which suited Hillary fine. They chose a table at the back. One that allowed them to keep their backs to the wall. Hillary felt inwardly amused. Soldiers. Guard the back at all times.

Maude didn't even ask if they wanted coffee. It slammed down in front of them, along with a couple of glistening menus. "Keep them tanks full," she grumped before stalking away.

Hillary and Trace exchanged looks. Trace shrugged. "I guess everyone has noticed how much running we do."

"It would seem so."

"You don't always have to come with me."

"I'd need a broken ankle to stop me," she answered. "I'm still wondering about your knees, however."

"They'll be fine." He paused. "I'm expecting notification that I'm being discharged as medically unfit, injury in the line of duty."

Hillary caught her breath. "No!" It was a sharp whisper.

He eyed her grimly. "I'll never jump again."

"That is terrible." She felt an ache for him.

"Yeah. But everyone has an expiration date. I believe I've reached mine. What good would I be except standing post at a forward-fire base?"

Maude appeared, demanding their orders. Hillary let

Trace handle it because now her mouth felt as dry as sand and any appetite she'd had was gone. He'd just shared that he was facing another catastrophe on top of the deaths of his two best friends.

And this *was* a tragedy. He was confronting losing his identity, one he'd carried for many years. The day would come for her, too, as it came for everyone, but she couldn't stand to think about the day when she'd no longer be Jegertroppen. That was who she was. Eventually it would be in the past, and she'd be a *former*. A *retired*. Which wasn't the same at all.

Easy enough for someone else to say, *Well, you're other things, too.*

Except this was different. It was bone-deep different. Everything in her life had been built around this one thing. To lose it would leave her feeling gutted. She wondered if there was any way to prepare for it.

She also wondered if Trace had been trying to prepare himself, or if he'd been living on strands of hope. *"Jeg synes sind på deg."*

He looked at her and she caught herself. English. "I feel bad for you."

One corner of his mouth lifted. "It sounded better in Norwegian." Then he shook his head. "Don't. It comes to us all."

"That doesn't mean it's easy."

"Well, no," he admitted just as Maude slammed plates in front of them.

Maude said, "Everybody's talking about how much running you two do. Seems crazy to me, but to each their own. Eat. You can't be that skinny from running and not need to top your tank."

Something between a snort and a laugh escaped Trace. "Thanks, Maude."

The woman sniffed as she marched away.

Hillary looked at the mound of food in front of them.

"She wasn't joking," Trace said. "Except nobody is going to run very soon after this much food."

A laugh escaped Hillary. "I wasn't planning to do it all over again too soon."

Everything was hot and fresh, and they both dived in with pleasure. "What will you do?" Hillary asked, referring to what he'd said about disability retirement.

"When I'm tromping the streets as a civilian again? I don't know. I guess I should start thinking about it soon. But it can't involve a desk."

The wry way he said it brought another smile to her face.

"I think I've learned that for sure," Trace continued. "No long periods at a desk. I'll have to dig up some other skills."

"I believe you probably already have them. Or you can develop them soon."

The problem was, Hillary realized, that she was not feeling those cheerful words at all. She couldn't imagine the gaping hole *this* was going to drill into Trace. She hoped he heard something different from the Army, but she feared he was right. Cogs had to work correctly or they were replaced.

"I could teach you to ski," she said suddenly.

That brought a grin to his face. "Norwegian spec ops?"

She shrugged a shoulder. "At least you could work out all that energy skiing cross-country. I don't think it would be terribly hard on your knees. And you could always teach younger soldiers."

"What they already know," he said dryly. "Thanks, but you'll have to do better than that."

She laughed. "You're right. Well, we could teach you to raise sheep."

What was she doing? she wondered. Picturing him in Norway? Oh, this was getting dangerous, and not the kind of danger she was trained to handle.

Together they walked down the street toward the Mannerly house, carrying plastic bags full of leftovers. Maude had been more than generous, and any thought of cooking later had vanished.

For which they were probably both grateful, Hillary thought with amusement.

Since it was blustery out, few people they passed did more than say hello before moving on. Fine by Hillary. The cold was beginning to bite her cheeks, and she wished she had chosen a balaclava instead of a watch cap. But then, she hadn't planned to stay for long.

The last autumn leaves were being ripped from the trees as they strode along the sidewalk. They didn't linger long enough to cover grass.

"Have you ever wondered," she asked, "where the leaves go when the wind carries them away?"

"Into some unfortunate neighbor's lawn," he answered. "I imagine it's like the snow. Usually it blows away until it gets caught somewhere. If you're lucky, it won't be on your driveway."

She felt her cold cheeks crack into a smile.

"Say," he said as they approached the house.

"Yes?"

"I've noticed you never say you're sorry in the way we use it. As in, 'I'm sorry something bad happened to you.' Is there a reason?"

"In Norway, at least," she answered, "to say we're sorry is not an expression of commiseration. It's an apology for having done something. A statement of taking responsibility for an action."

He was quiet a moment. "That's interesting. I never thought about it."

"Why would you? It's different in English."

"It also makes sense to me. You're right, *sorry* sounds more like an apology if you think about it. I wonder if it changes an individual's perception."

"I can't say. I just know I am not in the habit of apologizing for what I can't control."

"Do you hear it the same way in English?" he asked as they turned onto the short walkway to the front door.

"I've grown accustomed to the English usage. It doesn't confuse me."

He looked at her as he opened the door. "I don't think very much confuses you."

Then, out of her came a truly American phrase. "Wanna bet?"

He broke up at that and was still laughing as they carried the bags into the kitchen.

"Do you think in Norwegian?" he asked as they put foam containers in the fridge.

"Usually. The longer I am here, the more I think in English."

"As in *wanna bet*?"

It was her turn to laugh. "As in. But you've seen me slip a few times."

"I hardly think of it as a slip. And it's charming."

She felt warmed by his choice of words. But all too soon, coffee in hand, they headed back to the office and the endless search.

"We haven't seen that man in a while," she remarked as she slid into her office chair.

"I wish that made me feel better."

She knew exactly what he meant. If the man were an enemy, it was far better to have him in plain sight. If he were hiding, so much the worse.

AT SOME POINT, Trace began to mutter silently, then not so silently, at Allan. The thoughts he had weren't exactly nice, and occasionally they slipped past his lips as a quiet grumble.

Eventually Hillary, who was still moving through the stack of envelopes and sorting any other correspondence from Brigid, remarked, "Allan left you a mess."

"I'm wondering why the hell he didn't clarify this after Brigid was killed. Why hide it any longer? Unless he wanted to wait until he could report a full picture."

"I am wondering just how bad this will be when we piece it together."

Trace swiveled to look at her. "There's no need for you to take on this risk."

"I'm accustomed to risks. They don't frighten me."

Of course not, Trace thought. God, he wanted them both out of this mess, but he didn't want to betray Allan and Brigid. A lifetime of friendship was worth chancing a lot of danger.

Back to work building his own file of date-ordered emails. He couldn't escape that a warning must be hidden in this hodgepodge mess. Allan wouldn't have done this without reason.

Eavesdropping? Did he think the government might have been looking at his and Brigid's emails? If so, this mess was colossal.

But clearly Allan had been worried about something bigger than an individual. No single man could access protected emails. The military was very careful about that.

Which brought him around to the NSA, but that seemed

a whole lot bigger than would make sense, unless Brigid had stumbled on an extensive operation that could reach anywhere. Something that could rise to the highest corridors of power.

How likely was that?

How likely was it that two people would be killed over it?

His stomach began to turn sour. "I need to stop for a while."

Hillary looked at him. "Is something wrong?"

"Oh yeah. Two people dead. Just how big is this damn thing?"

She frowned. "I've been trying not to think about that."

"Maybe it's time we should both think about it. I don't care if my rapidly ending career terminates over this. But what about yours?"

THEY RETIRED TO the living room for some calisthenics. After that they repaired to the kitchen. Hillary hunted around to find a way to make hot chocolate. She found no cocoa powder, only an instant mix similar to what she sometimes encountered in field rations.

It would have to do. Besides, she knew how to make it richer—two packets to a cup and some of the heavy cream she had bought for cooking.

She washed the insulated mugs, used a handy electric kettle to heat the water and, when it was ready, she added a couple of spoonfuls of cream. The measurements were different from the metric ones she was accustomed to, but eyeballing worked just as well for this. She placed a mug in front of Trace, who seemed to be contemplating something over a far horizon, then sat with him.

Presently he said, "We may be looking at an octopus with a lot of high-level tentacles."

She nodded, having nothing to add.

"This should have occurred to me sooner in more than a passing way."

"Why? It's unthinkable."

"Until now, evidently. God, Hillary, we may be stepping into quicksand, and I don't want to take you down with me."

"There is always a way out of quicksand."

He shook his head. "You know what I mean." He shook his head once more. "I don't know why, but I was thinking of one bad guy. Or maybe two. I know we mentioned it, but I honestly didn't truly think beyond that to a chunk of upper-level command."

"Or a large independent contractor."

"Which wouldn't be much better. If it has important contacts within the military, then Brigid and Allan's cautious communications make sense."

She sipped her cocoa, hot and tasty enough to make up for the real ingredients. "Perhaps they didn't know but were merely being very cautious."

"Yeah, maybe. Until they both died." Now, at last, he sipped his own cocoa. "Not bad for a campfire quickie."

"It will do. I must say, Trace, that I find it just as appalling that a contractor might sell arms to the enemy. There is no excuse for whoever did this. None."

She stabbed her finger at the table, making a small thump. "A contractor stands to lose a lot, too. Huge contracts."

"Only if it gets out. Someone might cover for them. Everyone gets a few dollars in their pockets. The question is, how much money does it cost to get the right people to sell out?"

A question with no answer. Few of these questions had answers.

"Of course," he continued, "no military personnel need to be involved in reading their emails. Think about it. Who builds the equipment we depend on for secrecy?"

Ice ran down Hillary's spine. "Compromised communications?" There weren't enough curse words in Norwegian to express her feelings about that. Worse than arms sales. A threat to every single operation, every single soldier, out there. Out there anywhere in the world.

"You give me nightmares," she said.

"I'm going to have them, too. I'd suggest another run up the mountain, but look out the window."

She turned her head and saw snow blowing almost horizontally past the window.

Trace spoke. "And don't tell me you can do it. I know you can. But why risk a broken leg or a broken neck because we need to work off some stress?"

She didn't want to admit he had a point, but he did. Some conditions should only be challenged for training or for combat. Being foolhardy was never excusable.

"You know what I'm going to do?" he asked several minutes later.

"What?"

"I'm going to take a few hours off. Nothing we can do now is going to bring Brigid or Allan back. So I'm going to declare it time to relax. I'll uncover the fireplace and build a fire. We can pretend we're out in some lost cabin in the middle of a blizzard."

She nearly laughed despite the serious fears they had just discussed. "It sounds like home."

"Even better then. A fire, a drink…" He trailed off for a few seconds. "You know, I think Brigid and Allan kept some brandy for special occasions. You like brandy?"

"Very much, for sipping."

"Hell, I wouldn't toss it off like a shot. What a waste."

There was a woodpile out back, and Hillary helped Trace carry in some logs and kindling. She left the building of the fire to him while she went to change into her thermal undergarment with a sweater over it and pulled on some socks. If they were going to be cozy, then she was going all the way.

When the fire started crackling and flames began to leap, Trace went to a cabinet on the far side of the living room and squatted, giving her a nice view of his backside in stretched denim. "I knew it," he said shortly. "But it's brandy and Bénédictine, if that's okay."

"More than okay. I prefer it."

He also discovered some snifters and after wiping them out, he offered her a drink. She sipped with approval as she curled up on one end of the sofa.

"You don't mind taking some time off?" he asked as he settled into the recliner.

"I believe we have both earned it." Very much so. "I think your phrase is 'beating our heads on a wall.'"

A snort escaped him. "Just slightly." He stirred in his chair. "I feel like I'm desecrating space. This used to be Brigid's chair."

She pointed to the end of the sofa. "Then sit here."

"It's a stupid feeling."

"No. It's not. Now move."

He half smiled. "Orders again?"

"If they're needed." She sipped more liqueur. "This is quite pleasant with the fire."

At last he moved, sitting on the other end of the sofa. He lifted the brandy snifter to his lips. "You know the story of B and B?"

"I never looked."

"It's amusing in a way. A liqueur maker claimed he'd found the recipe in a destroyed Benedictine Abbey, then added the letters DOM for *Deo Optimo Maximo*, or 'God is great.' I guess it worked."

Hillary smiled. "The results hardly need the letters."

"Not anymore."

Quiet ensued, filled only by the crackling of the fire. Firelight danced over the wall, counterpointed by shadows. Slowly a realization began to creep through Hillary. She was feeling lonely. Lonely in a way she hadn't felt since leaving home for the army.

She guessed she needed her friends, her organization. Those who would understand and share with her. People she knew from the years behind her.

Trace was new, too new to reach that level of understanding, although he was slowly getting there when they talked.

She realized something else, too. It had been a long time since she'd had her arms around a man, or a man's arms around her. Her entire body had begun to ache for that intimacy, for the mindless pleasure sex could bring. She had been missing it for too long.

She had seen the reflection of desire in Trace's gaze from time to time, and Hillary was not one to hesitate once she had defined a need.

She set aside her snifter and scooted down the couch until she leaned against Trace. Hot, warm, hard. Their eyes met, his appearing surprised.

"Do you mind?" she asked.

"Hell no." He followed the declaration by putting his arm around her shoulders. "Get comfortable."

She did precisely that, leaning into him, resting her head on his shoulder. Male aromas reached her, enticing her further.

But she let it rest for the moment. Let matters follow their own pace. Take care she didn't intrude too far. Didn't demand what he might not be willing to give. Attraction was one thing. Following through was another.

He twisted a bit, drawing her into a more comfortable embrace. Her head slid down from his shoulder to his chest. His steady heartbeat filled her ear. She let her arm find its way around his narrow, hard waist.

The fire continued to burn, throwing orange light around the room, promising heat. Her heart sped up a bit, and her body began to ache all over with hunger. She wanted more from Trace than this exhausting, probably hopeless quest.

He had so much to offer, despite his nearly compulsive drive to save Allan's reputation. To end his own doubts. She had caught glimpses of the man behind the immediate problem, and she liked him. She wished she could know him even better.

"Hills?" he said, unwittingly shortening her name to the nickname many of her friends used.

"Hmm?"

"Is this what I think it is? Or do you just want comfort?"

She turned her head a bit as he looked down at her and met his gaze. "Comfort, of course. But this is exactly what you think it is."

"Well, hot damn," he said.

"I don't understand."

"You will," he promised.

Then, before she could draw another breath, he twisted more and kissed her on her lips. Her immediate response startled her. Warmth became a blaze hotter than the fire nearby. Until that moment she hadn't realized just how much she'd been longing for this. For Trace.

His arm tightened around her shoulders. She tightened her hold on his waist. He tasted of brandy, but she did, too, and as their tongues dueled, it became the last bit of the old reality and gave way to a whole new world.

He whispered her name, then pulled her sweater away from her throat, kissing and lightly licking her neck just below the ear. A delicious shiver ran through her, and her impatience grew as quickly as the heat.

She didn't want slow. She didn't want the teasing and tormenting. She wanted rough and ready and swift, an answer to hungers that were threatening to rip her apart with need.

She sat up, pulling her sweater over her head. "These thermals might be good for cold, but they're a nuisance now."

A laugh escaped him. "Sometimes all clothes are a nuisance."

TRACE WAS CHARMED. Enchanted. Never had he met a woman so bold, so immediately honest about her desire. Decisive.

No playing around with her, at least not this time. He joined her in pulling off their clothes as fast as they could. Hands and fingers tangled at times, drawing breathless laughs from them.

Then at last they were naked in the glow of firelight, but before he had time to really appreciate her beauty, she straddled him and claimed him.

Ah yes, he could get used to this. It was his last coherent thought as the pressure of need drove them hard, pushing them upward until they reached the peak together.

The explosion that ripped through him left him drained.

Hillary apparently felt the same way. She collapsed on his chest, their bodies melting into one another. Neither of them moved for a long time.

HILLARY STARTED DRESSING, a chill reaching her despite the fire. Trace looked at her.

"You're wrapping up too fast," he said. "I want to admire you."

"Nothing unusual about me. You can look later if you still want to, but now I'm hungry."

He laughed. Hillary. She was unusual in every way. "You're a piece of work, Valkyrie."

She grinned. "I hope that is a good thing."

"Trust me, it's good."

He watched her stride toward the kitchen and enjoyed the view. Those thermals concealed very little, and she had a toned, fit body with long legs, just enough of a curve on her hips and rump.

And she was totally unselfconscious.

Smiling, he dragged on his own clothes, just well-worn jeans and a plaid flannel shirt that had probably seen its best days fifteen years ago. But that was the thing about his career. Civilian clothes lasted damn near forever.

He discovered her scooping their leftovers onto plates and warming them in the microwave.

"Microwaves," she announced, "are transnational, unlike measuring spoons."

He hadn't thought of that. He used metric measurements all the time on duty, but in a kitchen? "Maybe we should get you a set."

She glanced wryly over her shoulder. "I will not be doing that much cooking."

"I should bake those brownies," he remarked. "Chocolate would be the perfect topper right now."

After they had eaten the remains of the leftovers, Trace took over. The only hindrance was finding his way around the unfamiliar kitchen. At last he discovered the measuring cup and held it up to her.

"Look at that, Hills. Both English and metric measurements."

"It must be an error."

God, he was feeling good. He couldn't remember the last time he'd felt this good. There was something to be said for a decisive Valkyrie.

He did manage to follow the admittedly simple directions and get all the batter into a glass baking dish. When he put it in the oven, Hillary took over the washing up. He caught her licking some batter off her finger.

"Tsk, Hillary. Raw egg."

She flashed a smile. "I think I'm immune to anything that goes in my mouth."

She might be right, given where they'd been. "Well, the batter is almost always the best part."

"When I was a young child, I would beg to lick the spoon. I believe many children do that."

"I would have if we'd ever made brownies."

Her expression saddened. "Your childhood must have been difficult."

He shrugged. "I didn't think so at the time. I just built my life differently. But I told you that."

"Children adapt well."

Too well, he thought, as images came to mind, images he preferred not to recall. Lives he could not change.

They sat over coffee while the mouthwatering aroma of brownies filled the kitchen. He wanted to reach out to her, to at least hold her hand, but he didn't yet know where the lines were. Maybe she was done now. She'd satisfied her urge and needed no more from him.

He didn't want to be the creep a woman couldn't shake off.

He also didn't want her to shake him off. That would come soon enough.

"What about your friends?" he asked as the thought occurred to him. "Do they know you're staying here?"

"I called my first night and said I might be staying with Brigid's family for a while."

Brigid's family. The description pleased him. "So you think I'm her family?"

"Brigid would think so, I'm sure. As would Allan. And…" she shrugged. "Brigid was my sister."

"Hold on now, this is getting incestuous."

She appeared startled, then laughed. "Don't be silly."

Damn, he loved the sound of her laugh. He needed to make her laugh more often.

"What did you think of England?" he asked.

"Well, like many places, it depends on where you are. My mother is very upper class. She speaks like the queen."

Now *he* laughed. "A very particular accent?"

"Very. Go away from the palace, and there are accents I still don't understand. But we have dialects in Norway as well. I would say Britain has many dialects."

The timer dinged, and Trace went to pull the brownies out of the oven. "Was there anything you liked about your visits there?"

"The old castles. Everyone likes those. But I was amazed to learn that the queen owns all the muted swans on open water. Every year a tally is taken."

"That's wild." He couldn't imagine it.

"Some things began so long ago, when only a few owned everything. At least the swans are protected."

"There is that."

TRACE WENT TO check on the fire. Hillary wondered if he would add more fuel or if this period of rest was over. He must be feeling the pressure to get back to their task. She was beginning to feel it as well.

She closed her eyes for a few seconds, enjoying the memory of her sex with Trace. Swift. Hot. So satisfying. How good it had felt when he held her. Upon occasion she liked to feel soft. Womanly. Those desires hadn't been scrubbed out of her.

She wanted more. A lot more. A chance to admire him, to explore him. A chance for him to explore her. Long, lazy, slow.

But not now. Clearly not now. They faced something so enormous that neither of them could let go, not unless they could find nothing useful at all. Then they would have no choice.

Her thoughts drifted back to that man who seemed to have been watching them. Probably nothing, but along the back of her neck, she felt a prickle of apprehension. A sense she had learned ages ago not to ignore.

But one man? After they had begun to wonder about the scope of what Brigid may have discovered? One man seemed like a small response that resulted in two killings. Were there more that they hadn't noticed yet?

Their respite was over. She felt it in her bones. Time to get back to it.

She thought of Brigid. Of the bright light that had been snuffed out. Of the fact that it may not have been an accident of war at all. Of Trace's conviction that Allan had not killed himself.

Her own growing conviction that the two deaths were linked.

Trace returned and went to the sink to wash his hands. "Time to get back to it?" he asked.

"Yes."

He pulled two small plates from the cupboard and put large squares of the brownies on them. "Coffee?"

"Of course. Need you ask?"

His smile reached only half-mast as he started another pot. "We'll take this into the office. I need to find some paper napkins or we'll get too sticky."

Hillary knew where they were, having seen them during her hunt for cooking utensils. She pulled out a drawer and helped herself to a few of them.

Minutes later, coffee and brownies in hand, they returned to the office. There had to be an answer of some kind in there. Even Brigid and Allan couldn't read each other's minds.

As they sat and bit into brownies, Trace spoke. "If this is as ugly as it's beginning to appear, we might be next on the killer's list."

"It's possible." The idea didn't disturb her. She'd been in situations where dozens of people had wanted to kill her. She wanted to live, but she didn't fear death. It often came swiftly and easily. She feared only surviving such an attack with her life in ruins.

"However," she said as she finished her brownie and wiped her hands thoroughly, "I cannot imagine that anyone is watching Allan's computer. Can you?"

Trace paused, then reached around and pulled a cable. "Not now for sure."

She shook her head slightly, then smiled. "If we'd found anything yet, that might matter."

"If we *do* find something, it *won't* matter."

No, it wouldn't. Not now. But the idea that someone might be monitoring Allan's computer didn't seem farfetched. Not if someone had monitored communications when Brigid had been overseas.

Or maybe they were just turning into conspiracy theorists. That was possible, too.

STAN WITHERSPOON WATCHED from outside again, ignoring the icy night, ignoring the whipping snow. His cheeks stung, and even his gloves couldn't keep his fingers warm. He shoved them into his jacket pockets.

What was going on in there? Through a crack in one of the curtains, firelight was visible. A love nest?

Maybe so. Maybe he was worrying over nothing. The two of them might just be involved in the early stages of a romance.

Entirely possible, given that woman's beauty. Given that she was probably one of the few people in this county who could run with Mullen.

Hell. Double hell.

He should leave now. No one here would find him, not after all this time.

But fear held him rooted. Fear that they *were* looking for something. Fear that they might find something.

Fear of what his boss would do if those two learned something and passed it along.

No, he couldn't leave. He didn't want to die. That hadn't been part of his bargain with the devil. But secrecy had been.

Secrecy. God, what a mess.

Chapter Eleven

Morning seemed to arrive too early, although a leaden darkness shrouded the land. The snow had lightened, but a look out the windows told a story from the night: it had been a heavy snow, drifting everywhere it could find a nook.

The sight pleased Hillary. The beginnings of winter always sheltered the world in a silence muffled in white.

Trace was annoyed. "I need a run. And I hope we have enough hanging around in this kitchen to make breakfast. Of course, I could always walk to Maude's. She'll make sure we're provisioned for a week."

Hillary stretched and yawned. "A walk would be nice. I'll go with you."

They dressed for the weather, locked up and set out. The air held that unique crisp smell of a first snowfall. Hillary had never found words to describe it, but she always liked it. Not only did the snow dampen sounds, but it dampened all the other odors of life as well.

Smoke drifted out of many chimneys. No one was about except an occasional patrol car with a plow on the front of it. Their own cars were under a blanket deep enough that only bits could be seen.

A perfect pure world. Right then, anyway.

Trace spoke. "We don't usually see this much snow, at least not this early."

"Climate chaos," she replied.

"Not climate change?"

She glanced at him, feeling a bit impish. "Look around you. This weather the world over is chaotic." She paused. "The glaciers on the mountaintops at home have begun to melt."

"That's a tragedy. One of our national parks, called Glacier, has no glaciers anymore."

"Sad. Very sad. Some days I try to imagine Norway being green year-round. The idea hurts."

"The gifts of life are fleeting."

"So it appears."

At Maude's they were chilled enough to order some hot food to eat before Maude filled bags for them. The diner was empty of all but a few hardy souls.

"I'd offer you lattes," Maude grumbled, "but the damn things would be ice by the time you get home. The food in the foam containers won't be much better. They're working on clearing the roads, but I don't know if it's worth digging out your cars yet. Where would you go? I hear the grocery has hardly any staff this morning. It's not like us."

Hillary looked up at her from over a hot bowl of oatmeal. "Not like you?"

Maude sniffed. "Snow doesn't shut us down. At least not usually."

"We also don't usually get this much of it," Trace remarked when Maude had gone back to her kitchen. "We're not exactly prepared for it."

"Everyone should have skis."

She was pleased when he laughed. She could tell the melancholy mood was overtaking him again.

"Have you no plows?" she asked. "I saw them on the front of two of your police vehicles."

"Oh, we have plows. Just probably not enough of them. As for the police, if there's trouble somewhere, they can't wait for a plow to get through."

She nodded. "I should have thought of that."

"You can't think of everything, Hills."

Once again her nickname. She liked that he had arrived at it all on his own.

"Especially," he added, "when our brains are fried. I believe I have most of the emails in order now."

"Then we should start reading in sequence."

"I think so."

The walk home felt less invigorating than when they had set out earlier. They each carried three bags of food from a generous Maude, enough to get them through a couple of days now that they weren't running.

For the first time, Hillary felt uneasy entering the house. She turned briefly while Trace unlocked the door and caught sight of something moving. Something dark. Then it was gone.

Not until they were inside did she speak. "I saw something or someone move in the bushes across the way."

Trace dropped the bags on the small lowboy in the short, narrow hall. "Footprints."

She had no difficulty following his thoughts because they were already hers. She set her bags beside his, and together they started out. They should have a clear trail to follow.

The footprints were there as expected. They were scuffed together and smashed down almost to slush.

"He has been here for a while," she said.

"Yup. Split up?"

It would double their chances of finding the man. She

nodded and started down the road in the general direction of the trail of footprints. Every so often she glanced to her right to check that they hadn't switched direction toward a copse of trees.

Not yet. Her instincts took charge, and when at last the footprints took a sharp turn, she followed them into the snow. Trace wasn't far behind. Then she reached the truck stop parking lot, already mush and ice from the heavy trucks beating it up.

She signaled Trace to swing to the left while she followed the outline of the parking lot to the right. Heavy trucks grumbled loudly, their engines and exhaust warming the air. And melting more snow.

No sign of footprints exiting the lot. Trace met her a minute or two later.

"Nothing," he said.

"Nothing," she agreed.

As one they turned to look into the truck stop diner.

"There is a crowd in there," she remarked. "No way to identify anyone."

"Nope."

"I only caught a glimpse," she told him. "It could have been anyone wearing a balaclava and dark jacket."

"That might well describe half the people in there."

"Any snow on him or his boots would have melted by now."

"Still not enough even if it hadn't. All those truckers. Many might still be dusted with snow, and their boots might be slushy from the parking lot."

Once more, Hillary walked around the lot in tightening circles, wondering if she could find any prints in the mess that appeared to follow a straight line from the ones they had been following. It looked like a stampede had run through that lot.

She hated to give up. Part of her training had involved tracking. She should have been able to find *something*. But not even the least little thing called her attention. Angered, she rejoined Trace, who had been doing the same thing.

"He knew where to run," she said.

He nodded. "Probably had it planned out in advance."

And they were, she realized, once again talking about the man, but now as if he posed a real threat. She imagined Trace wanted to get his hands on him. To shake him, perhaps, until the truth spilled out.

"Why," he asked as they walked home, "would the guy stay after he killed Allan? Hills, none of this is making sense."

"Only because we don't know the answers."

He snorted. "That's obvious."

She let a minor laugh escape even though she was feeling deflated. "True. So is the fact that little of this makes sense."

"We have a ton of speculation, that's all. And if Allan didn't leave a clearer message for us, I may follow him all the way to heaven and give him a good shaking."

She glanced at him and saw that he was trying to joke. Good. She hated to think he might be close to despair.

Once inside they took care of all the high-calorie food Maude had sent with them. It hadn't grown as cold as Maude had anticipated, but it did fill the refrigerator.

"Back to work?" she asked when they finished.

"I want a few minutes first. I want to think about that guy."

"Speculate, you mean."

He grimaced. "Obviously."

Inevitably another pot of coffee. Inevitably another round at the kitchen table.

Hillary spoke while they waited for the coffee. "When

my father and I are home together, we often gather at the table like this."

"From what I've seen, it's a popular place. Did you talk a lot?"

"Always. We played cards. Drank beer or aquavit. If it was an especially cold day and snowy outside, we gathered before a fire. Friends came over. I liked those days, but I mostly liked the private time with my father. There was never enough of it."

"Such good memories."

She eyed him. "Have you none?"

"A few." He didn't elaborate, though.

"How did you feel about your father disappearing?"

He cocked a brow. "Do you want the expected answer or the truth?"

"The truth."

"I was relieved."

That told Hillary as much as anything he had already said. She tried to imagine being relieved when your father left town. She couldn't. She had lived with the dread all her life that one day her father would never come back.

TRACE WATCHED EMOTIONS play over Hillary's face. A usually impassive woman, she was letting her inner life show. At least to him. A sign of trust?

But the man. Always the man. He kept popping up like a bad penny. Instinct told him the guy was definitely involved.

"What do you think of that man?" he asked her.

"He's around too much to be simply curious. He's also not very good at staying out of sight."

"I can't escape the question, though. If he killed Allan, why is he still here?"

She ruminated for a while. She poured coffee for them,

then recovered a container of pastry from the counter. "Sweets. Sometimes I need them."

He nodded understanding.

"Okay," she said as she settled across from him. "Reasons a killer might stay in town. Because he's not sure the story ended with Allan?"

"Good one," Trace said. "You'd have thought the results of the inquest would have been enough to send him on his way."

"Unless he fears there is some kind of evidence here."

He forked a piece of apple pie and drank some coffee before answering. "Then suddenly you show up and we spend a lot of time in the house. He might suspect what we're doing."

She made a face. "It's also possible he may think I'm your *kjære* come to visit."

"*Kjære?*"

He mangled the pronunciation a bit, but she didn't mind at all. She searched briefly for the English word. It wasn't one she had ever needed to use. "Sweetheart."

"Ah." He wiggled his eyebrows. "I should be so lucky. But that still doesn't explain why he's been hanging around for so long."

"No." She ate the rest of her pie, then got herself some fresh coffee. "All right. I agree, but this whole matter is strange. And if we are speculating…"

"Then anything is on the table. Could someone have told him about the emails?"

"You will make me shudder again. All the way to the top and beyond. So many lives at risk, so many operations no longer secret. I hate to think."

"If I believe that, then my anger over Allan's death will seem small in comparison."

"But we have to know for many reasons. All right, perhaps he has stayed because you made it so clear to everyone that you believe Allan was killed."

"Everyone in town appears to have heard about my meltdown."

"Oh yes, including the lovely Edith. I think even her dog knows."

"Oh for heaven's sake, Hills!"

The laugh shone from her eyes. "You made quite a spectacle, I gather."

He sighed and pushed his plate away. "I did," he admitted. "Nothing covert about what I believed. Bad soldiering."

"But good…" It was her turn to sigh. "I haven't the words for it. You are a good man. That's all it was."

"I was a little out of my mind at the time. Ignored. Helpless to make anyone consider anything besides suicide."

"From what Edith said, a lot of people believed you might be right."

"It would have been nice if they'd said so at the time. But what would have happened if they sided with me? An insurrection? Not likely."

She watched as he went to get himself more coffee. Nice view. Desire stirred again, but she pressed it down. "May I be bold?"

He looked at her, cup in hand, still beside the counter. "When have you ever been timid?"

"I can't remember. All right. We need to talk to your *sjef* of law enforcement. Your chief law enforcement officer."

"What good can he do?"

"He can hear what we suspect. Perhaps we might get some help with this strange man."

He looked out the window. "The snow has nearly stopped. Let me call him. Maybe he can spare some time."

Trace called the department and asked to speak to the sheriff. Gage Dalton answered after a few moments, coming straight to the point in his gravelly voice. "What's up, Trace?"

Trace almost hated to speak the words, given the hard time he'd given Gage right after Allan's death. "It's about Allan."

"Oh?" At least Gage didn't sigh.

"We think we may have found something. And we think we have a problem. Got some time for us to walk over?"

"I have a better idea. I'll drive over. At least I'm outfitted with tire chains and a plow. Give me twenty."

When Trace disconnected, he faced Hillary. "He's coming over."

"Good. It will be nice to have a new wall to bounce the ball off."

He was charmed by her phrasing. Occasionally her English took unexpected turns. Sometimes contractions deserted her, and other times they slipped easily past her lips.

Gage was prompt. Trace caught sight of him limping up the walk through the window and almost winced for the man. Trace's injuries had been treatable. Gage's had not.

Trace decided he'd better not wait much longer to shovel the sidewalk. It was perilous out there, and while he hadn't expected anyone so he hadn't hurried to get to shoveling, clearly he'd been wrong.

He opened the door before Gage could even knock. "Sorry about the walk. I waited too long."

Gage gave his patented crooked smile, only one side of his mouth lifting. The other side of his face had been burned, and shiny scar tissue evidently deprived him of some facial mobility.

"Don't worry about it," Gage said. "You have no idea what I've tromped through already today. And my *own* walk isn't shoveled yet. Knowing my wife, she'll have it done before I get back."

Trace grinned. "She's in great shape."

Gage lifted a brow. "She's always been in great shape. Now she stays that way at the gym. Yoga! Anyway, she says she'll have to die eventually, but she doesn't have to get old along the way."

"I like that attitude."

"You would, being the guy who runs around this county like a mountain goat."

By then they were inside. Gage had knocked as much snow as he could from his boots and then hung his parka on a wall hook beside Trace's and Hillary's.

"Coffee?" Trace asked.

"You need to ask? Cars need gasoline. I need caffeine."

Trace made the introductions in the kitchen, and soon there was a cozy gathering around the table.

Gage looked at Hillary. "So you're Brigid's soldier friend."

"Yes."

"A wonderful soul, our Brigid." Then he turned his attention to Trace. "You said you had some stuff to discuss about Allan. I'm assuming it's not the ground you already covered."

"Not exactly. Let's start with the fact that Brigid was killed in late January. I know how that made Allan's death appear, even more than six months later. But consider."

Gage nodded. "Go ahead."

"Allan left me this house, but he also included all the passwords to his computer files in his will. I'd have come in here sooner to check it out, but…" Trace trailed off for a moment. "Gage, this place is full of memories for me, and, worse, it felt like an empty dark pit. I didn't *want* to come in here. And when I did, Hillary reminded me how strange it was that Allan left me all those passwords."

Gage sat up a little straighter, wincing as he did so. "It's strange, all right. My inclination would be to let things remain locked and hope the equipment got trashed."

"Exactly. I had to conclude that Allan wanted me to find something."

"I can see that. So you started reading."

"I wish. I found all the computer files scrambled. No date sequence to all the emails. He'd scattered them in different folders with no organization whatsoever."

Gage now frowned. "That's odd. Do you think he was trying to bury something?"

"Yeah, I do. Then I found a sentence from him in one of his last emails. He told Brigid to let it go. To just let it go. That was one of Brigid's favorite sayings, and very unlike Allan's temperament. It felt like a warning."

"Maybe." Gage was clearly withholding judgment.

Hillary rose. "I want to show you something."

As she left the room, Gage looked at Trace. "She's British?"

"Half, she says."

"Nice accent. Kind of lilting."

Just like Gage not to miss a thing.

"She's a soldier, too?"

Trace hesitated. "Yeah, sort of."

"What? What am I missing?"

"She doesn't want anyone to know, but she's Norwegian special ops."

"I won't tell a soul. But damn! A Valkyrie?"

Trace nodded, but if anyone in this town needed to understand Hillary's background, he figured the sheriff was it.

Gage offered another of his crooked smiles. "Pity the

man who gives her any trouble in a dark alley. I've heard a little about them. But she's right. She doesn't want to become the subject of constant attention. Or of the grapevine."

"That's not what she's here for."

"I take it she agrees with you?"

"Maybe not at first. Now yes."

"Interesting."

Hillary returned just then holding an envelope. "It took me a few minutes to find it." She sat at the table and pulled the pages of the letter out of it, smoothing them. "This," she said, pointing as she moved the paper close to Gage. "The underlined part."

"'Too many guns,'" he read aloud. Then read it again. "Underlined. Heavily." After a moment, he swore. "I guess I know what you're thinking."

"Probably," Trace answered.

Gage leaned back, wincing again. "Discovering illegal arms sales would be enough to get a lot of people killed. Damn it all." Gage looked at Hillary. "I used to work undercover for the Drug Enforcement Administration. I'm suspicious by nature. This makes me *very* suspicious."

"Us too," Trace said. "But we need to comb through everything for more information, or we're at a standstill."

Gage nodded and rubbed the back of his neck. "More coffee?" he asked.

But he didn't ask Hillary, a gesture Trace appreciated. He went to get the sheriff more coffee.

"I need to think on this," Gage said presently. "I guess it was too easy to believe suicide under the circumstances. Especially since I knew how much trouble Allan was having with PTSD. Veteran suicides are all too common. But now…" He shook his head. "You're in a fine kettle of fish, and I don't know how I can help."

Hillary spoke. "There's one thing. A man."

Gage looked between them. "As in?"

"It doesn't sound like much," Trace admitted. God, they were handing Gage an awfully slim bit of evidence.

"Instinct," Hillary said flatly. "Trust our instincts."

Gage studied her for a moment. "Damned if I don't. I spent too many years having to rely on instinct. Go."

So Trace went, explaining the times they had seen the guy, but most especially that morning and how he had disappeared at the truck stop.

Gage rubbed his chin. "All right. A strange man. Not unheard-of around here since the college arrived. But this morning? I'd say you're going on more than instinct. A casual observer wouldn't have hurried away then covered his tracks."

"Exactly."

Trace was relieved that Gage didn't deliver a raft of reasons why it could have been innocent. If there was one thing Trace knew for certain, it was that he had grown awfully tired of being dismissed. He'd had an instinct about Allan. Now he had an instinct about this. By God, someone *had* to listen, and now Gage was.

Gage spoke. "You don't have a good description?"

Hillary answered, "If you suspect someone is watching you, do you stare back?"

Gage gave a short laugh. "Only in a restaurant." He sighed and took a swig of his coffee. "Okay, then. A stranger in dark clothes is showing an inordinate interest in you. When you show interest in him, he vanishes. That's a problem."

"And that's why I called you. I know you think Allan committed suicide, but—"

Gage lifted a hand, stopping Trace. "Let's be fair and

honest here, okay? There was no evidence at the time to suggest anything else. None. We sure as hell looked for it."

Trace felt Hillary's gaze on him. "I've been running amok."

Another chuckle escaped Gage. "No kidding. You were more than upset—you were maddened. It seemed like no one was listening to you. It would infuriate me, too. We heard you. *I* heard you. But without evidence, we had to go with what we knew for certain. Allan had PTSD. I don't know if you have any idea how bad it was. He'd been shot up and discharged. Then his wife was killed and he started drinking heavily. Isolated himself as completely as we would let him. I personally kept doing welfare checks because he and I had hit it off." He stared at Trace. "I gave a damn."

Trace lowered his head a moment. "I wish I could have been here longer."

"Seems like you were dealing with your own heavy-duty mess. Anyway, everything I knew? It looked like suicide. But yes, we tried to find proof otherwise. Now maybe you have it."

"Not really. Just some threads. I was acting like an ass, wasn't I?" Trace looked at Hillary. "I went berserk."

He was surprised to see her smile. "A human response. We all have them."

Gage added, "Don't apologize." He looked at his coffee cup.

Trace read the message and went to get him more. "You need an IV drip?"

Gage laughed. "Sometimes I think so." He drained his third cup. "All right. I'll have my deputies keep an eye out for a stranger who seems to be stalking you in some way." He cocked a brow. "Most of the time we don't get a very good description anyway, so looking for unusual activity works pretty well. In the meantime, you two keep reading what you've got. Maybe you'll tumble onto a better clue, but for right now, my suspicion agrees with yours."

He paused. "It just seems weird the guy would hang around so long. Unless there was more than one guy here to begin with. Can't tell yet."

A few minutes later he limped his way out the front door and back to his vehicle.

"What happened to him?" Hillary asked Trace.

"Sad story. When he was undercover for the DEA, he went home to see his family. Apparently his cover had been broken. From what I understand, there was a car bomb. Killed his wife and kids and left him a mess in more than one way."

Hillary said nothing as she absorbed the story. "My heart breaks for him," she said presently. "Bad enough for someone to try to kill him. Worse that they killed his entire family."

She turned and headed back to the office.

Trace followed. The search had to continue.

HILLARY HAD TAKEN an immediate liking to Gage Dalton. He seemed sensible to her and like a good man to trust. Given that he must have helped reach the verdict that Allan had died by suicide, it was surprising how ready he was to listen to Trace.

But it also said something that Trace had phoned him in the first place.

Trace was soon clicking away at files and folders again, dragging emails into his single folder where they'd be easier to review by date. Hillary resumed her study of the written letters.

Brigid had written a surprising number of them, as if she believed regular mail might be safer from scrutiny than emails. Or as if she had just liked to write her thoughts on paper, making them more enduring. It was amazing, however, because email had been a large part of everyone's life for ages now.

A slight chuckle escaped her.

"What?" Trace asked.

"Oh, I was just thinking of a time when I needed to write an actual business letter and I kept wanting to insert those emojis."

He smiled, too. "I remember the feeling. As if every sentence needed them for punctuation."

She tapped the stack of letters. "Brigid wrote without emojis."

"That's interesting."

"Irrelevant." Hillary shrugged. "It just struck me how they are changing everyone's writing, and I noticed only because they weren't there."

"You're going to make me laugh."

"Is laughter so bad, even now?" Some of the darkest moments in life were the best ones for black humor. It could help make life tolerable, but civilians would probably be appalled by it. Regardless, her comment hadn't been morbid humor. If it made Trace laugh, he needn't feel awkward about it.

Just about the time they both began to yawn and stretch, Hillary found another item. Her heart thudded. "Trace? She writes here that she has seen 'it' twice. She doesn't explain."

Trace leaned over and looked. "What's the date on that?"

Hillary did a swift mental calculation. "Three weeks before she died."

He swore and stood up, rolling his chair backward with his legs. "We're onto something."

He left the room, and after a minute she followed, only to find him in the refrigerator. He glanced at her.

"I've got to eat. My mind is getting fuzzy. You?"

Only then did she realize how many hours had passed. Her stomach announced them with a pang.

"Life is getting pretty boring in some ways," Trace said as they pulled containers out. "We run, we eat, we read. Man, you're here for the first time and I should be showing you around. Giving you something to look at besides the inside of that office."

"I don't expect it. We have a task."

He had just begun to open a container when he straightened. "I'm going to shovel the sidewalk, clean off the cars."

"Sounds good," she responded and joined him in dressing for the outdoors. "My body is going to calcify in that chair."

"It feels like it."

He looked at her as they stepped out into the frigid air. "I guess now we know how often people in love communicate."

She laughed. "All the time?"

"Seems like it."

Hillary threw herself into shoveling and sweeping with evident relish. Trace felt much the same. An ordinary task but one that loosened muscles, stretched his body. No running yet, but this worked a very different group of muscles. He almost wished there was more sidewalk and driveway.

Beneath the snow, ice had formed. Trace took the shovels back to the garage and brought out a bag of salt. Hillary had begun sweeping the snow from the cars with a long brush.

"There's an old military joke," Trace said. "So old that everyone has probably heard it."

"What is it?"

"You see that ice scraper you're holding? Well, the story goes that some guy is retiring. One of his men asks, 'Where are you retiring to?' And the soldier holds up an ice scraper. He says, 'I'm going to head south and stop at every gas station and ask them what this scraper is. The first place I find that says they've never seen one, that's where I stop.'"

Hillary laughed. It sounded even prettier on the fresh, cold air. "I haven't heard that."

"Maybe because you don't have any place far enough south for it."

"It would be hard to completely escape snow."

As they returned inside, wet pavement began to emerge from beneath the last of the frozen snow. The shoveled snow lined it like a white necklace. Overhead the sky promised more.

STAN WITHERSPOON WAS feeling fairly proud of himself. Hurrying into that messy parking lot had left no trail, and he'd had the sense to hide himself in the men's room just in case the two soldiers had seen enough of him to identify him on sight. He'd been relieved they hadn't come inside.

But he wasn't completely proud of himself. He'd allowed himself to be seen in a manner that had aroused enough suspicion to bring them looking for him. When he'd dared look toward the Mannerly house, which he could glimpse from the parking lot, he'd seen a sheriff's vehicle. His heart had stuck in his throat.

Stupid.

Stupid or not, he was among truckers who were mostly strangers in these parts, even more so than he. So he ordered himself a large breakfast, unsure when he'd eat again. It wasn't as if he kept his student apartment well stocked. Pointless to spend money on food he might have to abandon.

But now he had another problem to solve, and as the routine duty of eating soothed him, it cleared some of the fear from his mind. But not all of it. His hand shook a little as he lifted his fork.

He should just leave. Seriously. He hadn't heard of any trouble heading his way from Afghanistan. No ringing cell phone to alert him to a problem.

He'd tied up the loose ends and just needed to move on before he did something else stupid.

He wasn't cut out for this. Not at all. Three years in the Army hadn't prepared him for this. Damn, he'd been a clerk, a paper pusher, an inventory specialist. He'd never gotten closer to a fight than that argument with his roommate, a discussion that had earned him a punch in the gut.

No, he wasn't cut out for violence. It was one of the reasons he hadn't reupped even though he had no civilian prospects.

But it had gotten him this moneymaking job. It astonished him to find out how much more contractors were paid than the soldiers. Then he'd been offered a whole lot more money for falsifying the type of records he'd once kept honestly.

A simple enough task. Shave the inventory from the contractor shipment numbers.

Later had come the part about pulling a select but limited number of weapons from the crates in the equipment compound. As an inventory specialist, he had full access. Easy to remove smaller numbers of weapons, place them in a predetermined place and let the insurgents pick them up. He hadn't even had to deal with the money they paid. He never did know who was getting the money. He just knew what came down the pipeline every time he succeeded in delivering. But he had known enough about the insurgents to arrange Brigid's death.

He liked the money, though. A whole lot. It made up for a miserable life. In a few years he'd be able to retire. Nothing fancy, but he wouldn't have to worry about finding a job for years to come.

Then that Brigid Mannerly. Twice. The second time had been enough to warn him she didn't feel easy with what she saw through the chain-link fence. She wasn't just walking post. He knew the sentry schedule around the compound. Knowing was part of his success.

It hadn't been difficult to find out who she was, pretending he found her attractive. Nothing dangerous had begun rolling down the pipeline, but he set about arranging her death anyway.

Then his boss had told him Brigid was married and would be heading home to a husband in Conard County. He'd never heard of the place, but he found out quickly enough. Brigid's killing might not have been enough. Then he didn't feel safe even when he finally heard she'd been blown to bits.

The fear returned. Married couples didn't keep secrets from one another, did they? His boss didn't seem to think so.

Now here he was, a murderer. Twice. And contemplating two more.

God, he hoped he didn't have to do it again. And two of them? How could he get rid of two of them at the same time? They never seemed to be apart for long. Not anymore. He should have acted the first few days after that woman had arrived. Then Mullen had gone home at night. Now...

Now they rarely separated for any appreciable time.

Hell. Hell, hell, *hell*.

LITTLE MORE THAN a quarter mile away, refreshed by showers and lunch, Hillary and Trace dived in again. They were whittling away the most recent letters and emails, carefully reading every single word for hints.

"I don't like this," Hillary said later. "Not at all."

"The job?"

"No. Time for a fresh pot of coffee or I'll fall asleep."

"We've been working hard," he pointed out.

"Yes, but we're not finding the head of this nail."

Interesting phrasing. He wondered if it was something Norwegian or something she had come up with all on her own. He didn't ask. What was the point? He just liked listening to her.

She washed the pot before starting fresh coffee. Then she washed cups, which had been standing for a while.

"I should have washed up," he remarked.

She shrugged. "Does it matter? I noticed it and I dealt with it."

He was much the same himself. Training. Experience. This time he felt he'd fallen down on the job.

While the coffee brewed, he went to look out the kitchen window. Snow fell again, but gently this time. The kind of thing you wanted to see on Christmas Eve.

"Do you celebrate Halloween in Norway?"

"More so now than in the past. Movies brought your kind of celebration to us, but beyond a carved pumpkin and trick or treat, I believe you call it, we don't decorate much. We tend to prefer house parties the weekend before, possibly with costumes."

"Sounds very civilized."

She laughed. "It's a time of year we like horror movies. One of my favorites is called *Dead Snow*."

"That sounds shivery."

She grinned. "Suitably so. Zombies."

"Oh man, you've got them, too?"

"Some things become worldwide."

He turned fully from the window. "Did we export them to you?"

She shook her head slightly. "I don't know. The word seems to go back a very long way. Should we look it up?"

"And go back to a computer?" He pretended horror, drawing another laugh from her.

"There can't be much left to look through," he remarked, taking his coffee and remaining on his feet. Chairs had begun to look like an abomination to him.

"Reading back to front didn't help much. Maybe we need to go the other direction. Something was building, yes?"

"They both apparently knew something was going on. I wish they'd tell us."

She didn't sit, either, instead leaning back against the counter. "It is there. We've found three references. We must be overlooking something."

"Maybe it's encoded in invisible ink."

"That would fit." She poured her own coffee.

"If you were home in Norway right now, what would you be doing?" His curiosity was honest. How different might her life be?

"At this time of year in weather like this? Well, the days are getting shorter right now, much shorter than here. Much colder. Other than that, I don't think we're all that much different than the rest of Europe." Her expression turned wry. "We *are* a modern country."

"Never thought you weren't. Just curious about cultural differences."

"Maybe some. I don't know. I don't live here."

He laughed. "True. I'm just curious, is all."

"Anything to talk about to avoid going back to that

damn desk, hunting for—what is your expression? A needle in a haystack?"

"That's it, and that's what we're doing."

"I know." She sighed and refreshed her coffee. "I don't like being hunted by that man. I want to get to him and find out what he's doing."

The guy truly troubled Trace, too. The big question, apart from what Brigid and Allan might have discovered, was why that man had hung around so long if he was involved in either killing in any way. The lack of answers bugged him and goaded him.

As a man of action, he hated sitting on his hands. He believed Hillary felt the same.

"I don't like the feeling we're caught in a game of cat and mouse."

Her mouth twisted. "But we seem to be. Are there any weapons in this house?"

The question told him all he needed to know about her state of mind. "I think Allan had some long guns in a locker in the basement. Maybe some knives, too."

"Then we should prepare. If this man was involved in Allan's killing, possibly in Brigid's, he will stop at nothing."

No, he wouldn't. But it still didn't explain why he was here two months after Allan's death.

That question bugged him as much as anything. Did he think Allan had shared information with Trace? Or that Brigid had shared concerns with Hillary?

"He may think we already know what's going on. Maybe I shouldn't have let Gage park out front."

There were no answers, damn it. Still no answers.

"Brigid never shared any concern with you?"

"No. But perhaps she didn't want anyone else involved. Perhaps she feared exactly what happened."

Trace swore. "I was afraid you might say that. It's been running through my mind, too, especially given the secrecy she and Allan have displayed."

"It's awful to think," Hillary said sadly. "Horrible. For her to live with that fear…"

No answer to that, either.

AFTER A FEW more hours of reading Brigid's letters, Hillary stepped out on the front porch. The snow continued to fall, more heavily than earlier, but no wind whipped it around. A beautiful winter scene.

Reading Brigid's letters made her sense of loss more acute. Brigid's personality and her love for Allan shone through as brightly as an unwavering candle flame.

That flame had been snuffed out. Originally Hillary had accepted the loss as the wages of war. She couldn't do that anymore. A simmering anger burned inside her that not even the waning, snowy afternoon could wash away.

Her hands clenched into fists at her side, a repetitive gesture she had tried to quell. Occasionally it still took over, and this time she didn't try to stop it. An expression of powerful inner turmoil, the need to punch something was strong.

Staring at the snow, she wished she had put on her skis. A good long cross-country would do her good right now, washing her brain with fresh cold air, working her body until it relaxed.

She didn't think it would be wise to run right now, although the temptation nearly overwhelmed her. But a fresh layer of snow could hide an underlying layer of ice, and it would help no one if a misstep sent her to the hospital.

It certainly wouldn't help Brigid.

At last her hands stopped clenching. Her nose and cheeks were beginning to hurt from the cold. Damn, she wished again for that balaclava. But she hadn't expected to be here this long. Summery clothes awaited her in an airport locker. From the Mediterranean coast she'd expected to return to Afghanistan. Cold-weather military gear waited for her there.

One corner of her mouth lifted. Living out of what amounted to two or three locations. Packing light, traveling often. A wanderer who had a firm home base.

Difficult as this visit had become, one good thing had come out of it: Trace. She was glad to have met him. Glad to have had sex with him. Hoped for more before she departed.

There was a meeting of minds between them. A mostly comfortable meeting. She hadn't wanted to grow close, but she had. Oh well.

Calisthenics, she decided. The only alternative to reach physical fatigue.

The image of herself, the Norwegian soldier, headed inside without challenging the elements of snow and ice, amused her. Her friends in her unit would probably laugh at her.

Necessary risks were one thing, stupidity another.

Chapter Twelve

They must have learned something. The thought gnawed away at Stan Witherspoon's mind like a rat. Why else would the sheriff have come over? Why?

He could think of no other reason, although he tried. He began to wonder if he should get in touch with the boss and tell him about this mess.

Surely the man hadn't held Stan responsible for that woman happening to walk by at exactly the wrong time. She hadn't been expected. Not a sentry that he planned for.

But the thought of telling the boss about this made him quail. He'd probably meet the same fate as Brigid Mannerly. Besides, the boss had told him to sew it up.

With two more murders.

Stan couldn't understand why he was balking now. He'd already caused the deaths of two people. Why not two more? In for a penny, as the saying went.

Except that he still recoiled from the idea. He hadn't figured out a way to pull it off, either. All his scrambling thoughts just kept pushing out more fear. And an increasing amount of self-loathing.

Possibly worst of all was that he'd begun to fear himself as much as he feared his boss. Yes, he had to save his own skin, but the price was getting too high for a man who'd been hired merely to fudge inventory and move some weapons to the perimeter.

Much too high.

The money was certainly less of a motivator than it had been at the outset. Money would do him no good dead or in prison.

Why hadn't he thought of that before?

Fear had driven Stan to the first awful act. Then to the second.

And now to two more. He was in this up to his neck with no way out.

He had believed himself to be a smart man. Now he believed he was a damn fool.

And a murderer.

"I THINK I found something," Trace announced.

With wind blowing snow outside, the office in semi-darkness, Hillary pivoted. "Where?" she asked.

"In the pictures file, if you can believe it."

She scooted over to peer over his shoulder. She saw what appeared to be a photograph of a page from one of Brigid's letters.

"Middle paragraph," he said. "I guess Allan destroyed the original."

I know what I saw, Allan. The first time I just thought it was a contractor employee checking out a crate. It bothered me in some way, so I walked by a few nights later. He was pulling out weapons and placing them on a tarp.

"Just what we thought," Hillary murmured.

"No accusation, though."

"She was too smart for that. I don't have to tell you. Her suspicion is clear or she never would have mentioned it."

He nodded and leaned back in his chair. "And the fact that Allan photographed the page means he felt the same."

"Which explains why I haven't seen the original."

"Probably." Allan drummed his fingers on the desk, then closed the file. "For now I need to stretch, to give myself some more heartburn with coffee and maybe eat something. Do you have any idea how many picture files that man has? I swear, he's got photos going all the way back to high school."

Hillary rose and stretched. "How did you find that one?"

"It was labeled *not for distribution*. I assumed it was some kind of sexy photo I would wish I'd never seen."

She had to smile. "Chicken. Have you ever watched a movie?"

"Yeah, but my friends weren't starring."

That at least pulled a laugh from her. He followed her out of the office, then watched her go to the living room, where she worked on stretching every muscle in her body. *Not a bad idea*, he thought. He was beginning to stiffen. But the damn coffee first. Once he had it going, he joined her in stretching.

"I don't think my neck or backside will ever be the same again."

She appeared amused. "Maybe not."

He uncovered the brownies to serve with the coffee, but neither of them wanted to sit at the table. A tradition broken.

Instead they stood holding small plates of brownies and sipping from mugs that wound up on the counter or perched on the table.

There really didn't seem to be much to say. They'd proved their suspicion but still had nowhere to take it.

"This may be a fruitless exercise," Trace remarked. "Brigid may never have shared any specific details about which contractor she suspected. She might have continued to be vague."

Hillary arched a brow. "Are we giving up?"

"Hell no. I don't think Allan would have been so secretive if there wasn't something more in there."

She nodded. "That's my feeling."

She put her plate down beside her coffee on the counter and began pacing in the small space. "I don't know about your training, but I was trained to put small pieces together so I would know what other questions might need to be asked. I am seeing many questions, but no one to ask." She spread her hands ruefully. "Like being a detective, I suppose. Maybe worse, because we can't just run around asking these questions of everyone we might know."

"That would be like allowing someone to draw a bead on us."

"Precisely."

He finished his own brownie and went to the sink to wash his hands and wipe a damp paper towel across his face. "Part of me wants to keep pushing, after finding that photo. Another part of me is in serious need of a break in front of the fire. Your options?"

"The break. We need to stay fresh."

But something in the twinkle in her eye suggested she had more than a log fire in mind.

Well, so did he.

ONCE THE FIRE was dancing on the hearth, they curled up together at one end of the couch. Trace wrapped his arm around her shoulders, and she leaned into him, her arm around his waist, her head nestled on his shoulder. He leaned back in the bend between the sofa back and arm, and she tucked her legs up beneath her.

That tickled him. This woman who had seemed as firm and tough as anyone in her job had become soft. Melting. She trusted him.

He savored the connection and wanted to take time to enjoy the feeling. No rush. These moments seemed cast in amber.

Eventually, however, the heat in his body rose to the level of the flames in the fireplace. Taking care to be gentle, he touched her chin with his finger and turned her face up to his.

A lazy smile resided on her lips. Her eyes appeared drowsy.

Bending, he kissed her, his tongue finding its way past her teeth. He felt a quivering response that drew him deeper, the two of them dueling slowly, exploring each other with tongues.

Hell, he was ready to run rampant. He had to remind himself to move slowly. There was so much he wanted to do, such as exploring her every hill and hollow.

Hillary indulged him for a while, allowing him to undress her then himself. When he sat again, he began his journey, kissing her throat, then kissing her firm breasts and nipples.

He felt her response run through her, felt her arm tighten around his waist. *Beautiful*, he thought. She was perfect.

He pulled a bit away to look at her from head to foot. Athletic, muscles formed by long hours of training but curves in all the right places. He ran his palms over her while he continued to suck her nipples.

Her quivers grew stronger. Her fingers traced his back and chest, heightening his desire. Oh man…

She finished waiting. With a sinuous move, she withdrew from him and lay back on the couch, parting her legs. He reached out to touch her between her legs, stroking silky petals, finding her swelling nub. This time a shudder ripped through her.

Then she startled him. "Trace, enough teasing." She held up her arms, and he wondered how any man could resist that invitation.

Moments later he filled her warmth and felt her wrap herself around him. A guy could get used to this.

Then the world went away.

Later they cuddled before the fire, still naked. The time was precious. He already felt the ache of impending loss when she left. As of course she would.

But he realized he never wanted her to go away. A foolish, selfish desire.

Hillary then did a Hillary thing. She wiggled away from him and reached for her sweater and sweatpants. "It's time," she said.

"Time for what?"

Her smile was warm. "To move. To caffeinate. To eat something." She tilted her head. "You were right about this compulsion to eat. I never thought about it before."

Laughing, he rose, yearning for more of her but realizing she had other needs right now. Or maybe she sought some distance between them.

Much as he hated to think about it, he decided she was right. Their separate ways were far too separate.

He watched her prance from the room—really, it *was* a prance—and he grinned. She was a hell of a woman.

They ate slices of the whole pie Maude had given them. Warmed in the microwave, the apple pie was a perfect accompaniment to coffee.

"Tomorrow," Trace announced, "we're going to have

to find our way to the grocery. Or Maude's. I know you don't like cooking."

"I don't hate it," Hillary answered. "It's just not something I'm inclined to do. When my father and I are home at the same time, we take turns cooking for each other. Then it is special."

"It would be."

She smiled. "Maybe it's special now, too."

Well, that pleased him. Not because he wanted her to cook, but that it might not be a pain right now.

While he washed up, Hillary disappeared. When she returned, she was garbed for outdoors.

"Going somewhere?" he asked, suddenly nervous for her.

"To walk around the outside of the house. It is snowing heavily again."

He understood instantly and reached for a towel to dry his hands. "Want me to come along?" He was sure she didn't, but he was uncomfortable anyway. Of course she wanted to go alone. If someone had been prowling outside, she didn't want to take a chance that they might reveal their awareness. More, if something happened, one of them had to be free to react.

Masculine protective urges surged in him, but he battered them down. She wouldn't appreciate them at all.

Hillary exited through the mudroom and out the back door. He couldn't hear a thing, but he didn't expect to.

Stealth was their middle name.

OUTSIDE, HILLARY STOOD on the snowy stoop, giving her eyes time to adjust to the night. Snow still fell heavily, but the wind didn't blow, so it wasn't filling in anywhere feet had stepped. It would cover the divots with a fresh powder, but the depressions would still be there.

She didn't believe that guy had given up when they followed him to the truck stop. If he was the man who had killed Allan, he should have left long ago. But someone had stayed and was concerned enough to watch her and Trace. No, he hadn't given up.

Same man? It didn't make a bit of difference to her. A stalker was a stalker. They might pose different kinds of threats, but given what had happened to Allan, she would have gambled that he was here for the same reason.

At home a night like this would have been an invitation to snap on her cross-country skis. This night she had other matters in mind—more important ones.

At last her eyes adapted. Her peripheral vision had sharpened, ready to notice any movement to her sides regardless of the nearly lightless world.

The night had turned shades of blue and gray. Only an occasional snowflake twinkled with rainbow colors as it happened to catch faraway light.

Now she scanned to both sides. Little light escaped from the house, thanks to those heavy curtains. Here darkness and snow ruled.

If someone had walked along the back of the house, she couldn't see it. Shadows weren't deep enough. The snow was brighter than the sky above, but not enough to overcome her night vision.

She listened intently. Sounds of distant people and cars reached her. Occasionally she thought she heard a twig crackle, but that was probably from the leafless trees at the back of the yard. At least, that's where it seemed to come from. Cold could cause branches to protest, and she seriously doubted anyone was up there in those gnarly fingers. Not a good hiding place right now.

On high alert, her every sense engaged, she stepped slowly off the stoop. She was well practiced at walking through snow without the noise of crunching or swishing. Slow, careful, light steps, following no rhythm. Minimal sound.

The world slept beneath its winter blanket.

She moved steadily, first to the left corner, then to the right. If someone had been trying to watch them, he must be disappointed. Not that he'd go away. No, he seemed too determined.

After she'd covered the entire back of the house without seeing anything untoward, she moved around the right corner. Watching before she moved. Attuned to anything else that moved or that looked too dark against the snow. Nothing.

But before too long, she saw the first depression in the snow. Right under the kitchen window. Her heart accelerated just a bit.

Then another and another. Instead of continuing, she retraced her steps and went around to the other side of the house. More dips in the snowfall. A short stride, probably because of the difficulty of moving through the snow.

A bigger hole beneath one of the bedroom windows.

She'd seen all she needed to. She headed back to the stoop and went inside. A bootjack by the door offered her an opportunity to kick the snow from her boots, then she entered the kitchen.

Trace was waiting for her with clear impatience. "Well?"

"Someone's been trying to look in the windows. I stopped when I was sure."

He swore and looked past her for a few seconds. "He's becoming bolder."

"Or more desperate."

She began to strip off her outerwear, eager to get back to that fire with another cup of coffee. Or maybe some hot cider. Creature comforts. She took them when she could.

"Trace? We are not chasing shadows."

"Clearly we're not. If we could draw this guy out, maybe we'd learn the whole story."

Hillary shook her head a bit. "If he's willing to kill to keep his secret, how much talking will he do?"

"Maybe he's keeping someone else's secret and will talk in an attempt to save his own hide."

After hanging up her outerwear, Hillary pulled out a saucepan and poured cider from the gallon jug that was stashed in the pantry. "You want some?"

"Yeah, please. I'm getting sick to death of coffee. I never thought I'd say that."

As the cider simmered, she added a cinnamon stick. "We like cider in Norway. Many different kinds with different infused flavors."

"Maybe someday I'll come visit and find out."

But his thoughts were elsewhere, she could tell. Nor did she expect his full attention. She suspected his mind was running in a direction similar to hers. The man knew he had been spotted. Now the question was just how much he was hurrying his plan. Or how dangerous that had made him.

She passed Trace a handled glass mug of cider, then ladled some for herself. "We need to be truly alert now."

"Yeah. Yeah. This is not a good sign."

They returned to the living room but didn't cuddle. Instead they both stared in silence at the fire. It was burning low, so Hillary added a log, then sat again.

Trace eventually spoke. "I don't like being in the middle of a mission without a plan. Not one bit."

She understood. "But what plan can we make? We don't know enough. Put booby traps around the house?"

He snorted. "And catch some kid out throwing snowballs. Right."

"You know I wasn't being serious."

She got his attention then. "I believe, Hills, that you have too much sense to even consider doing such a thing. My sarcasm failed."

She lifted one corner of her mouth in a half smile. "Not really."

"Okay, we've got to do more than read letters and emails. We may or may not find a decent clue there, but this man has become a looming threat. He could well be more dangerous than anything we might learn."

Hillary sipped her cider, grateful for the tangy warmth. "So come up with a plan, *Herre* Airborne. I agree with you, but we need to find a way to do it."

TRACE HAD TO LAUGH. In the midst of a serious discussion, she still managed to make him laugh.

Or maybe he was walking on air. Or in free fall.

Just then he didn't care. He figured he was going to care a whole lot before long, but right now he was determined to enjoy this time with her.

He sat back with his cider, liking every moment they shared, especially the lighter ones. There was another side to the Valkyrie. One who was steadily creeping into his heart.

Man, he'd never expected this. There had been women in his life before, but none who stuck around and some he wouldn't stick around for. Nothing long-term.

This wouldn't be long-term, either. He thought of asking her how long she intended to stay, then backed away. The separation would come soon enough. Too soon.

"What about you?" he asked. "Do you have a plan?"

"Nothing beyond putting a man in jail. I suppose if he's watching us this closely, that we ought to be able to catch him."

"But how?" There was the crux.

"I wish I knew. Maybe your sheriff will find him."

"I'm not holding my breath. We're on our own, Hillary. I've been there before, and I'm sure you have, too."

She nodded. "Too often. When I'm interfacing with women, trying to learn something, I'm almost always alone. I don't want to seem like a threat."

"You certainly wouldn't learn much if you did."

She agreed with a slight nod of her head. "I suggest that after this cider, we go back to work. Maybe out of that will come some plan."

Trace doubted it. They'd already reviewed most of the stuff they had and had come up nearly empty-handed. Still, there was little else to do on a cold, dark night.

Well, there was something else to do, but he didn't want to push it. He also didn't want to start feeling guilty about his desires replacing their true mission.

"Want to break it up?" he asked. "I'll take a couple of hours while you nap, and then we can switch."

Now she gave a clear shake of her head. "I trust you about many things, Trace. But not about waking me up."

"Caught," he admitted. "Then let's get to it."

HILLARY WAS STILL past knowing how late or early it was. Between her initial time change and the hours they had been working, unless they went out for a run, she had no instinctive sense of the time of day.

No running tonight, that was for certain. Maybe when the morning came, whenever that might be, the roads wouldn't look so bad. Well, except for that ATV trail they'd been running along. She doubted anyone would clear that except someone with Ski-Doos or the like.

In the meantime, there was the desk until they both fell asleep in their chairs.

IT WAS 4:00 A.M. by the clock on Trace's computer when he exclaimed, "Will you look at that!"

Hillary rolled her chair over immediately to peer over his shoulder. "Trace?" she breathed.

"Are you thinking what I'm thinking?"

Indeed she was.

They looked at a photo of a smiling Brigid in full combat gear, her assault rifle held in both gloved hands across her body. A typical pose for a soldier to send home. Hillary's throat and heart ached.

But what caught Hillary's attention and apparently Trace's was the big sign behind her. It appeared to have been painted on plywood, supported by posts. It had faded and peeled a bit because of the harsh elements. Regardless, while Brigid's body blocked the logo behind her, the words above her were readable.

BRIGGS AND HOLMES

And just below that:

Defending Our Troops

Trace snorted. "*Who* does the defending?" he asked.

"My thought, too." Hillary rolled her chair back a foot or so. "Quite an unusual background for such a photo."

"Quite a loud message if you have any idea what's going on."

Hillary abruptly jumped up and hurried to the living room. The grief she had felt upon learning of Brigid's death crashed over her with renewed force. For days now she'd buttoned it down, shoving it beneath a heavy boulder in her heart, focusing on finding any information that would explain the loss of her friend.

But she could no longer bury it. *Brigid. Oh my God, Brigid.* Dutiful until the end. Fighting for right at great risk. Bearing a soldier's burden. Unwilling to look away even when her husband warned her. Trying to protect her fellow warriors unto her final breath.

Hot, heavy tears rolled down Hillary's cheeks as reality once again struck home like a punch in her midsection. This hunt for truth, as important as it was, had partly been a distraction from anguish.

Now, as that torment filled her, she felt her knees weaken. There weren't enough tears for Brigid. Not enough of them in this entire universe. Each salty drop mirrored a drop of Brigid's blood.

She didn't hear Trace approach. Only knew that he was there when his arms wrapped around her from behind and she felt his warm breath on her neck.

"Hills," he murmured, then turned her around, urging her to lean into him. His powerful arms held her, caring for her, and she took advantage of his strength, letting him hold her as sorrow ripped through her in successive, agonizing tidal waves.

"Hills," he murmured again, pressing his large hand to the back of her head, holding her even closer.

He let the pain rack her, didn't offer soothing words that wouldn't have helped at all. It seemed forever before she began to calm.

"I don't weep," she said hoarsely, her voice breaking. A few shudders still passed through her. "I don't."

"Of course not. This is all rain. I need to check the roof."

That pulled a watery half laugh from her. "I apologize."

"For what? For human feelings? Crap, even Valkyries can be human. You're not a goddess. Well, except when I look at you."

It was the right tone to take, and she rubbed her cheek

lightly against his shoulder. "Do you know what the original Valkyries are? They choose who lives and dies in battle."

"Sounds like a description of a soldier."

She sighed, then pulled gently back. "Brigid," she said. "That photo. Brave."

"Brigid was always a damn-the-torpedoes kind of woman when she believed in something. That was the thing. She might tell us to leave it, to decide if it was important enough to waste our time on, but when it came to a cause, nothing could stop her."

"Not even Allan, it seems."

"Not even Allan," he agreed.

Hillary wiped her face with the sleeve of her sweater, then gave in to a need for comfort. She leaned against Trace once again, leaning as she hadn't in her entire adult life. She had sought comfort from her father in her earlier life, but never since joining the Army. She had friendships, but no more.

Except Brigid. With her, Hillary had found a relationship that extended beyond friendship. She might never understand why she and Brigid had been drawn together, or why they had become so tightly knit so fast. It just was.

It had been such a good friendship, too. Probably what Trace had felt for Allan. Maybe for Brigid, too. And of their losses, Trace had suffered the greatest: two friends he had known his entire life. She couldn't imagine the gaping hole their absence had left in him. It was too much to conceive.

Yet here in the midst of his own suffering, he was offering her comfort. A remarkable man.

"Coffee or sleep?" he asked. "Or maybe a drink?"

"Drink," she decided, reluctantly moving back from his warmth and strength.

She chose a beer, not wanting anything stronger. He joined her, popping the tops on two bottles.

Though she was hardly ready to think about it, she asked, "What should we do about that sign?"

"It's not enough to build a case, but it sure gives us a direction."

Hillary closed her eyes briefly, summoning the photo to mind. "A huge clue," she said presently.

"But only a guide. I would say, however, that we have the right idea about what was going on."

"What's still going on." Hillary felt more anger burn in the pit of her stomach. "Brigid started this. We've got to finish it."

"Maybe we should check out Briggs and Holmes," Trace suggested. It was the only thing he could think of with what little they knew.

"We'll only find their public face," Hillary pointed out.

"Probably. But we might also find job listings that would tell us the kind of people they want to hire. We might even find some news stories that will tell us more."

Hillary raised her brows. "I think this company would want to stay very much below the surface."

"Or maybe they issue public statements. They must have stockholders. We ought to be able to discover what they were *supposed* to be doing over there."

She nodded slowly. "We might find some discrepancies. But we still don't know how to tie them to all this."

"Then let's damn well look for a way." He regretted the sharpness of his tone as soon as the words escaped him, but Hillary didn't appear troubled by it.

"We have to," she agreed finally. "It's all we have."

Two blocks away in a nearly empty apartment building built for better times, Stan Witherspoon prepared for another day of stalking without being noticed. He suspected it would be harder than ever now that the sheriff had been called. Maybe there was a hunt for him even now.

He sort of doubted it. Those two couldn't possibly prove that the man they had followed had anything dubious in mind.

Besides, another fear had begun to grow in him. What if Brigid had said something that his boss feared enough to tell him to take care of it? What if it could all somehow be traced back to the contracting company he worked for?

Just because trouble hadn't fallen down the line to reach Stan didn't mean there was no trouble brewing.

Worse, what if Brigid had said something that would point directly to the contractor? Just a few words in passing that someone else had thought needed to be reported up the chain?

The thought made Stan shudder, and not from the cold. There could be an internal investigation right now, right as he sat on his butt trying to stay warm.

Stan didn't doubt in the least that his boss would have a cover story that would point directly at Stan. Who, after all, had access to those crates? Who, after all, was capable of fudging the books?

He remembered all those times he'd sat around with other guys in uniform complaining about how much more contractor employees made than the stiffs in the service. Well, they had, and that had set Stan's sights on getting a job with one.

He'd never imagined that it would eventually extend to helping sell arms to insurgents. Not in his wildest dreams. But the money had been so great, he couldn't turn it down.

What if he'd stayed here too long? Yeah, he was required to return stateside for six months at a time, but that didn't mean nobody would notice the timing of his trip. Earlier than he'd been scheduled to take it. A claim of family problems.

That could be checked out readily enough if someone wanted to.

Stan swore every curse word he could think of and made up a few of his own.

He was a bean counter, for Pete's sake. Not a strategist. Not a planner. Not an assassin.

Sitting there in his darkened apartment, he wondered just how many potentially fatal mistakes he'd made.

The only way to save his skin was to get rid of those two people staying at the Mannerly house.

Except when he'd made his foray in the dark, he hadn't been able to see anything inside. How was he supposed to know where in the house they were, and whether they were sleeping?

He had no idea.

Nor was he a marksman who could kill them at a distance.

He had to separate them somehow. Get them one at a time.

He could do it. He just had to figure out how.

Chapter Thirteen

After a few hours of sleep curled up together on the queen-size bed, Hillary and Trace went back to work. Both of them were only slightly refreshed, but it was enough.

They ate the last of the leftovers in the fridge, which hardly qualified as a breakfast, then carried their inevitable coffee back into the office.

The first thing they reviewed was the photo of Brigid in front of the sign. Maybe there was another clue in it.

Trace enlarged it, and two pairs of eyes scoured it. Maybe that sign was the only clue Brigid had intended to send.

"If she'd sent more," Trace argued, "Allan would have figured it out. He wasn't stupid."

"What if he couldn't find out anything more to link this company to the arms?"

"I don't want to even think that. I want an answer to this mess."

Hillary sighed, rubbing her eyes. "So do I. I am just trying not to get my hopes too high."

"Hope? I'm beginning to wonder if I even know what that is. I'm just determined."

Hillary was, too, but she insisted on looking at the photo longer. She stared until she thought her eyes would turn into flaming coals from the intensity, but then she spied it.

"Trace."

He turned his head. "Yo."

"Look at the photo again."

"I've been staring at it for the last half hour."

"Just look." She pointed with a finger. "Shadows."

"Shadows?" But clued in now, he studied them closely. "There's something wrong."

"The light. The photo of her was taken at a different time of day than the photo of the sign. Look at the difference in the shadows. The time was far apart."

He leaned in, then murmured, "My God. My God."

"Tell me if you think I'm wrong, but the photo of the sign was taken under artificial light. As if some light source is shining on it."

"And Brigid appears to be photographed in the morning or the afternoon. You're right! She must have worked hard to layer the two pictures."

"And include the shadows," Hillary agreed.

"Damn, I wonder if I can take the layers apart."

"I don't know how. When she sent it, it was one photo." She picked up their cups. "I'm getting more coffee. And there must be something left in the cupboard."

"More brownie mix." But he sounded far away, as if lost in thought. Hillary's own brain was turning around, seeking some way to use this information.

Brownies? She could have laughed, then decided the chocolate and sugar might be helpful. She only wished she'd thought to buy a box of instant oatmeal, but at the time she'd believed she'd only be staying a few days.

She pulled the curtain back a bit to see the morning was clear and sunny. Maybe she should walk to Maude's and get them a meal.

Almost as soon as she had the thought, she discarded it.

If Trace was going to be diving into that photo, she wanted to be here for it.

But just as she was about to put the wet ingredients into a mixing bowl, Trace appeared.

"I locked up the photo under a new password. Now we're going to get out of here to buy some decent food. We can't live on brownies and leftovers, and neither of us really feels like cooking. Even if you do have cod in the freezer."

"I agree." Getting out would feel so good. Sunlight. Chilly fresh air. Snow crunching under her boots. She was not built to stay inside for so long.

"Maybe it'll drive out the fog in our heads."

"I could use that."

The walk to Maude's was wonderful. Hillary felt her head clearing, the staleness that filled her lungs and brain blowing away. It was cold, but people were about, apparently glad to escape from the winter storm. Rosy faces smiled. Cheerful greetings rang out. Trace answered them all with a smile and a wave.

Hillary was happy to see his hometown taking him back into their embrace. It must have been hard for him to feel like an outsider ever since he'd refused to accept Allan's death as a suicide.

Brief as the walk was, Maude's felt hot inside. Between her kitchen and all the people who preferred to eat in their shirtsleeves rather than winter coats and jackets, she probably kept her thermostat high.

As Trace came to the counter, Maude eyed him.

"Let me guess," Maude said. "Food for half an army and all of it takeout."

Trace laughed. "Plus lots of veggies. Whatever you've got. We've been missing them."

"Stick your nose out once in a while and you won't be

missing anything." Then she looked at Hillary. "Do I mis-remember, or do you like oatmeal?"

"Very much."

"Well, I've got a box for you to take back with you, if you know how to cook it."

Hillary smiled. "I think I can. Thank you."

Maude nodded. "Now you two go sit down while I get the food ready. Since I'm missing half my regular customers, it shouldn't take too long."

A few minutes later, a clone of Maude showed up bearing two tall insulated cups. "Hot lattes. My mother says you look like you're freezing."

Trace looked at Hillary. "Is my nose blue?"

She shook her head, a smile lurking around her lips. "I suspect mine's as red as yours, though."

They unzipped their jackets and enjoyed their coffee while they waited.

Hillary remarked, "You didn't ask for anything in particular except vegetables."

"That's because Maude will take care of us. Besides, everything on her menu is good. We might get a bit of most of it." He smiled. "Think of it as a treasure hunt."

About a half hour later they were heading back to the house with a whole bunch of plastic bags full of goodies.

"I can hardly wait to see what she gave us," Trace remarked. "Dang, that woman is softening with the years. I swear she used to be a fire-breathing dragon."

"Maybe she just likes you."

"Ha!" he answered. "Maude is famous for not liking anyone. Well, except Gage and the old sheriff. She must have a soft spot for cops."

"And maybe for soldiers, too."

Back at the house, they unpacked, peeking into the containers. No question but Maude had been generous and had given them a large variety of meals. As for veggies, there was a ton of broccoli, plenty of carrots and a few large chef's salads.

"Those salads won't last long," Hillary remarked.

"A good reason to start eating. That's ranch dressing on the side. Let me check what might be in the fridge."

He soon emerged with bottles of blue cheese dressing and creamy Caesar. "I hope one of these is to your taste."

"Blue cheese. In any form on almost anything."

Hillary left the box of oatmeal on the counter as a reminder to herself. She could eat it at any time of day.

They decided to dive into the salads immediately, along with the croutons Maude had packaged separately.

"Oh man," Hillary said. "Every cell in my body is happy."

Trace crunched on some lettuce, then agreed. "I think she included some sliced cheese, too. That woman thought of everything."

After cleaning up, they headed again for the office. Hillary paused. "I saw some pavement out there. The snow is melting."

"True." Trace flashed a smile. "We couldn't run all the way because I'm fairly certain a lot hasn't been plowed yet. Nothing out there but parks. Wanna go anyway?"

"Is that even a question? Calisthenics haven't been enough."

Twenty minutes later they were trotting along the road. *Such a beautiful day*, Hillary thought. Even the air felt a little warmer under the sun. As they fell into step together, she had the oddest feeling that she'd come home.

THEY WERE ONLY able to complete half their usual run, but they arrived back at the house feeling pleasantly relaxed anyway. A brief burst of freedom. Of self-care.

Hillary's mood had leavened considerably. The run had done her wonders, and Trace looked as if he felt the same. They'd been stapled to their chairs too much. Yes, it was important, but so was moving around, working muscles. The endorphins were pretty good, too.

After they ditched their winter clothes and boots, choosing to walk around in socks, they grabbed some coffee and headed to the office for another kind of marathon.

"I've been thinking about that photo a whole lot," Trace remarked as they marched down the short hallway and into the office.

But as soon as she crossed the threshold, Hillary froze. "Trace?"

"Yeah."

She pointed to the stack of letters that had been on her part of the desk. The pile was smaller, and many appeared to be gone.

Trace understood immediately. At once they both went on high alert and with hand signals agreed to take different parts of the house to find out if anyone was still there.

Hillary headed for the living room, a place full of many hiding spots, especially with the room darkened by the curtains.

Trace took the back of the house, where three bedrooms offered more hiding places. They moved slowly, silently, peering around corners before entering a room.

Hillary found nothing in the living room. Trace was taking longer in the bedrooms, so she went to check the mudroom.

There was no mistaking that the back door had been jimmied open.

She cursed under her breath, wishing she had her boots on so she could track outside. Well, she could get them now.

"Hillary?" Trace still spoke quietly as he came up behind her.

She pointed to the lock, then at her feet. Trace nodded and slipped away. Two minutes later he was back with both their boots and their insulated vests.

Outside the day was still crisp and fresh, dimming a bit as the afternoon deepened. Unmistakable boot prints covered the stoop and led away toward the trees. But there were also prints leading to one side of the house.

Again they split up, Trace heading for the trees, Hillary around the side of the house. Nothing but the footprints, the ones on the side of the house coming from the street, the ones at the back heading toward the trees.

Trace took off. Hillary waited in case he wanted backup of some kind. Not that he couldn't take care of just about anyone out there. But someone who was armed? Two people would do better. But the house still needed protecting. Much as she hated being the sentry, that was what was required just then. The invader might come back. Or if Trace called out, she needed to be ready and not already in trouble.

But the beautiful day, no longer as beautiful, remained silent.

At last Trace returned. He shook his head, and she waited for him to reach the stoop.

"A car," he said when they got inside. "A car. I'd call the sheriff, but it looks as if quite a few vehicles have been up and down that alley today, including the garbage truck."

"Apparently that man knows what we're doing, and he's getting desperate enough that he doesn't care if we know."

Trace's answer was harsh. "He won't be prepared for what he'll find in *this* house."

TRACE WAS ANGRY. Not a bit afraid or unnerved, but furious. Whoever had done this clearly knew something about what had happened to Allan and Brigid. There could be absolutely no other reason to break in here. Especially since nothing appeared to have been touched except Brigid's letters.

"God," he said. "That was a violation. Her privacy. His privacy. Even if they're gone now, no stranger has a right to invade their intimacy in such a way. No stranger has a right to invade their love."

Hillary nodded her agreement. She hadn't been any happier about reading through all those communications than he had been.

Trace attempted to lower his fury a few notches, but he didn't succeed. It wasn't just knowing that Allan, and possibly Brigid, had been murdered. No, it was the invasion. Matters they would have shared only with each other had now been stolen for some creep to read.

They returned to the office with bottles of beer, but Trace didn't face the computer. With his chair turned sideways, he looked toward Hillary but barely saw her. There was a blackness growing in him, a blackness he had felt only in the heat of battle. As if his soul were being scooped out, to leave a dark void behind. It wanted him to fall in. To never emerge again.

It was a hole he had felt only when the bullets were flying, when the bombs and grenades came his way. When death exploded the world and sometimes claimed his buddies. When all that was civilized was stripped away.

This creep was pulling him back there, to places in himself that he had never liked no matter how necessary. If that guy showed up right now, Trace would have throttled him with his bare hands.

"Hills?" he said, once again seeing her and not the pit inside him.

"Yes?"

"It would be murder if I kill that SOB."

She placed her bottle on the desk and leaned back in her own chair, studying him gravely. "Legally, it probably would be. I don't know your laws. Maybe if he comes inside this house when we're here, it wouldn't be. If he attacks, it wouldn't be."

"But there's always a set of conditions that protects *him*. Always."

"Rules of engagement."

The rules soldiers were supposed to follow. He sighed, rubbing his hands over his entire face. Trying to erase thoughts he didn't want to have. Rules of engagement. A guide that worked except in the heat of a battle.

"It can be a struggle," she remarked. "When we go to war, we are expected to be no longer civilized in many ways. When we come back, we are supposed to become civilized again."

"It can be a leap," he admitted. He looked to his blank computer screen again and realized he didn't want to dive back in. Not yet.

He turned his attention back to Hillary. "You have any PTSD?"

She shrugged. "I'm fortunate. It hasn't been disabling. You?"

"Yeah. I've been so wound up in this mess that it's been leaving me alone. I've been luckier than a lot of my buddies, though. A lot luckier."

But here he was, hovering on the brink of another pit that could suck him in. One that he'd been successfully battling. He forced his attention away from the internal war to the external problem. "There's got to be more information in that photo than we noticed."

"I think so. It was certainly pointed."

"Yeah. Brigid always knew what she was doing." Swiveling around, he woke up the computer and unlocked the photo. It hadn't changed any, but he tried to see it with fresh eyes.

"Can you change the colors in the photo?" she asked.

"I'm no geek, but I can try. Why?"

"Steganography."

A few seconds passed before he recalled the word. "As in a hidden message?"

Hillary nodded. "Those conflicting shadows may not have been intended just to identify a contractor. We can try changing the colors first to find out if anything looks out of place. Then we could try examining it pixel by pixel."

He stared at the photo. "It wouldn't be beyond Brigid to figure out how. She was always good with technology. Now I wish I'd gotten a degree in computer science."

An amused sound escaped Hillary. "I doubt steganography is one of the classes. Try looking it up online. There might be some suggestions how to do this."

A few minutes later, he groaned. "Damn, Hillary, do you have any idea how many ways there are to do it?"

"I was afraid you might say that." She looked over his shoulder and sighed audibly, warm breath on his neck. His mind leaped immediately to other things they might be doing, but he reined himself in. Kept going on the problem.

He spoke. "It had to be something Allan would recognize, would know how to decode. Naturally he left us a packet of directions."

The sarcasm in his tone was audible, and he wondered just how irritated with Allan he was becoming. "Okay," he said. "I already need a break. Maybe moving around will get my brain back in gear."

She lingered a few minutes looking at the photograph,

but soon joined him as he paced through the house, leaning her shoulder against a doorjamb and folding her arms as he passed by.

She spoke. "It has to be in the image. That removes quite a few methods."

"Sure. But that still leaves a lot of methods I don't know how to break through." He turned into the kitchen eventually and pulled out a container, inspecting the contents. Then he placed half a club sandwich on each of two plates. "Fuel up. We're about to take a long march."

This time he didn't reach for beer but instead started coffee. "God, I don't think I've ever drunk so much coffee."

"Neither have I. I'm starting to feel a bit of stomach burn."

"The food should help. If not, I'm sure there's some antacid in this house somewhere. What house would be without it, these times we live in?"

Another amused sound escaped her.

"What?" he asked irritably.

"You're actually charming when you're so frustrated."

"Charming?" Then he replayed his own words and tones in his mind. "Sorry."

"I'm not annoyed. I share your feelings. I just like the way you express them. Nothing held back."

Trace shook his head as he placed the plates on the table and dug out a couple of napkins. "Oh, I'm holding a lot back. I want to shake Brigid until her teeth rattle for not listening to Allan. I'm furious at him for not taking action with whatever information he had. He could at least have reported his suspicions."

Hillary grew so silent that he stared at her. "What?" he demanded finally.

Her words fell like bombs. "Perhaps he did."

HILLARY SUPPOSED THE sandwich was delicious, but it might as well have been sawdust for all she tasted it. She suspected that Trace wasn't feeling any differently. He ate mechanically, but he talked.

"If he reported it, something should have been done." Then he answered himself. "Unless he reported it to the wrong person."

"Possibly." She forced down another bite, then went to get a glass of water to help her swallow. The coffee remained untouched in its pot.

"Are you suggesting that Allan got killed because he told someone what he knew?"

"It's possible. I don't know. There must be layers to this arms sales business, but where are they? How deep is all this? How high does it go? I can't imagine he would have reported it to the contractor."

"That doesn't seem likely," Trace agreed. "What if we find a hidden message in that photo? Who do *we* report it to? How can we know it's not the wrong person?"

Hillary mulled it over for all of ten seconds. "I go to *my* chain of command."

"Are you saying Norwegians never get up to dirty business?"

"No. What I'm saying is that it's unlikely any of my countrymen would be involved in this *particular* dealing. Allan would have reported to someone he knows, most likely your military. Not in mine."

She paused. "I am not claiming any moral superiority. We also have our own arms manufacturers and deals with foreign governments. Weapons merchants are everywhere. It's just that this situation, involving an American contractor, would be unlikely to extend to the Norwegian military or companies."

He nodded grimly. "Okay. If we find something useful, you take it up your chain of command. Then duck, because if this extends across the alliance, we're going to take a dangerous ride."

"I think neither of us has ever avoided danger."

He then said something he figured she wouldn't like because she was so strong. But it burst from his heart anyway. "I couldn't stand it if anything happened to you."

She didn't bristle, not even a bit. Her answer was simple. "Nor I to you." Then she returned to Valkyrie Hillary. "We have a mission."

Easier said than done.

Chapter Fourteen

Stan Witherspoon was becoming an inveterate pacer. When the walls of his tiny apartment with its bedroll on the floor and its miniature kitchen covered with empty food containers became too confining, when he wasn't trying to see what that damn Mullen was up to, he paced in the courtyard created by the four surrounding apartment buildings.

There was hardly ever a soul out there, but Stan had paced enough to flatten all the snow into a hard, icy path around the perimeter.

He was a damn fool. A bigger fool than he'd ever guessed, and he was quite sure that he'd never overestimated his own intelligence. He knew enough to get by. He knew enough to fudge an inventory.

But he'd dropped out of college when he realized he'd never pass the CPA exam no matter how hard he studied. His father had wanted him to join the firm, but Stan knew better. He knew he was better off disappointing his father at the outset rather than after a mediocre performance during four years of college to be followed by failing the CPA exam.

His dad had at least looked impressed when Stan had told him about joining the contracting firm and the kind of income he was making. But money had always mattered to the senior Witherspoon, a trait he had passed along to his son.

Well, his dad wouldn't be impressed now, and neither was Stan. He was in a bind so tight that it sometimes felt like his head would explode from the pressure.

He'd taken care of the Mannerly guy according to his orders. It should have ended there. He should have just left town. Instead he'd had to stay. Because of that Mullen guy. Because he was making such a ruckus about murder.

Because he might know something.

But even non-Einstein Stan Witherspoon knew he'd made a major mistake earlier. Even though he'd been noticed, he hadn't been noticed enough to get himself in trouble. He doubted the sheriff was looking for him. Cripes, he'd made himself as invisible as he could, as unremarkable-looking as he could.

But today. Today he'd made a gigantic mistake.

Walking around outside, he wanted to pull out his own hair. He wasn't a burglar. What made him think he could break into that place and have anyone think it was a random robbery?

He should have taken something valuable. Like the TV. Or the sound system. Or even the computer sitting on that desk surrounded by papers. Except that he'd known that carrying that stuff from the house might have drawn the kind of attention he was seeking to avoid.

No, all he'd taken was some of those letters. The most recent ones from Brigid Mannerly. Hoping to discover what Mullen knew, if anything. To find out what the Mannerly woman might have revealed to her husband. Hoping that those two people staying there wouldn't notice. Why should they be interested in a stack of letters? Why was he stuck in this town making messes everywhere he went?

Because somebody up the chain had plucked a string somewhere. Because someone had made his boss nervous.

The cold penetrated the fog in his brain, and he realized abruptly that he needed to get inside. Afghanistan wasn't a hot climate, but he was finding it bothersome to adapt anyway. Or maybe it was his own fault for spending so much time outside accomplishing very little.

Except getting himself closer to trouble. When he got inside, he didn't even want to take off his outerwear.

He was cold to the bone, and he knew it wasn't the weather outside. No, this was the iciness of terror.

Death was creeping closer, and right then he couldn't imagine a good way to hold it off.

TRACE THREW UP HIS HANDS. Hillary almost followed suit. Her eyes burned and felt as if they wanted to fall out of her head. They'd been manipulating that photo for hours and seemed to be getting nowhere near any kind of message.

"And there's nothing useful in her letters," Trace grumbled.

"Not that I found. Emails?"

"I can start running through them again. Maybe I should just print them all out so that you can look with me."

"I wish that man hadn't taken her letters." Hillary felt sorrow tug at her heart.

"Me too, but, joy of joys, I found a folder where Allan scanned them all. They're still here, Hills."

"But you haven't read through them again?"

"Who's had time?"

She shook her head and stood up, shaking her arms and rotating her shoulders. "I'm convinced there's a message hidden in that photo. We just need to find a key."

"That's like going into a store and asking them to make a key without giving them a template to use. I'd just like to find a note from Allan saying flat out that this is what we need to do."

She barely managed a wan smile. "Considering how secretive they were being…"

"Yeah." Trace stood with her. "Calisthenics?"

It sounded like the best idea in the world. Hillary went to her bedroom to pull on her loose-fitting sweatpants and a T-shirt. Laundry again tomorrow or she was going to smell like the inside of a goat shed.

Eyeing Trace as they worked out was probably the most pleasurable thing she'd done since their walk to Maude's. The walk stood out in her mind the way a sparkling ornament stood out on a Christmas tree. And now this.

She'd heard the term *eye candy* somewhere, but now she knew what it meant. When they finally finished and began walking around the room to cool down, she told him frankly, "I'd like to climb into bed with you."

He straightened from the twist he was doing. "Seriously?" His brows had lifted, and a grin started to spread across his face.

"Seriously." Then she unleashed a light laugh and dashed toward the door. "I take the first shower."

"Maybe not alone," he retorted.

Nor did she.

THE WATER WAS WARM. Trace's soapy hands running over Hillary from top to bottom made her burn hotter far more than the water. How Trace managed to lather her and bend over in the small stall was something of a miracle in itself. But he did, even reaching the arches of her feet. When he began to wash her center, heat exploded into a firebomb.

But first she wanted to give him the same treatment. She took the slippery bar of soap from him and acquainted herself with every hard muscle, front to back. When she heard a soft groan escape him, she smiled with pleasure.

Hard, firm, perfect in every line. Staring into his face brought her a different kind of pleasure. She just plain liked his face. The sight of it warmed her in a wholly different way. Handsome. But more than handsome. Despite his hard edges, he could soften, and she saw it now.

They came together in a slick embrace, their kiss tasting like soap.

"Damn," Trace muttered. "We'd better get out of here before we slip."

She hated the thought but had to agree. But next was toweling each other off, massaging skin with soft terry cloth. Desire began to rumble like thunder on the horizon.

Then the ringing of a phone came from another part of the house. They both stilled and stiffened.

"That's not my phone," Trace said.

Grabbing a towel, Hillary swiftly wrapped it around her head. "It's mine. It may be my father."

"Go," he said with a laugh. "Go. There'll be time later."

She hoped so. Unless their brains started whirling over the mystery again. It never stopped niggling at her, at least not for long. The shower interval had been one of those rare times. Trace swept her away from reality with such ease. With such wonderful touches, as if he knew her body as well as she did.

She reached her phone, which was sitting on the night table beside her bed. She hadn't expected to need it except for an emergency, and her heart galloped as she wondered if something had happened to her father.

"Hills," said his warm, deep voice in her ear. "Where have you gone? Your friends say you went to America and decided to stay for a while?"

"Well, I'm in America and I decided to stay, Pa. Are you all right?"

"As fit as I've ever been. Staying young by climbing mountains. The snow is getting deeper. How can you give up your time in the South of France? Or is it more beautiful there?"

"It's…different. But there are mountains. Even some snow, but I don't have my skis."

He laughed. "If you were here, we'd take a long ski and camp under our favorite trees."

"I miss you, Pa."

"I miss you, too. But I won't miss you for long, I hope. A desk has taken over my life."

"No." Surprise hit her.

"Yes. My time has come. Now I write orders for everyone else."

It was her turn to laugh. "That sounds comfortable."

"Too comfortable. But the mountains are still here to keep me busy. When will you come back?"

"Soon, I hope. Keep my skis waxed."

Now his laugh was hearty. He knew as well as she that waxes must be chosen for snow conditions and temperature. No waxless skis for them.

"Be sure to telephone," he said before they disconnected. "I'm a father. I worry always."

Which made it all the more remarkable that he'd never objected in the least way to her decision to join the Jegertroppen.

She was still sitting on the edge of the bed naked when she looked around and saw Trace with a towel wrapped around his narrow hips. He had leaned his shoulder against the doorjamb and folded his arms. Only then did she realize that she'd been speaking in Norwegian. "My father," she explained.

"Is he all right?"

"He was wondering about me and when I'd come back. He said he's in a desk job now but the mountains keep him young." She tilted her head, staring at Trace, yearning, and then her mind produced one of its irritating flips.

"Trace? If we need to tell someone about this, it should be my father."

Trace straightened. "You're probably right. He'd be the last person in the world to want to put you in danger."

"I'm sure of it. And he knows a great many people. He would know who to trust."

Hillary looked almost sadly at Trace. The moment was gone. Standing, she reached for the last clean clothes she had. He had already headed to his own bedroom.

But she had only a limited amount of time to find out what had happened to Brigid and her husband.

Sometimes life wasn't nice.

Morning arrived with no more in the way of answers. Hillary moved laundry from the washer to the dryer. Without comment they'd begun to wash their clothes together. There weren't many.

"I would have done that," Trace said.

She closed the dryer door, turning it on, then faced Trace. "I know you would have. You can do the folding."

"Fair enough."

Exhaustion rode them both. Lack of sleep with a heavy dose of mental fatigue. Running around in circles wasn't very rewarding.

Hillary made her oatmeal and topped it with a coddled egg. Trace opted for some kind of hash full of fried potatoes. And coffee. Always coffee.

"One more stab at that photo," Trace said. "Later if you need to sleep first."

"I just want to finish this," she admitted. "Like you, I want answers. We don't have enough here to take to anyone. We may have an indirect answer to what happened, though. Is that enough for you?"

"Is it enough for you?"

Brigid appeared in her mind's eye, a laughing Brigid with a heart of gold. "No." Her answer was short.

"Me neither."

Hillary stirred her oatmeal, mixing it with the egg, then began eating. After a few minutes, she spoke. "Brigid wanted to join your Army Rangers. I think I mentioned that."

He nodded.

"Was she always trying to keep up with you and Allan?"

Trace appeared surprised. "I don't know why she would have wanted to. We were always trying to keep up with her. Anyway, she probably would have tried for the Rangers right off, except at the time they weren't accepting women."

"They are neglecting a good resource."

His answer was dry. "Funny how men often miss that. Maybe we should read more history. From Boadicea to Joan of Arc. And then all the Celtic women who terrified the Romans by riding naked into battle. Lots more, I'm convinced."

"Camp followers, as you call them, often fought alongside their men. What a disparaging name."

"Well, it keeps them in their proper place, doesn't it?"

One corner of her mouth lifted. "What is my proper place?"

"Valkyrie," he answered promptly. "I give you your due."

She didn't doubt it.

After a quick cleanup, both felt refreshed, so they went back to the office.

"I don't know how far we'll get before we crash," Trace remarked.

"Farther than we are. I'm too awake now."

They returned to the photograph, convinced that if there was any answer, it had to be there.

Hillary offered a suggestion. "Let's look closely at the shadow that Brigid is making instead of the entire photo. There may be a reason her shadow crosses the shadow of the sign."

"Like her rifle crosses her," Trace agreed, sounding rather interested. He printed out two photo-quality prints and handed her one. "Allan must have had a magnifying glass somewhere."

Hillary studied the picture as Trace hunted through drawers. "I'm going to need spectacles after this."

"I'll join you."

"What makes you think Allan might have had a magnifying glass? Few young people do."

He glanced over his shoulder. "Because he probably spent almost as much time as we have looking at that picture." He sat up holding a rectangular glass. "Found it. Now I think I'll print out all the color reductions we did, to see the differences side by side."

"Good idea."

There were three desk lamps, surprising given that only two people had ever worked here, but for the first time they turned them all on and twisted them until they illuminated the photos brightly.

He asked, "You want to use the magnifier first?"

She accepted it and bent forward, wondering if her back would ever be straight again.

FROM EACH COPY, Trace had already screened out colors, starting with one color at a time, then moving on to screening out colors that didn't noticeably affect the photo.

One of the articles had said that doing so might reveal an image within the image. So far no go. But ever one to press on against ridiculous odds, he had then pixelated the photo, dividing it into tiny squares.

But Hillary was right about the angle of the shadows. It wouldn't be beyond Brigid to have considered such a thing, aligning it as closely as she possibly could with her rifle. And crossing the shadows. There wasn't a doubt in Trace's mind that Brigid had sent a message. Or that Allan might have found it, given how he had labeled the photo.

Just as he was about to fade from fatigue, Hillary gave his heart a jump start.

"Trace, look at these pixels. I can almost make out a word. Am I imagining it?"

No, she wasn't.

EVERY HUMAN NEEDED REST. It was the reason sentries fell asleep on duty. It was the reason people crashed cars because they were having microsleeps as their brains tried to rest.

Hillary and Trace reached that point a couple of hours later. They had what looked like it might be a name, whether first or last, they couldn't tell. Clearly Brigid had linked it to the sign behind her. They needed more.

But when a person starts hallucinating when awake, the mind is screaming a message. Eventually they had no choice but to tumble into bed.

They wound up in Hillary's bed, spooned but too tired to take advantage of the moment. Too busy trying to think about what they had found. Sleep, however, was a merciless taskmaster and took them away before they could solve anything or enjoy anything.

It all would have to wait. Outside, snow began to fall again, wrapping the world in the cold silence of a grave.

STAN WITHERSPOON WAS jangling too much to sleep. His eyes felt gritty; his head ached, feeling ten times larger than it was. His hands wouldn't stop trembling.

All this for money?

He despised himself and considered suicide, then backed away. He was afraid of dying, or he wouldn't be in this mess.

He should have just walked off the job in Afghanistan. Just quit. Instead he'd been so full of himself he'd bragged about how he'd taken care of Brigid Mannerly.

At first the boss had been pleased. Stan needed that approval. But then everything had changed. The cage had been rattled.

Which brought him here, to a long road to nowhere. He wondered if he could successfully change his identity, then doubted it. He couldn't change his fingerprints, for one thing. Then there was the bigger problem: he had no idea how to get the necessary papers. He didn't know anyone or of anyone.

So there was just Stan on a dark Wyoming night while snow fell. It was probably his funeral shroud, he thought bitterly.

Then a germ of an idea was born. Just a germ. He tried to wrangle it into something he could use, but his mind was too far gone. He popped some pills for his headache, then lay down.

He damn well needed some sleep or he was going to lose it.

WHEN TRACE AND HILLARY AWOKE, thin gray light peeped through a small crack in the curtains. It wasn't going to be a beautiful day by the looks of it.

They lay face to face, their drowsy eyes meeting.

Trace spoke, his voice rough from sleep. "You know

what I'd like to do with you? But we're hot on the trail now and you've got to go home soon. And don't argue with me. Your father is already phoning."

Hillary would have loved an excuse but knew he was right. Her father was growing concerned or he never would have called. He'd been giving her freedom to live her life as she saw fit ever since she'd approached adulthood. He'd never watched over her every moment.

There'd be time to love each other again when they'd come to the bottom of this. Time if she had to wrest it from Freya herself.

Slowly she stretched then walked down the hall to the laundry room. Fresh clothes. A fresh day. A fresh search.

God, Brigid, what did you get us into?

Except Brigid hadn't meant to get them into anything. She'd wanted Allan to know what was going on. She probably never thought it would cost her life. She'd probably imagined that Allan could get to the bottom of it from a safe distance.

No distance was safe.

AFTER A BREAKFAST of oatmeal for Hillary, scrambled eggs with cheese for both of them and a stack of toast for Trace, they headed to the office. Each carried a mug of the endless coffee with them and resumed their close inspection of the photos.

"Okay," Trace said. "We've made out the name Stanley. It could be either a first or last name, which hardly gets us anywhere."

She nodded agreement. "Can you imagine calling Briggs and Holmes to ask if they have an employee with the first or last name of Stanley?"

"I don't need to imagine it. They'd either slam down the phone or laugh. Neither would be useful at all. Well, if

Brigid went to all this trouble, there must be another name in here somewhere."

They moved on to a different part of the shadow, hopeful as they had not been before.

A while later, Trace shocked her out of her intense focus, an intensity that was working her steadily toward a headache.

"You're beautiful," he said.

She pivoted, surprised, to look at him.

"Non sequitur, I know. But every time I glance at you, I see you all over again."

She felt her face heat slightly with an unaccustomed blush.

"Tell me to get back to work, my Valkyrie."

She drew a sharp breath. *His* Valkyrie? Oddly, she didn't mind at all.

"Okay, I'm out of line." He shrugged, smiling ruefully. "Brigid wanted to be like you, not like Allan and me."

"How can you know that?"

"Because I see all that's admirable in you. I'm sure Brigid did, too. Anyway, I apologize. Way out of line."

After a moment, she answered, "I didn't think so."

"Thank God. I don't usually just blurt things."

"You can blurt pretty things to me anytime you want." Then, following a strong, unrestrained impulse, she leaned forward and kissed him lightly on the lips. "My warrior from the skies."

That drew a broad smile from him. "That's the nicest way I've ever heard that." Then he shook his head. "Two warriors need to get back to work. I know you're leaving soon, Hills. Can't be avoided. But I'm going to miss you like hell."

Then, out of the blue, he was back in Afghanistan, in the midst of a firefight with shots raining down from the

ridges above. He'd never know what triggered it. It had gotten better over the months of rehab, but here it was again,
at the worst time possible. Was there ever a good time?

HILLARY SAW THE thousand-yard stare replace the usual
warmth in Trace's gray eyes, turning him icy, stiffening
him. Then he jumped up, knocking over his chair, hurrying from the room.

She followed immediately. "Trace?"

"Leave me the hell alone. Just get out of the way!"

He didn't know where he was going, just somewhere in
his attempt to escape the tsunami of memories that took
over his mind, that transported him to other places, other
horrors. Bleeding, the repeated vibration of a rifle firing
in his hands. The deafening sound of launching RPGs,
thunderous explosions. Blood and gore, bodies shredded.

It had escaped his control. He couldn't fight it now. It
had won.

HILLARY HAD A pretty good idea of what was going on, but
she knew there wasn't a thing she could do about it except
try to prevent him from harming himself while he relived
battles. Relived not being able to trust anyone, not even
the Afghans who had patrolled with him.

She'd learned that the hard way. She had a bullet scar
on her upper arm, a graze but still a lesson. Friendly faces
could conceal enmity.

Interesting, she thought distractedly, that neither of
them had asked about the other's scars except that once
when she asked about his face. It was as if they didn't see
them. As if they'd assumed and understood.

But as for Trace, he stumbled around the house then
broke out the back door, hurrying until he fell facedown

in the snow. In the posture of an infantryman holding a gun forward to shoot.

If she touched him now, he might turn on her, might perceive her as an enemy. She had to stand over him and watch. God, she wanted to be able to do something for him. Anything to yank him back.

He wasn't dressed for the snow or the cold. If he didn't rise from this ice soon, he could grow hypothermic. Maybe even get frostbite.

Finally she did the only thing she could think of. In her harshest, strongest *kaptein* voice she ordered him, "Mullen! Soldier, stand up, damn it. On your feet *now*!"

At first he only stiffened more. Then as the order penetrated, he rose to his feet cautiously, looking around.

Keeping her voice stern, she said, "The firefight is over, soldier. Get your butt back to the operating base." Thank God she'd listened to enough American officers to know the slang.

As he began to slip out of memories, his face slowly changed, losing its hard edge. It wasn't over yet, but at least he headed back into the house. She followed him, but he stormed into his bedroom and slammed the door in her face.

"Leave me!"

She didn't go away. Instead she stood guard, ready for anything. If he burst out of there looking to create mayhem, her hands would be enough. She clenched and unclenched her fists, preparing. Her heart ached for him.

These things took time, but she would have waited until the moon fell from the sky.

MORE THAN TWO HOURS passed before Trace emerged from his room. Without a word, Hillary motioned him to the kitchen and began to pump him full of hot chocolate. "Drink," she ordered.

Still appearing a bit dazed, he didn't argue.

She wondered if he'd eat oatmeal. He'd never shown any interest. He needed food. Food and sugar. She pawed through Maude's bounty and eventually came up with a couple of pieces of peach cobbler and heated them in the microwave.

She pushed the plate in front of him. "Eat."

At first he did so automatically, but gradually the present time returned. "You should have some of this."

"You need it more than I do. I'll find something else."

"Time for another trip to Maude's."

Relief flooded her. He was on the way back. All the way back.

Eventually he spoke again. "I'm sorry."

"For what? PTSD? We all have it to varying degrees. You just had a bad round."

He raised his gaze to her. "You too?"

"Believe it. I'm just lucky."

It was a while before he spoke again. Two more cups of hot chocolate. Then hot cider, as if the cold penetrated to his very bones.

"Did I hear you giving me orders?" he asked.

"Oh yes. You heard my best command voice. At least it brought you out of the snow."

He winced. "Like that, huh?"

"Oh well. You're in one piece. Mostly."

"I have no idea what triggers it."

"Who needs a reason? Maybe it's staring at that photo of Brigid. Maybe some sound I didn't notice. Or maybe nothing at all."

"Makes me sadly unpredictable. It's also embarrassing."

"I himmelens navn."

"What?"

She sighed. She'd spoken in Norwegian again. "Oh, for heaven's sake."

"Disgust, huh?" He appeared to brace himself for bad news.

"With your apology and embarrassment, yes. I was *worried* about you, especially when you were facedown in the snow. I was *not* disgusted."

"Thank God for that." A faint humor was beginning to reappear. "Something for you to eat?"

She returned to the refrigerator, pulling out a soggy-looking steak sandwich. "Share with me. My stomach aches right now."

"I'm sorry."

"Stop. I did that to myself. I could have just left you to it and gone back to the photo or found a book to read. You didn't *make* me feel anything." Except sorrow that he had to endure it.

"Pity. There are a lot of things I'd like to make you feel, and that's not one of them."

Relaxation began to return to her, and she smiled. "We'll try that later."

"Just don't skip town before we do."

"I could not imagine it." After a couple of mouthfuls of the steak sandwich—at least the meat was still good—she rose and opened the curtains over the sink. "Snowing."

"Maybe it'll never stop this year."

She laughed. "You're spoiled."

"Maybe so."

"My father is already speaking of putting on his skis. Of the two of us heading into the mountains to camp."

"In weather like this?"

"Of course. If we stayed in the house all winter, suicide might become a rising problem."

"Likely along with the endless nights."

She eyed him as she returned to eating. "You might like them."

He wiggled his eyebrows. "Especially the endless nights."

"You have a dirty mind."

"I'm proud of it, too."

After they cleaned up, they discussed what to do next.

"We need more food here," Trace said practically. "We've managed to eat through most of what Maude gave us. The diner or the grocery?"

She considered. "I am not happy to leave the house unprotected. Not after the theft of the letters."

"At this point, I don't care. We'll carry the photos with us in an envelope."

Thus it was decided. Hillary had to admit a walk would be very welcome. Stretching her legs with a steady stride instead of a run. Feeling the cold on her cheeks, breathing icy air, watching snow fall. As close to home as she would get here.

They bundled up and walked with a fast stride, this time to the grocery, joking about how neither of them liked to cook.

"Is there anywhere I can get cross-country skis?" she asked.

"Rent them, you mean? I think so. We can stop on the way back from the grocery."

That made her feel even better. Maybe Trace would join her. The traditional form of cross-country skiing, unlike the new form that was more like speed skating, was more like walking. Many people mastered it quite quickly.

At the grocery, they focused on items they could eat cold and items that were easy to cook, which included some frozen entrées. The butcher, Ralph, called them over and asked Hillary if she'd like him to order more fish for her.

"Please," she said with a smile. "Salmon and cod, if you can get them."

"Frozen or fresh?"

"I'd prefer fresh but frozen salmon will do. I already have frozen cod."

Ralph grinned. "I'll yank my contact's leg on that salmon again."

She felt pretty good as they departed the grocery with filled plastic bags. Then at the sports store, she found her rentals. She even persuaded Trace to try.

The boots were an easy fit for her, but the store owner eyed Trace.

"Do you have any idea how few people of your size want them?" He sighed and pawed through the boxes stacked nearly to the ceiling. "Hey," he said happily. "Size twelve. Now what about gaiters and socks and poles?"

They left fully equipped along with large backpacks that would carry almost everything they had bought at the grocery and the sporting goods store. The skis and poles they carried over their shoulders. Waxless skis, but beggars couldn't be choosers.

"Success," Trace said as they strode home.

"I think so. Now we have to decide when."

"Since the roads are a mess and we can't run, let's make it soon."

But when they reached the house, an envelope waited on the front porch, taped to the door.

"I think skiing just went off the schedule," Trace said.

Hillary pulled the envelope off the door. "Be careful when we open it. There might be fingerprints."

"I thought of the same thing. But gloves."

She regarded the envelope unhappily. Gloves. In this weather they were already wearing them. "The letter inside."

Trace was already unlocking the door. "Maybe. God, I hope it's useful."

Chapter Fifteen

Inside, they scrambled to put away frozen items or food that needed to be refrigerated. The envelope lay on the table as if it mocked them, seeming to grow brighter with each passing minute.

At last, with all the foodstuffs put away, their skis and accoutrements propped in the hallway, they sat as one to regard the envelope.

"What's your guess?" Trace asked Hillary. "A threat or information?"

"A threat," Hillary decided. "Given what happened to Allan and possibly Brigid."

"My feeling exactly." Rising, he went to get a filleting knife from the butcher block, then pulled on his glove liners once again. "Me or you?"

"You," she answered. She ran her gloved fingers over it. "Too thin to be threatening."

"Unless it contains powdered anthrax." A horrifying possibility.

"This man could have used that on Allan. He prefers blunter methods."

"I'd be inclined to agree, but we don't know that we're dealing with the same man."

When he said that, she reached out for the envelope. "Let me."

"Like hell."

She looked at him and realized he wasn't going to give ground on this. He'd already had a bruising day for his ego, and he was past caring that she was a soldier as well. She leaned back.

With the filleting knife in hand, he slipped it under a corner of the envelope and sliced carefully, a straight line across the top.

"Hold your breath," Trace said.

She knew an order when she heard one, and she obeyed, but only after saying, "Hold yours as well."

He cocked an eye at her. "You think I'm stupid?"

"Never, but if you're going to warn me, you should be warned, too."

His grin didn't quite make it. A good attempt, though. "What's sauce for the goose is sauce for the gander, right?"

She smiled back, although she didn't feel like smiling at all.

She watched intently as Trace slid a piece of paper out of the envelope. It sported a variety of colors. No powder showed or lifted into the air.

"Oh hell," he said, looking at the sheet. "Have we slipped into bad movie?"

"This is real."

"When did the movies ever care about that? No powder that I can detect. You?"

Impatient, Hillary rose and came around the table. Crooked cutout letters covered the page.

If you want to know what happened to Mannerly, meet me alone. More to come.

"Aw hell," Trace said. "Taunting."

"Basically useless, too. How long will he make us wait?"

"Until he tires of his game."

The hours ahead stretched until they looked like days.

THE GAUNTLET HAD been thrown, Hillary thought. A challenge.

"We've got to prepare anyway, Hills. I don't think he plans a meeting in the middle of town."

"Not likely." She pursed her lips. "Okay, he probably doesn't have our kind of experience and training."

"I doubt it," he agreed.

"The skis may be more useful than I thought. I can see it, Trace. You just have to accept it."

As if he followed her thoughts, he said, "Okay. He probably wants to meet *me*. You'll have to put your skills to the test. Ski ahead of the time of the meeting and find a good, concealed location."

"Exactly what I was thinking."

Trace's mouth twisted. "I don't believe he's going to be ready for an armed Valkyrie. I can just imagine you showing him your kind of hell."

"We need a weapon or two."

"Obviously I can't carry one. I'll look in Allan's gun locker. I'd be surprised if he doesn't have an AR-15 or AK-47. Semiauto. You want me to alter one to full auto?"

Hillary shook her head. "If I have a decent scope, I won't need more than one shot."

"Try not to kill him," Trace said dryly. "We need the information."

She answered just as dryly, "I learned a lot about shooting around body armor. Center mass won't do it. Nor will hitting an artery or his head."

"We understand each other."

THE WAITING HAD BEGUN. Trace was the first to admit that he wasn't good at waiting. He wanted action.

Hillary didn't seem any happier about it, but when she asked him to pull out the photos, he took them out of the plastic bag that had been tucked under his jacket.

"Might as well," he said.

An hour later, her phone rang again. He gathered it was her father, who must be unusually worried, to judge what she'd said about his previous call. He listened to Norwegian flow from her lips and decided it was a pretty language. He wondered if he'd ever be able to learn any of it.

When she disconnected, he said, "Your father?"

"Yes."

"I thought he didn't hover."

"Hover?" It took her a minute to understand, then she grinned. "Not usually. This time he's even more concerned because he can't imagine any good reason why I would be taking a holiday here. He must have looked up Conard City on a map."

"That would certainly raise questions. We're not on a list of anyone's preferred vacation destinations. At least we have mountains. What did you tell him?"

"That I'm on a mission. Then I thanked him for his concern and told him that I thought a squad of Norwegian special ops here would mess things up."

Trace laughed outright. "It certainly would. Sounds like a father to me."

She shrugged. "Just trying to be helpful. But this is hardly enemy territory."

Trace's expression changed. "I have no doubt that the two of us can handle this guy." He paused. "Before we get back into the photos again, I think I need to check the gun safe and give you a chance to adjust the scope."

They found a good selection of rifles, mainly for hunting. There was indeed an AR-15, semiautomatic. Legal in this gun-loving state and country.

From inside the mudroom with the door open so that no one could see, Hillary sighted through the scope. "I need to fire a few shots to be sure."

"There's a gun range just outside town. I doubt it's busy today. Wanna go?"

She nodded. This had to be done exactly right. Together they disassembled the rifle and cleaned it with the gun oil from the locker. Then they loaded it, still broken down, into a backpack so it wouldn't be identifiable. Trace added some high-powered binoculars when he picked up a box of shells.

THE GUN RANGE owner waved them in. "No charge today. All my customers are out hunting and aren't interested in practicing right now. Have at it."

"Let's wait," Trace said to Hillary. "Make sure we weren't followed. By the way, I hate waiting, in case I haven't said so."

"I as well. I didn't see anyone around on the way out here."

"Me neither, but extra caution never hurts."

They waited over twenty minutes while Trace scanned the surrounding area for any movement. Then Hillary quickly reassembled the AR-15 and loaded it with the bullets Trace handed her.

The clip could hold ten rounds. She took each shot at the target cautiously, adjusting the scope several times before she hit dead center three times in a row.

She locked the scope in place, and they once again disassembled the rifle. On the way back, they kept a sharp eye out for anyone who might be watching.

The road was deserted until they reached the edge of town. Even then the streets didn't appear busy.

"I think we made it," Trace remarked.

"I'm not too worried about it. He'll want you to come alone and probably unarmed. He won't be expecting me."

THE NEXT NOTE arrived overnight, left silently on the door. This one was also a mash of cutout letters, and the message was straightforward.

Six p.m. at old mining town. Mullen alone and unarmed.

Hillary looked at Trace. "You know where that is?"

"It's a landmark. Easy to get to, familiar to everyone, but it'll be deserted at this time of year." He looked at her. "Hills, it'll be deep twilight by then. Sunset is around six thirty. You know what the mountains do."

"I know. But it won't be dark enough to stop me." She glanced at the clock. "I should leave here soon to give me time to set up and get there without being noticed."

He sighed. "I don't like this. There are a whole lot of ramshackle and run-down buildings for him to hide in."

She shook her head. "I know what to do if he does. I'll be fast even on those no-wax skis, and skis are very quiet. I've done it before. Just give me directions."

That proved easy enough to do. The mining town was marked on the local map, and Allan had one folded on his desk, now buried in papers.

"There's no signal out there except on satellite phones. You won't have GPS."

"The map is all I need."

Of course it was, Trace thought. Of course. He went to find her a compass.

Chapter Sixteen

Hillary slipped away just after noon. She headed out the front in plain sight, and he watched her cart her skis and poles over her shoulder. Everything else was in a heavy backpack, her ski shoes and gaiters covering any outline of the rifle parts.

She walked away toward the east end of town, the opposite direction from the mining town. He saw her stop several people, and, whatever she said, they pointed east. Maybe asking them if there was a level place where she could use her skis.

Misdirection.

She strolled as if she had all the time in the world.

Then she disappeared from his sight. He could only guess where she'd gone to begin her westward trek.

Once again he had to wait. Only this time he worried as well. He eyed her cell phone left on the table so that if her father called again there would be no accidental ring in her pocket. Then he called the sheriff, Gage Dalton, and asked if there was any surreptitious way to get him a satellite phone and some zip cuffs. He didn't explain why, and Gage didn't ask. He just said, "Let me know."

Trace could do no more now except imagine the worst. What he couldn't face was the possibility that something might happen to Hillary. As upset as he'd been about Allan, he wasn't sure he could survive her loss.

HILLARY ENJOYED HERSELF. Misdirection was part of her training while keeping watch for a route where she could safely change her course. It felt great to be on a mission again.

She found her place, then headed south. She didn't want anyone to see her ski away to the west. This walk was longer, but houses and people thinned out until there was nothing. She kept going for another two kilometers, then stopped to put on her skis.

If anyone was watching now, it would all look normal. Perhaps the land to the east that people had pointed out would provide a less challenging snow cover. This area had brush sticking up through the snow.

Well, she'd dealt with that before.

Skis on and locked, poles in hand, she began moving steadily west. Familiar. So familiar to her from training, from missions, from childhood. Her body fell into comfortable rhythms, and the faint sound as she swooshed through the snow reminded her of better times.

So far it was wonderful.

The slope began to rise, also familiar. When she reached a thick stand of evergreens, she pulled out the folded map and the small compass from her pocket.

Experience told her she'd reach the mining town shortly after four. Soon enough to check the lay of the land and choose her ground.

In the meantime, she had nothing to think about except the pleasure of her movements.

And about Trace. He was like a jack-in-the-box in her head, popping up again and again. The face she had come to love. The voice that either soothed her or drove her to the brink of desire.

If anything happened to him, she doubted she would be happy ever again.

SHORTLY AFTER FIVE, Trace left the house, headed for the mining camp and thanked God he had four-wheel drive with studded tires on his SUV. Renting it instead of a car had been expensive, but given the time of year, he hadn't wanted to screw around worrying about money.

The roads were terrible after the fresh snow. Beneath that layer was ice, gripped by the studs. If it got too bad, he had tire chains.

Trace had been up to the mining town many times in his youth. Dangerous as it was, pocked by collapsing mines, teens still went there. A favorite hangout away from adults unless one of the deputies or game wardens happened on them. All the warning signs got ignored. A chain-link fence meant to protect people had been cut so many times that the county had given up. It lay rusted and flat in places, an unheeded alert.

As the snow deepened, nobody would expect teens to be there.

It was a great choice for an isolated meeting. It would give the guy a chance to watch him. Trace never believed the man would arrive unarmed. No, the perp intended to get rid of a problem. As he had with Allan. As he may have done with Brigid.

Anger simmered in Trace's veins, but it was an anger that cleared his head. Heightened his senses.

He'd been in situations like this before. They didn't scare him.

HILLARY SIGHTED THE mining camp at quarter after four. Plenty of time. She chose her position with the broadest view of the deteriorating town and the best concealment. Looking through her scope she surveyed the sinkholes, judging her skis would carry her safely over most of those pits. She memorized those she needed to be wary of.

Then she assembled the rifle and loaded it. Ready except for one thing.

She gathered snow-covered deadfall. She dug a body-size pit six inches deep. Then she crawled beneath the branches and waited. If the man came this way and happened to find her, he'd meet her rifle before he finished pulling away her cover.

The continuing snow protected her as well. She was prepared.

STAN WITHERSPOON SUFFERED anxiety as he waited at the mining village. He saw the SUV park about a hundred yards back in some wheel ruts that made it appear that damn vehicle might never get out. Good. He wanted Mullen stuck.

And he was glad to see Mullen alone. Nothing else around here had stirred in the last hour or so.

He surveyed the area and still saw no one and nothing as Mullen walked to the town and began pacing back and forth in front of the village. He'd come alone. The only question was if he was armed. Stan's mind leaped away from that possibility. He had to deal with it.

Stan was armed. He pulled a pistol out of his pocket and removed the safety catch. Only then did he hold it in front of him and approach Mullen. "Hands up!"

Mullen complied.

At this point Stan began to feel smart. He couldn't take Mullen and the woman out at the same time. That would have made him stupid.

But any way he looked at it, Mullen was the bigger threat given his background. Once Mullen was gone, the woman might just leave town. Or, if she knew anything and stayed, well, she was just a soldier. Stan was a soldier, too. Or had been.

One of the things Stan had learned in training was not to approach closely with a gun. Especially with a man like Mullen. He stood back at a safe distance.

"Do you want to know what happened to Allan? Why he had to die? Why Brigid had to die?"

"That's what I'm here for."

Stan was relieved Mullen made no move at all. One shot, maybe to his knee, whatever, would be enough to put Mullen down until Stan could kill him.

But Stan needed to get things off his chest. It wouldn't satisfy him just to kill. He hated being a murderer. He had to explain himself so this guy would understand.

"Brigid caught me moving arms to the insurgents. She saw me doing it twice, and I didn't think she was stupid."

"She certainly wasn't," Mullen answered.

Stan wanted to shrug, but his conscience was rearing up again, and he needed to get it all out. To explain how he had come to this. "I gave the insurgents an RPG and told them to take her out."

Trace drew a sharp breath. "Why, you…"

"Don't bother. I know what I am. I thought it was over. I have a boss, you know that?"

"I didn't until now."

Witherspoon heard the edge in Mullen's voice, saw the man clench his fists, even though they were up in the air. "Don't move or I'll shoot right now and you'll never know why I killed Allan Mannerly."

Mullen was silent for a few seconds but didn't move. "Go on." His voice was taut with threat, but Witherspoon didn't believe it.

Besides, he was going to die one way or another unless he got this cleaned up. Then he had a thought. "That woman isn't here somewhere, is she?" He started once again to scan the surrounding area but wasn't too worried. After an hour of observation, he was sure no one else was there. But he needed to ask anyway.

"She's a woman." Mullen's voice sounded scornful.

Just a woman. Mullen made a good point. Braver now, Witherspoon continued. "That Mannerly guy did something or said something. All I know is the cage started rattling, and I was caught in it. I didn't want to kill anyone!"

"I believe you," Mullen answered.

Stan didn't quite believe *him*, but it didn't matter. He needed to have his say, then he'd erase this part of the problem.

"My boss knew information had gotten out. He was uneasy. So he told me to get my butt over here, because he figured it was Brigid's husband who had warned someone else. I was sent to kill him any way I could."

Mullen growled but still didn't move.

"It was easy enough. The guy got drunk every night. I just told him I knew Brigid. He let me in. I don't think he ever noticed I was carrying my pistol." He paused. "Funny, but everyone around here has a gun, and some of them carry them in town. Nothing unusual."

Mullen gave a tight nod.

"So, when Mannerly got drunker, almost passed out, I finished it. Blew his brains out. Left the gun beside him. I thought I was done, but then you started yelling and my boss got even more worried."

Mullen never flinched.

"He was afraid you knew something. So now I have to take you out. I don't like it. I'm not a murderer, but he'll kill me if I don't get this done."

Trace's voice grew thin as fine steel. "You want me to feel sorry for you? You're the victim in all this?"

"You gotta understand. And it doesn't matter if you don't want to." He waved his gun toward a nearby building. "Now get in there."

"Why should I?"

Stan had never expected that response. He waved his gun again.

Then a movement caught his attention, and when he turned he saw the wrath of hell skiing swiftly toward him, a rifle pointed straight at him. It cracked like thunder.

He thought he felt sharp pain in his knee, but before he knew for sure, Mullen had jumped him and thrown him to the ground. His gun was still in his hand. He started to move it, wondering who to shoot first.

Then the woman was standing over him, her rifle pointing straight at his head, and said, "I wouldn't use that pistol if I were you."

Mullen had his hands around Stan's throat, but not too tightly for him to breathe. Just enough to scare him.

"Who's she?" Stan asked thinly. "I was watching before you got here. I never saw her come. You said she wasn't here."

"She's a Valkyrie, you jackass. Trust me, you'll have plenty of time in jail to look it up."

Mullen rolled Witherspoon over and used zip cuffs on his wrists.

Then Trace said, "I suppose we need to put a tourniquet on him."

"Regrettably," the woman replied.

"Gage gave me his sat phone," Mullen told them both. "I called just as I arrived here. Armed response is on the way." Then he began to tie something around Stan's thigh.

The pain in Witherspoon's knee pierced his shock, and he began to shriek. All he wanted now was an ambulance and a huge dose of morphine.

Chapter Seventeen

Hillary sat in the first-class cabin of an airplane on the way to Tromsø, north of the Arctic Circle. She was eagerly looking forward to seeing her father. She'd asked for and received an extension to her vacation. She suspected Pa had something to do with that. Maybe having him behind a desk could be useful.

She turned her head and looked at Trace in the seat beside her. He was already staring at her, and she felt a shiver of pleasure.

He spoke. "That Witherspoon guy sang like a bird."

She nodded. "Even sold out his chief."

"I think he figured that years in prison might be better than being shot some dark night by his boss."

"You may be right."

Silence fell between them. Hillary liked it when he took her hand, gave it a squeeze then just held it. He made her heart sing.

Her father had taken the story from her and assured her he would deal with it. She hadn't asked for details because she knew her father. By the time he was done, everyone involved in these arms sales was going to be exposed to criminal charges. Every single one.

Brigid and Allan would be avenged.

Trace spoke again. "Your father. Will he like me, do you think?" It was not the first time he had asked.

"I've said so."

She had no doubt. Her father would see in Trace a reflection of himself. More, he would think a special ops soldier was well suited to her.

But Trace would not be returning to the Army. One of the saddest things he'd said to her was, "I'll never jump again."

He'd decided a desk job would drive him nuts. "If I ever doubted it, all that work we did trying to catch this killer taught me. No desk for me."

Now he flew with her to Norway after putting in for his medical discharge.

And she had to hope that he would like her home, her country. He certainly hadn't bought a return ticket.

She squeezed his hand. "Don't be nervous."

"Who, me?"

She laughed lightly. "He's another soldier like you."

"Yeah? I've never had to face down a spec ops officer and tell him I want to marry his daughter."

Her heart stopped. "Trace?"

"You heard me. And you can handle it, so tell me if you want me to shut up."

"Never," she answered, squeezing his hand tightly. "Never." The song in her heart grew louder.

"I don't do crazy things like this." He grinned. "I love you, you know."

"You're giving me that idea."

"I'll give you more of an idea later."

MAGNUS KRISTIANSEN MET them at the gate, tall and straight, his hair only slightly darker than his daughter's. Hillary beelined straight for him, for his smiling face, pulling

Trace along with her. Her father gave her a big bear hug then looked at Trace.

"This is him?" he asked in Norwegian.

She answered in English. "This is Trace Mullen, the man I love. We're going to be married."

Now it was Trace's turn to feel a song in his heart. Especially when he looked at Hillary's father and saw a big smile.

"Just promise to live in Norway," Kristiansen said.

Looking at Hillary, Trace answered, "I think I can promise that."

* * * * *

DEADLY
DOUBLE-CROSS

LENA DIAZ

Chapter One

Mason Ford vowed to pay more attention next year when his assistant chose the date for the company's fall hayride, because it was incredibly difficult acting the benevolent boss on the anniversary of his brother's unsolved murder.

Then again, maybe having the hayride this morning was a good thing. A new, happy memory to help dull a horrific one.

He'd forgotten the charm and beauty of the eight-mile arts and crafts loop just east of Gatlinburg, Tennessee. And it certainly wasn't a hardship admiring the colorful fall leaves as a pair of enormous draft horses pulled the eighteen-foot wagon through the Smoky Mountains. It was the exact opposite of his Louisiana hometown's evergreens, swamps and bayous without a mountain in sight.

Moving here, escaping the daily reminders of his old life, was the only thing that had kept him sane through the years. Well, that, and being able to hire others like him, men and women whose law enforcement careers had been destroyed through no fault of their own. Being a Justice Seeker gave all of them a chance at redemption and an opportunity to continue their true calling—helping others.

The modern-day Camelot he'd created investigated crimes and protected others, with one important distinction from their law enforcement counterparts. The twelve Seekers who worked for him, his Knights of the Round

Table, would bend or break the law if necessary to keep someone safe. It was infinitely preferable to prevent a murder than to hunt down an offender *after* they'd violated a useless restraining order and killed someone. The Seekers sometimes played fast and loose with the law. But Mason's team helped their allies in law enforcement so much that they were usually willing to turn a blind eye.

The enormous success of his company was bittersweet since it owed its existence to his older brother's death. Mason had been the chief of police in his hometown of Beauchamp, Louisiana, when Landon was framed and convicted with blinding speed, then killed in prison while Mason was scrambling to exonerate him. It was his subsequent civil suit against the corrupt town leaders who'd been instrumental in his brother's sham of a conviction that had given him the millions to start his company. But he'd give up all his wealth, without hesitation, if it would bring Landon back.

Since that wasn't possible, he'd done the only thing he could to honor his memory. He'd secretly continued the investigation on his own, trying to figure out the identity of that one last person behind the conspiracy that had resulted in his brother's conviction and murder. But justice was proving to be frustratingly elusive. Which was why he'd soon head home for his annual appointment with a bottle of Jack Daniel's to grieve for his brother in private and curse his own failure to solve the riddle of Landon's death.

A burst of laughter sounded from the far end of the wagon. Former FBI profiler, Bryson Anton, was laughing at something his fiancée, Teagan, had said. Beside them, former secret service agent, Gage Bishop—Mason's closest friend and the very first Seeker he'd ever hired—grinned at his girlfriend, Harper. It was truly amazing to see Bishop looking so happy these days. Harper was exactly what the normally morose Bishop needed, a balm to his battered soul. It was a balm to Mason's as well, seeing how much his team seemed to be enjoying the outing.

Except, perhaps, the newest member of The Justice Seekers.

Eli Dupree sat by himself a couple of hay bales away from Mason, splitting his time between watching the scenery and surreptitiously glancing at the other Seekers. He was relatively new to Gatlinburg, having arrived only a few months ago. A former police officer and Louisianan, like Mason, Eli had been the victim of a crooked conspiracy in Baton Rouge. But unlike Mason, he hadn't been able to turn his misfortune into something good and had struggled to make ends meet.

Mason considered himself fortunate that Eli had looked him up and asked for a job. The timing was perfect, since Mason had been searching for a suitable replacement for their fallen Seeker, Seth Knox. And Mason was thrilled to help someone from his home state. He just hoped Eli would learn to appreciate Tennessee the way Mason did, and that he'd eventually fit in with the rest of the team.

When the wagon slowed and made the final turn off Highway 321 into the Family Dollar store's parking lot, where they'd all parked their personal vehicles earlier, Eli motioned toward Mason's black BMW. "Looks like someone's waiting for you."

A familiar red convertible was parked in the spot beside his with an even more familiar-looking platinum blonde standing between the two cars. Mason let out a deep sigh. Why had she chosen today, of all days, to show up again? It had been a couple of years since the last time she'd made the long trip here in her ongoing campaign to win him back. Plus, he'd heard she'd gotten engaged again. Apparently it had been too optimistic on his part to assume that would mean she'd finally stop what could only be called harassment.

A shadow fell across him. He looked up to see Bishop in full former secret service agent mode, dark sunglasses in place, pistol bulging beneath his light jacket, a deadly serious look on his face. "I can take care of this. Just say the word."

Dalton Lynch, a former policeman from Montana, stepped beside him, straightening the black Stetson he was never without. "Need me to block Guinevere's car while you make your getaway?"

Bishop gave Dalton a warning look over the top of his shades. "I've got this, cowboy."

Dalton bumped his shoulder against Bishop.

Bishop held his ground and returned the gesture, his frown growing fierce.

Dalton grinned, not at all intimidated.

A few feet away, Eli glanced back and forth between them. "Guinevere?"

Mason narrowed his eyes at Dalton, before answering. "Her *name* is Audrey Broussard. Years ago, *many* years ago, we were engaged."

"Lancelot must have frozen her credit cards," Dalton said. "No offense to your charms, boss, but I can give you several million reasons why she wants to be on your arm again."

Eli's look of curiosity turned to confusion. "Lancelot? Wait, didn't he sleep with Guinevere behind King Arthur's back?"

Dalton had the grace to wince before his expression sobered. "Let Bishop and me take care of this, boss. You don't even have to talk to her."

Mason's throat tightened when he realized the rest of his team had silently moved to stand behind Dalton and Bishop, letting him know they were there to support him, as well. Except for Bishop, none of the Seekers knew the details about what had happened in his hometown years ago. But all of them were making it clear whose side they were on.

He had to clear his throat, twice, before trusting his voice enough to speak. "I couldn't ask for a better team. You're always there for me and each other. But this...this is something I have to take care of myself."

They stepped back so he could make his way down the center aisle through the hay bales and dismount from the wagon. But before heading to his impatient-looking former fiancée, he turned around to address his employees. No, his *family*. His *chosen* family, rather than the one he was born into. He cherished every single one of them.

"I hope you all had a great time. Enjoy the Fall Festival in town today and Sunday. As a bonus, take Monday off, with pay. The last thing I need is a bunch of hungover gun-toting yahoos dragging into the office after partying hard all weekend."

Their cheers gave him the strength he needed to face whatever Audrey was about to dish out. When he reached his car, he nodded in greeting and leaned against his driver's door. "Audrey."

She mimicked his pose, leaning against the passenger side of her sports car. "Mason. Still wearing business suits everywhere, I see. Even on a hayride." Her red lips curved in a practiced smile.

"Image is everything." He returned her smile, taking in her stilettos and silky black dress that couldn't come close to keeping her warm. The early morning temp this time of year, this high up in the mountains, was probably hovering around fifty degrees, if that. He'd offer her his suit jacket, but he could see a fur coat draped over the passenger seat through the window behind her. She'd obviously chosen to go for looks, instead of warmth. And she did look good, always had. Even in grade school she'd been the prettiest girl on the playground.

"You're as beautiful as ever." On closer inspection, though, there were dark circles under her eyes that her makeup failed to completely conceal. And she seemed tired, pale. Even her hair seemed to lack the luster it usually had. Since he'd never seen her looking anything less than perfect, he couldn't help wondering if something was wrong. "Is everything all right? Do you feel okay?"

Her cornflower blue eyes widened and she self-consciously patted her hair. "I'm fine. Why do you ask?"

She was probably just tired after the twelve-plus-hour drive from Beauchamp to Gatlinburg. Maybe she'd driven through the night to get here and hadn't stopped at a hotel yet to rest. "No reason. Just small talk." He shifted against the car and crossed his arms. "I heard you and Thibodeaux got engaged. Congratulations."

"If that's what your baby sister told you in those gossip sessions over the phone, then she's either out of touch with the local grapevine or just being mean. Richard and I broke up a few months ago." She tilted her chin defiantly.

"Olivia doesn't have a mean bone in her body. But it's been a while since our last phone call, so I didn't realize your status had changed. I'm sorry that things didn't work out between you and Richard."

And he was. Even though Audrey had destroyed the friendship between Mason and Richard Thibodeaux, Mason sympathized with her over losing him. It had taken her years to get him to give her a ring. With him gone, there weren't many more prospects left in the small town of Beauchamp, since her main preferred qualification in a relationship was money, or at least the prospect of decent future earnings.

She shrugged, pretending it didn't matter. "He moved to

Texas. The man I left you for has now left me. That probably makes you happy, doesn't it? Poetic justice?"

"No, it doesn't. You deserve to find that special someone just as much as anyone else. I assumed that person was Richard. I'm sorry that it wasn't."

She stared at him a long moment, before blinking back the suspicious moisture in her eyes. "He was always my second choice."

"Audrey, don't."

"I mean it, Mason. You and I were good together. Really good. Give me another chance. Give *us* another chance. Forgive my one little mistake."

"Sleeping with my best friend, then throwing your engagement ring in my face in the middle of the town square isn't what I call one little mistake."

"It was only the one time. I turned to Richard for comfort. I was upset at you for filing that silly lawsuit. You sued half my friends. No one would talk to me anymore."

"I may have been a lovesick fool back then, but I wasn't blind. We both know it was more than once, with more than one guy."

Her face turned a bright pink.

"As to the *silly* lawsuit," he continued, "it was the only way I could obtain any kind of justice for Landon's death. Those so-called friends of yours helped conceal and falsify evidence. If it wasn't for them, my brother wouldn't have been convicted, sent to prison and slaughtered before I could prove his innocence. The infidelity I could forgive. You supporting the people responsible for my brother's murder? That, I can never forgive."

Her eyes flashed with anger. "It's so easy for you to judge me. Saint Mason can do no wrong, always better than anyone else. Maybe someone should judge you for a change, make you pay for what you've done to others."

Her lightning-quick mood swing surprised him, but no

more than what she'd said. Other than bringing criminals to justice, he'd always tried to treat others with respect, especially Audrey. No matter what had happened between them, he'd loved her once, had planned to spend the rest of his life with her. Part of him would always care about her. "I'm not sure what you're talking about. What do you think I've done?"

She opened her mouth as if to say something, then seemed to think better of it. When she regained control, she drew a steadying breath. "Obviously, coming here was a mistake. I shouldn't have wasted my time thinking you'd soften toward me. You probably never loved me in the first place."

He'd loved her *too* much. That was his downfall. His mind had known the relationship was doomed long before his heart would accept the painful truth.

"Why are you really here? Especially today."

She arched a brow. "What's special about today?"

Her tone told him what she refused to admit. She knew the significance of the date and must have chosen it hoping he'd be more vulnerable, maybe more amenable to whatever it was that she wanted. "Did you come here for money? Have you burned through what I gave you after I won the civil suit?"

Her face pinkened again. "It's been seven years since the lawsuit. If I had spent it all in that long a time, I'd hardly qualify it as *burning* through the money."

Since he'd given her close to a million dollars, he wasn't sure that he agreed. "How much do you need?"

She stared at him incredulously. "Are you seriously offering to pay me off?"

"It's not a payoff. It's an offer to help. If you're in financial trouble, I'm happy to give you some money. As a friend, nothing more. But after this, I'm done. It's not fair to either of us for you to keep coming up here. You should go home and never come back."

"Never come back." She gave him a tight smile. "Careful what you wish for."

He frowned. "What's going on in Beauchamp? Is someone bothering you? Do you need help?"

She clutched her keys in her hand and rounded her car to the driver's side. "If you think I'm here to hire The Justice Seekers, you've lost your mind. Your little company's a joke back home."

"A joke, huh?"

She gave him a mutinous glare.

He considered telling her his *little* company grossed over ten million dollars, in a bad year, and that his investments generated far more than that. It was true that half of his clients either paid little or no money, because they couldn't afford his usual fees. The Seekers never turned someone away based on finances if they had a legitimate, urgent need and Mason felt his company could help them. But the rest of their clients more than made up for that financial gap.

Wealthy businessmen were willing to pay a small fortune to protect their assets or to quietly resolve problems involving their families. Not to mention the lucrative hostage rescues the Seekers performed for corporations who didn't want the public to know their CEOs had been taken captive on a trip out of the country. They couldn't risk having their stock tank on that news. Business for the Seekers was good. More than good. But telling her that would only sound like bragging.

It didn't matter anyway. His hometown was no fan of him, no matter what he accomplished in life. The feeling was mutual. The secret trips he made to Beauchamp twice a year under the guise of vacations were just that—secret. Even his own family didn't know he was there, since none of them were willing to risk being seen with him any more than Audrey was, once he'd filed that lawsuit.

No one in Beauchamp ever saw past his alias and the movie-set-worthy disguise he'd paid a small fortune to obtain. Which was exactly what he wanted. He wasn't there for socializing. He went there to work on his brother's case, not that he'd made any real progress. It was taking far too long to get the locals to trust a supposed businessman on vacation twice a year and open up about anything they'd seen or knew. One of these days he'd have to put his life on hold and spend a couple of months in Beauchamp to really dig into the case. Maybe then he'd finally get justice for Landon.

"If you're not here for money, then why are you here? We both know you're not really pining for me. Not after all this time. What's going on?"

Again, she looked like she wanted to say something important, but she just shook her head. Without another word, she got into her car.

Mason had to jump back to avoid having his feet run over by her tires. He watched her tear out of the parking lot, going dangerously fast around a curve in the mountain road before disappearing from sight.

He stood there a long time, reflecting on their oddly short and bizarre conversation. But no matter how hard he tried, he couldn't make sense of it. Her past visits had been far less confrontational. They'd usually go to dinner, take a walk in the mountains, talk about old times—the good ones, before everything went bad. But no matter what he said or did, these trips of hers always ended the same way—with her storming off. If he lived to be a hundred, he didn't think he'd ever understand her. Which was a sad statement, considering they'd known each other for several decades.

Half an hour later he was standing at his kitchen sink,

holding a shot glass of whiskey. Before taking a sip, he made the same toast he'd made on every anniversary of his brother's death. "Landon, I promise I'll never stop trying to find out who really killed Mandy DuBois. I vow to get justice for you, and for our family. Rest in peace, big brother." He tossed the shot down, grimacing at the burn. But he knew from experience the next one would go down easier, and the next after that. The more drunk he got, the better the whiskey tasted.

He was reaching for the bottle to take it to the family room when a floorboard creaked behind him. He jerked to the side, grabbing his gun from its holster. A masked man dived at him, tackling him to the ground. Mason arched off the floor, bucking the man off even as other masked intruders swarmed into the room. He swung his pistol around and squeezed the trigger.

Pop, pop, pop.

One of the men dropped to the floor, groaning.

"Suck it up, Hank," another man yelled. "You've got a vest on, you wuss."

Mason lunged to his feet.

Someone slammed into his back, knocking him to the floor again. There were five of them, all wearing masks.

"Grab his arms, Gary. Good grief. He's just one man. Guys, help him."

Mason rolled and swung his gun around, but the one named Gary crashed down on his arm, knocking the gun away.

The rest threw themselves on his legs, his other arm, his ribs.

Mason bucked and thrashed, desperately trying to throw them off.

"Sit on his back, sit on his back! Hank, quit rolling around on the floor. Get the syringe. Hurry!"

One of the men slammed Mason's jaw against the floor. A coppery taste filled his mouth.

"Do it!" one of them yelled again. "Hurry up."

A sharp pain pierced the side of Mason's neck. He tried to jerk his head back but the weight of all the bodies on him was too much. A heaviness flooded his limbs. They'd drugged him. He tried to twist away but he couldn't seem to make his body obey his commands. He slumped against the floor, his muscles twitching, useless. His lungs seized as he gasped for breath, trying to draw in much-needed oxygen. Spots swam in front of his eyes.

"Good gravy, how much did you give him? We don't want to kill him. She wants him alive."

She? Were they talking about Audrey? Had the conversation in the parking lot been a test that he'd failed, and she'd sent these thugs to teach him some sort of lesson? He'd never known her to be violent in the past. Maybe this was related to his company, revenge because the Seekers had helped the police put someone's family member in prison.

He struggled to keep his eyes open, to fight back. But his strength melted away like ice on a hot road in summer. His eyelids fluttered closed and he surrendered to the darkness.

Chapter Two

Somewhere along the way, Mason had heard that there were over seven trillion nerves in the human body. As he blinked his bleary eyes at the ceiling above his bed, he was certain he could feel every one of them. Everything ached.

He blinked again, the bright sunlight pouring through the nearby window making it hard to focus. Wait. Bright sunlight? Normally he was up before dawn. Why was he lying in bed so late?

Maybe because his entire body was throbbing with pain?

If he'd wrestled with a baby elephant and it had jumped up and down on his back a few times, he couldn't imagine he'd feel more battered and bruised than he did right now. Maybe he'd wrestled *two* baby elephants.

He drew a deep breath and immediately regretted it. The pain nearly made him pass out. What had he done? Drunk the entire bottle of Jack Daniel's and a couple bottles of vodka as chasers? No. He'd only had one drink, hadn't he? He'd been standing at the kitchen window, tossing down a shot. Then he'd reached for the bottle and—

Someone had broken into his house.

No, that was wrong. They'd already been there when he got home. They were lying in wait. When he'd had his back turned in the kitchen, they'd attacked. At least five men. Gary, Hank and others whose names he hadn't heard.

They'd tackled him to the floor and the one named Hank had jammed a needle into his neck.

He gingerly felt along the back of his neck. Sure enough, it was sore. The way it would feel if a clumsy idiot not used to giving shots had stabbed him with a needle. He was lucky to be alive. Or was he? They would have killed him if that was their goal. He certainly couldn't have stopped them. God knows he'd tried his best. So why drug him, beat him to a pulp, then leave? It didn't make any sense.

He stared at the ceiling overhead, then frowned. The patterns were all wrong, too elegant, too…complicated. The ceiling should have been simple, not ornate. And white, not this creamy yellow color reminiscent of wa-tered-down lemonade.

This wasn't his house.

He jerked upright, then groaned as pain lanced through his body. Taking slow, shallow breaths, he fought through it and looked around. Instead of wooden blinds on the window by the bed, long golden curtains fluttered in the cool breeze. Music wafted through the opening, faint and hauntingly familiar. The kind he'd grown up with, had danced to, had sung out of tune to along with his drunk fraternity brothers in far too many bars on way too many nights. Jazz.

Familiar smells filtered in through the open window too. Hot asphalt. Garbage. Honeysuckle. And…beignets?

A sense of impending doom shot through him as he forced his aching body to his feet and crossed stiffly to the window. A black wrought iron railing ran along the balcony outside. He was in the second floor bedroom of someone else's home. Whose, he didn't know. But there was no doubt *where*, as he looked down into a narrow alley with garbage cans set out for collection, then across that same alley at the backs of other homes.

They were all brightly painted, with elaborate decorative molding and fancy wrought iron balconies, many adorned with cheap, colorful beads—the kind they tossed at Mardi Gras. As impossible as it seemed, he was in Louisiana. And if his memory was correct, this particular street was in historic downtown Beauchamp in Sabine Parish, not far from where Landon and his girlfriend used to live.

He swore and automatically reached for his pistol on the nightstand by the bed, both surprised and dismayed to find it there. Whatever was going on couldn't be good. Of that he was certain. He had to get out of here, fast, before whoever had brought him here came back.

Thankfully, there was no need to search for his clothes. He was still wearing the dove gray suit he'd worn at the hayride, although it was considerably more wrinkled now.

Cursing his aches and pains, he ran across the room and threw open the bedroom door. He was at the end of a long hallway but could see light coming from his left, probably the stairs. He bolted for them, taking two at a time. At the bottom, he started toward the front door, then froze.

A woman's body lay a few feet from the base of the stairs, in a pool of blood. The top of her scalp was gone, but there was enough hair remaining to show it was blond. Platinum blond. Or it had been, when she'd been in Gatlinburg.

"Audrey, good Lord, no." His voice broke as he stared down at her still perfect-looking face, turned toward him. Her eyes were cloudy and unseeing, no longer that cornflower blue so unique to her. There was no point in checking for a pulse. She was gone. The damage too severe.

What in the world had happened? Who would want to hurt her like this? He swore again and bowed his head, then sucked in a sharp breath when he saw the gun in his hand. The jagged, confusing images swirling through his mind suddenly crystallized into a coherent, terrifying reality.

Someone had drugged him.

They'd gone to incredible lengths to kidnap him and bring him back to the town he both loved and hated, a place crawling with enemies who wanted him dead.

They'd left him here, with a gun, with the dead body of his former lover, the same woman who'd confronted him in front of over a dozen witnesses in Gatlinburg on the anniversary of his brother's murder.

Ah hell.

Someone was setting him up. And the bastards had killed Audrey to do it. If he didn't get out of here, right now, he was royally screwed. He whirled toward the front door.

It flew open, slamming back against the wall.

"Police, freeze, don't move!" At least a dozen uniformed police officers surged through the opening into the house.

"Drop your weapon! Drop your weapon!"

He dropped the pistol and slowly raised his hands. "Officers, this isn't what it looks like. I didn't kill her. I don't even know how I got—"

Two of the police barreled into him, tackling him to the ground.

His aching ribs protested the abuse but he forced himself to go limp. Whoever was responsible for this insanity likely expected him to resist, giving the police an excuse to shoot him. This was a fight for his life, but not a physical one. He'd have to use all his wits to survive.

They rolled him onto his belly, jerked his hands behind his back and fastened handcuffs on his wrists with a painful click.

One of the officers patted him down while another barked orders. Still more fanned out, no doubt looking for accomplices. They needn't have bothered. Mason knew this story. He'd read it before. Except that time, it had been his older brother, Landon, who'd been found standing over a body. And it was his brother's girlfriend, Mandy DuBois, lying dead on the floor.

"Hank, Gary, get him up," the lead policeman yelled.

Hank? Gary? Mason jerked against their hold, but it was too late. They hauled him to his feet.

The leader stepped in front of Mason. "I'm Captain Paul Murphy. Remember the name. Because I'm the one who's going to see that you go to prison for murder, you slimy piece of scum. With any luck, maybe Louisiana will start carrying out the death penalty again, just for you." He motioned at Hank and Gary. "Get him out of here."

Chapter Three

Mason gritted his teeth as he was shoved out of the elevator onto the second floor of the police station by the two officers he now knew were Hank Abrams and Gary Donnelly. The one named Donnelly yanked his arm, hard. Mason pretended to lose his balance and fell against him, slamming the man's hip into a nearby desk, equally hard.

"My bad." Mason smiled.

Donnelly cursed and shoved away from the desk. "You did that on purpose," he accused, as Abrams tugged Mason's other arm.

Mason held his ground, ignoring Abrams. "You and I both know that you and your little friend here were in my home in Gatlinburg. Drugging me and setting me up for Audrey's murder. You may have the upper hand right this minute. But that won't last. By the time I'm done, you'll both either be in prison or dead."

"Is that a threat, Ford?"

"It's a promise, Donnelly. And if you yank my arm one more time, I'm going to break your damn nose."

Donnelly's face turned red. "I dare you to try."

"Take one step closer and I'll take that dare."

He hesitated, looking unsure.

"Cluck, cluck." Mason purposely incited him.

Sure enough, Donnelly lunged forward. Mason jammed his elbow against the other man's face with a sickening crunch. He yelled and grabbed his nose, which was already dripping blood. Donnelly glared his rage, then charged Mason again. Abrams intervened, letting Mason go to grab Donnelly in a bear hug. He harshly whispered for him to knock it off and stop making a scene.

Mason took full advantage of the chaos as a couple of other officers in the near-empty squad room headed toward Donnelly. Backing against another desk, Mason feigned a look of boredom as he grabbed a pair of sunglasses he'd spotted moments earlier and clutched them between his cuffed hands.

While Abrams tried to settle Donnelly down, Mason snapped one of the arms off the glasses, then snapped it in half again to give himself a thin, clean edge. He slid his makeshift shim into the ratcheting mechanism of one of his cuffs, jamming it in as hard as he could while trying not to grimace at the pain when the cuffs ratcheted tighter.

"Hey, hey, what's going on over there?" a detective from the other side of the room called out.

Abrams shoved his partner back, giving him a warning glance as they both straightened. "Just a minor disagreement. We're cool." He waved away the other officers who'd come over to help, then glanced at Mason, as if just remembering he was there.

Mason did his best to keep his arms and shoulders steady so he didn't give any indication that his hands were furiously busy behind his back. He shoved the shim again, between the metal teeth and the ratchet. The cuff ratcheted one more slot, then another, then disengaged. The metal arm of the cuff opened and slid off his right wrist. He grabbed it between his fingers just in time to keep it from clinking against the other cuff, while keeping his hands linked together. To anyone looking at him, he was still handcuffed.

Abrams argued with the detective who'd crossed the

room to check on them while Donnelly pressed some tissues to his nose.

Mason glanced behind him to the corner of the room where his office used to be. Sure enough, gold letters on the solid, steel security door still said Chief of Police. Hopefully the inside of the office hadn't changed either, or his hastily concocted plan was going to end almost as soon as it began.

He didn't know who was behind his kidnapping, or Audrey's murder, but his experiences long ago told him one thing for sure. If they got him into a holding cell, he'd never come out alive. There were too many crooks still running this town, in spite of everything he'd done to try to clean it up. And the mysterious "she" the masked men at his home had mentioned was still calling the shots for the police she'd bought and paid for.

"Come on, Gary," Hank gritted out. "Cool your heels. Let's just get him to booking."

"Chief Ford? Is that you?" Another detective crossed the room, a big burly man Mason recognized as one of his former deputies, Harvey Latimer. Back then, everyone had called him Al because of his resemblance to the Twinkie-eating policeman in the movie *Die Hard*. When someone found a collection of Twinkies in his desk, it had sealed the nickname.

"Al?" Mason asked.

He grinned. "You remember. What are you doing here?" He stopped in front of Mason, his grin fading. "And what the hell are you doing in handcuffs? Donnelly, Abrams, have you lost your minds? This is one of our former police chiefs. He's the one who cleaned up this place, got rid of the riffraff around here." He gave them both a contemptuous look. "Not that it stopped more from coming after he left."

"Mind your own business," Abrams muttered. "He killed someone. Was caught red-handed."

"What he meant to say," Mason corrected, "was that these two jokers and a handful of others broke into my home in Tennessee, beat the hell out of me and drugged me. I woke up here, in a house I've never been in before, with the police crashing in the door. Once again, someone in my family is being framed for murder. Only this time, it's me. Amazing how this stuff always happens in Sabine Parish, don't you think?"

Al's frown became incredulous as he turned toward his fellow officers. "What's going on, Abrams? Donnelly? You know anything about him being attacked and kidnapped?"

Donnelly rolled his eyes and grabbed another handful of tissues from a nearby desk. "What a crock." His voice was muffled. He rolled his eyes again and threw the tissues down. "It's halfway across the country from here to Gatlinburg. If someone broke in his house yesterday, he wouldn't be here in Beauchamp today. Do the math. It don't add up."

Mason arched a brow. "I don't remember mentioning Gatlinburg, or the timing."

Donnelly's face reddened.

"It's a twelve-hour drive," Mason continued. "More than enough time for me to be here now. *Do the math*. Or didn't you pass basic math in elementary school?"

He took a menacing step toward Mason.

Al shoved him and moved between them, his back to Mason. "That's enough. Looks to me like we need to get the chief to figure out what's going on—"

Mason yanked Al's gun out of his holster, then slung his left arm around Abrams's throat, jerking him backward. Using him as a shield, his gun aimed at Abrams's temple, he backed toward the corner office.

Al put his hands on his hips. "Now, Chief Ford, why'd you have to go and do a thing like that? I was on your side."

"Sorry, Al. But this is life or death. Mine. And I'm not

putting my fate in the hands of two of the men responsible for kidnapping me and setting me up. As far as I know, one of them murdered Audrey Broussard too. At the very least, they know who did." He jerked Abrams, making the man grunt in pain. It was surprisingly satisfying.

The handful of officers at other desks pointed their guns at Mason, who was almost to the office now.

"Hey, hey," Abrams choked out. "You're pointing those at me too."

The officers glanced uncertainly at each other, then slowly lowered their weapons.

Mason's back bumped against the door, stopping him. "Al, is Holloway still the chief?"

"Nah. He was over his head from day one and was bound and determined to take this place down with him. We've had a string of chiefs since then. No one sticks around very long. Our new mayor brought in Mitch Landry a couple of years ago, from nearby Many, hoping he could finally finish cleaning out the cockroaches around here after the good cleaning you gave the place." He eyed Donnelly. "But those nasty things are hard to get rid of."

Donnelly glared at him as if he wanted to shoot him.

"Is he in his office?" Mason asked. "I need to talk to him, make sure he knows what's really going on."

"He's out of town at a convention, in New Orleans, over four hours away."

Donnelly frowned. "I thought—"

"Well that would be a first, wouldn't it?" Al gritted out. "Shut up. And wipe your dang nose before you drip blood on the carpet."

Donnelly blasted him with a string of obscenities as he wiped his nose, leaving a red smear across his face.

"I'm happy to wait until the chief's available." Mason turned the knob behind him and pushed the door open. He gave Abrams a huge shove and jumped inside, then slammed the door. After locking it, he tucked his gun in his waistband and grasped a filing cabinet to the left of the door. It was full, far too heavy to scoot across the low-pile carpet. Instead, he heaved and strained, toppling it over like a tree. It fell sideways with a deafening bang, the drawers hanging half open and folders spilling onto the floor. He'd pretty much destroyed the cabinet. But it did the job, blocking the door from opening.

"Well, this is awkward."

He whirled around at the sound of the feminine voice behind him. When he saw the young woman sitting behind the desk by the window about fifteen feet away, he swore.

Her brows arched and she tucked her wavy, long brown hair behind her ears. "Not the reaction I'd normally hope for from a gorgeous man like yourself. Then again, the handcuffs dangling from your left wrist are a relationship nonstarter for me. I'm Hannah Cantrell. And you are?"

"Really sorry that I didn't realize you were here before I blocked the door." A muffled banging noise sounded behind him, rattling the door on its frame.

"That makes two of us. But since they're ramming the door, I'm guessing you aren't going to move the filing cabinet to let me out."

"That wouldn't be my first choice." The banging sounded again. "Excuse me a moment. I need to take care of this." He drew his gun, keeping it pointed away from her.

"You're not going to shoot anyone, are you?" she asked.

"Not on purpose."

She motioned toward the door. "Then by all means. Carry on. I'll wait."

He gave her a puzzled look, but nodded. Half turning, keeping her in his peripheral vision, he yelled, hoping Al could hear him. "Get away from the door or I'll shoot."

The loud bang sounded again. The door held fast as

designed when he'd beefed up the physical security during his tenure as chief. But the frame around it shuddered. He looked back and spoke in a low voice. "Hannah? They haven't built a third story on this place since the last time I was here, have they? I didn't see the outside of the building when they drove me into the parking garage."

"Not that I've noticed. And I work here every weekday, so I'm pretty sure it's just two stories."

"Thank you."

"You're welcome."

"You might want to cover your ears."

She obligingly put her hands over both ears. He pointed his pistol toward the ceiling and squeezed the trigger.

The gunshot was incredibly loud in the confined space. His own ears were ringing. But at least the siege on the door had stopped. "The next time someone tries to knock the door down, I'll shoot right through it," he yelled.

A moment later, Al's voice called out, sounding muffled. "We'll stop trying to get in. Just don't shoot, all right?"

"Did you call the police chief?"

"What?" Al's voice was barely audible.

Mason cleared his throat, regretting that he'd put such a solid, thick door on the office as he yelled his question again.

Al answered, "He's on his way. But like I said, he's a good four hours out, only a little less with lights and sirens. Traffic and road conditions and all that."

"Just let me know when he gets here." He shoved the pistol in the back of his waistband and headed to the desk. "Hannah, thank you for your cooperation. I have no intention of hurting you."

"Good to know. Who are you?"

"Oh. Sorry. Mason Ford."

Her eyes widened, and he realized they were an incredible shade of green.

"*The* Mason Ford? The former police chief who brought this town to its knees with an FBI corruption investigation eight years ago? And sued it, successfully, for millions of dollars in a wrongful death suit? *That* Mason Ford?"

He winced. "One and the same. Trust me. Coming here today in such a public fashion was never my intention. My visits normally stay below the radar."

"Visits? Then you've been back here since you left? I mean, since your, well, rather ignominious departure?"

He hesitated, realizing he'd already said more than he'd intended.

"Forget I asked," she said. "None of my business. But why are you here now, in this office? With a hostage no less?"

"Hostage? Oh, you. Right. Well, it wasn't my plan. And it's a long story."

"I've got time. Four hours, apparently, until the current chief arrives."

"Are you the chief's assistant? Is that why you're in his office?"

"Assistant? What makes you think I'm not his boss?"

"Are you?"

She smiled. "No. I'm a crime data analyst. I came in here to print out some reports since my printer's broken. Unfortunately, my timing couldn't have been worse."

"Sorry. Both for the male chauvinist assumption that you were an assistant, and for ruining your day by locking you in here with me."

"Handsome and also able to admit his mistakes when he makes them. Where have you been all my life?"

He couldn't help grinning. "You're cracking jokes while locked in a room with an armed man, twice your size, who's on the run from the police. Are you not intimidated at all?"

"Nope. I've got Wesley."

"Wesley?"

She pulled her hand out from beneath the desk and pointed a pistol at him. "Meet Wesley, otherwise known as a Smith and Wesson M&P9, the best 9mm pistol on the market, in my opinion. Makes that Glock 17 shoved in the small of your back look like a toy."

He slowly raised his hands, the cuffs rattling against each other on his left wrist. "This just keeps getting better and better."

"You probably should have kept your gun out until you were sure that I wasn't armed. You underestimated me."

He couldn't help smiling again, even though his situation was far from amusing. "I guess that goes along with the assistant assumption. What now? You want me to move the filing cabinet?"

"Eventually. Right now I'd appreciate it if you'd scoot away from the desk so my finger doesn't get too itchy on the trigger."

He stepped back several feet. "And I'd appreciate it if you'd move your finger to the gun's frame. At this distance, you can still put it back on the trigger before I could jump you. But it could save my life if you get a muscle spasm in your hand, or just squeeze without thinking about it."

"Good point." She moved her finger. "Better?"

"Yes. Thank you."

"Now take your Glock and pitch it underneath the desk. Slowly."

He did as she asked, then raised his hands again. "What now? You hold the cards."

"I'm debating."

"What are the options?" he asked.

"You tell me. You must have had some kind of plan before you backed in here. What were you going to do?"

Not seeing that it mattered at this juncture, he decided to go with the truth. He moved toward the other side of the room. Her pistol followed his every step. He placed his hand on the wall about six feet up. "I'm going to press this panel. Don't let that trigger finger get itchy."

"I'm as steady as a frog on a lily pad."

"That's what I'm afraid of. Here goes." He pressed the panel and it slid back into the wall, revealing a dark opening behind it.

Her brows raised. "You know about the hidden hallway?"

He frowned. "This isn't a surprise?"

"No. But history was my minor while pursuing my Criminal Justice degree. Specifically, Louisiana history, with a special emphasis on my hometown, Beauchamp. Building architecture is part of that, including all the major landmark buildings, like this one. The hidden hallways with secret panels that open up onto the stairwells are common in a lot of structures around here. Most are marked on the original blueprints, pretty easy to find if you care enough to do a little research. Most people don't."

He looked down the dark hallway. "Most people? Who around here *does* know?"

"Me, obviously. My dad, because I share pretty much everything with him." She tapped her free hand on top of the desk. "Come to think of it, that's probably it."

"Then I don't have to worry about Hank or Gary sneaking up on us?"

"No. You don't."

He stepped closer to the desk, keeping a watchful eye on her pistol as it followed him across the room. "I don't suppose you have a car in the parking garage downstairs and would consider letting me borrow it?"

"I have an SUV, yes. But, no, you may not borrow it."

"Fair enough. Would you consider letting me go? I could disappear down the hallway and figure out my own transportation once I'm outside the building. You could tell the chief that I pointed my gun at you and you had no choice."

"Hmm. Well, that might be hard to pull off."

"Why is that?"

"Because the chief is standing right behind you."

Mason whirled around. A long gun was aimed directly at his gut by a man nearly as big as him, standing in the opening to the secret hallway.

"Put your hands up, Ford," the man ordered.

Mason slowly raised his hands. "I thought you were in New Orleans."

"I was having breakfast down the street. Al lied."

"You can't trust anyone these days." He glanced over his shoulder. "I'm guessing you lied too, when you said only you and your father knew about this hallway."

"I didn't lie."

"I was *really* hoping you wouldn't say that. The last names—you're married?"

"Widowed." She waved toward the man with the gun. "Former police chief Mason Ford, meet current police chief Mitch Landry. My daddy."

Chapter Four

Hannah returned her gun to her purse as her father yanked Mason's arms behind him and clicked a new pair of handcuffs into place. She winced in sympathy when she saw the wince on Mason's face, quickly hidden. Normally her dad wasn't that rough with prisoners. If anything, he treated them far more politely then they typically deserved. But she supposed he was a bit more aggressive this time because he felt he was protecting his daughter. Then again, maybe it wasn't her father's rough treatment that had caused Mason pain. His face, even one of his hands, had faint bruises, as if he'd recently been in a fight.

"Al told me on the phone how you got away. Pretty neat trick shimming a sunglass arm beneath the ratchets to work that cuff off your wrist," he told Mason. "Never heard of anyone doing that before. I'm going to have to order a different type of handcuff in the future."

"I've got a lot more tricks where that came from. Let me go and I'll be happy to teach you."

"Nice try." He motioned with his long gun toward the secret hallway.

"Daddy, wait. Please."

He held his free hand up, making Mason stop. "I need to get this man to lockup, Hannah. We can talk after."

"I don't want you to lock him up."

Mason looked just as surprised as her father.

She rounded the desk, hesitating when her father angled his body partway between her and Mason.

"Don't get too close," he cautioned. "This guy's a big fellow. Even in restraints, he's dangerous."

Mason nodded, echoing her father's advice. One former chief of police agreeing with the other that she should be more careful around a prisoner. That spoke volumes to Mason's character, not that she needed any proof. She knew all about him, even though this was her first time meeting him.

She leaned back against the front of the desk. "I assume since you called him Mr. Ford when you came in that Al told you who this man is?"

"If you mean a murder suspect, he did. That's why he's going to lockup."

"He used to be the chief of police, the one before that joke, Holloway, came along and undid half the things Mason had done to fix this place."

"I know who he is, Hannah. That doesn't change anything. He was caught holding a gun, trying to leave a murder scene. His ex-fiancée is the one who was shot and killed. Open-and-shut case."

"Open-and-shut." Mason shook his head. "I've heard that before. From the district attorney who helped the mayor and others frame my older brother for murder. Before I could prove his innocence, he'd been killed in his prison cell. I'm no more guilty of murder than he was. But you'll be just as guilty as the corrupt officials I helped the FBI lock up years ago if you let whoever framed me start this cycle all over again. How long do you think I'll last in a cell? I guarantee I'll never make it to court. Someone went to far too much trouble to get me here to risk what I might uncover in a trial."

Her father's face flushed. "You're missing one critical fact in that speech you just made. *I'm* the chief of police now. And I don't tolerate conspiracies or railroading innocent people into prison. You'll get a fair trial. I'll make sure of it."

In spite of her father's earlier warning, Hannah stepped closer and put her hand on his arm. "Like Julian did?"

His eyes flashed with anger. "I was on vacation when that happened."

Mason glanced back and forth between them. "Who's Julian?"

Hannah waited. She'd thrown down the gauntlet. It was her father's job to pick it up.

He sighed and met Mason's questioning gaze, long gun still pointed at him. "He was the town drunk. Got arrested for a hit-and-run, a little girl. She died. Julian was found the next morning hanging in his cell. Later, we proved he wasn't even involved in the accident."

"Suicide?" Mason asked.

Her father's throat worked. "No."

Mason's eyes widened. "Vigilante justice in Sabine Parish. Again. I see."

"No, you don't see," her father snapped. "That happened a few months after I started as chief. I was still untangling the mess around here because half of *your* deputies had been imprisoned or fired and most of the replacements were pathetic. The city hired an imbecile to replace you and a host of other incompetents after that. I did the best I could at the time, given the situation. The guy who killed Julian is sitting in prison right now, doing life without parole."

"Who killed Julian?"

"One of my father's most trusted deputies." Hannah dropped her hand from her father's arm. "Don't give me that hurt look, Daddy. It's the truth. Yes, you've done a lot to fix the problems around here. But there's a long tradition of corruption in this town, and it will take decades to weed it all out, if it's even possible. Knowing Mason's past, and all the people around here who think of him as their enemy, are you really willing to bet his life that you can protect him if you lock him up here? Look at the bruises on his face. I imagine he's hiding worse ones beneath his suit."

Mason's dark brows arched in surprise. "Observant. I bet you're a great analyst."

"I will be, once I get more experience under my belt. Thanks for the compliment."

"Stop," her father warned. "Quit treating him like a friend instead of a criminal. I'm sure he resisted arrest or he wouldn't have gotten hurt. My deputies don't beat up prisoners."

Mason scoffed.

Her father narrowed his eyes in warning.

Mason directed his next comment to her. "While I appreciate that you want to argue on my behalf, I have to wonder why you're doing it. We don't know each other. Why do you want to help me?"

"I'd like to know that myself," her father said. "What in tarnation is going on here?"

"Olivia."

"My baby sister?" Mason asked.

"Since she's twenty-three, I don't know that *baby* really fits anymore. But, yes. She was one of my best friends in college. And you can get that skeptical look off your face, Mason. I know I'm a lot older than her, but I didn't go to college right after high school, like she did." She waved her hand in the air. "Doesn't matter. Regardless of the age difference, she and I hit it off our freshman year. She was so quiet and, well, seemingly fragile and in need of a friend that I had to introduce myself. I'm exceedingly glad that I did."

He smiled sadly. "Olivia took Landon's death harder

than anyone else in the family. She's never gotten over it. *Fragile* is an apt description."

She gave him a sympathetic look. "I was pretty lost myself when we met. My husband died several years ago and I was trying to get my life together and return to the job market. I think Olivia helped me far more than I've ever helped her."

"Sounds like Olivia. She has a good soul and a soft heart." He gave her a sympathetic look. "I'm sorry about your husband."

She nodded her thanks.

"Oh good grief." Her father frowned at both of them. "Enough already. Hannah, why are you so interested in helping Mr. Ford? You said it had to do with his sister?"

She crossed her arms, unable to hide her irritation with her father. "She's bent my ear many times telling me about her amazing second-oldest brother, who took on the whole town and won. I've heard all kinds of things about his work as well, in Tennessee. He's a good man. The least you can do is give him a few minutes to explain what's happened, from his perspective. Then decide how to proceed."

Her father rolled his eyes. "You'll never let me hear the end of this if I don't, will you?"

"You know I won't."

He motioned toward the desk. "Sit behind that so there's a few more feet between you two and a solid obstacle to slow him down. I'll give him a few minutes to say his piece. *Then* I'm taking him to lockup."

"Thanks, Daddy." She hurried behind the desk and sat. To her surprise, her father uncuffed Mason. Well, he removed *one* of the cuffs, then attached it to the arm of a heavy chair in front of the desk.

Mason's mouth quirked in a wisp of a smile as he rattled the cuff against the chair arm.

Her father sat in a guest chair across from him, but at

least he wasn't pointing the long gun anymore. Instead, he had it propped across the two arms of his chair, ready to swing in his direction if needed.

"Don't even think about trying to shim those cuffs off, or breaking the chair arm to escape. I don't care what tricks you think you know. You can't outrun a bullet."

Mason glanced at the gun, then nodded.

"Start talking," her father told him. "And make it fast. Al will buzz my phone soon if I don't check in. I sneaked up that back hallway without telling him I was in the building yet."

"I'll tell you what I know, which isn't much, unfortunately. From what I gather, today's Sunday, right?"

Her father frowned, then nodded.

"Okay, then *yesterday* morning I was in a Gatlinburg, Tennessee, parking lot, surprised to see Audrey Broussard, my former fiancée, standing by my car. She said she wanted another chance at reconciliation. I told her no, as I've done every other time she's come to see me. I went home, was attacked by five masked men in my kitchen and drugged. I specifically remember feeling a needle being jammed into my neck. Next thing I know, I wake up here, in Beauchamp, in a house I've never been in before. Audrey was dead on the floor from a gunshot wound and I was holding a gun. I'm sure once you run ballistics, you'll find the bullet was fired from my pistol."

"Because you shot her."

His eyes glittered with anger. "Because whoever killed her is framing me. And I can tell you the names of two of the men involved. Gary Donnelly and Hank Abrams."

Her father's eyebrows shot up. "Two of my deputies? What are you talking about?"

"They were wearing disguises in my home. But I heard their voices, and one of the other men called them Hank and Gary. I heard those same voices, and their names again, at the murder scene."

Her father chewed on that for a moment, then said, "First of all, we only have your word that you were attacked and kidnapped. Second, if they wore disguises, you can't identify them. I'm not willing to condemn two of my deputies on something that flimsy. And this whole thing doesn't pass the smell test anyway. If someone wanted to frame you for Ms. Broussard's murder, it would be far simpler to murder her in Gatlinburg, if she was there visiting you. Why go to the trouble of drugging you and transporting you here? It doesn't make sense."

"Sure it does," Mason countered. "I've got a company, friends, allies in Gatlinburg. Here?" He scoffed. "Even my own family won't risk being seen with me. They know all the enemies I've got in Beauchamp, the families of the people sitting in prison because I brought the FBI in here. My enemies will vandalize my family's property and make their lives a living hell. That's the reason I left in the first place. Even after I won my civil suit against the town, the harassment against my family wouldn't stop. Framing me in Gatlinburg? Next to impossible. Framing me here? Slam dunk."

Her father was shaking his head before he finished. "Why frame you at all? And why kill Audrey? You've been in Gatlinburg how many years?"

"My brother was murdered eight years ago. The criminal trial, my subsequent civil trial and the aftermath from it took another year."

"Seven years then, give or take. Did something happen recently to put you on someone's radar back here?"

"Only Audrey visiting. Nothing else that I know of."

"Seven years after you leave, someone, what, finds out Audrey is heading to Gatlinburg to visit you, so they decide to kidnap you, bring you back here, kill her and frame you? If a woman hadn't died, I'd be laughing my head off. The whole thing sounds ridiculous."

Mason's voice was hard as steel when he responded. "So does framing my older brother for shooting his girlfriend. And yet, here we are. Same town. Same setup. Different victims."

"All the people behind your brother's frame-up went to prison a long time ago."

"Not all of them. The real murderer was never caught. No one would roll over and give up his name. Everyone who went to prison was part of the FBI corruption investigation I headed. The only way I could get any kind of justice for what happened to my brother was through the civil lawsuit. No one ever did time for what happened to him, or to Mandy DuBois, his girlfriend. That's a cold case. And from what I've seen, no one here is even trying to solve it."

Her father's face turned red. "It's still an open case. But there has to be new evidence to lead in a new direction or there's no point in having someone working it."

"Have you even *read* the case files?"

"As I said earlier, I've been working on cleaning up the mess that still remains from after you left and the new mayor appointed a string of idiots to replace you. Working your brother's and Ms. DuBois's cases hasn't been a priority. I'm sorry, but that's the way it is."

Hannah held her hands up. "Can we lower the temperature in here a few degrees and get back to Mason's predicament?"

"Predicament?" Her father's voice was just as hard as Mason's. "He's been arrested for murder and needs to be locked up. Nothing I've heard changes that. Why would a killer, a full eight years after the original murder, decide to do the exact same crime all over again to the brother of the man he originally framed?"

"Maybe it's not the same killer," Mason snapped. "Maybe he's a copycat. How am I supposed to know?"

"I don't think either of you are asking the right questions," Hannah said. "Yes, if killing Mason was the primary goal, or the only goal, then killing him in Tennessee makes sense. But the person who orchestrated his kidnapping had to gain something by bringing Mason here and framing him for Audrey's murder. What does he gain?"

"That's easy," Mason said. "He humiliates my family, and me, once again. It took years for my family to live down the notoriety of everything that happened. Now all of that will be rehashed and my family will likely be harassed again."

"Someone has a vendetta against you, your family, or both. Maybe they have a vendetta against Audrey too, and once they realized she was going to visit you, they used that to their advantage."

Her father gave her a long look, then shrugged. "Makes a little more sense. But who hates Mason and Audrey enough to do all that?"

"What about her most recent fiancé?" Hannah asked. "Wasn't Richard Thibodeaux your best friend, Mason?"

"A long time ago, yes."

"He broke up with Audrey and left town. Maybe she brought your name up one too many times and he felt threatened. Maybe he blames you for destroying their relationship and wanted revenge on both of you."

Mason shook his head. "Richard would never do that. I've known him most of my life. Yes, Audrey played us against each other and destroyed our friendship. But that didn't make us enemies. We both moved on, moved forward. As for Audrey, she could be…difficult, when she didn't get her way. She had her share of altercations with people in town. But I can't think of anyone who actually hated her, or wanted to hurt her. As for my enemies, the list is too long to contemplate. Half the town resents me or blames me for the people who went to prison and the pay-out the town had to do in my civil case. The fact that the town's insurance company covered the judgment doesn't seem to matter to anyone. They take it personally that I sued Beauchamp."

"Is there a point to any of this?" her father asked. "It's all speculation. The simplest explanation, the most obvi-ous, is that Audrey humiliated Mr. Ford in Tennessee and he wanted revenge. Or, heck, maybe she was blackmail-ing you. There are rumors that you're a wealthy man, that you've grown that civil suit money into a heck of a lot more than you started out with. Is that true?"

Mason gave him a crisp nod.

"What if Audrey has something on you and threatened your financial empire? And you felt you had no choice but to stop her, for good?"

"Since I offered her money in Gatlinburg, and she turned me down, that pretty much eliminates a black-mail angle."

"So you say."

Mason's fingers gripped the chair arms so tightly his knuckles whitened.

Her father, likewise, tightened his grip on the long gun resting across his chair arms. "I still say that you followed her here and killed her."

"I don't even know where she lives these days."

"That's hard to believe since you were found in her house."

Mason swore. "That's news to me. And I've already told you, I wasn't there of my own accord. I was drugged and kidnapped and brought here against my will."

"Or you followed her from Gatlinburg."

"You're kidding, right?" Mason gave him an incredu-lous look. "How could I follow her all the way from Tennessee to Louisiana without her losing me along the way? Or spotting me in her rearview mirror? Talk about far-fetched."

"Maybe you put some kind of tracking device on her car."

"Right. She shows up unannounced, confronts me in a parking lot with my whole company watching, and I happen to have a tracking device handy and put it on her car? And no one notices? How far down this rabbit hole do you want to go to make your version hold water?"

"I'm just throwing out hypotheticals. Whether I'm right or wrong about any of it doesn't even matter. The truth will come out during the investigation. In the meantime, there was plenty of probable cause for your arrest. And you can sit in jail like anyone else until you either make bail, or the judge denies bail and you wait until this thing goes to trial." He stood and worked on the cuff attached to Mason's chair.

Hannah shoved to her feet. "How was the arrest made? Mason, what happened, specifically?"

Mason stood and turned around so her father could cuff his arms behind his back.

"Mason?" she pushed. "What happened?"

Her father stepped back, cradling his gun in his arms. At least he wasn't pointing it at Mason. Yet. "Go on. Might as well finish."

It took a few moments for Mason to answer. He seemed to be struggling to tamp down his anger. She couldn't blame him for being angry. She'd be furious if she was in his situation. As much as she loved and respected her father, she was certain that this time he was wrong. Of course she had the advantage of hearing for years about the good work Mason had done, both here and in Tennessee after starting some kind of company that helped people in need, regardless of their ability to pay.

When his dark gaze finally met hers, the anger was still there, but tightly leashed. He was like a caged tiger, ready to explode, but determined not to vent his frustration at her.

"When I woke up this morning and realized I wasn't in my own house, I instinctively reached for my gun. It just happened to be sitting on the bedside table. That was a huge red flag and I knew I was in trouble. I had to get out of the house before whoever was plotting against me came back. I rushed downstairs. Then I saw Audrey." Pain flashed in his eyes but was quickly hidden. "As soon as I recovered from that shock, the police were busting down the door and arresting me."

"I'm sorry about Audrey," she said.

His jaw tightened and he gave her a crisp nod.

"You said the police arrived as soon as you found her. How did they know to go there?" she asked.

"Al said there was a 911 call," her father chimed in.

Hannah stared at her father. "And you don't find that strange? Given the circumstances? Where did the call come from?"

He pursed his lips. "It was anonymous."

She crossed her arms. "No kidding. Wasn't the 911 call with his brother's frame-up also anonymous?"

Her father's face reddened again. "I'm not familiar enough with that case to say."

Mason's gaze flashed to her father but he didn't say anything. Maybe he didn't see the point of arguing anymore since her father still wasn't backing down.

Pounding sounded on the door to the office. "The chief's closer than I thought, " Al yelled. "He'll be here soon. Why don't you open up and we'll wait for him together?"

A few seconds later, her father's phone buzzed in his pocket. He checked the screen. "Al's asking where I am. Says he's ready to bust down the door. He's tired of waiting and he's gambling you won't actually shoot anyone."

"Dad, you have to help Mason, give him a fighting chance. Do you really want to risk another Julian?"

He frowned. "That's a low blow."

"I know. I'm sorry. But I can't imagine with your sense of fair play that you aren't wondering whether this is a frame-up. Can you really be certain no one will harm him if he's locked up?"

The door rattled again as something hit it.

Her father looked at Mason, then shook his head in exasperation. "Go on, Ford. Stall him. I'll text Al that I got waylaid downstairs taking care of a problem, that I'll be up soon."

Mason hesitated, glancing at her father's gun as if he didn't trust him.

He pointed it toward the floor. "I'm not going to shoot you unless you give me a good reason to. Go on."

Mason crossed the room and yelled through the door, telling Al to give him more time.

Hannah smiled. "Thank you, Daddy."

"You misunderstand. He's going to jail. I just want a few more minutes to wrap my head around this, get as much information as I can."

"One phone call can straighten all of this out." Mason stopped a yard away from her father.

"You can call your lawyer after you're booked."

"I'm not talking about a lawyer. I mean my team, The Justice Seekers."

"The what?"

"My company, in Gatlinburg. We perform investigations and offer protection to those who've run into hard times, when conventional avenues haven't worked out."

"Conventional avenues? You mean the law?" He sounded derisive. "You protect *criminals*?"

Mason's eyes looked cold enough to freeze her father in his tracks. "We help *innocent people* who can't get what they need through normal channels. Like abused women and children. I can get one of my men to check the security system at my house and prove I was kidnapped. That should go a long way toward establishing reasonable doubt about my guilt."

"Even if what you say is true, I can't imagine a group of five guys going after you without looking for something like security cameras and taking them out, first thing. I doubt there's any video to see."

"They wouldn't have seen the cameras. They're hidden, outside on the property and inside the house. The electronic feed goes straight to the network at Camelot."

"Camelot? What the heck are you talking about now?"

He sighed heavily. "My company's headquarters."

"Are all rich people as eccentric as you?"

Mason's eyes flashed with anger again.

Her father's hold on his long gun never wavered. There was no sign of him giving in. "If you've got a camera system that fancy, you must have an alarm. And yet you said they surprised you."

"You're right. My alarm should have sent a text to my watch when they broke in." He held up his right wrist, showing them the watch in question, a sleek black band so thin it looked more like a bracelet than a watch.

"There was no text. All I can figure is those men knew how to disarm the system. Just call my company. Get them to check the server. They can log in remotely, get the security feed within minutes and send it right to your phone."

"Daddy—"

"All right, all right. You've got me curious. I don't see where a phone call can hurt. Who will I be talking to?"

"Bishop." He rattled off the number as her father punched it into his phone.

"Just *Bishop*? Is that his first name or last?"

"It's what he'll answer to."

Her father mumbled something again about eccentrics, then spoke into the phone when someone answered. A few moments later, he and Mason were both bent over the phone's screen, watching the security recording, while Hannah leaned as far over the desk as her father would allow so she could see it too.

She sucked in a shocked breath, watching the proof of everything Mason had said. Masked men swarmed an incredibly upscale kitchen, punching, kicking and jumping on Mason. If there'd been one less of them, they might not have won. He was holding his own amazingly well against such overwhelming odds. But the bad guys eventually got him on the floor, and just as he'd described, one of them jabbed a needle into his neck. He went limp, his eyes closing.

"Son of a gun," her father said. "You weren't lying. Any idea who the one guy was talking about when he said some woman wanted you taken alive?"

"I'd forgotten about that. But when he said it, I wondered whether Audrey was mad at me for turning her down and hired someone to beat me up. It feels disloyal even saying that. She was never violent. It's just as likely that someone's mad that my company helped put one of their loved ones in prison and wants me to suffer, at Audrey's expense."

"Maybe." Her father didn't sound convinced. Neither did Mason.

"Your guy, Bishop, just texted me another link, said it's from the outside of your house, before the guys broke in." He clicked it, then held the screen up for all of them to watch the next video.

A dark-colored SUV drove up the driveway.

"Dad, isn't that a Ford Expedition? Like Audrey Broussard owns?"

"I thought she drove a red convertible."

"So did I," Mason said. "That's what she's always driven. It's what she had in the Gatlinburg parking lot when she spoke to me."

"She's got two cars. I only know because I was at the dealership a few months ago getting my Tucson serviced and saw her buying the Expedition. Like you, I was surprised and asked her if she was trading in her convertible. She said no, but that she needed something bigger for her interior decorating business to carry samples."

"Since when did she have her own business?" her father asked. "I thought she lived off investments and money from the guys she dated." He shot a glance at Mason. "No offense."

Mason's mouth tilted in a wry smile. "None taken."

Hannah shrugged. "I'd heard she'd started up some kind of business early this year but didn't press for details. We were friendly, saw each other around town on occasion. But I wouldn't call us friends."

Mason nodded toward the paused video. "If that is her SUV, I don't know what to make of it. Maybe she'd hired men here and had them drive up with her. She planned to have me brought to her home, thinking she could try again to convince me to stay with her."

"After having some guys beat you up?" Hannah shook her head. "I can't imagine anyone thinking that was a good way to restart a relationship."

"Honestly, I'm grasping at straws right now. I don't know what to think."

"It's a common enough type of vehicle," her father said. "Doesn't mean it's hers. Let's watch the rest of the video."

Five men exited the SUV. But the driver stayed inside, dark-tinted windows and the camera angle protecting his, or her, identity. The group of men headed around the back of the house, their movements picked up by yet another camera. Three wore masks, two carried them in their hands. The reason soon became clear. They must not have wanted their masks to obscure their vision as they performed the meticulous task of disabling the security system. Once that was done, they both turned toward the house and raised their masks, but not before the camera got a perfect shot.

It was Abrams and Donnelly.

Mason didn't seem surprised.

Her father looked shocked, and obviously furious. He stopped the video, his mouth clamped so tight his lips formed a hard line.

"Dad? Are you okay?"

"No, Hannah. I am *not* okay. Give me a minute. Just one dang minute. I have to think." He shook his head a few moments later. "That explains the alarm not going off. Abrams used to work for an alarm company. Knows every kind of system on the market, backward and forward. He and Donnelly are bosom buddies. Must have taught him everything he knew. That rat-faced jerk."

A faint knock sounded through the office door again. "What's going on in there?" Al's muffled voice called out. "Open this door, Chief Ford."

Her father put his phone away. "This is a hell of a mess. I don't know who to trust anymore. I knew I'd coddled Abrams and Donnelly too dang much. But the pickins' are slim around here with the pathetic salaries the city pays deputies, and no compensation for overtime. I pretty much hired anyone who'd agree to the pay scale. Still, with all the issues those two have with everyone else on the team, I should have dug deeper, should have realized they were dirty and canned them both long ago."

Mason shook his head. "Half my police force was on the take for years, and I didn't know. This isn't on you. It's on them. Don't blame yourself."

He eyed Mason. "How many years did it take you to not blame yourself?"

Mason didn't answer.

"That's what I thought. Here you are trying to console me and you still blame yourself." He rubbed the back of his neck. "The buck stops here, don't it? A chief is always responsible for the actions of his men." He lowered the long gun so the muzzle was pointed at the floor. "If I let you go, do you have someplace you can lie low, where no one will think to look? Not with family either. That's the first place anyone would search."

Mason's brows shot up. "I've got a cottage a block from the historic district that I bought not too long ago. It's probably six blocks from here, listed under an alias that I created for my occasional trips down here."

"That won't work. It's way too close to the station and we patrol the historic district more heavily than the rest of town because of all the tourists. The chances of being spotted are too high."

"Before I bought the house, I stayed at a place I own north of town. It's in a rural area. Secluded. No neighbors. And the deed is buried under a maze of shell companies, so it won't come up on a property search as belonging to me."

"No one around here knows you own it? Family? Friends?"

"No one *anywhere* knows I own it. I don't come to Beauchamp to socialize. I come to work on my brother's case."

The implied insult—that no one else was working on his brother's case—seemed to hang in the room. But her father ignored it. "How far out are we talking?"

"Ten miles, give or take."

He scrubbed his jaw. "That might work, at least for the short term. What about transportation? How will you get there?"

"I'll figure something out."

Her father shook his head. "Not good enough. You need to disappear and I need to know you're safe. I won't have your murder on my conscience."

"I can drive him where he needs to go." Hannah grabbed her keys and slung her purse over her shoulder. "We'll open the window and make it look like he jumped out and got away. The facade is covered with clinker bricks. They stick out every foot or so, like little stepping-stones. Someone desperate enough could use them to scale the wall. In theory, at least. It's a believable scenario. The three of us can head down the back hallway so no one learns about the secret passageway. When Al breaks the door down, he'll find an empty room and an open window. He'll assume Mason climbed out. Then you'll come up in the elevator to handle things while Mason and I are getting out of Dodge."

Her father stared at her, eyes wide. "When did my crime analyst turn into a criminal mastermind?"

"Not criminal, Daddy. Just a mastermind." She smiled. Her father shook his head, but returned her smile.

Al banged on the door, louder this time. "You've got one minute, Ford. Then we're coming in whether you want us to or not. And if you shoot at us, we'll blow this door to bits, you right along with it."

"Mason," her father said, dropping the Mr. Ford formality. "The bruises. Did my men do that when they arrested you?"

"No, sir. Your men showed remarkable restraint at the murder scene. They followed protocol. My bruises are from when I was attacked at my home."

Her father gave him a grateful nod, relief palpable on his face. "Hannah, how sure are you that Olivia's right, that Mason's really a good man?"

Mason's gaze shot to hers.

"One hundred percent. If we had time, I'd tell you the

stories about his bravery, and how he's helped save dozens of lives, including those of many of the people working for him. He's a good man, Daddy. The best. I know it."

Mason's eyes closed briefly, and he let out a ragged breath, as if in relief.

"Let me do this, Daddy. I'll drop him off and come right back. No one will even know I helped him. Please. If you turn him over, it'll be like when his brother was arrested all those years ago. Or when Julian was arrested."

Pain flashed in his eyes, which had her feeling horrible. But a man's life was on the line. She'd do whatever it took to make her father see reason.

He cleared his throat. "You'll come right back?"

"Promise."

"All right. Open the window. Hurry."

She rushed to the window, unlocked it, then shoved it up. When she turned around, Mason—no longer in handcuffs—was standing by her father at the entrance to the secret passageway. She hurried over to them.

"Al doesn't bluff," her father said. "He's going to bust in that door. Let's get you two out of here. I'll do what my daughter suggested, head up in the elevator and pretend like I just got freed up from some crisis downstairs. I'll buy you some time. Hannah, call me when you get wherever you're going. Don't tell me where you're at. But call me. Then get back here as soon as you can."

"Will do." She kissed his cheek. "I love you, Daddy."

He gave her a curt nod, which meant more to her than anyone else's proclamation of love.

The three of them stepped into the hidden passageway. Her father sealed the entrance just as a loud noise sounded from the office. True to his word, Al was breaking down the door.

They took off running.

Chapter Five

Mason hopped into the front passenger seat of Hannah's dark blue Tucson, barely getting his door shut before she took off through the parking garage.

"Easy," he said. "We don't want to attract attention. Let's go the speed limit, okay? We'll be long gone before Al can bust in past that filing cabinet and discover I escaped."

"Right. Sorry." She slowed down to the five miles per hour posted in the garage. At the end of the row, she headed toward the exit, glancing down each side aisle as she went.

A shadow moved off to their right. "Stop!" Mason yelled.

She slammed her brakes, skidding to a halt about ten feet from the man who'd led the arrest brigade against Mason. Captain Murphy. He stood in the middle of the lane, legs braced wide apart, both hands clasped around the pistol he was aiming at Mason.

"Out of the vehicle, Ford. Keep your hands where I can see them."

Mason swore. "I knew this was going too well." He reached for the door handle.

"Hang on." Hannah slammed the accelerator.

The Tucson jumped forward, throwing Mason back against the seat.

Murphy dived to the side, rolling out of the way to avoid

being hit. She blew past him through the exit, out onto the street. Horns blared. A car swerved, narrowly missing her. She screeched around the corner, then headed north through town.

"Hannah, you almost ran over a policeman. We need to pull over and de-escalate what's about to become a very dangerous situation."

"I would have swerved if he hadn't jumped out of the way." She slowed, but only to check both ways at a stop sign, before speeding through the intersection.

"This escape attempt was over the moment Murphy saw me. We need to stop, call the police and let me turn myself in. I'll tell them I saw you in the garage and tried to steal your car. You pulled your gun and I got it away from you, then held you at gunpoint. But after I forced you to speed out of the garage, almost hitting Murphy, you convinced me to give myself up. You'll be in the clear."

"I'm not letting you turn yourself in."

Sirens sounded in the distance. Either Murphy, or Al, or both had alerted patrol. He looked through the rear window but didn't see any flashing lights. Yet.

The SUV bounced over potholes and careened around another corner. He grabbed the armrest to keep from being thrown against the door. A quick glance at Hannah told him they were in trouble. Stress lines creased the corners of her eyes and she seemed on the verge of hyperventilating.

"Hannah." He tried to make his voice sound soothing. "I need you to slow down. Ease off the gas."

"Can't. Don't you hear them? They're not far behind." She bit her lip and checked the mirrors.

The wobble in her voice wasn't reassuring with her bumping through narrow residential streets and weaving around parked cars.

"Hannah?" When she didn't answer, he said it more softly. "Hannah?"

She frowned and weaved around another car.

Ever so carefully, he feathered his fingers down her cheek, then pressed the back of his hand against the side of her neck. "Hannah? Take a breath. In, out. Look at me for just a second."

She blinked as if coming out of a trance and shot him a glance. "Y-yes?"

"This looks like a family neighborhood. What if a little kid runs out from behind one of those cars?"

She blinked again, then reduced her speed. "Thanks." Her voice sounded hoarse. She cleared it and tried again. "I didn't think about that." She flexed her hands against the steering wheel.

He let out a relieved breath. She'd calmed down, at least a little, and was driving more carefully. He'd still prefer she slow down more, or pull over. But he'd made some progress. "Up ahead, on the right. That looks like a good place to pull over."

Her brows drew down in a frown. "You're giving me tone."

"Tone?"

"Your voice. It's the way your brother Wyatt talks to Olivia when she's gone off her medication or hits a rough patch. I'm not having a psychotic break. I'm just…a little nervous, okay?" She shot him an aggravated look. "I'm trying to save your life. Everything I've heard about you tells me it's a life worth saving. So how about instead of fighting me, you help me."

"I *am* trying to help. Don't throw away the years of hard work you've put into going back to college and starting a brand-new career as a crime data analyst."

She winced.

"Stop the car. I'll surrender. You're the innocent victim I took at gunpoint. This all goes away."

"For me. Not for you! The DA will tack kidnapping onto your other charges. That's federal, with big-time penalties. I'm not going to lie and say you forced me into helping you escape. That would make me as bad as whoever killed Audrey and framed you. I'd rather rot in jail than face myself in the mirror every day knowing I traded your life to get myself out of trouble."

"Let's say we manage to outrun them. Then what?"

"I thought you said you had a place north of town where we could hide out."

"I do. But *you* have a *life*, here, in Beauchamp. A career. I never planned on you staying with me. *Neither did your father.* You promised him you'd drop me off and go right back. He wouldn't want you to do this."

She swallowed hard. Was he finally getting through to her?

"Daddy will understand. I'll stay with you, for now. My life will be waiting for me after this is over."

Apparently he *hadn't* gotten through to her. "Not if you're charged with a felony, aiding and abetting a fugitive."

"I'm helping an innocent man. It will all work out. But not if they kill you like they did your brother."

He shook his head, both impressed and appalled by her naivete. He'd been idealistic once too, believing justice would always prevail. But he'd learned that right didn't always triumph over wrong.

She headed up a straightaway, leaving the neighborhoods behind and entering a more rural, sparsely populated area. "Should I keep going north? You said ten miles, right?"

"Give or take."

"Help me, Mason. Us getting caught won't fix this. I'm not going to lie when they ask me what happened."

"What about your dad? Will you tell them he let me go? At best, it would destroy his career. At worst, he'll face charges."

She drew a shaky breath. "He'll do what works for his conscience. I'll do what works for mine. Where's your hideout?"

"Are you always this stubborn?"

"If an innocent person's life is at stake, you'd better believe it."

He couldn't help smiling. "You sound like one of my Justice Seekers."

"There you go. I can work for you when this is over. Maybe not as a crime analyst. But I can put my criminal justice degree to good use helping in some other way. Problem solved."

"Hannah—"

"Where to, Mason? Where's the hideout?"

"Good grief. You're like a dog with a bone."

"Not exactly flattering."

"An intelligent and extremely attractive woman with a favorite gun she named Wesley?"

She smiled. "Much better. Which way?"

He settled back against the seat, conceding. For now. "Highway 191."

Moments later, she zoomed up an access road and swerved onto 191, heading north, almost slamming into the side of a semi blowing its air horn at them.

"My bad." She waved at the trucker before zipping past and speeding down the highway.

When Mason could breathe normally again, he released his death grip on the armrest. "Where'd you learn to drive? NASCAR?"

"Pfft. NASCAR's got nothing on me. I was the local drag racing champion before I turned eleven."

"You say that like it's a good thing."

She grinned, which had him feeling infinitely better. She'd seemed so lost earlier. But the farther they got from town, the more twisty the road became, the less stressed she seemed. Her mood had definitely lightened and she seemed more like the flirty, fun woman he'd pegged her to be when he'd barricaded himself in her father's office.

A siren whined somewhere behind them again. She glanced in the rearview mirror. "Dang it. Someone must have called in about my high-speed jaunt through town."

"Or that semi driver reported a Tucson driving recklessly down the highway."

She grinned again, enjoying this mad dash far too much. "Maybe. Either way, I think they've figured out where we are, or at least what road we're on."

"Last chance. Are you sure you want to do this?"

"Really? You're going there again?"

"Apparently not. First, we need to toss your phone. Murphy's probably already putting a trace on it. When the phone's in motion, even if you're not using it, it pings off the cell towers and—"

She threw her phone out the window, then rolled it back up.

He blinked in surprise. "I figured I'd have to argue with you."

"I'm a reasonable person." She glanced at him. "Don't give me that look. Turning you in wasn't a reasonable request. Throwing out my phone so they can't track us makes sense. What's next?"

"Get off the highway. There should be a turnoff a couple of miles ahead that we can—"

"Hold on."

He braced his hands against the dash right before she

slammed her brakes. She jerked the wheel hard left and went bouncing down a curvy dirt road that seemed to miraculously appear in between thick pines and bushes that scraped the sides of the SUV.

"Or we can take this one," he said drily. He checked to make sure she had her seat belt fastened. Then he grabbed his own and clicked it in place. As they rounded a curve, he was relieved to see the highway disappear in his side view mirror. And even though he could still hear sirens, they were fading. "Where does this road go?"

"Don't know. Never even noticed it before."

He shook his head, finding it impossible not to smile at her enthusiasm. "What happened to the scared woman from just a few minutes ago? You're actually enjoying this now, aren't you?"

"*Scared* might be a little too harsh. I was…cautious, not used to running from the police, or such high stakes. And, yes, this is the kind of driving I like best. Get me on a Gator or a dune buggy and you'll have to peel me off."

Another jolting bounce had the top of his head brushing the roof. "If you don't slow down, you may have to peel *me* off the roof. Besides, we don't know how long this road is or how quickly it might end."

"You had to say that. Hold on." She slammed the brakes.

They slid toward a stand of thick pines marking the end of the road. Just when it seemed they were about to test out the airbags, she slammed the accelerator and jerked the steering wheel. The Tucson fishtailed and shot to the right, its rear bumper banging against one of the trees before they rocketed a few feet down into what appeared to be a dry creek bed.

Except there weren't any dry creek beds around here, not with the high water table and bayous surrounding the area.

It must have been another access road to someone's

acreage at one time. The waist-high weeds and small sap-
lings she was plowing through attested to its disuse. He
studied the woods zipping past the window.

She bounced in a deep rut, making everything squeak.

He winced, his battered body feeling the abuse just as
heavily as the Tucson. "I suppose I'll have to buy you a
new SUV when this is over."

"Honey, you can buy me anything you want. A new Tucson will do, with all the goodies. Oh, and a phone. Don't
forget the phone."

"With all the goodies?"

"Of course."

He laughed. "You got it."

The creek bed, or forgotten access road, ended and they
were suddenly in the woods with no obvious path. She was
forced to slow even more, picking her way around trees,
fallen logs, and occasionally mowing down thick bushes
blocking their way.

About ten minutes later, he glimpsed a bog. Flashes of
white were probably snowy egrets, which were common
around here.

His watch vibrated against his wrist. He glanced at the
screen, then looked out the window and saw a blue stripe
painted about ten feet up on a pine tree.

"I still hear sirens," she said. "Faint, but definitely sirens. Off to the east I think."

"The highway. It's running roughly parallel to us. I
don't think they found where we turned off or they'd be
on our bumper by now."

"If they were, I sure couldn't outrun them. We could
probably go faster walking at this point. Maybe we should
ditch my car."

"I don't think we'll have to do that."

"Why do you say that?"

"Because I see a building through those trees."

She frowned, then nodded when she saw what he'd told her about. They bounced up a slight incline on their right to get around a fallen log. When she came around the other side, they were in a large clearing that could have held a dozen cars if it was a parking lot. She stopped about twenty feet from the building, a dilapidated-looking barn whose sagging roof seemed ready to collapse in a stiff breeze.

Thick woods surrounded the barn. Through a gap in the trees on the left, sunlight sparkled off brackish water, revealing the bayou he'd spotted earlier. It was dotted with swamp tupelo trees and bald cypress draped in Spanish moss. There would be lily pads and duckweed too, although he couldn't see them from here. Even with the car door closed and the windows up, the damp mustiness of the bayou drifted in through the air vents.

An unexpected pang of longing settled over him as he drank it all in. In Gatlinburg he'd have a coat on right now. Here, he could wear short sleeves just about year-round. Tennessee was glorious with its seasonal colors, waterfalls that could take his breath away, mist-covered mountains outside his back door. But there was something about the bayous of Louisiana, the music, the food, that tugged at his heart. Even with the horrors that had happened to him and his family in Beauchamp, his blood hummed with pleasure at being in this unique brand of paradise again. It was, quite simply, home.

Hannah thumped the steering wheel in frustration. "The good news is that I think we lost them. I don't hear any sirens. The bad news is I got *us* lost in the process. I don't even know if I can backtrack at this point. I had to make so many turns to get around obstacles. I have no idea where we are."

"About a mile from Pete's Bog. The Sabine River is to

the west just past the bayou, maybe a quarter mile as the eagle flies. Highway 191's five miles to the east."

Her brows arched in surprise. "How do you know all that?"

"Because I own that barn and the forty acres surrounding it. Welcome to my hideout."

Chapter Six

As barns went, the one that Hannah was standing in took the prize as the worst she'd ever been inside. Not that she'd been in many. But there were enough of these antiques still around that she'd explored a few, mostly as a teenager up to no good. Unlike this one, though, none of those had seemed ready to fall down. If it wasn't for Mason assuring her this building was far more solid than it looked, she wouldn't have parked her Tucson inside. And she wouldn't be here in the shadows with twenty-foot-tall stacks of moldy hay surrounding her.

"You don't look impressed."

She turned at the sound of his humor-filled voice as he finished securing the massive, sagging doors behind them. "I think the hay bales are the only things holding this place up. I suppose that could be called impressive."

He grinned but remained standing by the doors. "That's all you see? Hay bales?"

She turned in a slow circle, trying to make out details in an interior lit only by what little sun could filter through the small, dirty windows set high up in the walls. "I see dirt floors, dry-rotted walls and rafters, hay that should have been thrown out months or years ago. Not that I'm complaining, since no one would ever think to look for us here. But, well, okay, yes. I'm complaining. It would be nice if it was a whole lot cleaner. As it is, we'll probably have to sleep in my car. And I'm not looking forward to using the woods as an outhouse, or hunting squirrels for dinner." She squinted up at the crisscross of cracked, weathered beams holding up the rusty metal roof. "Are you *sure* this thing isn't going to crash down on top of us?"

"This building is only about six years old."

"You're kidding. What happened to it?"

He laughed. "It was designed to *look* like it should be condemned. The actual bones of the structure are made of steel, set in concrete footers. The rotting wood is for aesthetics, so no one finds this place and starts asking questions about a pristine new building in the middle of nowhere. Even if a hunter or fisherman got curious and broke in, they wouldn't think there was anything of value in here. But they'd be wrong." He winked and stretched his arm up to press a board on the wall. A click sounded. Then a low mechanical hum filled the barn.

That wink had her stomach doing flip-flops. Which was ridiculous. It wasn't like he was flirting with her. He was just being charming, trying to put her at ease. Like when she'd been on the brink of a nervous breakdown trying to evade the police on her wild ride through town. He'd gently touched her face and spoken in that deep, soothing voice—centering her, grounding her, giving her an anchor to bring her back from the edge.

Anyone else with his physical presence—tall, broad-shouldered with biceps that strained against his suit jacket—might have intimidated her. But she'd respected and admired this man's character long before she'd ever met him. And it didn't hurt that his exquisitely handsome face could have been designed by Michelangelo. To top it all off, he was wearing a business suit. How sexy was that?

"Are you impressed now?" he asked, as he stepped beside her.

Her face heated. Had she said all of that out loud?

He motioned toward the back of the barn. She turned, then stared in amazement. "Looks like at least half the hay has been moved on the right side of the building. Wait, is that…is that a door?"

"It is. The first three levels of bales have swung back to reveal the true beauty of this place—a hidden door that leads to a hidden room. Even the ceiling is concealed. If someone climbs into the loft and looks down, all they'll see is hay. And if anyone crosses onto the property, I'll be notified. The boundaries are marked with blue paint on some of the trees. Motion-activated cameras hidden in those trees will send a text to my watch, including pictures, so I can see whether it's someone trespassing or just wildlife."

"Sounds like you thought of everything."

"Not everything. I never expected someone to drive in from the south when the only paved access is on the north side of the property. It took me a while to realize that so-called road we were on was taking us here."

She followed him to the door and motioned toward the left side of the barn. "The bales on that side haven't moved. Is there a hidden room over there too?"

"Something like that. I'll show you later." He pushed open the door and waited for her to enter.

It was dark, which had her worried about creepy crawlies skittering across her shoes. But she gathered her courage and stepped inside. After the door clicked closed, another click sounded. Light filled the space, revealing a pristine, white room with polished concrete floors. It was long and narrow, maybe thirty by fifteen feet.

She glanced up. Modern canned lights were recessed into the smooth white ceiling. A row of neat, open shelves ran along the left wall, holding a few boxes of nonperishable foods, medicines and a couple of cases of bottled water. There were stacks of electronics, as well. She spotted some phones, at least two laptops. Beneath all that was a long black counter with an assortment of mini kitchen appliances, including a microwave and a beverage cooler.

The end of the room formed the main living area. It boasted a surprisingly large, U-shaped sectional that looked custom-made for the space, with built-ins on the wall above it providing even more storage. A coffee table with a stack of place mats indicated it did double duty as a dining table.

"Dinner might be boring tonight, but you won't go hungry. No need to hunt for squirrels," he teased as he grabbed two bottles of water from the cooler and a bottle of pain pills from one of the shelves.

He handed her one of the water bottles while he washed down several pills.

"Those jerks really did a number on you in Gatlinburg. How bad does it hurt?" She took a deep sip from her own bottle, surprised at how thirsty she was. Apparently fleeing from the police did that to a person.

He set his bottle on the counter. "A good night's sleep will do wonders. But the pills are a welcome crutch for now. What do you think about the place?"

She set her bottle beside his. "I'm honestly impressed. But why buy a house in town if you already had this place? Especially since it had to cost a small fortune to build."

"I come to Beauchamp once or twice a year to research my brother's case. Originally, I used this barn as my home base, with the goal of staying out of town as much as possible. I didn't want to rub salt in old wounds, or upset my family. But even though I was discreet about meeting with potential witnesses, I found most weren't willing to disclose much information. My investigation stalled. For the last few years, I've been working on a new approach. I hired a movie makeup artist to design a reusable disguise. And I created an alias, with a background that could withstand most internet and basic database searches, along with ID that matched my new name, Christopher Johnson."

"Christopher's fairly common around here. Johnson isn't."

"I was going for a Tennessee name. My alias background is from there."

"Good choice then. I'm guessing with the alias and disguise, you felt comfortable buying the cottage, living in town thinking no one would recognize you?"

"Exactly. You'd be amazed how many people will gossip with a tourist on a hunting or fishing trip, especially if he invested in the community by purchasing a home. It's slow going, getting people to trust and open up. But things are definitely working better with an alias than without one. I've got high hopes something will break loose in the near future." He made a face. "Correction, I *had* high hopes. Who knows what will happen now."

"I just hate that you and your family have suffered the way you have. It's so unfair."

He shrugged. "It is what it is." He reached above the counter and pressed a button on a small electronic keypad she hadn't noticed earlier.

She glanced around, expecting one of the walls to move. "I think something's broken. Nothing's happening."

"The stacks of hay are moving into position outside this room to conceal the door."

"I don't hear the mechanical hum."

"Soundproofing. No sense in having a secret room if someone outside can hear us in here."

"Makes sense. This would be a perfect little apartment if it had windows. But even without natural light, everything's so bright and looks so clean."

"Even with constant ventilation and climate control, it gets pretty dusty between visits. But I was here not long ago, which is why it looks presentable right now. That door over there is the bathroom, with a stackable washer and dryer. That'll come in handy tonight. You can wear my robe or something else from the closet in there while we wash your clothes. It's not ideal, but at least you'll have something clean to wear."

She nodded, but her body flushed with delicious heat thinking about wearing something he'd worn. She cleared her throat. "What about door number two over there? Bedroom?"

"Mechanical room. Houses all the high-tech gizmos that make this place work. I won't bore you with too many details, but the air-conditioning, heating, even the motor for the concealment system is in there with special ventilation and more soundproofing. We've got internet too, with a state-of-the-art fire wall to protect the connection. The satellite dish is camouflaged at the top of a pine tree."

"But no bedroom."

"No bedroom. I didn't see the point in wasting valuable square footage when I can sleep on the couch. But don't worry. I'll take the floor tonight. There's extra bedding in the bathroom closet."

She rolled her eyes. "No way. That sectional is plenty big enough for both of us. I wouldn't dream of letting you sleep on that hard concrete floor, especially with all those bruises."

His eyes widened, but he didn't argue. From the way her pulse was speeding up at the prospect of sleeping so close to him, maybe she shouldn't have suggested it. Today's events and the potential repercussions, already had her mind churning. Add to that the temptation of an incredibly sexy, compelling man that she'd essentially been crushing on for years and she'd probably get zero sleep.

She crossed the room to put some distance between them and sat on the sectional. "Now that you have the house in town for when you're investigating, does your team stay with you there or do they pile in here with sleeping bags?"

To her dismay, he crossed the room and sat beside her, completely scattering her focus.

"Neither. I've never brought them with me."

For a man with dark brown eyes, it was amazing how expressive they could be. Had she noticed those gold flecks before, around the iris?

"Hannah?"

"Sorry, what?"

Those expressive eyes crinkled at the corners as he smiled. "You were asking about my team. Was there something else on your mind?"

Him. And she was pretty sure he knew it. She shoved her hair back behind her ears. What had she been asking? Oh right. His team. Wait. What had he said? "Your team doesn't come to Beauchamp with you? Ever?"

"I'd hoped to bring a few of them at some point to help me. But after creating The Justice Seekers, it took far longer to recruit and build the team than I'd anticipated. Not to mention the time involved just to run the company. Later, the idea of pulling anyone off other cases to work on mine never felt right. My brother is gone. Nothing I do will bring him back. It's hard to justify diverting resources when our clients need our help."

"I understand the dilemma. But *you're* important too. You have every right to expend resources to resolve this, especially considering it's ripped your family apart. Olivia said you almost never talk to your parents or your other sisters, Ava and Charlotte. And the only time you talk to your younger brother, Wyatt, is when he brings Olivia up to visit you."

"The others have called, or been up to visit too."

"Really? How often?"

When he hesitated, she held up her hands. "Sorry. That

was way too personal. It's easy to forget that you just met me when it feels as if I've known you for a long time."

His mouth quirked in a half smile. "Olivia talks about me that much, huh?"

"You're her favorite topic."

His half smile morphed into a full-out grin. "I bet that makes Wyatt furious. Especially since she lives with him. It's probably a sore spot between them."

"You don't seem to mind."

He shrugged. "Wyatt blames me for hurting our family. He says that if I hadn't started the FBI investigation and launched the civil suit after Landon's death, then my family's friends wouldn't have turned against them. It took a long time after my parents told me to stop visiting for the community to no longer treat them like pariahs. I imagine if you'd listened to Wyatt all these years instead of Olivia, you'd probably think I'm the devil."

"Not a chance. Even if Olivia hadn't bragged on you, I've seen for myself your integrity and character. You were willing to let Murphy lock you up because you wanted to protect *me*, knowing it could cost your *life*. Do you realize how incredible and rare that is? For a person to put others first, even if it means sacrificing themselves?" She scoffed. "I'll bet the real reason your brother resents you is because he knows he's not half the man you are. And it's your family who's hurt you, not the other way around. They've abandoned you, even though everyone knows you send them gobs of money all the time. I mean, come on, your parents' house is practically a mansion. Your mom was a teacher, like mine was. And your dad worked in some factory downtown. I can't see them affording that place on their retirement alone. Your money is good enough for them, but you're not? How hypocritical is that? As far as I'm concerned, they should be falling all over themselves begging for your forgiveness."

He stared at her so intently her face heated with embarrassment. "Oh gosh, I did it again. I overstepped. I shouldn't have said—"

Her next words were stopped by his lips against hers. The kiss was so unexpected that she barely managed to respond before it was over. But for such a short kiss, it packed an incredible punch. Her body felt incinerated from the inside out and she was tingling all over. But more than that, the aching sweetness of his touch had her heart melting. It was as if she'd felt everything he'd felt—the longing, the heat, but also the hurt and pain he'd suffered for so long. If his family, if the people who'd rejected and blamed him all these years for their own failings were here right now, she'd make it her quest to have them leave feeling ashamed for their actions. Or, better yet, she'd have them groveling at Mason's feet for the injustices they'd piled on him.

His hand shook as he gently feathered her hair back from her face, then dropped his hand to his side. "Thank you," he said, his voice raspy. "I can't remember the last time anyone defended me like that. And I didn't know how badly I needed to hear that until you said it." He let out a ragged breath, his lips curving in a wry smile. "But this shouldn't be about me. What matters is figuring out how to extricate you from this mess without destroying your future." He cleared his throat, his jaw tightening. "And we need to find Audrey's killer."

She stared at him in wonder. He was *still* more concerned about others than himself. But what surprised and dismayed her was the raw emotion in his voice when he'd said Audrey's name.

"You still care about her, don't you? After all these years, and the things she did to… I mean—dang it. Forget I went there. I don't know what's wrong with me today. I swear I'm not usually this awful." She fisted her hand on the couch, ashamed that she'd been about to say something very unflattering about a woman he'd loved, maybe still loved.

He tilted her chin up until she met his gaze. To her immeasurable relief, there was no anger, or censure in his eyes. There was only understanding, tinged with grief. "It's okay, Hannah. I'm well aware of Audrey's past. It's not exactly a secret around here that she cheated on me. And just like you believe in me, I'm getting a crash course today on believing in you too. You've got a good heart. You're only trying to look out for me. I understand that." He pressed a whisper-soft kiss against her forehead, then gently threaded his fingers through hers. "My feelings for Audrey are...complicated. I don't know that I can explain it. We basically grew up together. Her past is inextricably linked with mine. No matter what happens in the future, I imagine I'll always care about her."

She stared down at their joined hands, blinking back the tears burning in her eyes. "Hearts are complicated, aren't they? Truth be told, Johnny and I probably had more hard times than good. But through it all, we loved each other." She shook her head in wonder. "Here it is, six years later, and that love hasn't faded. The pain has, thank God, or I wouldn't be able to function." She raised her head and met his gaze. "That's what I want for you. Some kind of closure over your brother's death, and Audrey's, so your pain will fade too."

His answering smile was sad, but determined. "I hope so too. I assume Johnny was your late husband?"

She nodded. "Johnathan James Cantrell. But he always hated the name Johnathan." She smiled in remembrance. "He wouldn't even let me call him Johnathan in our wedding vows."

Mason laughed softly. "Sounds like he had strong views."

"Oh, he did. We both did. Two hardheaded people can

make for a lot of fireworks. It actually helped our relationship that he was gone so often. Those were our cooling-off periods between fights. But the homecomings were amazing." She winked, delighted when he laughed in response. It was good to see the shadows finally lifting from his eyes.

"He worked on oil rigs, in the Gulf, mostly. Good pay, great benefits. Until he was killed in an accident, and I realized we didn't have nearly enough life insurance. When you're young, you think you'll live forever. We weren't prepared at all. I was a homemaker, suddenly with no income, and no real job training. I had to start over, go back to school while working part-time to make the insurance money last as long as possible. Thankfully my parents let me move in with them until I was able to get my own... oh shoot." She tugged her hand free and stood. "Parents. I told my dad I'd call as soon as we got here. And there's no telling what Murphy told him. He's probably confused and worried sick."

"It's okay. You can call your dad right now and explain what happened. I need to make a few calls myself." He got up and strode to one of the shelves of electronics. He pulled two phones out of a box, pocketed one, and brought the other to her. "It's a burner. A little more sophisticated than most. It has all the bells and whistles you're used to on a typical smart phone. But it's untraceable, for the most part."

"For the most part?"

"There's really no such thing as a phone you can't trace. But as long as your father doesn't try to trace your call and you don't call anyone else, we should be fine. I can go into the outer part of the barn so you can talk without—"

"*No*. I mean, if you don't mind waiting a few minutes, would you please stay? Dad might want to talk to you too. And honestly, I could use some backup if things get testy.

I didn't get my stubbornness and hardheadedness from my mom's side of the family."

He chuckled and sat back down. "No problem."

She dialed her father's personal cell and put it on speaker.

"Chief Landry."

"Daddy, I've got you on speaker here with Mason. I'm—"

"Hannah, thank God. Where are you? No. Don't answer that. Are you okay?"

"I'm fine. We're fine. Sorry it took so long to call."

He let out a ragged breath. She could picture him raking his hands through his hair, creating a halo of short white spikes all over his head.

"Dad, something, ah, unexpected happened when we were leaving the station, so I can't come back just yet."

"*Unexpected?* Are you kidding me? Is that what you call nearly running over Captain Murphy?"

She grimaced. Mason put a reassuring hand on hers. "I'm really sorry, Dad. I didn't know what else to do. He was pointing a gun at Mason. I just…reacted. I didn't think."

"Mason should have surrendered as soon as Murphy spotted him instead of getting you pulled into this."

"You're absolutely right, sir," Mason said, before she could reply. "I should have surrendered. What kind of spin is Murphy putting on what happened?"

"Before you answer, Daddy, I want to make it clear that Mason was trying to surrender. He was about to get out of my Tucson but I took off. It was my decision and mine alone."

Mason frowned, obviously not pleased with her taking the blame.

"I'm glad to hear he was trying to do the right thing," her father said. "You should have let him. Not knowing what really happened, I told Murphy that you must have been kidnapped when you went out to get something from your car. He knows you carry a gun in your purse. I said Mason probably took it and forced you to nearly run Murphy over during the escape."

"Oh for goodness' sake, Dad. Even if he hadn't jumped out of the way, I would have swerved. He was never in danger. What a pansy."

Mason coughed. It sounded suspiciously like he was trying to hide a laugh.

"Young lady—"

"It's *true*. I wish you hadn't lied for me. I don't want more charges piled on Mason."

"I can, and should, take the heat for this," Mason interjected.

"Agreed," her father said. "This is a huge problem now. There's a BOLO out for Hannah's SUV and half the force is out searching for the two of you. I need to end this before the mayor decides to call in the state police. That's something, as a law enforcement officer, that I just can't allow to happen, knowing you haven't really been abducted. Mason needs to bring you back and surrender so we can deal with this, without making it worse."

Mason nodded his agreement.

It was her turn to frown at him. "No. Absolutely not. You and I both risked *everything* to help him escape because we knew it was the right thing to do. He's innocent. You saw the video."

"The video proves he was attacked. It doesn't prove that he didn't shoot Ms. Broussard."

Mason's mouth tightened in a firm line, obviously not happy with that statement.

"He would never hurt Audrey, Dad."

"You sure about that?"

She met Mason's gaze. "I am 100 percent positive that he didn't hurt Audrey."

He stared at her in wonder, then took her hand and pressed a kiss against her knuckles. She felt that kiss all the way to her soul.

"Okay, okay," her father said. "I'm trusting your instincts. Heck, if I didn't, I wouldn't have let you go with him in the first place. But your safety comes first. You need to get back here before some nervous Nellie stumbles over your location and pulls the trigger with you caught in the middle. I don't care if you think you have the best hiding place around. Even with just my local guys out searching, I'm confident they'll find you. Most grew up around here. They're outdoorsmen, hunters, with their own scent hounds. Tracking is what they do for fun. It scares ten years off my life just thinking about you being hunted down, knowing what could happen if someone gets spooked. I promise I'll do my best to ensure Mason's safety in jail, but you have to come back."

"I'll bring her back, sir. I have a car here. They won't be looking for that like they are her Tucson."

She frowned. "You have a car?"

"I do."

"Excellent," her father said. "We need to figure out the best way to do it, though. With so many officers out searching, even if you're in a different vehicle, they might spot you. I'd say wait until dark, since most of the searchers will have to stop their efforts until daylight. But that could be just as dangerous. Any vehicle out late at night might cause suspicion and draw attention."

"How about during the morning shift change?" Mason asked. "Most of the uniforms should be at the station, finishing up reports from the night before or preparing to go on patrol for a morning shift. You still do turnover at 0700?"

Her father laughed. "You haven't forgotten much, have you, *Chief Ford*? Yes, seven o'clock. That'll work."

"No," Hannah protested. "I refuse to let him go to jail. And he can't just drop me off at the station without someone seeing him."

"You're being stubborn, Hannah," her father accused.

"Yeah, well. Wonder who I get that from?"

A heavy sigh sounded from the phone. "I want you back, safe, without the whole state out gunning for both of you. We need a plan."

Mason shot her an apologetic look. "I have an idea."

Chapter Seven

Hannah yawned and shifted her weight on the hood of her Tucson in the dilapidated-looking barn, waiting for Mason to finish putting on his so-called movie-worthy disguise and join her. She yawned again and shook her head. Just as she'd feared, she'd gotten almost no sleep last night. But not because she was lying on the other side of the sectional craving Mason's touch. Instead, she'd been angry—at her father and Mason, but mostly at herself for agreeing to this outrageous idea.

If it worked, she'd be home free. No criminal charges for having helped Mason escape. But it meant telling more lies, which she hated. And it would do exactly what she'd been trying to avoid—make things worse for him.

The only reason she'd finally agreed was that if she didn't do this, he swore he would turn himself in.

"Still mad at me?"

She stiffened at the sound of his voice.

"Since you're not looking at me, I guess the answer is yes."

She let out a pent-up breath. "I'm not mad at you. I'm mad at myself. Everything I did to keep you from getting into more trouble was for nothing."

"You saved my life. That's a lot more than nothing."

"It only counts as saving your life if we don't throw

that away today. It's risky having you drive me into town, even with a disguise."

"I'll be fine. Because of you, I'm here this morning, alive, not locked up at the mercy of an unnamed enemy. You've given me what few people around here ever have— a second chance. I promise you that I'm not going to squander it."

Tears burned her eyes. She wiped them away before they could fall. "The BOLO is for my SUV. It should be safe for *me* to drive your car to the police station while you stay here. I'll explain that I panicked when I saw Murphy in the parking garage and—"

"They'll arrest you for aiding and abetting a fugitive. I've looked at every angle I could and truly believe this is our best option. It's the only way for you to avoid criminal charges. And don't even ask me to leave you alone at the cottage. I need to be there until you're safe and back with your dad. Otherwise, you'd be too vulnerable."

"Only because of this ridiculous plan you concocted."

He remained silent, not backing down.

She tried arguing it another way. "We're just delaying the inevitable. They'll eventually realize that I helped you."

"I agree. The truth is going to come out. I certainly have no intention of remaining a fugitive my whole life. But if we can delay the truth until I figure out who killed Audrey, and can prove it, everything changes. A reasonable District Attorney would drop all charges against me at that point, and is highly unlikely to levy charges against you or your father, since you were protecting an innocent man whose life you believed was in danger. Given the history with my brother and this town, that's a rational assumption. Especially since we already have proof that two of the current deputies are involved in my abduction. Last night you said Warren Knoll is a reasonable DA. Have you changed your mind?"

She shook her head. "No. He seems fair and honest. He works in Many, half an hour from Beauchamp, so it's not like I see him every day. But I've worked with him enough on special projects to feel that I can judge his character. And there's never been a whisper of scandal about any of his cases."

"Then there's hope this will all work out. Sticking to the plan is our best chance at a good outcome all around." He put his hand on her arm. "Are you ever going to look at me?"

She sighed and grabbed her purse before sliding off the hood. Swiping at her eyes again, she turned to face him. She jumped about a foot and let out an embarrassing squeak of surprise.

He laughed, a deep rumbling sound that was the only thing familiar about the stranger looking back at her. The bearded, gray-haired man with a slightly puffy face bore no resemblance to the dark-haired, clean-shaven, tongue-swallowingly gorgeous man she'd been hearing about for years and had finally met in person just yesterday. Even his eyes were different. Instead of warm brown, they were dark blue. And the pudgy stomach was more fitting on someone like her father than a man as buff and virile as Mason.

"You look like a grandfather who's lived a hard life in a doughnut shop."

He laughed again. "I guess that means the disguise works."

"It's *Mission: Impossible* worthy. But what about your voice? If any of the police who saw you at the station hear you speak, you'll be in trouble."

"I'm used to letting my Southern come through to cover my natural Louisiana accent whenever I visit. Seems to have worked for me so far."

The sexy Southern drawl he'd just affected had her

wanting to purr and curl around him. "O…kay. Works for me." She cleared her throat. "What about your height? You can't change that. You're, what, six-two?"

"Three-ish, a tad over."

"Wow."

"Good wow or bad wow?"

"Oh, it's definitely *good*." His grin and knowing look told her he realized full well that tall men were her kryptonite. If her face got any hotter, she was going to burst into flames. "I meant *not* good. Cops are naturally suspicious. Someone might be inclined to take a closer look at you because your height makes you stand out."

He reached off to the side of the Tucson and held something up.

She frowned. "A cane? I don't—"

"It's part of my disguise, for the exact reason that you just mentioned."

Grasping the cane in his right hand, he leaned heavily on it and paced in front of her. His disjointed gait and slightly stooped posture completed the look. She doubted even his hero-worshipping baby sister would recognize him.

"Okay, okay. You obviously know what you're doing."

He winked, which had her nerves jumping for a whole other reason.

Glancing at his watch, he said, "We need to get going soon or we won't make it to the cottage around shift change. Ready?"

"Shouldn't you take off the watch? It's rather expensive looking and distinctive. You had it on at the police station."

He arched a brow. "Good catch, Ms. Crime Analyst." He took it off and shoved it in the pocket of his baggy, completely unflattering jeans.

She *really* missed the suit.

He pressed some buttons on his phone. A mechanical

hum sounded. The hay bales on the left side of the barn shifted and moved. In the newly revealed opening sat an older model, charcoal gray four-door Nissan Altima. Nothing fancy or eye-catching about the sedan. Definitely not the type of vehicle that would attract attention.

He'd explained last night that he always came to the barn, first thing, on his trips. He'd exchange whatever vehicle he'd driven here, whether it was his personal Mercedes or a rental car, for the Altima. Then he'd put on his disguise and head to the cottage. If the police ever pulled him over, they'd find the car's registration matched the fake driver's license under his alias.

She rounded the car and opened the passenger door.

"Hannah."

She looked over the car's roof in question.

"In order for the plan to work, you can't sit in the passenger seat. Someone might see you as they drive by the car. There are also surveillance cameras all over, both public and private. Especially in the historic district since thieves tend to prey on the large number of tourists there. The cottage is just a block off that. One of the first things the cops will do in an investigation is check for video to corroborate or disprove someone's story. That will include Christopher Johnson."

She closed the door. "Makes sense. I can sit in the back seat, or even lie down, maybe covered with a blanket. But how will I get into your house without being seen?"

"That part's easy. It's a newer build with an attached garage. I can use the remote control, drive right into the garage and close the door behind us."

"Sounds good." She opened the rear door.

He slowly shook his head.

She frowned. "What now?"

"If any of those cameras show a mounded blanket in

the back seat, it could raise questions when police review the videos."

She watched with growing trepidation as he moved to the back of the car. And opened the trunk.

She blinked. "You can't be serious."

"I'm afraid it gets worse."

"Worse than me riding in the trunk of your car? What could possibly be worse?"

"Those videos have time stamps. They'll show exactly when the Altima goes into the garage. The call to 911 should happen almost immediately after that, as if I'd just found you inside."

"Okay, so?"

"With the police station so close, and everyone on high alert about you missing, there will be cops at the house in less than a minute. We won't have time to stage anything. We have to stage it now." He reached into the trunk and pulled out a nylon rope.

Chapter Eight

Hannah's face heated with shame as a crime scene tech carefully cut the nylon rope off her, putting each piece in a brown paper bag. Officer Arthur Mallory sat beside her on the couch, awkwardly patting her shoulder. Her dad had invited him to share their Christmas dinner last year because Mallory's wife was out of town on an emergency business trip and he would've been all alone. Other patrol officers and detectives she knew equally well moved through the house searching for clues about where the man who'd kidnapped her had fled.

She was looking right at him.

He was standing on the front porch, clearly visible through one of the windows, talking to the first officer who'd responded to Mason's 911 call. The same officer who'd shown her around the station her first day on the job. He was a good man: honest, trustworthy, caring. And he was no doubt thanking *Christopher Johnson* for inadvertently scaring off a wanted fugitive when he pulled into the garage. And for calling 911 on behalf of the young woman they all knew and loved at the Beauchamp Police Department.

She hung her head, squeezing her eyes shut.

"Just a couple more," Mallory assured her. "I'm sorry it's taking so long. The tech has to be careful not to cut you. And he's trying to preserve as much of the rope and potential hair and fiber evidence as possible for the state lab to examine."

Her eyes flew open. Lab? She hadn't thought about that. Then again, did it really matter? The DNA on the rope would be hers and Mason's. Which furthered the narrative about him forcing her to drive him out of the parking garage and then holding her in a vacant house until the heat died down so he could get out of town without being caught. The fact that her Tucson wouldn't appear on any videos of the area would be explained by saying he parked in woods and forced her through back yards to get here. Their cover story answered every possible question, except for one. How would they explain all male DNA in the house belonging to Mason, and none to the man who owned this house and had found her?

Would *Christopher Johnson* even have to provide a DNA sample? The whole story would fall apart if they tested him and it matched Mason. They'd know she'd lied all along. But since she told them when they got here that Mason was the one who'd tied her up, there wouldn't be any reason to ask Johnson for a sample. Would there?

It was all so confusing. What had she been thinking to agree to this outrageous plan? They were all going to jail. No, to *prison*, which was infinitely worse. Mason, her father and her. Good grief. What had she done? By convincing her father to let her help Mason in the first place, she'd doomed them all. But if she hadn't helped him, he'd be dead.

Or would he?

Mason firmly believed he'd have been murdered if he'd been put in jail. Was he wrong? Should she have let her father lock him up as he'd originally wanted? Would Mason be okay? She and her father would certainly be in a better position right now, no question.

If only she could talk to Mason again. He had a way

of making the crazy make sense. He could reassure her like no one else. The only way she was going to make it through this was if she believed she'd done the right thing. But she wasn't even sure about that anymore. She shook her head in frustration.

"It's okay," Mallory soothed again. "Almost done."

She nodded her thanks when she really wanted to scream.

The front door flew open, making her start in surprise. When she saw her father standing in the opening, the tears that started flowing down her face were real. She'd never been so relieved to see him in her whole life.

He rushed to the couch and dropped to his knees in front of her. The tech snipped the last of the rope, and suddenly she was clinging to her father with his arms wrapped around her. As she cried against his shoulder, his shaking hand rubbed up and down her back. Her father was always her rock, and here he was shaking. Which just had her crying harder.

Officer Mallory spoke to him in low tones, giving him an update. She tuned them both out, drinking in the comfort of her father's arms around her. It was several minutes before she was finally able to stop crying. She had to force herself to let him go, and sit back.

He grasped her upper arms, his gaze traveling over her from head to toe. "He didn't hurt you?"

She shook her head. "No, Daddy. He didn't hurt me. I promise."

He smoothed her hair back from her face. "Thank God you're okay. The EMTs checked you out already?"

"The 911 dispatcher sent an ambulance but I turned them away. I don't need anyone prodding me or sticking me with needles when nothing's wrong."

Grasping her hand in his, he pulled her to her feet. "You need to see a doctor to be sure." He addressed Officer Mallory. "Tell the detective assigned to interview Hannah that he can question her in my office after she's checked out at the hospital."

"Dad, no. Please. I don't *need* to go to the hospital."

"Yes. You do. And I'm taking you."

Her shoulders slumped in defeat.

Mallory cleared his throat. "My apologies, Chief. I should have insisted that she be examined."

"It's okay. I know how stubborn she can be."

"Dad—"

"Come on." He pulled her toward the door. As they stepped onto the porch, she risked a quick glance at Mason. But he didn't even look her way.

A chorus of cheers had her stumbling to a surprised halt. Her cheeks heated with embarrassment as about a dozen police officers in the front yard clapped and smiled, elated that the analyst they'd been working with for the past year had been safely "rescued."

She was totally going to hell for this.

Her father ushered her through the crowd toward his police-issued SUV. Once inside, she collapsed back against the seat and closed her eyes. She was such a fraud. When the truth eventually came out, they'd all hate her. And she couldn't blame them.

The SUV rumbled as it pulled away from the curb.

"I know this is tough," her father said. "But it's going to be okay. We'll get through this. Together."

She let out a deep breath and opened her eyes. Then she straightened. "Dad? This isn't the way to the police station. Please tell me you're not *actually* driving me to Sabine Medical Center. Many's half an hour away and there's no telling what kinds of tests and scans they'll insist on doing. I just want to get my interview over with and go home."

"I'm not taking you to Sabine Medical Center."

She relaxed against the seat. "Thank goodness."

"I'm taking you to Beauchamp Clinic."

"Dad."

"Consider the clinic a compromise. But we *are* going and you *will* be seen by a doctor. We're doing this by the book so it looks legit. If someone thinks it's not, you could be arrested for a felony. You get that, right? It won't matter that I'm the police chief. We have to convince people like Captain Murphy to believe you. If we don't, you and I will both be in serious trouble."

The reminder about the danger to him quelled any further complaints. "I'm sorry about all of this. I never meant for things to get so out of control."

He reached across the middle console and patted her hand. "I knew the risks when I took those handcuffs off him instead of taking him to lockup. After seeing that video, there really wasn't any choice. I couldn't stand by and simply hope that none of my other deputies were as rotten as Abrams and Donnelly. If that decision comes back to bite me, so be it. But you're not to blame for this situation. The blame lies squarely on whoever killed Ms. Broussard and framed an innocent man."

Tears threatened yet again. She breathed through it, holding them back. She'd never been a crier, but no one would believe that if they'd seen her yesterday, or today. Next to losing her husband, this was the roughest thing, emotionally, that she'd ever faced. Apparently she wasn't as tough as she thought.

Her father steered around some potholes, bumping through one of the town's worst intersections. "I didn't see Mason at the cottage. I thought he was going to pose as the homeowner and supposedly discover you so you wouldn't be vulnerable and tied up while he went somewhere else to call 911. Did he change his mind? Leave you alone? If he did, so help me, I'll—"

"Seriously? Dad, he was on the front porch talking to one of your officers. You didn't see him?"

He gave her a surprised look. "The guy with the beard? And the cane?"

"Yes."

"I remember glancing at him as I nodded at Jennings. Nothing sparked any recognition. Guess he was right about that disguise of his."

"And?"

He rolled his eyes. "And he didn't abandon you. I shouldn't have jumped to that conclusion. Okay?"

"Okay. And you're right, that was an incredible disguise. I doubt his own mother would recognize him." She wrinkled her nose. "Not that she visits him enough to even remember what he looks like. I've probably seen him more these past few days than she has in the past eight years."

His brows arched. "I take it he's not close to his family?"

"The other way around. It was their choice. I kind of hate them for turning their backs on him."

"*Hate*'s a strong word, Hannah Rose."

She smiled. "I know I'm in trouble if you're using my middle name. Usually Mom's the one who calls me Hannah Rose."

He shot her a pained look. "Speaking of mothers, *yours* is worried sick about you. I called her when I got official word that you'd been found safe. But she'll still need to see you for herself. So will your sisters."

"You told them I was kidnapped?"

"Honey, I didn't *have* to tell them. It's all over the news. They called me in a panic last night. Mary drove in from New Orleans around midnight. Sarah got here an hour ago from Baton Rouge. Their husbands stayed home with their kids and dogs. I hated lying to them, especially your mom, but I had to. We need everyone to act the way they would if you'd really been abducted. It's a lot easier if they don't have to pretend."

She groaned. "This hole we're digging is getting deeper and deeper."

"I know. I'm trying to figure a way out of it. It all hinges on finding out the truth about Ms. Broussard's murder. At my request, Detective Latimer is heading up a large team of detectives on this case. It's their top priority."

He turned down the side street that led to the clinic. "Will you stay at our house for a few days? It would make your mother calm down after such a scare."

"I'll come for a quick visit. But please don't try to guilt me into staying with you and Mom longer than that. I need some normalcy in my life after this roller coaster we've been on. Besides, Sarah and Mary will be in the spare rooms. You don't need me piling on your couch. And, honestly, if I have to endure a couple of days of questions from them, I'll probably cave. I'll be lucky if I can hold it together long enough to survive the questioning at the station later and not spill the beans to Mom and them."

"I get it. I do. If your mom tries to force the issue, I'll take your side, try to help her understand that you need your space." He crossed through another intersection. "We're just a few blocks from the clinic. I promised to give that Bishop guy an update about the search for Mason this morning. This seems as good a time as any." He nodded toward his personal cell phone sitting in the console. "Would you mind pressing the first contact under favorites? You can put it on speaker mode."

Moments later, Mason's employee answered the call. "Bishop."

"Bishop, this is police chief Mitch Landry in Beauchamp, Louisiana, calling to give you that update I promised."

"Mason got away safely. The kidnapping ruse worked

and you're taking your daughter to the hospital to be checked out."

Her father frowned. "Your boss was talking to one of my patrol officers last I saw. No way did he have a chance to call you. How do you know all of that?"

"It's my job to know."

He rolled his eyes. "Let me guess. Mason has one of those fancy, hidden alarm systems at the cottage, transmitting to you?"

When Bishop didn't say anything, her father swore softly. "It's *my* job to keep my daughter safe," he snapped. "Mason didn't tell me he was letting you in on the truth about this kidnapping farce. I don't want anything getting out and hurting Hannah."

"I understand your concerns. But you can't expect us to trust your legal system, not given what's happened in the past. We're going on the offensive and will do whatever it takes to get justice for Mason. Beauchamp, Louisiana, is about to become really uncomfortable for a lot of people."

Her father's jaw worked. Hannah didn't think she'd ever seen him this angry. "Be warned, Bishop. I'll fight for justice too, because it's the right thing to do. But protecting my daughter comes first. Are we clear?"

"Crystal, sir."

"But you're not going to promise that she won't get hurt in this fight of yours, are you?"

"I don't think either of us can promise that."

Hannah put her hand on his shoulder to stop whatever he was about to say. Listening to Mason's employee sounding so calm and in control, somehow had a settling effect on her. She'd never met this Bishop guy, but his confidence was comforting. More importantly, Mason trusted him. That went a long way with her. And knowing that she and her father weren't in this fight alone was a huge relief.

"It's okay, Dad. Like you said earlier, we both knew we

could get in serious trouble when we helped Mason escape. All we can do now is keep trying to protect him, and each other, and hope for the best."

He turned into the Beauchamp Clinic parking lot. "All right, Bishop. We're all going to do what we feel we have to do. When can I expect my town to be invaded by these Justice Seekers?"

"We're already here."

Chapter Nine

Being poked and prodded at the clinic had been a demoralizing experience, especially since it was unnecessary. But Hannah would go back for more torture if she could avoid what was next: an interrogation by one of Beauchamp PD's finest.

She clutched her father's hand as the police station's first floor elevator doors closed. He pressed the button for the second floor.

"It'll be okay, Hannah. Even if things don't go the way we hope they will, neither of us has a criminal record. The DA would take that into account when considering whether or not to press charges."

Neither of them acknowledged what he hadn't said, that even if they both avoided prison time, both of their careers would be over if they were convicted of a crime.

The elevator dinged and she let go of his hand. She drew a bracing breath just as the doors opened, and another painful gauntlet began. In spite of shift change being long past, the squad room was full. Officers who should have been on patrol hurried to greet her, hug her, tell her how they'd prayed for her safe return.

Her father helped as best he could, steering her toward his office—which sported a brand-new door and frame to replace the ones that Al had busted. She was about ten feet from sanctuary when a familiar face a few desks away had her stopping so fast that her father ran into her.

"Hannah, goodness, what…" He went silent when he saw what she saw, or rather, *who* she saw.

Mason Ford.

Except that he was Christopher Johnson to the detective talking to him. His cane rested against the desk and he seemed completely at ease, gesturing with his hands as he answered whatever question was being asked.

Hannah spotted Al standing a few desks away, talking to some patrol officers. Two more deputies who'd worked here when Mason was the chief of police were in the squad room too. What was he thinking, risking his life like this? What if one of them realized who he was?

"Ms. Cantrell? Is that you?"

She jerked her head toward Mason.

He grinned and rose from his chair and leaned on his cane. "Good to see you looking so well."

Her father put his arm around her shoulders, which was probably the only reason she didn't fall down. She cleared her throat. "Um, Mr.—I'm so sorry. I forgot your name."

He gave her a grandfatherly smile. "After what you went through, I wouldn't expect you to remember. It's Johnson. Christopher Johnson."

"Mr. Johnson, thank you again for…rescuing me. I'm in your debt."

"Wasn't nothin'. All I did was walk into my living room and call 911. Glad I could help."

Her father, perhaps because so many people were turning to watch, stepped forward and offered his hand. "I didn't get a chance to thank you at the cottage. I'm Chief Landry, Hannah's father. Thank you for helping her."

Mason switched hands on his cane, wobbling as he shook her father's hand. "Glad I was there."

Al noticed the exchange and hurried over. "How about

you finish up that statement, Mr. Johnson. I need to talk to the chief."

"Sure, sure. That's fine." He eased down into the chair, grimacing as if his arthritis was acting up.

Hannah couldn't believe how comfortable he seemed in a room full of people dedicated to throwing him in jail.

"Come on, Hannah," her father urged, steering her toward his office again.

A moment later the three of them were cocooned inside. She gratefully took one of the seats in front of her father's desk while he sat behind it.

Al surprised her by sitting in one of the other guest chairs. "Are you feeling up to answering some questions, Hannah? Did the doctors say you're okay?"

She glanced at her father before looking back at Al. "You're the one who's going to interrogate me?"

He smiled. "No, ma'am. An *interview* is reserved for suspects. You're the victim in this. I'd like to have a conversation with you, ask some questions to make sure I have all the facts right. Your father can stay, unless you don't want him here."

"Oh no, he can stay. I'd like that."

"Good, good. This shouldn't take long. But if you're not feeling well or ready—"

"Oh, I'm ready." She smiled. "I'm glad it's you who's questioning me. A familiar, friendly face will make this much easier."

"Glad to hear it." He pulled a small electronic device from his shirt pocket. "I'm going to record our conversation. Is that okay?"

Her smile dimmed. "Um, sure."

He pressed some buttons, then set the recorder on the arm of his chair. "For the record, this is Detective Harvey Latimer questioning Ms. Hannah Cantrell in the matter of her alleged kidnapping by Mason Ford."

She winced at his "alleged" remark, but understood it had to do with Mason being presumed innocent until proven guilty.

After stating the date and time for the recording, he rested his massive forearms on his knees, making her feel crowded and a little uneasy. His earlier smile seemed like a distant memory. It had been replaced with a hard look that was all business.

"Now, then, Hannah. Let's start with the incident in the parking garage, where you almost ran over Captain Murphy."

Ten minutes later, she was squeezing the arms of her chair so hard she was amazed they hadn't broken. If this was supposed to be a *conversation*, she couldn't imagine what an interview would be like. It had her wondering if he'd seen through her lies and was trying to make her crack. But her father didn't seem concerned. Maybe these were softball questions after all. But it sure didn't feel that way.

A knock on the door had Al frowning. But Hannah was pathetically grateful for the reprieve. Her father called out and the door opened to reveal Officer Mallory. He smiled when he saw Hannah, then addressed her father.

"Chief." He motioned toward the squad room. "There are some people here to see you."

"We're a little busy right now."

"Sorry for interrupting. But I felt you'd want to know about this. The leader, I guess you could call him, is adamant about talking to you, immediately."

"Leader?"

"Some guy who calls himself Bishop. I don't know if that's his first or last name. Apparently he works for a group called The Justice Seekers."

Her father's face was carefully blank. "Justice what?"

She realized the only way they could both know about

the Seekers was if they'd heard it from Mason. Thank goodness her dad had thought of that.

Mallory leaned against the doorframe. "Seekers. They said that's the name of a company Mason Ford created. Apparently they investigate crimes and protect people, or something like that. Most of them are former law enforcement or ex-military. They're demanding to speak to you."

Her father swore and seemed genuinely aggravated. She knew he hadn't been looking forward to Bishop and the rest of Mason's team showing up, so he probably wasn't acting. Then again, maybe he was. Police lied to suspects all the time. Maybe extending that to other things wasn't a stretch. The realization that her father was a good liar wasn't comforting. And it had her wondering whether every officer and detective she knew was just as skilled.

No wonder so many police who'd worked for Mason years ago had been corrupt without him realizing it. It also helped explain how her father's two deputies concealed their own corruption. Who else around here was in on what had happened to Mason? And how could she trust any of these people in the future? Then again, how could they trust her?

She sighed and tuned back in to what her father was saying, something about putting the visitors in a conference room.

"Chief, we don't *have* a conference room big enough to hold all of them."

"*All* of them? How many are there?"

"Well, if I counted right, there are at least a dozen of the Justice Seekers and—"

"A dozen?"

Mallory nodded.

Hannah exchanged a surprised glance with Al. Both of them leaned to the side to look at the squad room through the open doorway. She was stunned to see so many men and women milling around that she didn't know. Some of the men were as tall as Mason. One of them wore a black Stetson. Another stood slightly apart from the others, leaning against a wall, his expression unreadable. She instinctively pegged him as Bishop and wondered if she was right.

Her father tapped his hand on his desk as he considered the problem. "We can fit a dozen people in the clerk of courts conference room on the first floor. Al's lead detective on the case, so he needs to be at the meeting too. It'll be tight. But I suppose a couple of those so-called Seekers can stand if need be."

Mallory cleared his throat. "The, ah, Justice Seekers aren't the only ones here to see you. They brought some other people with them."

"Other people? Who?"

"Mr. Ford's lawyer. Actually he has two of them—one from Tennessee and another from right here in Louisiana. I guess she's his *official* lawyer because she's licensed to practice law in this state while the other lawyer isn't. There's also a homicide detective from Gatlinburg. One of our own judges, the District Attorney—"

"Wait. Warren Knoll is here, and a judge?"

Mallory tugged at his collar. "That's not the worst of it, Chief."

Her father gave him an impatient look. "Then what *is* the worst, Mallory?"

There was a commotion in the doorway behind him. He moved back and another man stepped into the opening, his dark suit and tie in stark contrast to his crisp white shirt.

"I think he means me." He pulled his credentials from one of his suit pockets and held them up. "Jaylen Holland, special agent with the FBI."

Chapter Ten

From his seat in the squad room, Mason observed the chaos erupting around him. The detective he'd been talking to was now arguing with Dalton. Another was backing away from former FBI profiler, Bryson Anton, who was adamantly arguing that any imbecile could see that Mason wasn't a murderer. Even Bishop hadn't escaped the mayhem. Patrol officers were buzzing around him like angry gnats, demanding information about the Seekers. In response, Bishop was being Bishop. He ignored them, focusing instead on the open doorway to the chief's office.

Not the kind of reception Mason had hoped for. Emotions were running high, which had people choosing sides rather than realizing they were fighting for the same thing—truth and justice. And yet, in spite of the chaos, progress *was* being made. That shouldn't have surprised him, since he'd put Bishop in charge. He just wished that he could have warned Hannah about the newest development. He'd only found out about it himself while texting Bishop from the men's room down the hall.

Bishop had assembled the Seekers and a few others and met with District Attorney Knoll this morning. It went relatively well, but the DA had surprised everyone by immediately assembling his own team and heading to Beauchamp PD. The boulder was rolling down hill and picking up speed. All Mason could do was prepare for damage control—and hope the damage wasn't catastrophic.

Bishop straightened, a signal to Mason that the chief was about to emerge from his office. He stepped out, followed by FBI Special Agent Holland, who'd worked with the Seekers many times in the past. Behind him were Al and Hannah. She looked pale and worried. Mason wished he could reassure her.

Al charged off toward his fellow detectives and officers, rounding them up and ushering some to grab chairs while sending others to the elevator. After a brief exchange with the chief, Dalton and Bryson led the Seekers in helping the detectives move desks to the side and form a circle of chairs in the middle of the squad room. Mason hobbled out of the way, careful to lean on his cane in keeping with his disguise.

"Ladies and gentlemen," the chief called out above the noise. "If you're one of the detectives investigating the Broussard murder, please stay. Likewise, if you're a Seeker or one of their guests, please stick around. Everyone else, take an early lunch or head out on patrol. As soon as the room's available again, I'll have a department text sent out to let you know."

Muted grumbling met his announcement. But those not invited to stay began heading toward the elevators or stairs while others moved toward the circle of chairs.

The chief seemed surprised to see *Christopher Johnson* still there. He motioned to one of the departing patrol officers. "Escort Mr. Johnson to the break room and tag one of the detectives to finish his interview in there."

Mason tapped his finger on the desk, twice, to signal Bishop. No way in hell was he missing this. His future—and possibly Hannah's—was on the line.

"We want Mr. Johnson in the meeting," Bishop called out. "We might have questions for him."

The chief frowned. "I don't think that's a good idea. He's a civilian—"

"So are we. This isn't business as usual. And we have a limited amount of time before our Gatlinburg guests have to leave. If we need to call Mr. Johnson back later, it will delay things."

"I still don't think—"

"Let him stay." Knoll, who'd been quietly observing the chaos, stepped forward. "I'm all for saving time. Today's events have already wrecked my schedule. I'm sure I'm not the only one."

Before the chief could protest again, Mason headed to the circle of chairs.

Hannah hesitated. "Dad, should I go home?"

He dug in his pants pocket for his keys and handed them to her. "Take my SUV. I'll call you when this is over so you can pick me up."

She took the keys and started toward the elevator.

"Wait a minute." Knoll motioned to her. "I'd like Ms. Cantrell to stay. She has far more to add than Mr. Johnson. Let's all sit down, shall we?"

Her eyes widened with concern, but she followed her father and sat beside him.

Mason would have given anything to hold her hand right now. As if thinking the same thing, her father squeezed her hand, smiling encouragingly. But when the DA took the seat on the other side of the chief, his smile faded.

Chief Landry glanced around the room. "I guess I should get us started. I'm not really sure what—"

"No worries. I've got this." Knoll smiled, but there was no amusement in it. "I'll get things rolling. If you don't mind, of course."

"Um, sure. Please. Go ahead." The worry lines on Landry's forehead deepened.

"Excellent. All of the people in this room have a connection to the ongoing murder investigation of Audrey Broussard, or the suspect, Mason Ford. On behalf of those who don't know everyone in the room, and as a reminder for those of us who've only recently met, I'll make some introductions."

He shifted in his chair, as if settling in for the long haul. "I'm Warren Knoll, District Attorney over the 11th Judicial District, which basically means all of Sabine Parish. To my right is the honorable Judge Richard Guidry. To my left is police chief Mitch Landry, then his daughter, Hannah Cantrell, who's also a crime data analyst for Beauchamp PD. I see esteemed defense attorney Bernette Armstrong over there." He smiled. "We've been on opposite sides of a courtroom more times than I can count but are still cordial, so that's saying something. To her left is Jaylen Holland, special agent with the FBI. I believe you're from the Knoxville office?"

Jaylen nodded. "I've got special permission from the local field office to advise on the case involving the abduction of Mr. Ford. The FBI's interest is because he was taken across state lines. Also, based on some of the evidence, we might have another corruption case brewing against Beauchamp PD. I'll want to interview deputies Abrams and Donnelly in the very near future."

"Yes, yes. We'll see that you meet with the illustrious deputies in good time. Let's see, Mr. LeMarcus Johnson—can we call you LeMarcus to distinguish you from the other Mr. Johnson in the room, who's a witness in this case?"

"Of course."

"I believe you're Mr. Ford's personal attorney, with assistance from Mrs. Armstrong since you're not licensed in our state. Is that correct?"

"It is, sir. I'm also employed as one of the Justice Seekers."

"Right, I'd forgotten that. Bishop, you're the leader of the Seekers—"

"No, sir. Mason Ford's our leader. But I'm heading up our current case."

"My apologies for not making that distinction."

"What are Justice Seekers?" Al asked.

Knoll motioned to Bishop. "I'll let you take that."

Bishop sighed, as if he was tired of answering that question, which Mason imagined he was. Few people around here had likely ever heard of his company.

After Bishop's explanation, Knoll said, "To save time, Bishop, can we skip introducing the rest of your team unless they speak during the meeting?"

"Yes, sir. I would, however, like to mention that seated two chairs to my right is Detective Erin Sampson, from Gatlinburg PD."

"Very good," Knoll said. "From our side, we have a large team of detectives working this case. The lead detective is Harvey Latimer. Most of us know him as Al, for reasons I've honestly forgotten. Something to do with Twinkies, I believe."

Al grinned and raised his hand in greeting to everyone. "Yippee-ki-yay, folks."

Mason couldn't help smiling at the *Die Hard* movie reference.

Chief Landry motioned toward one of the people Knoll hadn't mentioned. "Captain Murphy, I don't believe you're working this case. You can go."

"He's my guest," Knoll said. "He stays."

Landry's mouth tightened. Mason imagined he was fuming inside, being treated so casually when this was his police department. The DA should have met with the chief privately first. The fact that he hadn't revealed an alarming lack of respect. And yet, Knoll had seemed fair and reasonable in his meeting with Bishop, according to

Bishop's texts. But for some reason he wasn't extending that same courtesy to the chief. That had Mason concerned that the DA might know more than either Mason or Bishop had thought.

Knoll crossed his legs at the ankle. "Let's get started. When I arrived at my office this morning, Bishop and a lot of the people in this room *demanded* to speak to me. They proceeded to show me some compelling videos and launched a long list of complaints against Beauchamp PD, my office and pretty much anyone in law enforcement in the state of Louisiana. I was then threatened with a lawsuit that would drain Sabine Parish's coffers back to the Stone Age if I didn't immediately intervene in the miscarriage of justice going on here in Beauchamp. I've left out some of the more colorful language that was used." He arched a brow. "Bishop, did I summarize that accurately?"

Bishop gave him a reluctant smile. "Close enough."

Knoll glanced around the room. "One of the many *interesting* topics we discussed was presented by Special Agent Holland. Since the FBI has interceded here before, he was well versed in this town's rather sordid past regarding the appalling handling of the Mandy DuBois/Landon Ford case, which he proceeded to remind me about—not that I needed the reminder. The case is notorious around here even though I wasn't the DA at that time. Near the end of the meeting, my office was informed that Ms. Cantrell had just been rescued after allegedly having been abducted yesterday by Mr. Ford. Knowing her father, Chief Landry, would want to be with her, I asked Captain Murphy to fill me in on some of the details of the past few days. It was quite enlightening."

Landry exchanged a concerned glance with Hannah before looking at Knoll again.

The DA continued. "I think everyone here is well aware of the alleged abduction of Mr. Ford in Gatlinburg. And

Gatlinburg Detective Sampson has already made her outrage painfully clear to me about Mr. Ford's subsequent
treatment here in Beauchamp."

"Don't forget," she said, "that I also brought a warrant
for Abrams and Donnelly, and an extradition request."

"I haven't forgotten. But my main goal at the moment
is to keep my parish from becoming embroiled in yet another expensive lawsuit. And more importantly, ensuring
that innocent people aren't hurt, as they have been in the
past under the leadership of a previous mayor and an em-
barrassingly large number of corrupt public officials, even
former deputies within this police department."

The chief was frowning again, his gaze fixed on Knoll.

"In regards to Mr. Ford and what occurred in Gatlinburg, videos prove without question that he was viciously
attacked, drugged, abducted and transported across state
lines. There's also zero doubt in my mind that two of the
men involved in those crimes are deputies of Beauchamp
PD. They have, rightfully so, been placed under arrest. It's
my recommendation they be fired immediately. My office
will assist Detective Sampson with extradition proceed-
ings. Chief Landry? Any issues with that?"

He shook his head. "None."

"Do the lawyers present have anything further to say
on that particular topic?"

LeMarcus and Armstrong both shook their heads.

"Moving on, I've got a few things to say regarding the
tragedy of Ms. Broussard's murder. We will of course do
everything in our power to fully, and lawfully, investigate
what happened. And I personally guarantee that none of
the shenanigans that happened in the DuBois/Ford case
years ago will happen again. Evidence will *not* be tam-
pered with, fabricated, or disappear on my watch. Bishop,
your team will be given unprecedented access to work
alongside our detectives on the case. I understand your

goal is to prove your boss innocent. Our goal is to find out who murdered Ms. Broussard. If your faith in Mr. Ford is justified, I don't see any reason those goals should conflict with one another."

Bishop's brows raised. "No, sir. They shouldn't."

Knoll looked at Detective Latimer. "Al, you'll get a copy of the videos from Gatlinburg that I mentioned. In one of them, you'll see a black Ford Expedition. The Seekers had an expert enhance footage taken in downtown Gatlinburg that same day. While I don't understand how this particular puzzle piece fits with everything else, there's no question that the SUV was registered to Ms. Broussard, and that she's the one who drove Abrams, Donnelly and three as yet unidentified masked men to Mr. Ford's home, where they proceeded with the aforementioned assault and abduction of Mr. Ford."

Al's eyes widened in surprise. Either he hadn't heard about the SUV, or no one had told him the theory yet that Audrey might somehow be involved.

"Another thing to consider in your investigation, Al, is the video of the assault. It clearly shows Mr. Ford's pistol was taken from him by Abrams. And yet, that same pistol is miraculously in Ms. Broussard's home when Mr. Ford awakens from his drug-induced state. If the ballistics come back proving Mr. Ford's gun killed her, that's extremely suspicious. Given all of the other circumstances leading up to him being in Ms. Broussard's home—including her history of contentious visits to Gatlinburg, as relayed to me by the Justice Seekers—I'm inclined to have more than reasonable doubts that Mr. Ford is the one who pulled the trigger. I strongly encourage you to look at both of our jailed deputies as suspects in the murder."

Stunned didn't come close to describing how Mason felt right now. From what Bishop had told him, Mason had been expecting a fair shake. But he hadn't expected the DA to essentially declare Mason not guilty.

Al straightened. "Sir, while I admire and respect Chief Ford from when I worked for him, I'm not prepared to say he didn't do this. The investigation is just starting. And you have to consider his most recent actions when judging his character. He kidnapped Ms. Cantrell."

"I'm not asking you to stop your investigation. What I'm telling you is that the bar is extremely high on this one. In order for my office to take this to court, you'll have to show me solid evidence, untainted by Abrams's and Donnelly's actions, that definitively proves guilt."

Al crossed his arms. "Understood."

"As to your comment about him kidnapping Ms. Cantrell, I've got a few thoughts to share on that."

Mason's stomach sank. This was the part he'd wished he could warn Hannah about. As if realizing he was looking at her, she glanced his way, her eyes wide with uncertainty. But he couldn't even nod his head without risking giving himself away. It was torture sitting there and doing nothing.

Knoll turned to face Landry. "Chief, when exactly were you going to tell me about the hidden hallway behind the wall in your office?"

Her father's face reddened. Mason exchanged a surprised glance with Bishop. The DA hadn't mentioned the secret entrance in the earlier meeting. Bishop had assumed he'd bought the theory that Mason had climbed out the window. Now the DA's poor treatment of the chief began to make sense.

Knoll leaned slightly forward to look at Hannah on the other side of her father. "You and I have discussed the history of this town. I know you studied it in school, as did I. It shouldn't come as a surprise that I also know a lot of these buildings have hidden panels off the stairways that access secret hallways. Just like the one that leads into your father's office."

Her father stiffened. "Now, wait a minute—"

"You might also be interested to know, Hannah, that our security guys sent me footage from the cameras in the parking garage. I'll bet you didn't think about the cameras when you and Mason exited the back stairs and got into your SUV, did you?"

The chief slumped like a balloon losing air.

Hannah tilted her chin defiantly as she addressed Knoll. "No, actually. It never occurred to me."

He laughed, seemingly amused. "The cameras also recorded you nearly running over Captain Murphy."

"I was in control of my vehicle at all times. If he hadn't moved, I would have swerved. He wasn't in any real danger."

A gasp across the room had her looking at Murphy.

"Oh, come on, Paul." She rolled her eyes. "How often did you and I drag race in high school? I whipped your butt every time and never crashed. And you know I'd never hurt you, or anyone else. You *know* it."

His face reddened. A few of the people in the room chuckled. "All right. In hindsight, maybe I made too big a deal out of it. But you can't deny you were helping a fugitive escape."

"No, I can't and won't deny it. And I'd do it again if given the chance."

"Hannah," her father cautioned.

She shook her head. "No, I've been silent too long."

"Ms. Cantrell." This time it was LeMarcus who spoke up. "As a lawyer, I strongly urge you not to say anything else without your own attorney present."

"I appreciate the advice," she said. "But I'm not taking it." She leaned forward to look at Knoll. "Enough of these games. You obviously know that I helped Mason escape. What you don't know is that as soon as Captain Murphy saw us, Mason wanted to surrender so he could keep me from getting into trouble. I'm the one who refused to stop. Why? Because I had every reason to fear for Mr. Ford's life. You mentioned this town's tarnished past. Mason's brother was railroaded to prison in a setup like the one playing out against Mason. Landon paid for the corruption with his life. I wasn't about to let that happen to Mason, not if there was anything I could do to stop it. Go ahead, arrest me if you want. But I won't apologize for doing the right thing."

Knoll's eyebrows had arched so high they were practically at his hairline by the time she finished. "Is there anything else you want to add to that speech?"

She leaned forward again. "As a matter of fact, there is. Mr. Ford never pulled a gun on me. He didn't kidnap me. Instead, he risked his own life by putting me in that cottage so I could go home to my family. He did that because he was worried that a search party might shoot me by accident. What you see here, Mr. Knoll, is a pattern. Every time someone needs help or protection, Mason Ford's first reaction is to help them, no matter the cost to himself." She turned her head and glared at Al. "*That* is the measure of his character. How dare you impugn him by suggesting otherwise. Your time would be better spent doing your job—finding out who killed Audrey and dropping all charges against the innocent man who has only ever loved her, even when she didn't deserve that love. He is the absolute last person who would harm her." She crossed her arms and sat back. "Now I'm done."

Mason, along with everyone else in the room, stared at her in shock. His heart had seemed to crack a little with every fierce declaration she'd made, every argument she'd said in his defense. He'd been agonizing about how she'd handle the revelation about the parking garage cameras, which was the information Bishop had told him right before the meeting. But in his worst-case imagined scenario, he'd never expected her to admit to everything, leaving herself completely vulnerable to prosecution.

He had to do something. He couldn't sit here hiding behind a disguise while this incredible, strong, amazing woman was going to battle for him, and putting herself at risk. He jumped up from his chair, only to be pushed back down by Bishop. Mason hadn't even seen him coming toward him.

"Oh, so sorry. Mr. Johnson, was it? I didn't realize you were getting up too. Were you heading to that coffee bar over there like me?"

Mason narrowed his eyes in warning.

Bishop narrowed his eyes too. He wasn't backing down. "Come on, I'll help you." He pulled Mason to his feet and shoved his cane in his hand.

It was either go along with Bishop's ploy, or deck him. While Mason debated his choices, Dalton was suddenly on his other side.

"Feeling a little shaky, Mr. Johnson? Here, we'll both help you." They each grabbed an arm, and even though he was just as big as either of them, together they were a force to be reckoned with.

When they were all three in the alcove, Mason jerked his arms free. He glared at them. Dalton grinned. Bishop busied himself making three cups of coffee. Mason leaned past the edge of the wall, frowning when Dalton blocked his way.

"I'm just going to see what they're doing," Mason gritted out in a harsh whisper.

Dalton moved, but not enough for Mason to easily get past him. He shook his head in exasperation, and peered around him to see what was going on.

Knoll shifted in his chair. "I think I've got the information I needed to make some decisions. I'll start with Mr. Ford. The kidnapping charge will be dropped. However, the murder charge stands."

Once again, the room erupted in chaos, with nearly everyone talking at once. Mason let out a deep breath, while Dalton swore beside him.

Knoll held up his hands, motioning for everyone to be quiet. When they settled down, he said, "I'm not saying he's guilty. But I can't ignore that he was found holding a gun over a murdered woman's body. Al will continue his investigation and once he's done, I'll make the final decision on whether to proceed with prosecution or drop all charges. However, I'm going to do something I've never done before in a murder case. I'm recommending that Mr. Ford be released on bail."

Mason blinked, waiting for the catch.

Knoll turned to the judge, sitting on his right. "I've been assured by Bishop that Mr. Ford has the means to have left the country if he'd wanted to. Therefore, as bizarre as it seems to say this after the earlier escape, I don't consider him a flight risk. Instead of fleeing Louisiana when he easily could have, he stayed here in the parish, presumably to prove his innocence."

The judge nodded his agreement. "You and I discussed this before we came here and my opinion hasn't changed. However, out of respect for Ms. Broussard's family, the amount has to be high, commensurate with the crime."

Mrs. Armstrong called out, "How high?"

"One million dollars."

Hannah visibly recoiled in her seat and shot Mason a worried glance.

He winked.

Her eyes widened.

The two lawyers conferred for a moment, then Armstrong spoke. "Agreed. I'll have a commercial bail bond arranged as soon as this meeting is over, with the usual required percentage paid in cash so that my client can be free until trial. Or until the charges are dropped."

Knoll arched a brow. "Your client can pay one hundred and twenty thousand dollars, cash, right away?"

It was LeMarcus's turn to reply. "*Our* client can pay the entire million in cash if he has to. But obviously we prefer a bond." He pulled a sheaf of papers out of his suit jacket pocket and handed them to the other lawyer.

Armstrong glanced through the papers, then took them to Knoll. "That's Mr. Ford's current bank statement. As you can see, the required 12 percent won't be a problem. I request that the court accepts that the client will pay and grants freedom immediately."

"That's pretty brazen." Knoll shrugged. "Judge?"

He considered it a moment. "Mrs. Armstrong, do I have your word that it will be paid? Right after this meeting? Knowing you could be disbarred for lying to the court?"

"You have my word."

"Very well. The court accepts those terms. Consider Mr. Mason Ford officially free on bond. But he'll have to show up in person, to prove he hasn't fled the country, and to give me confidence he'll be here for any required court appearances."

"Agreed."

Mason exchanged glances with Bishop and Dalton, and tapped his face. They nodded in understanding and formed a human wall in front of him, casually holding their coffee cups and effectively blocking anyone from seeing him.

"Next up," Knoll said, "my decision about Ms. Cantrell."

Mason couldn't see what was going on, but he listened intently as he pulled the fake paunch out from under his shirt.

"Hannah," Knoll said, his voice taking on more of a friendly tone. "We've worked together enough that I feel confident you're telling the truth. You strongly believe in Mr. Ford's innocence, and that his life could have been forfeit if you hadn't intervened. Therefore, I'll overlook your involvement in his escape, *and* the fake kidnapping. No charges will be filed against you."

Mason smiled and worked at a piece of glue on his neck, wishing he could see her. She'd probably been too overcome with emotion since she didn't say anything. His own relief was immeasurable. Maybe Bishop and Dalton had been right to intervene when they had. Otherwise, the outcome might not have been this favorable for either him or Hannah.

"As to you, Chief," Knoll said, "that video in the garage showed more than two people in the stairwell. You were there too. Except you went through the door to the lobby instead of into the parking garage. Obviously, you had the same concerns as your daughter. However, she's a civilian and you're a trusted member of law enforcement who deliberately helped a prisoner escape and then covered it up. If you had concerns, you should have followed the chain of command by contacting both the mayor and me. Together, we would have ensured his safety and avoided this huge hullabaloo about an alleged kidnapping. *You're fired.*"

"No," Hannah cried out. "You can't do that."

"Technically, you're correct. Only the mayor can fire your father. I spoke to him on the way here and he's in full agreement. He's in the process of sending over the signed paperwork and initiating an immediate search for a new chief. In the meantime, he's already appointed an acting chief, Captain Murphy. I swore him in over the phone."

Mason clutched the counter, guilt riding him hard. He'd created The Justice Seekers to help others who'd had their law enforcement careers destroyed. And here he was, destroying Landry's career. How could Landry, or Hannah, ever forgive him? Hell, how would he forgive himself?

The sound of footsteps crossing the room had Mason lifting his head. Dalton whispered, "Landry's giving his golden eagle lapel pins, badge and gun to Murphy."

"Chief, I didn't ask for this." Murphy's voice was laced with misery. "I'm truly sorry."

"Not your fault, Paul. I'm sure you'll do a good job. That's what matters."

Mason angrily shucked off the last of the glue on his face and turned around, still hidden behind his men.

"Just one more matter to take care of," Knoll said. "Mrs. Armstrong, LeMarcus, the judge has a busy schedule. He needs to know whether to wait here for your client to make the required bail agreement appearance. How long will it take to have him report to the police station?"

Mason strode past Bishop and Dalton to the chair that *Christopher Johnson* had vacated earlier and sat. "You wanted to see me?"

Chapter Eleven

Hannah endured another bone-crunching hug from her mom in her parents' foyer. She and her father had barely made it through the front door before her sisters and mother converged on them. If this was how they reacted after being told she *hadn't* been kidnapped, she probably wouldn't survive if she actually *had*.

"Help," Hannah silently mouthed to her sisters over her mom's shoulder. "Can't. Breathe."

Mary giggled.

Sarah gave her a smug *serves-you-right* look, but finally relented. "Come on, Mom. Your enthusiasm is about to kill your baby. I think you've broken at least three ribs already."

Her mom gave her one last hug, then reluctantly let go, wiping at her tears. "I'm just relieved you're okay. We've been worried sick."

"I know, and I'm so, *so* sorry. Everything happened really fast. Thinking about how it would impact you all didn't even enter my mind until later. But I promise, I never meant to hurt you with my lies."

"It's okay, sweetheart." Her mother looped her arm through Hannah's and tugged her from the foyer into the family room with her sisters and dad following. "I couldn't be prouder of you for standing up for what's right. You're a real hero."

Mary plopped down on one of the two couches. "*I'm* proud of her for snagging a real hottie. I hear that Mason Ford's ten times sexier than his brother Wyatt. And that's saying something. Wyatt's an 8, maybe even a strong 9. What's Mason, a 20?"

Hannah's face heated. "I didn't *snag* anyone."

Her mother shook her head at Mary. "Stop teasing her. I'm being serious."

"So am I." Mary grinned as Sarah sat on the opposite end of the couch. Their dad rolled his eyes from the other couch.

Her mother joined him, leaving Hannah no choice but to sit between her troublemaking sisters. They were both winking and grinning as if they were still in high school instead of married, and in Sarah's case, a mom.

"Hannah, dear," her mother said, "your dad mentioned something on the phone about Mr. Ford getting bail. Is he heading back to Tennessee? He lives in Gatlinburg, right?"

"He can't leave town," her father told her. "Condition of bail."

"Oh, I guess that makes sense. Well, I can't imagine him staying with that awful family of his. Where *is* your Mr. Ford, Hannah?"

She gritted her teeth as her sisters grinned. "He's not *my* Mr. Ford. There's nothing going on between us."

Sarah leaned in close. "But you wish there was."

Hannah shoved her but Sarah only laughed.

"Settle down, children." Since the order came from their father, they straightened up. But Mary couldn't resist one last salacious wink, with her face turned so her father couldn't see her of course.

Hannah shook her head in exasperation.

"Maybe we should offer him one of our guest rooms," her mother said.

Hannah blinked. "I don't think he—"

"He could stay with Hannah," Sarah interrupted. "She's got plenty of room. Don't you, sis?"

"Why, yes. I do, Sarah." She gave her sister a warning look, before turning to her mom. "But since he owns a cottage near the historic district, I don't think he'll be homeless anytime soon. That is, if he really is out on bail. At the end of the meeting with the DA, there was a revelation of sorts and the DA was ticked. He ordered everyone out of the squad room except for Mason, his lawyers and the judge. Dad and I don't know what happened after that."

"Oh dear," her mother said. "I do hope they worked out the problem." She patted Hannah's father's hand. "I'm sure one of your officers will get the scoop and call you with an update soon."

His face flushed and he tugged at his collar.

Hannah's mother narrowed her eyes suspiciously. "What's going on?"

He blinked. "What do you mean?"

"Don't give me that innocent look. You're hiding something. There's more to this business with Mason Ford than you've told us."

He sighed heavily. "I'm not trying to hide anything, Rachel. I was just waiting for a better time to tell you. These past few days have been emotional for all of us. I didn't want to dump bad news on you right now."

She made a disgusted face. "Mitchel James Landry. Since when have I been a delicate flower to wilt at the first hint of trouble? I've been a cop's wife most of my life, kissing you goodbye every morning and praying you'd come home safely. There's nothing worse you can throw at me than that. I can handle anything"

"Yeah, well, maybe not this."

Hannah bit her lip, knowing what he was about to say. Her heart ached as her father took her mother's hands in his.

"Rachel, honey, my career in law enforcement is over. I got fired."

Her mother burst into tears.

"Ah, honey. Don't cry." He pulled her against him and rested his chin on the top of her head.

Hannah exchanged a miserable glance with her sisters. *It's my fault,* she mouthed silently, a single tear sliding down her cheek. But rather than look outraged, they did what they always did when one of them was hurting—gave her their love and support. They sandwiched her between them and put their arms around her shoulders. The three musketeers, one for all, and all for one. She'd never been more grateful for the gift of her sisters than at this moment.

Her father shot her a helpless look and rubbed his hand up and down her mother's back. "I'm sorry, honey. I may not like what happened, but the mayor was right to let me go. Helping a fugitive escape and covering it up, well, obviously that's not something that should be tolerated in a chief of police. But, like Hannah, my conscience is at peace. We both did what we felt, and still feel, was the right thing to do. But hurting you is the last thing I ever wanted."

"Hurting me?" Her mother pushed out of his arms. "I'd despaired that this day might never come. I've been after you to retire since I retired from teaching ten years ago. But just when I thought you might finally agree, the Beauchamp mayor recruited you to move back here to try to straighten out this corrupt little town. I bet I cried for a week when you said yes."

He stared at her. "You cried? I never knew that."

"Because I didn't want you to know. Your job is to protect others. Mine is to protect you, to be supportive so you can save lives without worrying about me. But it's well past time you quit working so hard. We deserve to spend our golden years together."

"Golden years? We're not *that* old."

"Old enough. And the longer you're in law enforcement the worse the odds are that you'll get shot or seriously hurt. It's a relief that you won't be going back. I'm absolutely thrilled."

"I'm relieved that you're not upset like I thought you'd be. But, Rachel, honey, I don't know that we have enough in savings to do the things you'll want to do during our retirement. I should probably try to get a security guard job for a while or—"

"No, Mitch. You're not getting some job you're way overqualified for. We'll make do on my teacher's pension and your 401K and limit ourselves to whatever we can afford to do. As long as we have each other, we have all we need."

He gave her a skeptical look. "I've only been unemployed for a few hours. I'm not ready to make life-altering decisions about our future just yet."

"We'll figure it out together, starting tomorrow morning. Instead of leaving the house at the crack of dawn for work, you can catch up on some sleep. And when you're all rested and ready to face the day, I'll have a big old-fashioned breakfast waiting for you."

He cocked his head. "Eggs, bacon, biscuits?"

"And homemade gravy. Oh, and baked red-potato slices with onions and cheese. Your favorite."

"Darlin', you start feeding me like that and you'll have to roll me out of bed. I won't be able to move. But I sure will enjoy it." He kissed her and pulled her against his side.

"Are we invited to this amazing breakfast you're cooking tomorrow?" Sarah teased.

"You bring those adorable grandchildren of ours and I'll cook anything you want."

Sarah winced. "Thanks for that reminder. Daniel's got to be pulling his hair out with the kids about now. When I heard about Hannah, I headed out of there so fast I'm not even sure I said goodbye." She hugged Hannah's shoulders. "Now that I know she's okay, I'm going to head home before my husband files for divorce. But if that breakfast offer extends to the weekend, we'll bring the kids over then."

"That would be wonderful," her mom exclaimed. "Mary, what about you and Ian? Can you come too? You could bring those gorgeous retrievers. I haven't seen my fur-grandbabies in ages."

"Of course. It'll be fun. I need to head home now too, but this weekend is definitely a date." She hugged Hannah tight. "I'm so proud of you and Daddy for standing up for what's right." She crossed to the other couch and hugged their dad. "The mayor's an idiot to let you go. As far as I'm concerned, he doesn't deserve you, so good riddance."

"I second that." Sarah hugged him, then grabbed her purse from the end table. "You give us his address. I'll bring the toilet paper. We'll do his house up as pretty as you please."

Her mother gasped. "Sarah, don't you dare. None of you had better dare. Please tell me you've never actually done anything like that before."

Hannah laughed. "The stories we could tell."

"I don't think I want to know. Go on. I don't want the husbands mad that we kept you so long."

"I think I'll head out too," Hannah said. "I'd like to be in my own space to unwind after all this."

"Do what you need to do. But come back this weekend to celebrate your father's retirement."

"Hey," her dad complained. "I haven't agreed that I'm retiring just yet. I have to think on it."

She patted his hand. "Of course you do, dear. But we're still celebrating this weekend."

He chuckled. "I'm on to you, Rachel. You just want me fat and lazy so I never leave home again."

"Clever man." She kissed his cheek.

Hannah was relieved at how things were turning out. But after the goodbyes were said and she stepped outside with her sisters to leave, she suddenly realized that she didn't have a car. An officer had driven her and her dad home because he had to turn in his police-issued SUV. And her Tucson was still parked in Mason's barn.

Mary waved as she backed out of the driveway, then drove away.

Sarah was about to get in her car, when she looked around. "Where's your Tucson?"

"Actually, I just realized I haven't gotten it back from Mason since the, ah—"

"Fake kidnapping?"

She sighed. "Yeah. That. I'll head back inside and have a rental sent over. I don't want to take mom, and dad's car."

"No way. I can drive you home."

"It would add an hour to your trip since it's in the opposite direction of where you need to go. Besides, I need the rental anyway. There's no telling when I'll see Mason again and be able to get my car. I'd prefer to get the rental rather than be stranded at my house without transportation." When her sister hesitated, Hannah hugged her. "I'm a big girl. I've got this. Go. Give my favorite niece and nephew a hug, and kiss that sexy brother-in-law of mine. I'll see you all soon."

"I bet when Mary has kids, you'll tell her the same thing about them being your favorite."

"Probably. But Daniel will always be cuter than Ian."

Sarah laughed. "You're right about that. Take care, little sister. Call if you need me."

"Always."

After watching Sarah drive away, Hannah went back inside. Her parents were still on the couch, her mom's head against her dad's shoulder. They looked so content it made her heart swell with happiness instead of the guilt that had been consuming her.

"Car wouldn't start?" her dad asked. "Oh, wait. You don't have a car. Goodness me, I totally forgot. I'll get my keys and—"

A knock sounded on the door.

"Stay there. I'll get it." Hannah returned to the foyer and opened the door. Her stomach did a little flip when she saw who was there. "Um, hi."

"Hi yourself." Mason smiled, looking unbelievably sexy in a chic, linen suit that had to have been tailored for him to hug his broad shoulders so well. His team must have brought some of his clothes with them from Tennessee. Or maybe he'd gone back to his barn-apartment and gotten something. Either way, she definitely approved.

"*Good grief,* you look good."

His answering grin and knowing wink had her face turning warm.

"So do you. Always. I hope you don't mind that I'm here. I asked around at the station and was told an officer drove you and your dad to this address. It's your father's place, right?"

"It is. Mine's half an hour from here."

"And you don't have your Tucson because it's in my barn." He motioned toward the Altima parked in the driveway. "Rather conveniently, I have a car and would love to drive you home. That is, if you're not staying here."

"Honey, who is it?" her father called out.

She leaned past the doorway to see around the foyer wall. "It's Mason, Daddy."

"Well ask him in."

She turned back to Mason. "I'd love a ride. That was really nice of you to come all the way out here. But, um, would you mind coming in for just a minute? Otherwise I'll get lectured on my bad manners."

"Well we wouldn't want that." He winked again and stepped inside.

When she introduced him to her mom, she fairly swooned. Hannah couldn't believe her mother was blushing, or that Mason actually kissed the back of her hand like an old-world gentleman. Not only was he funny and clever and sexy, he knew how to turn on the charm. Thank goodness her sisters weren't here or they'd have teased her mercilessly, or fawned all over him like her mother was doing right now. She met her father's laughing gaze. He shrugged, obviously finding her mother's behavior amusing.

"I stopped by to offer Hannah a ride home because I still have her car," Mason told them. "But I also wanted to thank you, Chief Landry."

Her father winced at the title, but Mason continued.

"Very few people would have done what you and your daughter did. You both saved my life. And in return, you lost your job, your career, your livelihood. I owe you a debt I can never repay. But I hope this helps make up for your tremendous loss."

He pulled an envelope out of his suit jacket pocket and handed it to her father.

He frowned as he opened it and pulled out a piece of paper. His gaze shot to Mason's. "A check?"

"I know it's impersonal, but it's all I can do right now to try to make up for what happened."

He held the check toward Mason. "I didn't help you for financial gain. And even if I had, this would be way too much. I can't accept this."

"I don't think you understand, sir. By accepting that check, you're doing me a favor. You're helping assuage some of my guilt for the harm that helping me did to you and your family. My company's mission is to assist people in law enforcement who lose their jobs while trying

to do the right thing. You're the poster example of that."
He motioned toward the check her father was still holding.
"That's no more than I'd give one of my Seekers as a typical signing bonus. It's my way of thanking them for their
service. It's an honor to be able to do the same for you."

"Mason." He cleared his throat, his voice raw. "I appreciate what you're trying to do. But I can't—"

Hannah's mom grabbed the check and looked at it. Her
eyes widened in shock. "Yes, Mitch. You *can*. Do you realize what this means for us? You can retire without worrying whether we've saved enough. We can travel and
check off both our bucket lists. It's a miracle. Don't you
dare give it back."

Mason smiled. "Your wife is a wise woman, Chief. I
suggest you follow her advice. And please don't worry
about the amount. I can easily afford it."

Her father frowned. "Rachel, I thought you said as long
as we had each other, that's all we needed."

Her mother's cheeks took on a rosy hue. "That's still
true. But it doesn't mean that extra money wouldn't make
things a whole lot easier, and more fun." She handed him
the check. "It's your decision. I won't be mad either way.
But I think you're crazy if you say no."

He laughed, then handed it back to her. "For safekeep-
ing."

Her smile lit up the entire room.

Her father shook Mason's hand. "You've made my wife
happy. There's no better gift than that."

Hannah leaned against Mason's side and hugged him.
He smiled down at her before meeting her dad's gaze.
"There *is* one more thing, sir. I would appreciate it if you
and your wife would leave town for a while. Take a vacation. My treat. All expenses paid."

Her father eyed him warily. "Why?"

"A precaution. Abrams and Donnelly have escaped."

Hannah sucked in a breath. "What happened?"

"That's what I want to know," her father said.

"I don't have many details. The DA and I were finishing our meeting when Murphy sent for them so that Special Agent Holland could conduct an interview. An officer came running into the squad room a few minutes later, saying one of the guards was hurt and the prisoners were gone."

Hannah noted the worry lines on both men's faces. Her mother looked pale.

"Why are you concerned that they'd come after my parents? Dad didn't do anything to them."

"I had them arrested. We've had run-ins before, on other cases. They're a tight-knit pair and seem to egg each other on. I've reprimanded both of them in the past. If they're desperate, and out for revenge, I can see them coming after me. It wouldn't be the first time a criminal blamed the man who caught him instead of taking responsibility for his own actions." He kissed her mom. "Honey, how about pack us a bag. Just enough for a few days. We can stop back for more later if it looks like we'll be gone for a long time."

"A vacation sounds good to me. I can ask my friend Martha to come over and water the plants while we're gone. Hannah, can you let Sarah and Mary know we have to postpone the weekend plans? Maybe you can all come see us wherever we land."

"Sure, Mom. Whatever you need."

"Thanks, Hannah. Dear, I'll have us packed in ten minutes." She hurried down the hallway to their bedroom.

Her father pulled out his cell phone. "I imagine I've still got allies at the office. I'll get a status on the search for our two escapees." He opened the sliding glass door and stepped onto the back deck.

Hannah took one of Mason's hands in hers. "If they're

out for revenge, you could be a target too. They risked everything to frame you, and yet it was your security video that brought them down."

"I agree. It's one of the reasons I wanted to see you. How would you like to stay with me for a while?"

She blinked, a delicious heat spreading through her. "*Stay* with you?"

He took both her hands in his, threading their fingers together. "I'm going to lie low until these two fools are caught. My lawyer's renting an estate outside of town for my team and me. One of the Seekers is setting up security right now. There's a guesthouse on the property, a good distance from the main house." He cleared his throat. "It's easily big enough for two."

Her fingers jerked in his as she drew a shaky breath.

As if unable to resist the temptation, he pressed a whisper-soft kiss against her forehead, before pulling back. She shivered in response.

"Tell me if I'm reading the signals wrong," he said. "But I believe that you and I have a connection, something special, rare, something that could be…" He shook his head as if struggling for the right words. "I want to explore this… bond, this attraction, whatever it is between us. I'm asking if you'll share the guesthouse with me, at least until Abrams and Donnelly are rounded up again. Maybe even for the duration of the investigation, if you want. It's definitely what I want. Assuming you don't tire of me." He gently feathered her hair back from her face. "This shouldn't be happening, with everything else going on. It's the last thing that should be consuming my thoughts, keeping me awake at night—"

"What's keeping you awake at night?" Her voice was barely above a whisper as she stared up into his beautiful, incredibly expressive eyes.

He cupped her face in his hands. "*You*, sweet Hannah.

You're what keeps me up at night. I'm falling for you. Please tell me I'm not the only one."

She stepped close, reveling in the heat of his body. Craving the feel of his skin against hers. Wanting more, so much more, but well aware that either of her parents could walk in at any moment. She settled on smoothing her hands up the front of his shirt, caressing the hard contours of his chest. "Mason?"

"Yes?" His voice was a deep rasp of need.

"You're not the only one."

He let out a ragged breath, tightening his arms around her. Ever so slowly, he leaned down, angling his mouth toward hers. Closer, closer. The tension built between them until she thought she might scream if he didn't kiss her, *right now.*

Bam!

He grabbed her and dived to the floor, his body wrapped protectively around hers.

Bam! Bam!

She stared up at him in shock. "Gunshots?"

"Rifle fire." He shook his head in disgust. "And I don't have a gun because of the bail agreement." He raised up, looking toward the front windows.

"Mason, my purse. You can use my gun." She looked around, trying to remember where she'd left it.

He scrambled onto his knees and peered over the back of the couch. "Hannah, stay here. Don't move."

"Wait, I'm getting the gun." She reached for her purse on the end table but Mason didn't wait. He took off running toward the back of the house. *The back of the house?* Her father!

She shoved to her feet and ran past the hallway just as her mother ran out of the bedroom. Hannah stumbled to a halt.

"Did I hear shooting?" Her mother's eyes were wide with fear.

"Mason's checking it out. Go back in the bedroom, Mom, please. Get down on the floor."

Hannah ran to the back door, then pressed her hand to her throat. Her father was lying on the deck, not moving, blood saturating his hair, his shirt. Mason was kneeling beside him, pressing his wadded up suit jacket against her father's wounds.

She jerked open the sliding glass door so hard it slammed against the frame and bounced back against her. She shoved it back again. "*Daddy*. Mason, what—"

"Call 911."

So much blood. Oh God. Daddy. Daddy. She started shaking. Spots swam in front of her eyes.

"Hannah!"

She jumped at his shout, frowning in confusion. "What are you— He can't— I don't— *Daddy*—"

"Hannah. Listen to me. Your dad's been shot. Do you understand?"

She blinked, then nodded. "Yes, he—"

"I've got to keep pressure on the wounds. I need you to call 911. Hurry!"

His words galvanized her into action. She ran inside and grabbed her phone.

"Hannah?" Mason yelled again.

She sprinted to the back door, phone in hand.

His agonized gaze met hers. "Tell them to send a chopper."

Chapter Twelve

Mason straightened his tie and tugged his latest suit jacket into place outside the main entrance to the surgical waiting room. Alexandria's Rapides Regional Medical Center was the closest level one trauma center to Beauchamp, but it had still been an hour and a half's drive. Thankfully, the medical chopper got Landry here much faster than that. He was in surgery long before Hannah and her mother arrived, followed by her sisters. Mason had been delayed because he'd had to get special permission from the DA to leave the parish. Since Al was seated about ten feet from Hannah's family, it was a good thing he'd taken that extra precaution. Otherwise, Al would probably arrest him. He still might try if Mason didn't head him off.

A quick glance confirmed that Dalton and Bryson were inside the waiting room, discreetly keeping watch. But he didn't see his newest Seeker, Eli. He was supposed to come here after bringing Mason a fresh suit that wasn't covered with blood.

The sound of voices down the long main hallway had Mason looking that way. Eli was facing him, talking to a dark-haired man with his back to Mason. He seemed familiar, but at this distance, without being able to see his face, Mason didn't have a clue who he was. When Eli spotted him, he said something else to the man, then hurried over.

"Hey, boss. The suit looks good."

"I appreciate you bringing it." He motioned toward the stranger who was continuing down the hall away from them. "Was there a problem?"

"What?" He glanced where Mason had gestured. "Oh. Just some guy asking for directions to the men's room. I'd just come back from there myself so I knew where it was." He looked toward the waiting room, then back at Mason. "Bryson and Dalton knew I was leaving. Is…is that okay?"

"Of course." Mason smiled reassuringly, hating the twinge of suspicion just because his newest Seeker, and fellow Louisianan, was talking to someone he didn't recognize. Not knowing the *whys* and *whos* behind Audrey's murder and the frame-up had him leery about trusting anyone he didn't know all that well. Eli certainly fell into that category, having only been on the team for a few months.

"Have you seen Bishop? I called him from the DA's office and asked him to act as bodyguard for Landry."

Eli grinned. "Bishop's in surgery."

"*In* surgery?"

"He told the doctors that he's not leaving Landry's side and they'd better make sure the chief pulls through or he'll hold them personally accountable. They had him scrub up and gown up. And since you somehow convinced the hospital administrator to honor our concealed carry permits inside the building, Bishop's even packing in the OR. His pistol is wrapped in sterile plastic, but he still has it on him."

Somehow had been a generous donation in Mitch Landry's name. Heck, they might even name a wing of the hospital after him as a result. But the outrageous expense ensured the Seekers could conceal carry in the hospital and that they had full access to just about anywhere they needed to go. Mason had been determined to remove any barriers that could interfere with the Seekers here in Alexandria protecting the Landry family. The rest of the team was still in Beauchamp, pounding the pavement, going door-to-door, examining the evidence collected by the crime scene techs. They were doing everything possible to prove Mason's innocence.

"Thanks, Eli. Keep up the good work."

The look of relief on his face had Mason feeling even more guilty for being suspicious. But it didn't take the suspicions away.

He headed into the waiting room, nodding at Bryson and Dalton, who immediately spotted him. Hannah saw him too, and motioned for him to join her and her family. He held up a hand to let her know it would be a minute.

Al had pushed to his feet as soon as Mason walked in. His hand was hovering near the bulge beneath his suit jacket, no doubt his service weapon. Stopping in front of him, Mason handed Al his get-out-of-jail-free card, the signed agreement from the DA that said he could leave Sabine Parish for the purpose of going to and from Rapides Medical Center.

"Is this legit?" Al frowned at the paper. "I've never heard of Knoll doing this before."

"Feel free to call and check."

"Maybe I will." He handed it back and sat. But instead of taking out his phone, he crossed his arms and frowned his displeasure at the far wall.

Mason sat beside him.

Al's mouth tightened and he continued his study of the peeling wallpaper.

"I'm sorry about everything that's happened, Al. I meant no disrespect to you or anyone else at Beauchamp PD. But when your life's on the line, you'll do almost anything to survive."

"Yeah, well. Apparently that includes not trusting old friends. And bringing in a lot of outsiders who think they're better than the rest of us."

"Not better. Different. And can you blame me for wanting people by my side who aren't from Beauchamp? After my family's history here, including *recent* history? Honestly?"

Al sighed heavily. "You make it dang hard to hold a grudge."

Mason held out his hand. "Truce?"

Al smiled reluctantly and shook his hand. "Truce. As long as you keep me in the loop going forward and don't pull any more stunts."

"I'll keep you in the loop as much as possible. And I'll only pull a stunt if someone's life is in danger and I don't feel I have another choice. Fair enough?"

"Fair enough." He motioned toward Hannah and her family. "They're glaring daggers at me like they think I'm about to arrest you. I can only imagine what would happen if I tried. Go on. They don't pay me to sit and gab with murder suspects." He smiled, letting Mason know he was teasing. Partly, at least.

Instead of joining Hannah, Mason crossed to Dalton and leaned down so no one would overhear. "Eli was out in the hall talking to a dark-haired man in jeans and a blue blazer a few minutes ago. Have you seen that guy?"

"No. Is he someone you know?"

"Not sure. He seemed familiar but he was far away and I didn't see his face. Eli swears he was a stranger needing directions."

"Height? Weight?"

"Six foot one, tops. Weight's hard to judge because of the blazer but he had an athletic build, smaller than me."

"I'll check around, see if some of the nurses or other patients spotted him."

"Thanks, Dalton. Be discreet. It's probably nothing, and I don't want Eli thinking I suspect him of something."

"But you do?"

He shrugged. "I'm being extra cautious."

Dalton clasped his shoulder. "I've got this." He stood and crossed to Bryson. After whispering to him for a moment, Dalton left the waiting room.

Mason headed to the corner of the room to greet Hannah and her family. His heart nearly broke when he saw the tears in their eyes and the stark fear etched in their expressions. After a quick greeting to all of them, he knelt in front of Rachel Landry so they were at eye level.

"Mrs. Landry, is there anything I can do for you? Anything you need while you wait for word on your husband?"

She twisted a tissue in her lap. "You saw him, after he was…you saw him. I haven't talked to any doctors. No one will tell me anything. The volunteer at the desk over there will only say he's still in surgery. How bad is it? Do you think…do you think he'll make it?"

Hannah touched her shoulder. "Mama, don't ask him something like—"

"It's okay." He smiled at her, then took her mother's hands in his. "I'll tell you what I do know, Mrs. Landry. I know that your husband has a reputation for being an honorable, devoted family man who loves you and your daughters very much. I've also heard he's a fighter, fighting for what he believes in, for what he knows is right and for what matters most to him. *You're* what matters most. I know that he won't give up, and he'll do everything he can to try to come back to you."

She let out a sob and reached for him. He pulled her close, letting her cry against his shoulder as he gently rocked her back and forth. Hannah and her sisters smiled through their tears. He hated that they were all going through such agony. They were good people. They didn't deserve this. No one did.

After she'd calmed down, she moved to sit between Sarah and Mary and closed her eyes with her head on

Mary's shoulder. Mason took the seat she'd vacated and sat beside Hannah, holding her hand while they waited for news. Sarah smiled at the two of them, then laid her head back and closed her eyes.

Another hour went by before the volunteer that Mrs. Landry had mentioned gave them an update. Essentially it was the same as before, that he was still in surgery. But that meant he was still alive. And where there was life, there was hope.

Paul Murphy walked into the waiting room a few minutes later. He spoke quietly to Al before coming over. Hannah stiffened. Mason squeezed her hand and straightened in his chair.

"Mr. Ford, Hannah." He greeted her sisters, then smiled sadly at their mom. "Mrs. Landry, I want you to know that everyone at the station is pulling for your husband. It's been an honor working for him these past few years. I've certainly learned a lot. If it was in my power, I'd reinstate him immediately, and I know I'm not the only one who feels that way."

Her chin wobbled and she gave Hannah a helpless look.

Hannah cleared her throat, getting his attention. "My mother appreciates your sentiments, Paul. But she can't talk right now. It's too hard."

"I understand. My apologies if my being here puts additional stress on you all. I want you to know that we're working hard to find out who's responsible for what happened to Chief Landry. The obvious suspects are the deputies who escaped. But we're not jumping to conclusions. We're exploring every lead."

He motioned to Al, who was watching them. "Detective Latimer would like to ask you some questions about what happened while it's still fresh in your minds. He's been waiting, out of respect for what you're going through. But we really need to jump on this. Which of you saw what happened to the Chief?"

"No one." Mason said. "He was on the back deck. Mary and Sarah had already left when it happened. The shots were fired while Mrs. Landry was in her bedroom. Hannah and I were in the main room. Neither of us saw the shooters. We only saw the aftermath. But I did hear tires squealing right after the shooting, so it seems likely it was a drive-by."

Paul's expression mirrored his disappointment. "You didn't see the vehicle?"

"No. I couldn't even tell you which direction they were going, though obviously they had to drive down the street that runs behind the Landry home in order to have a line of sight into the backyard. If you haven't already, I recommend you canvass the neighborhood for any doorbell security videos or other home security cameras. Check out businesses within a five-mile radius for surveillance cameras to determine what vehicles were in the vicinity shortly after the time of the shooting. You might get lucky and trace some license plates to potential suspects."

"I think we're already doing all that, but I'll put a bug in Al's ear to be sure. How soon after the shooting did someone call 911?"

"I'd say one to two minutes." He glanced at Hannah. "Does that seem right?"

"A shot rang out. You tackled me to the floor to protect me just as two more shots sounded. I swear you were on the back deck within seconds of that."

"Who called 911?" Murphy asked.

"I did," Hannah said. "Mason was helping my father, trying to stop the bleeding." Her mother's face blanched. Hannah reached across Mason to squeeze her arm.

Mason met Murphy's gaze. "You're looking for a rifle, guarantee it. There's no mistaking that sound."

"Good to know. There were three shots? With a pause in between the first and the rest?"

"That's my recollection. Hannah?"

"Yes. One shot, a pause, then two more."

"Is there anything else you can add?" Murphy asked. "Is there any point in sending Al over to question you?"

Hannah shook her head no.

"I'll add one thing," Mason said. "Chief Landry was on the back deck, alone, talking on the phone for several minutes before the shooting happened. They don't have a fence around their property, nothing obstructing the view. Whoever pulled the trigger knew exactly who they were shooting."

Murphy shook Mason's hand. "Thank you. I'll relay the information to Al. And we'll let all of you know as soon as we have anything substantive in this investigation."

No sooner had Murphy left, taking Al with him, than a doctor in green scrubs entered the waiting room. He spoke to the volunteer at the information desk. She pointed them out, but instead of coming over, the doctor told her something else and left. She rounded the desk and started across the room toward them.

Hannah clutched Mason's hand, her expression filled with dread as she and her family prepared themselves for whatever they were about to hear. Mason knew that look, knew that feeling. He also knew the soul-shattering blow of being told that a family member hadn't made it. He prayed that Hannah and her family weren't about to receive that devastating news.

The lady stopped in front of them, her polite smile as benign and difficult to interpret as the *Mona Lisa*'s. "Mrs. Landry, Doctor Stanton would like to speak in private to you and your family about your husband."

Chapter Thirteen

Hannah sat with her mom and sisters in the tiny meeting room as Doctor Stanton gave them the update they'd both wanted and dreaded. Mason leaned against the far wall. He'd offered to give them privacy and wait outside, but they'd all emphatically told him they wanted him there. Hannah felt it was a testament to his strength and kindness that he was the rock her family was leaning on, even though they barely knew him. She, of course, felt like she'd known him for years. And so far, every wonderful thing that Olivia had said about him had proven to be true.

"I don't understand," her mother said, her voice raw. "His *ribs* are broken?"

Sarah patted her hand. "If you'll quit interrupting him, maybe it will all make sense, Mama."

Stanton looked at them over the top of his glasses. "I know this can be confusing."

"Can you start over, please?" Hannah asked. "I think we're all having trouble with the medical terms you're throwing out."

"Sure. I'll try to summarize it without the jargon. Mr. Landry made it through surgery without any major complications. After he leaves recovery, he'll be moved to intensive care for around-the-clock monitoring. The bullets nicked his spleen, left kidney and fractured a couple of ribs. There was a lot of bleeding from the head wound as well as the internal injuries so we had to give him several pints of blood. Whoever called for the medical chopper no doubt saved his life. If he'd gotten here a few minutes later, I honestly don't think we could have saved him."

Hannah smiled her gratitude at Mason, then caught her mother's confused glance. "What is it, Mom?"

"The gunshot wound to his head. He didn't talk about it other than the bleeding." She clutched her ever-present tissues. "Is he...will he ever be the same again? Will he wake up?" Her voice broke and Mary hugged her close.

"I'm so sorry if I gave you the impression that he was shot in the head. He wasn't. The head injuries, based on what the EMTs relayed about the scene, were likely a result of him slamming his head against the deck when he fell. His scalp was lacerated and bled extensively. He's got a concussion, and there's a possibility his brain could swell. But we'll monitor him closely and act quickly if the worst happens."

Her mother blinked. "The worst? What does that mean?"

"Poor choice of words on my part. There are many things that can go wrong. Your husband suffered serious injuries and will need rehabilitation in order to make a full recovery. But while I can't make any promises, I'm optimistic he'll make a full recovery."

Her mother's expression still seemed confused, but there was also something else there. Hope. "Are you... are you saying he's going to be okay?"

"I'm saying he has an excellent chance of being okay, yes, ma'am."

She covered her face and started crying again.

While Hannah's sisters comforted her mother, she shook the doctor's hand. "Thank you so much, Doctor Stanton. When can we see my father?"

"You can head to the ICU waiting area now. As soon as he's in a room, someone will let you know."

The long wait was excruciating, but finally they were brought to the ICU to her father's room. Seeing him lying there, still unconscious, hooked up to monitors broke Hannah's heart. He was alarmingly pale. Wires and tubes formed a spiderweb around him. But he was alive. The doctor was optimistic. And it was all because of Mason that her father had made it this far.

While her mother and sisters hovered by his bedside, Hannah pulled Mason to the other side of the room by the door.

He looked down at her, his brows raised in question. She cupped his face and stood on tiptoe to give him a quick kiss. As she pulled back, his lips curved in a surprised, but achingly sweet smile.

"What was that for?" he whispered.

Her heart was full as she looked up at him. "Thank you. Thank you for running outside to help my father even though the shooters could have still been there. Thank you for working tirelessly to keep him from bleeding out before help could arrive. Thank you for somehow knowing exactly what to say to reach me through my panic and getting me to call 911. And thank you, thank God for you, that you knew to request the helicopter so we didn't lose time waiting for an ambulance, only to realize the chopper was needed. Mason, there's no question that my father would be dead right now if it wasn't for you. *Thank you.*"

She kissed him again.

"I'd ask for one of those too, but Daniel might not like it."

Hannah jerked back at the sound of Sarah's voice.

Sarah smiled through her tears and put her arms around Mason, giving him a tight hug. His eyes widened in surprise, but he hugged her back. When she let go, she rolled her eyes at Hannah. "Stop looking so jealous. It's obvious who puts that spark in his eyes. And it's not me."

Hannah felt her face heat. Sarah laughed and put her arms around her shoulders. "Thank you, Mason. I heard what Hannah said and I second it 1,000 percent. So do Mom and Mary. We know how lucky we are to still have our father with us. No, not *lucky*. Fortunate, and grateful that you were there to save him."

He shook his head. "I don't deserve such praise, but I'm honored just the same."

Sarah started to say something else, but a knock sounded on the door.

Mason gently pushed them behind him, once again being the fierce protector even though he had two men stationed outside the door to watch over them. Let alone one of Beauchamp PD's officers by the nurse's desk watching out for Donnelly, Abrams or anyone else who might intend her father harm.

After opening the door a crack and speaking to someone, he gave Hannah a surprised look. "Do you and your family feel like having a visitor?"

"A visitor? Who?"

"My sister. Olivia."

After a brief greeting with his sister, Mason stepped out of the room so she could visit Hannah and her family. Dalton was leaning against the far wall and subtly motioned toward the nurse's desk a short distance away. There, speaking to one of the nurses, was the man Mason had seen earlier with Eli. Same dark hair, jeans and blue jacket. But this close, Mason realized the man wasn't just familiar.

He was his brother. Wyatt.

Chapter Fourteen

Mason leaned against the far wall beside Dalton, watching his brother flirt with one of the nurses at the nursing station. "Looks like you found the guy who was talking to Eli."

Dalton arched a brow. "Looks a lot like you."

"I never thought so, growing up. My older brother, Landon, was practically my twin."

"And the woman who was with him?"

"Baby sister. Olivia. There were six of us—Landon, me, Ava, Charlotte…" He nodded toward the nurse's desk. "And Wyatt."

His brother laughed at whatever the nurse had said, then started across the hall toward Landry's room. Bishop shifted his weight, blocking the door.

Wyatt put his hands on his hips. "Hey, man. Do you mind? I need to get in there."

Bishop pointed across the hall.

Wyatt looked over his shoulder, then slowly turned around. He hesitated, then with a noticeable lack of enthusiasm, closed the distance between them. "Mason."

"Wyatt. You don't seem surprised to see me in Louisiana."

He hooked his fingers into the belt loops on his jeans. "Considering your name was all over the news for kidnapping someone, can't say that I am. Wanted for murder too. *Audrey's* murder. Now *that* was a surprise. Chief Ford, a common criminal. Who knew you could ever fall so low." He motioned toward the Beauchamp police officer sitting a short distance away. "I assume he's taking you back to jail after you finish doing whatever you were brought here to do?"

Dalton stiffened. Bishop took a step forward, as if to intervene, but Mason subtly shook his head.

"I've missed you too, Wyatt. How's your financial advisor business these days?"

He frowned. "Aren't you even going to deny the charges? Protest your innocence?"

"Would it matter if I did?"

Wyatt swore. "Nothing ever shakes your calm, does it? I know you wouldn't kidnap anyone and you certainly would never hurt Audrey. Heck, I doubt you'd cross a street unless you were at the corner with the walking sign flashing."

His brother would be shocked to know what lines he'd cross these days for true justice. But at least his brother didn't believe he was a murderer. "Then why do you seem so aggravated? What's the problem?"

"Problem?" His jaw clenched. "The grapevine says a couple of corrupt deputies abducted you and forcibly brought you here, then set you up to be charged for murder. And it never occurred to you to ask your own brother for help? Or call your family and tell us what was going on?"

"I was too busy trying not to get killed to worry about catching up."

He rolled his eyes. "What *is* going on? And why are you here, outside Chief Landry's room, instead of in jail?"

Mason debated telling him anything. His brother had rarely ever expressed concern for him in the past. But he relented and told him the nickel version of what had happened.

Wyatt winced. "That's just crazy. I'm glad the DA

seems to be working with you, though. And let you out on bail." He motioned toward Dalton. "Is he one of your *Justice Seekers*, here to rescue you?"

Dalton pushed away from the wall and offered his hand. "The name's Dalton Lynch."

Wyatt shook his hand.

Instead of letting go, Dalton held on, until Wyatt met his gaze. "I'm a very good friend of your brother's, as well as his employee. As for rescuing, he took care of that himself. He also rescued Chief Landry, saved his life. *That's* why he's here, in the hospital." He let go, and leaned back against the wall.

Wyatt eyed him as if he was a rattlesnake and had just bitten him. From the way their knuckles had whitened when they'd shaken hands, Mason imagined there'd been some kind of challenge going on. There was no question that Dalton had won.

"Behind you," Mason said, "guarding the Chief's door is Bishop. Another good friend. Also a Seeker."

Wyatt held out his hand. Bishop crossed his arms.

His face reddening, Wyatt turned back to Mason. "Real friendly fellas."

"The best."

Wyatt shook his head, clearly exasperated.

"Now that you know why I'm here, why are *you* here? Hannah didn't mention that she knew you. Are you friends of one of the other Landrys? Or is Olivia having another bad spell?"

"Hannah? You're on a first name basis with the chief's daughter? You don't waste time, do you?"

If Wyatt could have seen the deadly look in Bishop's eyes behind him, he'd probably have taken off running. Mason didn't answer his brother's childish question.

His brother sighed. "Yes, Olivia's having a tough time. I try to give her space. She's got her own suite of rooms at my house. But I watch over her, check on her. It's what family does. They stick together."

Ignoring his latest gibe, especially since it was his family's choice to ignore him, not the other way around, he asked, "Has she been to her therapist? Is she taking her meds?"

"That's where we're going after we leave here, to her doctor. I'm going to request that he adjust her medication, at least for the short term. As soon as she heard about Hannah's dad getting shot, she lost it. Took forever to calm her down. Luckily she's not one to listen to the news or plug in to local gossip, so she hasn't heard about Audrey or what's going on with you yet. I'd appreciate it if you don't tell her any of that, at least until we've been to her doctor."

"I can't imagine Audrey's death would bother her any more than any other stranger's. She didn't like Audrey when we were together, and that's ancient history."

"So is Landon's death but that still bothers some of us."

Dalton swore under his breath.

"Wyatt," Mason said, "I'm well aware that you blame me for Landon's death because I was the chief of police and couldn't keep him from being convicted. And you blame me for Olivia's problems afterward. But this isn't the place or time to go into all of that. I just wanted to know if Olivia is okay. If there's something I can do to help, please let me know. You've been taking care of her for a long time, so I'll defer to your wishes. I won't tell her about Audrey and the charges against me until you think it's okay to do so. But I don't know if the Landrys will mention it."

Wyatt studied him a moment, then blew out a long breath. "If they tell her, I'll deal with it. You're right that she's never been a fan of Audrey. But the circumstances of Audrey's death are similar, at least at first blush, to what happened with Mandy and Landon. I'm worried the similarity could send her into a tailspin. Since she's already having trouble coping with Hannah's family troubles, adding her favorite brother's on top of that would likely send her over the edge. I'd like to avoid a hospitalization for her if I can. It's been years since we had to do that."

Mason winced. "I didn't think about it that way."

"You should have."

Dalton stepped forward, forcing Wyatt to back up or be hit by the brim of Dalton's Stetson. "Mason's too nice and polite to stand up for himself with his so-called family. I'm not. And neither is Bishop. I suggest you either figure out how to be respectful or move down the hall, before Bishop and I lose the last of what little patience we have left with the likes of you."

Wyatt gave him a disgusted look. But he was wise enough to realize that Dalton wasn't bluffing. He crossed to one of the chairs by the police officer and sat, looking anywhere but at Mason and the others.

Mason leaned against the wall as Dalton did the same. "You know I don't need you to fight my battles."

"I know. But if he'd said one more nasty thing to you, I'd have ended up arrested. So I figure I was doing you the favor of not having to bail me out."

Mason smiled. "If you put it that way, thanks."

"No problem."

Mason eyed Wyatt's profile, wishing he knew how to heal the rift between them, a rift that had begun the moment that Landon was charged with murder. Olivia had been inconsolable and Wyatt had been the one to calm her down when their parents and sisters were wrapped up trying to help Landon, and Mason had been trying to find the real killer.

Olivia had fallen apart, and the one left to pick up the pieces was Wyatt. He'd appointed himself her guardian angel, moved her in with him, and had been performing that duty ever since. Hannah was right when she'd said Olivia was fragile. She'd been so young when Landon died, only fifteen. Now, at twenty-three, she seemed to be doing well when he spoke to her on the phone or saw her during one of her rare visits to Gatlinburg. But obviously she was struggling more than he'd realized.

When the door finally opened, both Olivia and Hannah stepped outside the room. Hannah hugged Olivia, and then Olivia hugged Mason.

"Sorry to leave before we can catch up," she said. "But I, ah, have an appointment. See you later?"

"Of course. I won't leave town without making sure I see you first."

She smiled and went to Wyatt, who led her away without a backward glance.

"Brr." Hannah rubbed her hands up and down her arms. "A bit frosty between you and your brother. And Olivia didn't seem to have a clue why you were here, so I didn't mention anything about what's happened to you. None of us did."

"I appreciate it. Wyatt's trying to keep that from her for now, to protect her. I'm sure he'll resent me even more because of it. He owns a financial investment company and has to take time off whenever Olivia needs help."

"Your other sisters can't help her? Ava and Charlotte? I remember Olivia saying they're both married and live in other towns, but couldn't they come home if Olivia needs them?"

"I suppose they could. But Wyatt and Olivia are really close. He considers it his job to take care of her."

"Well if he chooses to be the only family member to watch after her when she needs assistance, that's on him. She's got your parents and two sisters who could help. And I'm sure you would too if she reached out to you."

"I've tried to get her to move to Gatlinburg and stay with me. But she doesn't want to leave Beauchamp."

"Well there you go. Your family has made it impossible for you to live here, so you've done all you can. Stop feeling guilty."

He arched a brow. "What makes you think I feel guilty?"

"I see it in your eyes, hear it in your voice when you talk about her. Nothing that has happened to your family is your fault. I really wish you could believe that."

"Most of the time, I do. It's harder when I'm here. Ready to go back in the room to see your dad?"

"I am. But I wanted to finish that conversation we were having at my parents' house first, before…" She swallowed. "Before my father was shot. Is that offer to stay at the guesthouse with you still open?"

Heat flashed through him. He had to clear his throat before trying to talk. "Of course, but I thought you'd want to stay with your family now."

"Tonight, definitely. After that, it depends on how well he does. The nurses aren't happy with how many of us are in there with him. They want to limit the number of visitors. Mom is staying. She shut them right down when they said she couldn't. They agreed to bring in a cot for her. My sisters and I will take turns sitting with her, bringing her food and fresh clothes. Sarah and Mary will go home soon to pack bags for a longer-term stay. I know Sarah has to get a babysitter to watch her kids so her husband can go back to work. I'll need more clothes too. It's all just…so complicated. And even though I want to be here for my family, I'm itching to get into the investigation too. I want to use my degree for something really useful—finding out who shot my father and helping clear the charges against you."

He tucked a few loose strands of her hair behind her ears. "I've got a whole team working on that. You don't have to do anything."

"I want to. This is as personal for me now as it is for you. If you're worried about my safety, then include me.

Let me work with you. Because if you don't, I'll investigate on my own."

"Sounds like blackmail to me."

"It's my first time being a blackmailer. How am I doing?"

He smiled. "I'd say pretty well. But I'm not sure it counts, since I'd rather have you with me anyway." He motioned toward the Beauchamp police officer, who was openly watching them. "Unfortunately, I can't stay much longer. The DA never intended for me to be here long-term. I need to return to Sabine Parish."

"Hopefully I can join you soon." She stepped close and pressed a quick kiss against his lips. "Thank you, Mason. For everything." She squeezed his hand, then headed back into her father's room.

Mason let out a ragged breath. When he felt Dalton's stare, he held up a hand to stop whatever he was going to say. "Don't make me hurt you."

"I have no idea what you're talking about." Laughter was heavy in his tone.

Mason crossed to Bishop, with Dalton following. "I'm heading back to Beauchamp. If you don't mind standing guard tonight, I'll send Jaxon to spell you early in the morning."

"I'll stay as long as you need me."

He clasped Bishop's shoulder in thanks. "I'll update the hospital administrator to smooth the way so Jaxon can conceal carry while he's here too. Dalton, can you stand guard until Bishop gets some dinner? Then head directly to the estate?"

"No problem. As long as he doesn't take too long."

Bishop rolled his eyes and stepped away from his spot by the door so Dalton could take up his stance.

Bishop glanced at Mason as they headed down the hall. "What's happening at the estate?"

"Team meeting. I'll have someone include you by phone. We need to talk strategy, make assignments, figure out who's doing what. I want to get those bastards, Donnelly and Abrams. And figure out who murdered Audrey. It's time to catch a killer."

Chapter Fifteen

Hannah had been surprised later that week when Bishop picked her up at the hospital and said the remote property outside of town that Mason had rented was the infamous Fontenot estate. Everyone in Beauchamp had heard about this place, though few had ever seen it. *Fontenot's Folly*, as the locals called it, was rumored to be a mishmash of architectural styles that formed a ridiculous joke of a house. The owner had spent a small fortune designing, redesigning and furnishing the home in an attempt to convince his wife to move from New York to Louisiana for their retirement. It had taken one trip to Beauchamp for her to decide this wasn't the place for her. Fontenot's Folly had remained vacant ever since.

She'd assumed the home had fallen into disrepair in the decades since it had been built and was probably ready to be dozed by now. But as Bishop parked his black Dodge Charger in the circular driveway behind nearly a dozen other vehicles, the view through her passenger window proved all of her assumptions were completely wrong.

The main house was absolutely gorgeous and pristine. Although definitely a mishmash of styles, from French Colonial to creole cottage, it somehow managed to blend them perfectly. Traditional white clapboard siding was interspersed with floor-to-ceiling windows across a sweeping veranda that appeared to wrap around the entire first floor. White pillars held up the second floor gallery on the front of the house that boasted intricate wrought iron railings. Blush-colored brick stairs led to the solid glass double-front doors.

The acreage surrounding the home was just as stunning, dotted with century old oak trees dripping Spanish moss. But by far, what was most impressive about it was the gorgeous man who'd been leaning against one of the pillars when they'd driven up, and who was now heading toward her door.

Mason.

She got out of the car and turned to thank Bishop, but he was already shouting distance from the car, heading toward the backyard in the direction of some absolutely delicious-smelling food. Something spicy and familiar.

"Welcome to the Seeker's temporary headquarters."

She turned around, her heart speeding up just to be standing so close to him. "Mason. It's so good to see you."

"Same here. I've missed you. It's been, what, three days?"

"Four. Not that I'm counting."

He smiled. "Your father's doing better I heard?"

"Much. He's conscious and talking. No deficits from the head injury. He's in a regular room now, out of ICU. Still, even with him doing so well, it was hard to leave. But he insisted."

"He did?"

"He knows I want to help, to work on the investigation. He teased me that he was weary of me hovering around him, that he could rest much easier knowing I was here, with you and the Seekers. He basically kicked me out."

He moved closer, until their bodies were nearly touching. "I'm liking your father more and more."

"Mason?"

"Yes?"

"Would you please kiss me?"

His mouth curved in a sexy grin. Then he nearly brought her to her knees with one of those breath-stealing winks. "It would be my extreme pleasure."

He pulled her to him, one arm sliding around her back, the other cupping her head. And then he was kissing her the way she'd always wanted him to kiss her, since the first time Olivia had shared his picture and bragged about how honorable and wonderful he was. This kiss was nothing like the short, tame ones they'd shared before. This one was hot, wild. It shattered the memory of every kiss she'd ever had, searing her nerve endings and rocking her to her core.

When the kiss was over, she slumped back against the car to keep from falling down. He seemed just as shaken, bracing his hands on the roof on either side of her, struggling to catch his breath.

"Wow," she said, when she was able to talk again.

His shoulders shook with laughter. "Wow yourself, Hannah Cantrell. That was…there are no words."

"I have some. How about, where's that guesthouse where you said we'd stay?"

He groaned, then swore.

Her face heated with embarrassment. "Okay. Once again, not the reaction I was hoping for." She pushed his arm out of her way and started toward the main house.

"Oh, no you don't." He scooped her up in his arms and cradled her against his chest. "Don't be angry. I didn't swear because I *didn't* want to be with you. I swore because I *do*."

She hesitated, then looped her hands behind his head. "Then what's the problem?"

"The problem is that there's a catered crawfish-boil dinner-slash-party waiting for us behind the main house. Everyone's been working so hard that I felt some downtime for a few hours would benefit all of us. The entire team is here, minus Han, whose taking up guard duty at the hospital. And after the get-together, we're all going to review the status of the investigation. Our, ah, *tour* of the cottage will have to wait a bit longer. This has been planned since early this morning, long before I found out you'd be coming back to Beauchamp today. I'd cancel, but everyone's been looking forward to this."

"Oh goodness. I wouldn't dream of asking you to cancel. I'm sad to have to wait a little longer, but once again you're proving what an exceptional boss you are to think about your team like this. I think that's admirable, and sweet."

"Sweet enough to win me another kiss?" he teased.

"Definitely." She tightened her arms behind his neck and kissed him, pouring all her pent-up longing into every caress of her lips against his, every sweep of her tongue in an erotic duel as old as time.

The sound of laughter coming from the backyard had her pulling back to look over his shoulder. "Someone's having fun."

"Not as much fun as we're going to have once dinner and the meeting are over."

Her belly tightened. "Then we'd better hurry."

He grinned and set her down. They took off running.

In spite of her initial hope to hurry through the get-together and subsequent meeting so she could have some alone time with Mason, she couldn't remember laughing or enjoying herself this much in a long time. And she hadn't realized how keyed up and stressed she'd been until she'd begun to relax right along with Mason's team. He was a smart man to realize that his people needed some downtime, however brief. Hannah didn't think she'd have thought of it herself.

It had been hilarious seeing the looks on some of the Seekers' faces, particularly Dalton's, when Eli showed them how to eat mudbugs, or crawfish as most around here called them. When he broke off the tail and pulled out most of the meat, no one seemed to mind that. But when he sucked the shell and broke the claws to get every last piece from inside, Dalton turned green. He flat out refused to try them. At least until several of the others made fun of him. His face had turned red with indignation. Mimicking everything Eli had shown them, he managed to eat one of the Cajun delicacies. To his surprise, he'd loved it.

The sun had gone down long before they began gathering in a circle around a firepit, just a stone's throw from the bayou behind the main house. A seat by Mason seemed to miraculously open up when Hannah headed to the circle. It was obvious from the knowing looks and smiles that it wasn't a secret that she and Mason were interested in each other. Apparently gossip traveled just as fast among the Seekers as it did through Beauchamp.

When everyone fell silent, Mason started the meeting. "I hope you all had a good time tonight. Thanks, Eli, for helping extend a bit of Louisiana hospitality to everyone. I hear Dalton has such an affinity for the food that he just might move here when this is all over."

Dalton thumped his Stetson. "Yeah, right. Maybe after Eli ropes a calf and rides a bull with me in Montana, I'll consider it."

"You're on, cowboy." Eli grinned.

Dalton shook his head.

"I'd like to thank you all again too," Mason said, "for being willing to temporarily uproot your lives to come all this way and help me out. God willing, it will be over soon and we can all go home."

Hannah's smile dimmed at that. Mason glanced at her and she smiled as he continued his speech. But the smile was definitely forced. Just thinking about him leaving Beauchamp cast a heavy pall over the gathering for her.

Having been half in love with him for years, she'd been thrilled to finally meet him in person and confirm that he was every bit as wonderful as she'd expected. Then she'd become focused on helping him prove the charges against him were false. With everything that had happened, she hadn't stopped to think much beyond that, about what the future might hold for them. She'd figured that two people as attracted to each other as they were, well, that the pieces would fall into place for them. But as she thought about it now, she realized that was likely a fantasy, rather than reality.

Their outlooks on Beauchamp, and Sabine Parish, were polar opposites. Her family was here, her friends. The food, the culture, the music—everything about this place spoke to her heart. She couldn't imagine ever living anywhere else. And yet, the same wasn't true for Mason. He'd spent the last seven years hundreds of miles from here. He'd built a life, no doubt never expecting to return, not permanently anyway. Even if the charges were dropped against him, would that change how he felt about Beauchamp? How his family felt about him? Unlikely. How could there be a future between them with one of them in Louisiana and the other in Tennessee?

She twisted her hands together in her lap. Maybe staying in the cottage with him wasn't a good idea after all. Loving him, then losing him, would likely destroy her. Perhaps she should put the brakes on before it was too late for her heart to survive, if it wasn't already too late.

"Are you sure, Bryson? My brother? Wyatt?" Mason said.

Hannah blinked in confusion, realizing she'd missed whatever they'd been talking about.

Bryson nodded. "There are quite a few people on the list of Audrey's known associates that the local PI gave me. We're all having problems getting the locals to open up to us, but he's well-known around here and seems plugged in to the gossip scene. I have no reason to doubt that list. But when I saw Wyatt's name on there, it set off a few red flags. So we're digging deeper to determine his exact relationship with her."

"Wyatt didn't mention any kind of relationship with Audrey when we spoke. Let me know what else you find out."

"There's something else." He glanced at Brielle, who nodded.

Mason frowned. "What?"

Brielle, a former Gatlinburg police officer, spoke up. "You might be surprised to hear this, Mason, but Kira and I have been looking into the original case against your brother, Landon. The coincidences between that case and yours are too blatant to ignore. They could be related."

"Agreed. I've wondered myself whether the same killer was responsible for both murders. What's that got to do with what Bryson said about my brother?"

She motioned to Bryson.

He sighed. "After seeing his name on that list, and knowing the similarities between the current case and the old one, I dug into Wyatt's finances."

Mason stared at him a long moment. "He's a financial advisor. Runs his own business. He's always done really well, from what I could tell."

"Well, actually, that's the problem. He hasn't always done well. It's not obvious at first glance. But you know our resources, our experience as a team, following the money. As near as I can see, your brother's business has never been a particularly thriving enterprise. He doesn't even have that many clients. And yet, he has an expensive home, car, a very comfortable lifestyle. Unless you're giving him money, I can't explain it."

"I'm not. I've offered money to all of my family. Wyatt refused."

Bryson nodded. "Well, his rise in fortunes seems to

have begun about two years before your older brother was framed for Ms. DuBois's murder."

Mason grew still. "Two years?"

Bryson nodded.

Hannah glanced back and forth between them. "Is that significant?"

Mason didn't say anything.

Bryson looked at her and said, "When Mason brought the FBI into town to investigate corruption, they found it had basically begun two years earlier, when the mayor started his little crime syndicate."

"Wait. You're not saying his brother was..." She pressed her hand to her mouth.

Mason glanced at her. "He's insinuating that Wyatt was as corrupt as the others, way back when, and that he worked with the mayor to line his own pockets. Aren't you, Bryson?"

"I'm still in the early stages of the research. I could be completely wrong. Look, I'm sorry. I shouldn't have even brought it up. I'll go back and—"

"Stop." Mason scrubbed his face with his hands, then looked at all of them before speaking. "We're a team. We're in this together. And you all know I've been trying to solve my oldest brother's murder for years. If solving it takes you into uncomfortable territory for me, so be it. If Wyatt was involved in the corruption and didn't get caught in the FBI net, then I want to know about it. I can't figure out how that involves Audrey, and rather doubt that it does. But I'm not going to ask you to not follow every lead wherever it takes you." He nodded at Bryson. "I appreciate that you're doing as thorough a job as you can. Please keep doing it."

Bryson nodded but didn't look happy about it.

Brielle squeezed his shoulder, then cleared her throat. "Kira, Bryson and I have all been working on looking into Landon's frame-up because of its similarities to yours.

And I was wondering if you could give us a quick history lesson about what happened. Maybe that will help. We know the basics—that your brother was found standing over his live-in girlfriend's body at their home, and she'd been shot to death. But aside from reading the case file, we don't have much else. Is there anything you can add around that, to frame it for us?"

Hannah perked up. She'd like to know more about what had happened too. It wasn't one of those subjects that Olivia talked about. And not something others around town brought up in daily conversation.

"Well, to *frame it*, I'll quote former Louisiana representative Billy Tauzin who once said that 'half of Louisiana is under water and the other half is under indictment.' Unfortunately, that's not too far off. The state has a history of corrupt politicians from the governor's mansion on down, and Beauchamp is no exception. When I was asked by the mayor to be the next chief of police, my ego was big enough to think he'd asked me because he saw my amazing potential, even though I hadn't been a police officer long enough to typically be considered for that kind of position. I learned the hard way that the real reason he asked me was *because* of my inexperience. He assumed I either wouldn't notice the corruption, or I'd ignore it."

Hannah put her hand on top of his arm. "He was wrong on both counts, wasn't he?"

"He was. But not right away. In the beginning I was full of myself, blinded by the shiny gold eagles on my uniform. I looked up to the mayor. I was so impressed by his professionalism and willingness to help people that I got Olivia a job working for him as an intern while still in high school so she could put that on her college applications. Once I realized what a snake he was, I asked her to quit. She refused, as any typical rebellious teenager would. So I pulled out the big guns to force her to quit."

Brielle grinned. "You told your parents?"

He smiled. "I did. I didn't have proof yet about his illegal activities, but I'd seen and heard enough to know something was seriously wrong. My parents called the mayor and told them their minor child—she was fifteen at the time—no longer had their permission to work there. He had no choice but to let her go after that. She resented me for a long time."

"She doesn't anymore," Hannah said. "She practically worships you."

He held his hands out in a helpless gesture. "She seems to. But I've never felt I deserved that. I think she's so devastated over Landon's death that she clings to her two remaining brothers."

"What happened to the mayor?" Brielle asked.

"He killed himself at home one night. That was after Landon's case was adjudicated, and his death. The mayor was going to be arrested soon. He must have realized that and took the easy way out. He left a wife and two small kids. His death left a huge gap in the FBI's investigation. Many of the answers to their questions went to the grave with him. It was apparent that he was involved in the framing of my brother for Mandy DuBois's murder. But we never found out why he did it, and who the real killer was. His suicide was a lose-lose for everyone involved. But there was one thing that came out that made me glad I'd forced Olivia to quit working for him. Some of his interns came out saying he'd made inappropriate advances toward them. I asked Olivia if he'd ever tried anything. Thankfully he hadn't. She got out in time to not become one of his victims." He shook his head in disgust.

Hannah pressed a hand to her heart, hating that anyone had been preyed upon by the mayor. She'd never heard that before. She was so glad that Mason had pressured Olivia's parents to have her quit working for him.

Jaxon sat forward in his chair, hands clasped with his arms resting on his knees. "You said you proved Landon didn't do it. How did you prove that without finding out who the real killer was?"

"Actually, it's something you'd appreciate, Jaxon. You're the video whiz kid around here. It was a video that proved he was innocent. I was able to show he had an alibi for the moment that Mandy DuBois was shot. Unfortunately, too late to save him. After his conviction, I started over from the very beginning, trying to find out what was missed. When I canvassed the neighborhood where Landon and Mandy lived, I spoke to his neighbor across the street. Turns out, one of his surveillance cameras had a perfect angle of Landon's second floor. It clearly showed all the lights were out upstairs. Then you hear a gunshot. The light goes on and Landon jumps out of bed and runs through the bedroom doorway. Seconds later, he's back, grabbing his phone and calling 911 before running back downstairs. There was only one shot fired that night and it was clearly fired *before* Landon went downstairs. Mandy's body was on the first floor, in the main living area."

Jaxon frowned. "But if the video provided an alibi, how was he convicted?"

Hannah threaded her fingers through his, sensing Mason's pain as he relayed the story. He let out a deep breath and squeezed her hand.

"The video was never presented at the trial. The only way I got a copy was because the neighbor, who'd given the video to the police, had kept a copy on his computer. He said when he heard that Landon was convicted, he was surprised. What he hadn't known was that the video was destroyed and the defense never knew it existed. If that neighbor hadn't saved a copy, to this day we wouldn't have proof that Landon was innocent. That video is what clued me in that there were some in my own police force who were crooked, concealing evidence in the case. It was also pivotal in me winning the civil suit against the town."

"Was there other key evidence that helped you win the lawsuit?" This time it was Dalton who asked the question.

"Gunshot residue. The video clearly showed what clothes my brother was wearing that night—a white T-shirt and blue boxers. His T-shirt didn't have a pocket on it. At trial, the prosecutor presented a white T-shirt and blue boxers as the outfit Landon wore that night. But the T-shirt had a pocket. Landon had several T-shirts and boxers that were similar and didn't realize they'd switched the clothing. The outfit presented in court was GSR positive, supposedly proving he'd fired a gun. But since the shirt wasn't his, it was obvious someone put gunshot residue on another shirt they switched out, to make him seem guilty. Losing the video could have been argued away as an innocent mistake that someone totally forgot about. Switching his clothes was proof positive of evidence tampering."

"Geesh." Dalton shook his head. "And these are the people with your fate in their hands right now."

"Yeah, well. Most of those people are in prison. But, yes, it's scary to think that a similar setup is in the works again. And I don't know who's behind it. There were several other things my lawyers and I presented at the civil trial. But the most significant in my mind was that our crime scene reconstruction specialist proved Mandy was shot from about fifteen feet away. Based on the angle of the body in the crime scene photos, her killer was standing in the kitchen. But the police found Landon standing right over her, which is inconsistent. It's just one more thing that casts doubt on the crime scene."

"What about the murder weapon?" Hannah asked. Her face heated and she looked around the circle. "I'm sorry. I'm not part of your team. I shouldn't be asking questions."

Mason very deliberately lifted their joined hands and

kissed her knuckles, with everyone watching. "You're on *my* team, Hannah. You can ask any questions you want."

She gave him a grateful smile, but silently berated herself for interrupting.

"The gun was Landon's. He identified it during the trial. It was a Sig Sauer 9mm. He got it as a present, all of us brothers did, from my dad when we each turned twenty-one. Landon kept it downstairs, in an end table drawer. One theory is that an intruder, a would-be burglar, found the gun, then hid in the pantry when Mandy and Landon came home. After Landon went to bed, maybe Mandy heard something or saw him sneaking out and he shot her, then quickly wiped the gun and tossed it down beside her before running out the back door."

Bishop gestured to him, taking a turn at asking a question. "Regardless of who the shooter was, why would the police falsify evidence to frame your brother? Why go to all that trouble?"

"I've asked myself that same question many times. There are two answers that seem plausible. One is that the burglar theory is accurate and the police who framed Landon did it either to get back at me because of the ongoing FBI investigation, or to distract both me and the agent who was looking into the corruption."

Bishop nodded. "Makes sense. What's the second theory?"

"There was no burglary. Mandy was the intended target and the plan all along was to frame Landon so the real killer wouldn't take the fall." He shrugged. "That one is pretty thin. I've never found anyone who wanted to harm Mandy. I've got no evidence to back that up."

"But your gut is telling you that's what happened, isn't it?" Bishop asked.

Mason slowly nodded. "It is. I've always felt that someone came there with the intent to kill Mandy."

Everyone fell silent, as if they were all reflecting back on that fateful night and trying to fit the pieces together.

"Mason?" Brielle asked. "There's one additional piece of evidence you haven't mentioned that has been bothering me since I began looking into this. Mandy DuBois's clothes, what she was wearing the night of the shooting."

He frowned. "What about them?"

"She was still clinging to life when your brother found her. They cut her clothes off at the hospital. The outfit was bagged and tagged and kept all these years with the rest of the evidence. It's still there. I saw it yesterday at the police station, when they let me review everything in a conference room. Given what you've said about other evidence being falsified or hidden or thrown out, I figure that no one considered her clothing to be of any evidentiary value or it might have gone missing. If you're okay with it, I'd like to take her clothes to a private lab to have them perform extensive DNA testing of the bloodstains."

"A private lab, because our state lab is backed up for months?" he asked.

"Exactly. Plus, they're neutral in this. We could get results in days if you're willing to throw enough money at it. Maybe even hours. It's not the testing itself that takes long anymore. It's the requests queued up, and lack of funding."

"I don't mind the testing and I'll certainly pay for it. But if the shooter was fifteen feet away when he pulled the trigger, it's not like his DNA will be on her clothes."

"Agreed. But going along with your theory that someone came there to kill her, maybe they talked to her first. Maybe they got close up, touched her clothes, got their sweat on them. He could have backed away before firing so he wouldn't get blood on him. I know it sounds crazy and is probably a huge waste of resources. But I'd like to at least give it a try. Who knows. Maybe it will lead us to the killer."

"Okay. Do it. If the police fight you on it, talk to our resident FBI agent. Holland should be able to convince them to sign the evidence over to the lab for testing."

"Will do. Thanks."

"Thank *you*."

Dalton thumped his Stetson, getting everyone's attention. "If we're through talking about your brother's case, I'd like to talk about yours. Bryson shared the PI's report on Audrey Broussard with me, and I feel like there are a lot of gaps in the timeline leading up to her death that someone who knows her might be able to fill in. Beauchamp PD has been cooperative and provided me the address of her parents. Her being an only child, that's pretty much the only family she has here in town. But I didn't want to talk to them without asking you first. Are you okay with that?"

"No. I'm not." Mason sighed and scrubbed his face again. "Sorry, Dalton. I know you're trying to help. But when nearly everyone else in this town turned their backs on me, including Audrey, her parents were about the only ones who didn't. They suffered a lot of fallout for publicly supporting me during the civil trial and all the hate that was directed at me because of it. I can't even imagine the pain they're feeling right now. And I don't want to be responsible for causing more. That's the only reason I haven't contacted them myself with my condolences. I'd like to help them in any way that I can. But given that I'm the only suspect in their daughter's murder, it's beyond inappropriate for me to go near them. And I don't want anyone on my team imposing on them either."

"Understood. I'll work with Bryson on the timeline without bothering the Broussards."

"Thanks, Dalton." He looked around the circle. "I know more of you have updates on the things you're investigating. But it's getting late and I don't want to keep you any longer. Let's regroup tomorrow morning and finish the meeting before everyone heads into town. I've got a local café dropping off breakfast here at nine. It'll be set up in the dining room. Get a plate and we'll meet in the gathering room, since that's the only place inside big enough to hold all of us comfortably. Sound good?"

There was a chorus of agreement and the Seekers began drifting up to the main house in groups of twos and threes. When it was just Mason and Hannah left, he gently pulled her to her feet.

Her belly jumped with a mixture of longing and dread. Then she met his gaze, and realized she wasn't the only one with reservations. His expression was serious, with none of the teasing or heat from earlier.

"What's wrong?" she whispered.

"We need to talk."

Chapter Sixteen

Hannah's purse and small suitcase were sitting by the front door inside the cottage. Bishop must have put them here for her at some point during the evening. She'd completely forgotten to get them out of his car.

The cottage was cozy yet luxurious—from the modern bright white kitchenette in one corner to the cushy-looking white leather sectional in the center of the room. The bedroom door stood open, revealing a four-poster king-size bed with frothy white curtains and a down comforter, just waiting to wrap someone in its embrace. And not far from where she and Mason stood just inside the cottage, a silver serving tray sat on a decorative table, holding a bottle of champagne in a bucket of ice. Two champagne flutes sat beside it waiting for a loving couple to enjoy them.

A single tear slid down her cheek. Everything was perfect. And yet, it wasn't.

Mason stepped behind her and gently pulled her back against him, his hands caressing her shoulders. "That mirror over the fireplace tells me my fears were well-founded. That's not a tear of joy sliding down your beautiful face."

She drew a shaky breath and wiped her eyes before turning around. "I think we've both come to some kind of realization tonight, thus the tears. You first. You said you wanted to talk."

"The look on your face at the meeting tonight was full

of regret and worry. The later it got, the more worried you looked. It dawned on me that you were probably starting to dread agreeing to go to the cottage with me. I've been pushing you too hard, too fast. You're not ready for this step, and I never should have expected you to be. Not with everything else going on."

She frowned. "What? No. No, that's not it at all."

It was his turn to frown. "Then…you still want us to stay here? You want to make love with me?"

"More than anything."

A look of relief crossed his face. "Then my radar is really out of whack. I thought you were having second thoughts." He reached for her, but she quickly stepped back. He slowly lowered his arms. "Okay. Now I'm really confused."

She let out a shuddering breath. "I'd like nothing better than to lock us both in here for a week without coming up for air."

"And that's a bad thing?"

"It is," she whispered brokenly. "It's bad because, for you, it would be a pleasant interlude between two consenting adults who *really* like each other. But for me, it would be the culmination of years of longing, of building you up in my mind until—"

"Ah. I understand. Olivia built me up so much that reality doesn't hold a candle to the fantasy." He smiled sadly. "It's okay. My ego can handle the rejection. It might take a while, but I'll move on. Eventually. Stay here as long as you want. Come up to the main house during the day and brainstorm the case, if you'd like. We can just be friends. Somehow." He winked, but it didn't have the heat or the sexy charm his winks usually had. "You're safe here. We have perimeter cameras that will sound an alarm if anyone comes within a mile of this place. I can stay in the main house. No hard feelings." He started to turn away.

"Mason, wait." She grabbed his arm. "I wasn't finished. You have it backward. Reality *eclipses* the fantasy. You are more than I ever dreamed you could be. And I'm not just talking about how ridiculously gorgeous you are."

His eyes widened, but she hurried to explain before he said anything else. "It's what's inside your heart, your mind, your soul that are so amazing. Don't you see? I'm falling for you. The real you, not the Olivia hero worship you. And if we make love, I'm afraid my heart will tumble over the edge and I'll fall completely in love with you."

"Hannah, I—"

She pressed her fingers against his mouth, stopping him. "We can't make love, Mason. I have to protect my heart, while I still can. Unless you can tell me that you plan on moving back to Beauchamp after your name is cleared and you're a free man. Can you do that? Promise me you'd be okay moving here if we fall for each other? That you could see a future for yourself in this town? With me?"

He stared at her a long moment, before slowly shaking his head. "No. I can't see a future for me in Beauchamp, or even in Louisiana. But I could live anywhere else, if I was with someone I loved. Do I see forever when I look at you? Honestly, I'm not sure yet. Everything's happened so fast. But the *idea* of forever, with you, doesn't scare me. And that's saying something. Since breaking up with Audrey years ago, I've never, ever, felt the way I feel when I'm with you. Why not just enjoy the moment, our time together, and see where it leads? If it leads to forever, then we can move anywhere you want. We can figure out all of that later."

"No. We can't. After nearly losing my father this week and seeing my mother beaten down, so in need of the love and support of her family, there's no way I could leave them. And I know they could never leave Sabine Parish. They were born here in Beauchamp and moved to Many right after high school, then returned a few years ago so dad could be chief. Their parents grew up here. So did their parents, and their grandparents and theirs. My roots are here, deep roots. I have no choice but to stay. And it's a choice I gladly make. Where you look around and see corruption and the evil of the past, I see my hometown, lifelong friends and a loving family. Knowing I could never leave, and that you could never stay, it's pointless to explore this relationship any further. All it would do is break my heart. It broke once, when I lost my husband, and it took years for me to recover." She looked up into his tormented gaze, her tears flowing freely now. "If I *had* you, if I loved you with all my heart, then lost you, it would wreck me."

He stared down at her, his expression unreadable. Finally, he smiled. "My offer to stay, to help in the investigation, still stands. I hope to see you at the main house, that you won't feel awkward and not want to join the rest of us. We'll get through this." He took her hand in his and pressed a whisper-soft kiss against her knuckles. Then he left her.

Chapter Seventeen

Going to the main house the next morning was probably a mistake, but Hannah couldn't pretend she didn't care about the investigation. She wanted to know who'd shot her dad. And she wanted to know who'd killed Audrey and was trying to frame Mason. Even if there was no future for her and Mason as a couple, she cared deeply for him. And she wanted to support him in any way that she could. Maybe, even with all those smart Seekers digging up clues, she'd still be able to spot something they didn't. As long as there was even a slight chance that she might help in some way, she'd risk the awkward reception she might get from Mason—and the others once they realized their relationship had changed.

Everyone was already assembled in the cavernous main room when she arrived. Since they were taking turns giving summaries about their individual work on the case, as they had around the firepit last night, she quietly made her way across the room to an empty chair. But when she sat, Mason, who was several places away on a love seat, motioned to Dalton sitting beside him. Dalton moved to another seat, and Mason looked at her, clearly an invitation for her to join him. Relief flashed through her and she quickly crossed to him, returning his smile with one of her own. Things weren't the way she wanted them to be between them. But at least he wasn't treating her like a stranger.

Bryson was talking about some kind of financial reports on various people who'd been seen with Audrey in the weeks prior to her death. Hannah tuned him out for a while, but as she looked around at the Seekers, she realized that one of them was missing. She leaned close to Mason and whispered, "Where's Brielle?"

"She's in New Orleans at a private lab, getting Mandy DuBois's clothing tested."

She nodded and tried to pay attention to Bryson, but finances didn't interest her in the least. What she wanted to know was whether they'd figured out some good suspects. Still, when he said the name Wyatt Ford, it definitely got her attention. She remembered Bryson had mentioned Wyatt's finances, and that his company was having problems. He'd even mentioned he might be associated with the old mayor in some way. Had he found out something concrete?

Mason was riveted on what Bryson was saying. Hannah listened as carefully as she could, hoping whatever Bryson had found out didn't implicate Wyatt in Mandy's murder. Because that's where this seemed to be headed. And something that awful—that one brother could frame another for murder—wasn't something she'd wish on her worst enemy. Mason had suffered enough in his life already. Surely the Fates wouldn't add something like that as an additional burden on his shoulders. Because, after all, if Wyatt had framed Landon, what was to stop him from framing Mason eight years later?

Bryson cleared his throat. "I know it's a lot to take in. I still have a long way to go to get it nailed down. It's taking forever to weed through the mayor's finances and Wyatt's. But it doesn't look good. There are withdrawals of large sums from the mayor's accounts that seem to match deposits to Wyatt's a few days later. And yet, the mayor doesn't appear on any list of clients of Wyatt's financial advisor company. I've turned the information over to Special Agent Holland to see if he can dig deeper. I've gone as far as I can without crossing a line." He arched his brows at Mason as if in question.

Mason shook his head. "Let Holland work that angle. I don't see an urgent need right now to take more risks on our end. The last thing I want to do in Beauchamp is break any laws, no matter how tempting. Let's keep it legal."

Hannah blinked in surprise. She'd understood that Mason's company might bend a law now and then to protect a client, maybe even break one if it was a matter of life or death. But Mason's future, his life, was at risk here. She'd have expected him to be okay with pushing the limits. But as usual, he put everyone but himself first and apparently didn't think his own situation was worth the trade-off of putting some of his own people in a tenuous situation. She admired him for that. But it also bothered her that he might not be putting every resource he had into his own defense.

"I'm willing," Bryson assured him. "If you change your mind, let me know."

"Thanks, Bryson." Mason scanned the room. "I know we've found ties between Wyatt and Audrey." He cleared his throat. "Has anyone found any ties between Wyatt and Mandy DuBois, Landon's girlfriend who was murdered?"

Everyone exchanged glances but no one offered any information.

"All right," Mason said, sounding relieved. "I believe Jaxon was next. Hannah, you'll want to hear this. He gave me a preview earlier this morning."

Jaxon, a former marine MP, stood to give his summary, probably a formality he'd learned from the military, because most of the Seekers were more laid-back. But as he began, Hannah was more interested in Mason.

"Are you okay?" she whispered.

"Because of Wyatt?"

"Yes."

He leaned close to her ear. "I know it looks bad. But things looked bad for Landon, and for me too. And neither of us were killers. For all I know, someone else is behind both frame-ups and is purposely lining up Wyatt to take the fall when things go bad. Maybe someone has a vendetta against our family and is going after all three brothers. I'm trying to not let emotions cloud my judgment. But I'm also giving him the benefit of the doubt. I'd never want to accuse someone of something they didn't do. It's a miserable feeling."

"You're an amazing man, Mason Ford," she whispered.

He stared at her so long, her face heated. But she couldn't read his expression well enough to know what he was thinking. It bothered her, because she'd always been able to read him before now.

Jaxon said something about videos in her neighborhood, which had both her and Mason paying attention again. He told them about various knock-and-talks he'd done, going door-to-door trying to find anyone who might have snapped a picture out a window or had a doorbell surveillance system that might have caught a car driving by or the shooting itself.

"What it boils down to," he said, "is a mountain of video in that part of the city. And it paid off. I was able to point Beauchamp PD to two specific recordings that were high quality and left no doubt about who shot Chief Landry." He looked directly at Hannah. "Abrams and Donnelly were in the car together. Abrams was driving. Donnelly shot your father."

She started trembling, even though it was basically what she'd expected. "Th...thank you, Jaxon."

"Yes, ma'am."

Mason put his arm around her shoulders and she gratefully leaned into his side.

A loud knock sounded on the door.

Bryson, who was the closest to the entrance, disappeared into the foyer. A moment later, he led Chief Murphy into the room.

Murphy seemed surprised as he looked around. "I didn't expect this big of an audience. Mason, Hannah, I've got some developments to speak to you about. Am I talking to everyone or just you two?"

Mason crossed to him and shook hands. "We have no secrets here. Everyone stays."

"Very well."

Mason sat beside Hannah. One of the Seekers got up from a nearby chair and offered it to Murphy so he could be closer to them. He nodded his thanks and sat.

"First, Hannah, has anyone updated you on what the Seekers found out last night?"

"That your deputies shot my father?"

He winced. "Yes. I wanted to let you know they've been caught. They'd holed up at an old fishing cabin on Donnelly's uncle's property. We found them before sunup this morning. Al's been interviewing them and the DA made a deal—if they came clean about who was with them in Gatlinburg, and why, he wouldn't seek the death penalty for them trying to kill your father. And before you get mad about that, your father gave his consent to the deal an hour ago."

Mason took her hand, helping to calm her immediate outrage. She threaded her fingers in his and let him take the lead.

"What was their explanation, Chief? Who hired them?"

"Audrey did. Actually, she hired our notorious two former deputies, and they brought in three more guys. Under oath, knowing if we catch them in a lie the death penalty is back on the table, they swore that Audrey hired them as her backup plan to kidnap you if you turned her down in Gatlinburg. Her idea was to, ah, seduce you and convince you to stay with her. She felt that if you woke up in Beauchamp, you'd be inclined to spend time with her and work things out."

Mason frowned. "That's bizarre. And even if it's true, why would Abrams or Donnelly, or one of their thugs, kill her and then frame me?"

"I'm getting to that part. But before I do, I want to speak to the autopsy results. Mason, Audrey had glioblastoma, stage 4."

He stared at him in shock. "Brain cancer?"

"Yes. The medical examiner called around and discovered that she'd been getting treatment in Lafayette at Our Lady of Lourdes JD Moncus Cancer Center. The date of her diagnosis was right around the time she bought that SUV—something that Al, Detective Latimer, was able to validate. My guess is that she didn't want people seeing her red convertible in Lafayette and asking questions. She kept her illness to herself, didn't even tell her parents. It might have been because she didn't want anyone pitying her. Or maybe she didn't want people hearing about her illness and not hiring her for decorating jobs. The ME says her cognitive skills would have definitely been impaired. At her last treatment, her doctor told her next time she needed to come back with someone else driving her or he'd officially work with the state to take away her license. She missed her next appointment and didn't answer their calls."

Mason's hand tightened on Hannah's. "She was pale and tired-looking in Gatlinburg." His voice was quiet and strained. "I asked if she felt okay and she insisted that she did."

"You didn't know," Hannah told him. "She didn't want you to know."

Murphy rested his forearms on his knees. "I think you can feel better knowing she wasn't in her right mind when she arranged your abduction."

He stared at Murphy. "If what you're saying is true, how did she end up shot to death and me framed for it?"

"The blood spatter evidence shows a void in front of Audrey."

"The killer was standing in front of her, close to her, when he shot her."

"Someone was standing in front of her, yes. The evidence shows they were about four feet away. There were gunpowder burns beneath her chin, where the barrel was pressed against her skin. Blood sprayed back into the barrel. Gunshot residue was on her hands, her clothes and the floor right beneath her. There's also a scrape mark in the blood, showing after the shooting the gun was picked up from the floor. When you picked up the gun in the bedroom upstairs, there wasn't any blood on the outside or we'd have found blood in the bedroom, or even on your hands. There also weren't any prints on the gun and no GSR. There wasn't any gunshot residue on you either."

Mason gave him a hard look. "Murphy, are you trying to tell me that Audrey killed herself? And that someone else wiped the gun and tried to frame me as if it was murder?"

"That's exactly what I'm saying."

"You're wrong. She wouldn't do that."

Hannah touched his forearm. "I don't think he's finished. Let's hear him out, okay?"

His tortured gaze met hers, and he gave her a crisp nod before looking back at the acting chief.

Murphy smiled at Hannah and continued. "What we don't know yet is who framed you. Donnelly and Abrams swear they had nothing to do with that. They said they responded to the anonymous 911 call and were shocked to find Audrey dead and you standing over her. Rather than do the right thing and admit that they'd been part of the crew who kidnapped you and had brought you there—which likely would have kept you from serious consideration as a suspect—they remained silent, so they wouldn't get in trouble."

Murphy shook his head in disgust. "Other than you holding the gun, there is zero evidence to show you did this. None of the forensics point to you. There'd be no reason for you to clean the gun and then be found with it. If you shot her, you'd have run right then, not risked being found in the house. And the evidence shows whoever was there when she shot herself was standing too far away to have held the gun under her chin. No matter how you look at it, there's just no way that you shot her. Whoever was there watched her shoot herself, and for some reason thought to frame you for it after the fact. They likely called 911 as part of that. We'll work hard to figure out who that is."

He stood and pulled a gun from his pocket. Reversing directions, he held it handle first toward Mason. "The DA said it was okay to give you back your weapon."

Mason didn't take the gun. "I'm out on bail. I'm not allowed to have a firearm."

"The DA has dropped all charges against you. Mason Ford, you're a free man."

Chapter Eighteen

Hannah saw Chief Murphy out and thanked him. But when she went back into the main room, there was no sign of Mason. Many of the Seekers had left for other parts of the house. Others sat around the expansive room, working on laptops or talking on their phones.

Dalton caught her attention from across the room and motioned toward the wall of glass that looked out over the bayou. Mason was standing on the dock in one of his gray suits, his hands in his pockets, staring out at the cypress and tupelo trees. Yesterday morning, she wouldn't have hesitated to check on him. This morning, she didn't know if he'd want her there.

She started to sit, but the serious, quiet and somewhat intimidating Bishop crossed to her.

"He doesn't want any of us with him right now," he told her.

She nodded. "I figured. He wants to be alone. Because of Audrey. Finding out she killed herself has to be a huge blow, regardless of the state of their relationship when she died."

"You seem to know him really well, in spite of only meeting him a relatively short time ago."

Her face heated. "Yes, well. I've kind of hero-worshipped him from afar for a long time. His baby sister, Olivia, is a good friend and talks about him. A lot." She cleared her throat. "And now I'm talking way too much. Since he doesn't want anyone to bother him, I'll just sit and wait."

"You misunderstood me. He doesn't want *us* out there, the Seekers. But I'm quite certain he'd want *you*. He'd never ask. But if you're inclined to join him, even if you don't say anything, it could make a difference."

Impossibly, her face heated even more. "I don't think so. Last night, well, he won't want to see me. Honestly, I probably should just go home." She started to turn away but he moved to block her.

"Ms. Cantrell. I found him in the library this morning, asleep on the couch. So I already knew something had gone wrong between you two. But he still cares about you, very much. And as his best friend, whose known him for many years, I'm certain that he needs you."

He needs you. She looked toward the wall of glass, at the lone figure on the dock, and had to blink back the threat of tears. "Thank you, Bishop."

Without a word, he walked away.

She paused by a mirror on one wall and checked her makeup, then fussed with her hair, before realizing a couple of the Seekers were smiling at her primping. She squared her shoulders, then headed outside, praying she wasn't making a mistake. The last thing she wanted was to hurt him, or make things worse.

When she reached the dock, she made no effort to soften her footfalls. She didn't want to surprise him, and wanted him to have the opportunity to tell her to go away.

He didn't.

Instead, as soon as she stopped beside him, he pulled her against his chest.

A pent-up breath shuddered out of her, and she slid her arms around his waist, holding on tight, telling him with actions, if not words, that she cared about him, that she would do anything in her power to take away his pain.

It felt so good to be held by him, to feel the tension slowly easing from his body. Maybe Bishop was right and she was helping after all. He kissed the top of her head. But instead of letting go, he took her hand in his and faced the bayou again.

"I'm so sorry about Audrey," she whispered. "I can't imagine your pain."

He squeezed her hand. "It hurts more than I expected. But I think what hurts the most is that people will remember the wrong things about her, that she orchestrated my kidnapping and fired the gun that killed her. That's not who she was."

"It's was her illness, the brain tumor. People who matter will realize that and remember her kindly."

"You're a good person, Hannah Cantrell. Having you here helps. Thank you."

This time, it was her turn to squeeze his hand.

They stood a long time, watching the Spanish moss dip and sway in the slightly cool breeze. A giant white egret landed in the top of one of the cypress trees. Insects buzzed and flitted from lily pad to lily pad, while somewhere in the distance a bullfrog croaked.

"I can't make sense of it." His deep voice broke the silence.

She let go of his hand and turned to face him. "Tell me."

He glanced over at her. "Audrey was a fighter. It was something I admired about her, how strong she was, and driven. I keep thinking about her being told she had terminal cancer and imagining her reaction. And I just can't see her giving up."

"The suicide."

He winced, then nodded.

"The tumor—"

"Doesn't matter. I'm telling you, if ten doctors told her she was terminal, she'd find an eleventh doctor who said there was hope. She would have fought to the very end for every second she had left, for every breath in her body. She wanted to live. Even if the tumor was affecting her judgment, her self-preservation instinct would have kicked in. I can't see any way that she'd have killed herself. Period."

"Okay. If anyone would know, you would. So the alternative is—"

"Someone murdered her and made it look like a suicide." He put his hands on her shoulders. "I know what I said sounds outlandish. But I also know something else— how crooked and underhanded some of the people in this town have been in the past. Like Abrams and Donnelly. Trusted public servants who were basically thugs for hire. What if someone wanted Audrey's murder to look like a suicide?"

"Why would they? What do they stand to gain?"

He let her go and raked a hand through his short, dark hair. "I don't know. I feel like I'm back where it all started, drowning in questions without enough answers."

"Let's talk it through," she said. "Does anyone benefit financially from her death?"

"No. My guys did a full financial investigation on her. She barely had enough life insurance for her burial. She made a good living, and she had investments that helped her keep a good lifestyle. But her assets weren't enough to tantalize someone into killing her. Not in my opinion."

"Okay, revenge?"

Again he shook his head. "She could be abrasive, but never mean. I can't imagine her doing anything that would make someone resent her enough to go after her like that."

"Love? People kill the ones they love all the time. It's a powerful emotion and can make people do things they wouldn't normally do."

"I don't think so."

"Well, that only leaves one other motive that I can think of. Someone wanted her quiet. She knew something, and they didn't want anyone else to find out about it."

He cocked his head, studying her. "You're not trying to talk sense into me and tell me it's a suicide."

"Why would I? You knew her better than anyone. And I'm right with you on the corruption around here, or incompetency. Maybe both. If you think someone killed her, then I'm 100 percent behind you on that. Even if she pulled the trigger, someone forced her to do it. Somehow."

He slowly shook his head. "You're amazing. Thank you."

She slid her arm around him and gave him a quick hug before stepping back.

"All right," he said. "I'll call Chief Murphy and tell him my suspicions. I'll ask him to order another autopsy, have the crime scene techs go over the scene again. Look at everything with a fresh perspective. They've missed something, an important piece of information that will prove it wasn't a suicide."

"Don't you think calling Murphy is risky? What if he tries to pin her murder on you again?"

"With everything else he said about the scene, I don't think he will." He took his gun out, studying it. "Someone used my gun to kill her. It's still so hard to believe." He idly turned it upside down and ran his fingers over two deep parallel lines cut into the bottom of the grip.

"What are those?" she asked. "I've never seen a gun with grooves like that."

"My dad's a retired machinist and a big proponent of concealed carry for self-defense. He taught all of us about gun safety. Remember earlier I said he gave us each a gun on our twenty-first birthdays? My sisters picked out different types. But us guys all wanted the same kind. To tell them apart, my dad machined those grooves onto the bottom of each gun, corresponding to each son's birth order."

"Ah. One for Landon, two for you, three for Wyatt?"

"You got it. If any of us are carrying when we go to visit him, he makes us put our guns in a special box on a table in the foyer. Or, at least, he did, back when we all were in Beauchamp. When we left, we'd check the grooves, make sure we took the right gun." He ran his thumb across the grooves, a half smile curving his lips. "I'd forgotten about that."

"Good memories?"

"Good memories. There was always some kind of tension in our house, but overall it was a good place to grow up. It's only after what happened to Landon that it all went to hell." He holstered his gun, then pulled out his phone and frowned at the screen.

"Something wrong?" she asked.

"Olivia's been texting me but I didn't realize it. She's at my parents' house. Apparently she's finally heard about me being charged, then let go and doesn't understand what's going on. She asked if I'd come over and explain everything. My parents said it was okay."

"Okay for you to come over? They should be *begging* you to come over. Or better yet, they should have been at the police station day one demanding answers and trying to help you."

"You don't understand the hell they went through when the town turned against all of us. They don't want to go through that again. I'm surprised they'd even risk me being seen going over there."

Hannah was careful to keep the anger from her voice when she spoke again. "Are you going?"

"I don't see a reason not to. I'd like to see Olivia, make sure she's okay. Calm her fears." He sent a quick text before putting his phone away. "I can call Murphy on the way there and discuss Audrey." He cleared his throat, suddenly seeming unsure of himself. "Do you want me to drop you off at your house? I had your SUV moved there, so you won't be stranded. With Abrams and Donnelly captured, you should be safe."

"Actually, if you don't mind, I'd like to go with you to your parents' house. As your…friend, I want to be there for you." She put her hand on his arm. "Please."

He smiled. "My very special friend. I'd like that. Let's go."

Chapter Nineteen

Mason and Hannah sat on a couch in his parents' family room, with Olivia between them and his parents sitting on the adjacent love seat. While Hannah held Olivia's hand, Mason worked to calm her fears and avoid a meltdown. For once, he actually sympathized with his parents. They'd been desperate when he'd arrived, not sure how to help Olivia. Her usual shadow, Wyatt, was in a meeting not answering their calls or texts, and they were at their wit's end.

It took nearly an hour to explain everything, answer her questions and get her back to her usual, bubbly self. Like a switch being flipped, it was as if none of the earlier hysterics had ever happened.

"How long will you be here?" she asked, as if he was on vacation and they hadn't just gone around and around about Audrey's murder.

He was saved from answering when Wyatt walked in. He stopped, his jaw tightening when he saw them.

Olivia's face lit up with happiness. "Wyatt. Look. Mason finally came to visit."

"I see that. Mason, Hannah." He gave his parents a hard look as he crossed to Olivia and kissed her forehead. "Everything okay, sweetie?"

"Everything's perfect. It's so good to see Mason again. Isn't it?"

"Of course. It's time for your meds. I got you a refill on my way over."

"Oh, thanks, Wyatt." She stood and took the little pill-box he handed her, then headed into the kitchen.

He crossed to the love seat and kissed his mother's forehead. "Mom, good to see you. Dad."

She smiled just as brightly as Olivia had. "Sorry to disturb your busy schedule with all those messages. I didn't know what else to do."

"It's no problem. I came as soon as I could." He sat in the recliner that faced the couch and eyed Mason with a lack of enthusiasm. "I heard some of what you were telling Olivia as I was parking my gun in the foyer. The charges against you have been dropped?"

He nodded, not particularly interested in striking up a conversation with his brother.

"I guess you'll be leaving soon, then. Heading back to Tennessee."

"We've got a few more loose ends to tie up."

"Like what?"

"Like finding out who set me up for Audrey's forced suicide."

Wyatt stared at him. "Forced suicide? What does that even mean?"

"I thought you heard everything in the foyer. The ME said she actually shot herself, and then someone tried to frame me after the fact. That same person is likely the one who somehow coerced her to shoot herself and then wiped the gun clean and left it for me to pick up. The FBI's looking into all of it as part of the conspiracy charges, so hopefully it will be figured out soon. There's some DNA evidence that proves someone else was there. Just a matter of time before we get a profile. Then, it's a matter of getting a warrant for a DNA sample from all of Audrey's known contacts. Shouldn't be too hard. The PI we hired already provided a list to the Chief." He frowned. "Come to think of it. Your name was on that list. I didn't realize you and Audrey were an item."

Mason caught Hannah's surprised look, but she quickly masked it, nodding as if in agreement with his bogus claim about the DNA. Wyatt, on the other hand, wasn't masking his surprise well at all. The fact that he'd gone pale had Mason all the more determined to keep his team digging into his past. Something wasn't right here. And although he'd never peg his brother as a killer, he'd bet his entire fortune that Wyatt knew something and for some reason was hiding it.

"Your source is misinformed," Wyatt said, his usual indifference back in place. "I've seen her around town a few times, but we certainly weren't an item."

Mason shrugged. "That's for the FBI to decide I suppose. Doesn't matter anyway. Obviously your DNA wouldn't be a match."

"Obviously not."

Hannah blinked innocently. "Wasn't there some DNA evidence in Landon's case the police are looking at too?"

Mason grinned. She was playing Watson to his Sherlock.

"Landon?" Wyatt swore, then glanced at their mother. "Sorry." He looked at Mason again. "Are you digging up ancient history? Dragging our family through that awfulness again?"

"When I saw you at the hospital, I thought you said the family was still concerned about what had happened to Landon? Don't you want to know who killed Mandy and framed him?"

His father's face scrunched in anger. "Mason, don't you dare go stirring up trouble again."

"Mr. Ford, are you kidding—"

Mason put his hand on Hannah's arm to stop her.

She clamped her mouth shut.

He winked, and she relaxed against him, letting out a deep breath.

"What DNA?" Wyatt asked. "Hannah said there was something in Landon's case."

"Now, son—"

"Dad, I want to hear this." Wyatt motioned to him and their father fell silent. "Go on, Mason. What all-important piece of evidence have you dug up that's worth making our lives miserable again? And jeopardizing my business? I could lose clients."

"Just some testing being performed on the clothes that were cut off Mandy DuBois in the hospital. We should have results anytime now. They're testing every drop of blood, looking for DNA from whoever fired the gun that killed her. Just like with the DNA in Audrey's case, they feel they'll be able to wrap everything up really soon."

Hannah nodded. "Yep. It's all coming together. Isn't that wonderful?"

"Thrilling," Wyatt said, his eyes flashing with annoyance.

Olivia stepped into the room from the kitchen, her hands tight around a glass of ice water. "Wyatt? What's he talking about? Mason, you didn't say anything to me about DNA."

Wyatt stood and crossed to her. "Don't get worked up. It's standard police stuff."

Mason gave her a reassuring smile. "I didn't mean to worry you. We think we'll be able to point to Mandy's real killer is all. And figure out who tried to frame me in Audrey's case. After that, we'll never have to worry about these cases again."

Wyatt put his arm around her and narrowed his eyes at Mason.

Hannah nudged him. "I'm expecting that package at my house. I have to be there to sign for it, remember?"

"Oh yeah. Right. We need to go." They both stood. "Mom, Dad, we'll see ourselves out. Take care, Olivia." He and Hannah headed out of the room and into the long foyer. He couldn't wait to get out of the house and away from the people he called family.

He'd just reached for the doorknob when Hannah stopped him.

"Wait, your gun." She opened the box on top of a decorative table against the wall. His and Wyatt's guns were both there. She started to pick one up, then hesitated, her eyes widening. She gave him a sharp look before setting it down and taking the other one instead.

"Is there a problem?" Wyatt stood at the other end of the foyer, looking at them.

"Uh, no, of course not." She seemed shaken as she handed Mason his gun.

He gave her a questioning look but she shook her head, so he didn't say anything.

"Another great visit with you, Wyatt." Mason pulled open the door. "Let's do it again real soon." He ushered Hannah outside.

Chapter Twenty

As soon as they were out of sight of the Ford home, Hannah let out a pent-up breath. "That was fun."

He grinned. "It was once you started playing detective with me. I think we really rattled Wyatt."

"You think he killed Mandy? And threatened or confused Audrey into shooting herself?"

"I guess it's possible, especially if Audrey was heavily medicated. But I'm more inclined to think since the mayor was the one heading up the conspiracy to frame Landon, and Wyatt's obviously financially involved in the dealings the mayor had, that he knows something about why Mandy was killed and who killed her. And why Landon was framed. The bastard's more worried about escaping justice for his own crimes than catching whoever is indirectly responsible for Landon being murdered in prison."

"I think there's far more to it than that." She looked out the window. "I know we were bluffing, saying we had to go to my house. But since we're about to pass the turnoff and it's closer than the estate, let's swing in there. I need to show you something."

Without a word, he turned down the next road, then moments later headed up the long unpaved driveway that led to her home. He winced as the rental car hit a pothole. "I can see why you have an SUV. Ever think about having this thing paved?"

"It would ruin the old-world charm."

He smiled and pulled to a stop in front of her house. "I don't like you living out this far from other homes. Doesn't feel safe."

"I've been here for years, never an incident. Come on. This is important."

When they were inside, she pulled him to the couch and tugged him down beside her.

His brows shot up in surprise. "You really are in a hurry. What's so important?"

"Take out your gun."

"What?"

"Take out your gun."

"O…kay. It's loaded. Be careful."

She shook her head. "I don't want it. I want you to turn it over, look at the bottom."

Frowning, he turned it over, careful to keep the muzzle pointed away from her. "Ah, hell. I've got Wyatt's gun. I'll have to see him once more before I leave to give it back to him."

"Mason. That's not Wyatt's gun."

"Well of course it is. There are three grooves on the bottom. Mine only has two."

"Look closer."

He held it up to the light, tilting the gun back and forth. He suddenly stiffened.

She nodded as if he'd spoken. "I saw it too, in your parents' foyer. I took his on purpose to show you. The first groove is just like the one you showed me on your gun earlier today. The other two are different. Close, but different. Definitely not done by the same tool."

He slowly shook his head. "It's Landon's gun. Wyatt must have made more grooves to make it seem like his own gun. Which means the gun at Landon's trial was actually Wyatt's. No one ever thought to look at the grooves on the bottom to be sure. We all assumed it was Landon's. Just that someone else had faked the evidence to make it seem that Landon's gun was the one that killed Mandy. My God, Hannah. Wyatt must have killed Mandy, and framed Landon."

"I knew I should have gotten rid of the dang thing years ago."

Mason and Hannah jerked around to see Wyatt standing in the opening to her hallway. He aimed an identical-looking gun, Mason's gun, at Mason's head. "Drop it or I shoot your girlfriend."

Mason pitched his dead brother's gun onto the floor. "How'd you get here ahead of us?"

"A little shortcut I know about. It's hell on a car's undercarriage, but I knew my only chance to get the drop on you was the element of surprise."

"Why did you keep Landon's gun? So no one would be suspicious when you no longer had it? Considering your own gun was locked up in evidence?"

"You always were too smart for your own good. I had to carve those grooves on the bottom so no one would ask why I no longer had my gun. But all the while I prayed no one would think to check for grooves on the one at the trial. Honestly, I was stunned that no one did. I was on pins and needles for months expecting that to happen. All these years, no one noticed the difference in the grooves I'd made. Until Hannah did back at Dad's house. I knew she was acting funny as she picked up your gun. Of course, after you left and I looked at mine, I knew she must have figured it out and would tell you. I thought you'd run to the FBI or police as soon as you signed for the package you mentioned. Luckily, you didn't."

Mason shifted on the couch as Wyatt moved into the room, obviously trying to shield Hannah.

She cursed herself for being in such a hurry to come

inside that she didn't even bring her purse from the car. If she had, she might have been able to get her own gun and surprise Wyatt.

"What did you do?" Mason asked him, probably stalling for time as they both tried to figure a way out of this that didn't end with either or both of them dead. "After you killed Mandy, you realized you'd have to leave your gun there since ballistics would match it, and take Landon's?"

"You think you have it all figured out, don't you?"

"I'm getting there. Unfortunately, not soon enough to save Mandy and Audrey. Or Landon."

His eyes flashed with anger. "Audrey killed herself. You told us that tonight. It was a suicide."

"Not if someone else was there, and they coerced her. Someone had to wipe the gun clean and put it upstairs after she shot herself."

"Well it sure wasn't me."

"What about Mandy? There's no other explanation for you having Landon's gun. You shot her, then framed your own brother and let him go to prison for it. You might as well be the one who killed him in prison. If it wasn't for you, he wouldn't have been there."

"Not true. I didn't kill Mandy. I haven't killed anyone."

"If that's the case, why are you pointing a gun at us?"

His jaw tightened. "Because I need you to listen. All this digging and DNA crap you're so proud of, all it's going to do is destroy what's left of our family. You need to stop and fix it, before it's too late."

Mason subtly shifted again, and Hannah realized he was trying to position himself closer to her end table. A heavy paperweight in the shape of a small ball was sitting there. Was he hoping to throw it at Wyatt?

"It's the DNA that's got you scared, isn't it? When I mentioned testing all the blood on Mandy's shirt, you went pale."

"For good reason. Just whose DNA do you think you'll find if you complete those tests?"

"Yours. Obviously."

"Wrong." Wyatt's hand tightened on the gun as he stepped closer. "Olivia's."

Mason had been slowly moving his hand toward the side table, but Wyatt's statement stopped him cold. "What the hell are you talking about?"

"The truth. Olivia's blood is on Mandy's shirt. If you don't stop this train you've got going down the tracks, it's going to run over her and destroy her."

"Put the gun down. I'm not calling the police. Put it down and tell me what you're talking about."

"No way. I don't trust you. But I will tell you what happened. Because you're forcing my hand. If you'd left it alone, she wouldn't be in danger. All these years I've done nothing but try to protect Olivia. And you came down here and destroyed my efforts in a matter of days."

"Wyatt—"

"Olivia killed Mandy. Her blood is on the shirt because they fought. They were tangled up with each other when Mandy got a good punch in and bloodied Olivia's nose. It bled all over her shirt. Mandy was so angry she pulled Landon's gun out of the side table. Olivia was forced to shoot her, in self-defense. But she panicked, and ran."

"There are all kinds of gaps in that story. You're covering for yourself."

Hannah pressed a hand to her chest. She couldn't believe what she was hearing. And from the disbelief and horror in Mason's voice, he couldn't either.

"No. I'm not. Since Olivia wasn't old enough for dad to have given her a gun yet, she stole mine and used it to threaten Mandy. She didn't mean to hurt her, but she did. After she shot her, she dropped the gun, then panicked and grabbed it again and ran. Except she grabbed Landon's by mistake and left mine. And by running, she left Landon to find Mandy and you know the rest. That's why she's been so torn up all these years. She can't handle the guilt of what she did, that Landon went to prison and died for her crime. I swear to you, Mason. If I could have saved Landon, I would have."

"I'm not buying any of this," Mason said. "I know you were involved in the corruption, that you and the mayor were laundering money. And someone faked GSR results against Landon. And misplaced evidence that would have exonerated him. Olivia couldn't have done that."

Wyatt swore. "You really have been digging. As for my activities, sure, I laundered some money for him. There's your confession. Too bad the statute of limitations has expired on those crimes. Trust me. I checked. After Olivia killed Mandy and I realized it was my gun she'd used, it shook me to the core. I cleaned up my act and dedicated myself to helping her."

"Is he right?" Hannah asked. "About the statute of limitations."

Mason nodded. "He did his homework. But there's no statute of limitations on murder."

Wyatt's throat worked. "Which is why I'm trying to talk some sense into you. You and that fancy company of yours and all these people you brought to town to work on your investigations, you need to put the brakes on. Somehow. Or you're going to send Olivia to prison."

"Make me believe you, Wyatt. Make me believe your story. Then we can discuss Olivia. But first, put the gun away."

"So you can attack me? Or shoot me? No thanks. I know all about that famous sense of justice you have. You still think I'm the bad guy in this. Until you believe otherwise, you're going to try to take me out."

Mason swore. "Then at least turn the muzzle away from my head."

Wyatt relented, and turned it, but only a little. In a heartbeat he could point it right back at him.

"Go on. Convince me that our fifteen-year-old sister at the time is a murderer. And then explain how you're not the one who framed Landon for the murder. Because there's no way Olivia did."

"I'm not saying she's a murderer. It was an accident."

Mason waited, without saying anything else.

Wyatt glanced at Hannah as if hoping she could help him make Mason see reason. "You made Olivia quit her job working for the mayor to protect her. Well it was too late. She was already having an affair with him."

Hannah gasped in shock.

"You're lying," Mason gritted out.

"I'm not. I'm telling you the truth. Mandy found out. I don't know how, but she did, and she called Olivia and told her she was going to tell the police and they'd arrest him for statutory rape. Olivia fancied herself in love with the mayor and didn't want anything to happen to him. She stole my gun and confronted Mandy. After she shot her, by accident, she ran out. She made the anonymous 911 call to try to save Mandy. It didn't occur to her that Landon might end up taking the blame. She ran to the mayor, told him what had happened. Naturally, he wanted to protect his secrets from coming out, so he told her not to tell anyone. Later, once Landon was charged, he convinced her to keep quiet, saying he'd make sure he got off. But of course we all know how that turned out."

He held his free hand out in supplication. "Why do you think Olivia had so many issues after Landon's death? It was guilt. All this time, she's been struggling with that guilt. It's a terrible burden."

"Drop the gun, Wyatt." Olivia's voice rang out.

He jerked toward her, then turned the gun away. She was standing in the hallway where he'd emerged just minutes earlier, holding her own gun. "What are you doing, Olivia? Put that away."

"No." Her hands shook as she held both of them around the pistol. "I knew you were up to something when you drove off right after they left." A single tear slid down her cheek. "I won't let you kill Mason."

"Kill Mason? Sweetie, I'm not going to shoot him. I just wanted him to listen to me telling him…"

"What?" Another tear slid down her face. "Telling him how awful I am? That I'm the reason Landon died?" She sobbed, the gun dipping.

Mason stood.

Wyatt whirled around, pointing his gun at him. "Stay there."

"No." Olivia sniffed and steadied her gun at Wyatt again. "I don't want him hurt. I didn't save Landon. But I can save Mason." The gun was shaking so much that Hannah was surprised it didn't go off.

"What about me?" Wyatt asked. "I've helped you all these years. And now Mason's trying to frame me, say I had something to do with Audrey's death. Does that seem fair, Olivia?"

Her lower lip trembled. "No," she whispered. "It's not fair."

A look of relief crossed his face. "He's trying to hurt you, and me. Shoot him, Olivia."

She swung her gun toward Mason.

Hannah slid to the floor at his feet, her hand covering her mouth.

"Whoa, whoa," Mason cajoled, holding his hands out placatingly toward Olivia. "Both of you put your guns down and let's figure this out."

"Go on," Wyatt urged. "Shoot him. All your pain, everything that's happening, is his fault."

"Mason's fault?" Her lower lip wobbled, as if she was fighting the urge to cry.

"That's right," Wyatt said. "It's Mason's fault."

"Don't listen to him, Olivia. He's trying to blame you for Mandy's murder. He said you shot her."

Her face crumpled. "Because I did."

Mason slowly shook his head. "No. You didn't."

"I did. She was going to tell on me. We fought. I got scared and I—"

"You pointed a gun at her. But you didn't fire it."

A look of confusion crossed her face. "I didn't?"

"He's lying to you," Wyatt called out.

Hannah didn't have a clue what Mason was trying, but he shifted on his feet, and the toe of his right shoe nudged Landon's gun out from under the coffee table where it must have landed. Another subtle shift and he nudged it again. She realized he was very much aware that she was on the floor, and knew that might give them a chance. Carefully, ever so slowly, she inched her fingers toward the gun that Wyatt had altered.

"I'm not lying." Mason's voice was calm, like when he'd talked her down at his parents' house earlier. "And I can prove it. Where were you standing when Mandy was shot?"

Her brow wrinkled. "Right beside her. We were arguing. She hit my nose. The gun went off." She shuddered.

"And was Mandy holding a gun?"

She shook her head. "No."

"Olivia, you don't know what you're saying," Wyatt said. "She had Landon's gun. Remember?"

"No, I…she didn't have a gun. I had Landon's gun. I took it from the side table where he normally keeps it."

"Olivia—"

"Shut up, Wyatt. I'm trying to think."

His face reddened.

Hannah stretched her hand a little more. She couldn't screw this up. She couldn't let Wyatt see her moving toward the gun on the floor.

"Olivia." Mason's voice was soft, gentle. "The gun the police ran ballistics on, the gun that killed Mandy, was Wyatt's gun."

She shook her head. "No. I had Landon's gun."

"That's right. But the person who killed Mandy was standing in the kitchen opening. I had a crime scene reconstructions specialist prove that. She wasn't shot at close range. Wyatt was standing in the kitchen. He must have found out you were going there and followed you. I'm not sure. Only he knows that. But Wyatt's gun is the one with the three grooves on the bottom that dad carved, and that's the gun left at the scene that night. It was the gun that fired the fatal shot. You grabbed Landon's gun, thinking it was Wyatt's. He let Landon take the blame, and then made you think all these years that you'd shot her, when he's the one who shot her."

She was shaking her head back and forth. "No, no, no. You said you would prove it."

"I can. We'll get the gun from evidence and see it has three lines on the bottom, lines that Dad made. It's Wyatt's gun in evidence. When we were at the house earlier tonight, Hannah saw the gun Wyatt had in the basket, on the foyer table. And she saw that two of the grooves weren't like the others. That's because Wyatt carved those grooves himself. Hannah took his gun to show me, and left mine. Wyatt's holding my gun. And his gun, the one he's carried for the last eight years, is under the coffee table. It's Landon's gun, the one that Wyatt used to kill Mandy. And the only way he can have Landon's gun is if his gun is the one they thought was Landon's at the trial."

He looked at Wyatt, his face mirroring his disgust. "You

let a fifteen-year-old think she'd killed someone when you're the one who did it, likely to protect your money laundering scheme. You knew the mayor was molesting her and didn't want Mandy to report him and ruin your little venture together. When you somehow realized that Olivia was going to confront Mandy, you followed her, and decided to take advantage of the situation. You were able to keep Olivia silent about the mayor by feeding her guilt about the crime. And you let Landon take the fall. Good grief, did none of that ever bother you?"

His face scrunched up with anger. "Landon. Knew."

Hannah and Mason both froze and stared at him.

"It's true," Olivia whispered. "I told him, in jail, what I'd done. I said I'd confess and get him out, but…" She blinked, and a look of dawning crossed her face. "But Wyatt convinced both of us it would work out. The evidence would prove Landon didn't do it. If I just stayed quiet, he'd get off and I wouldn't get into trouble." She lifted the gun ever so slightly, aiming it at Wyatt's head. "You killed her and let me think I'd killed her. And then you let Landon die."

He whipped his pistol around to point at her, his face contorted in rage. "I could have killed both of you that day, you and Mandy, to keep the mayor's secret. But I didn't. I protected you, and kept protecting you, all these years."

"You used me," she yelled. "To cover your crimes. And you let Landon die."

"No. You did. Just who do you think killed him in prison? Your lover, that's who. The mayor was worried that Landon's appeals against his conviction would reveal the truth about his relationship with you. Landon's death is your fault. Not mine."

She let out a keening moan. But she kept the gun trained on him.

"Stop it, Wyatt," Mason ordered, his face red with

anger. "How dare you try to pin any of this on Olivia. She was a kid, fifteen. The mayor wasn't her lover. He was her rapist. If the truth had come out, he'd have been convicted of statutory rape and you would have gone to prison for the illegal schemes and money laundering you both did together."

Olivia's eyes widened. "Money laundering? I don't understand. Wyatt? What did you do?"

Wyatt swore and narrowed his eyes at her.

Hannah was finally able to grab Landon's gun. But she didn't raise it. Her angle was all wrong. The only person she could clearly hit from where she sat was Olivia. Not Wyatt. She kept it down on the floor and pressed it against Mason's leg. He shifted again and slowly sat down.

Wyatt glanced at him. "Don't move."

"Just sitting."

Wyatt frowned.

"Drop your gun, Wyatt," Olivia ordered again. "You have to pay for your sins. Mason's going to arrest you."

"Arrest me?" He laughed. "He's not even a cop anymore."

She frowned.

Wyatt centered his gun on Olivia's chest. "You made me do this."

Bam! Bam!

Olivia's eyes widened in shock. The gun dropped from her fingertips as she stared at Wyatt.

Wyatt frowned in confusion as he watched her, obviously looking for blood. But there wasn't any. He blinked, then blinked again. He staggered forward, then looked down at his chest where a red wet stain was slowly spreading across his shirt. He turned his head toward Mason, and only then noticed Landon's still-smoking pistol in his hand. The gun he'd scooped up just as Wyatt was about to shoot Olivia.

Wyatt slowly crumpled to the floor.

Chapter Twenty-One

Hannah clasped her arms around her waist as she sat on her front porch steps beside Mason nearly two weeks later. It was the only way she could keep herself from reaching for him. After all, it would only cause her more heartbreak. Because there was no way he was staying here now, not after Wyatt's death and he'd had Olivia temporarily committed to a mental hospital. And there was certainly no way *she* was leaving *her* family. They were two people who deeply cared about each other, but could never be together. Sometimes life really sucked.

His rental car was a few yards away, packed and ready. He'd stopped to give her an update on the case and to say goodbye on his way to the airport.

"How's Olivia holding up?" she asked.

"She's having a tough time. It'll take a while to beat the addiction to the drugs Wyatt was feeding her." He shook his head. "I still can't believe none of us realized he was doping her all this time, rehashing his mythical version of Mandy's murder, reinforcing her guilt so she wouldn't think about what really happened that night and out him as the killer. If she hadn't gone into withdrawal after Wyatt's death when her pills ran out, we might never have known she was addicted to drugs. We might never have figured out the truth."

"Well you're helping her now. Fighting your parents in

court yesterday to get guardianship over her so she could get the treatment she needs had to be incredibly hard. But now Olivia will have a chance at a real future. You really are her hero. You're giving her back her life."

"Tell that to my parents. As far as they're concerned, the hearing was one more nail in my coffin. Especially after Wyatt's death."

"They should be thanking you for saving their daughter instead of blaming you."

He pressed his cheek against the top of her head. "You're a good friend, Hannah Cantrell."

The word *friend* had her wincing. Luckily, he couldn't see her face right now.

"I got a call from Knoll a little while ago."

"Uh-oh. Why would the district attorney call you?"

"Don't sound so worried. It was about the DNA testing. My bluff about them finding DNA in Audrey's case turned out to be fact. They found touch DNA on Audrey's forehead. It matched Wyatt."

"Wait. Are you saying he's the one who was at her house when she was shot? He kissed her, then what? Convinced her to kill herself?"

"We may never know the full truth. But he was lying about the money laundering being in the past. He was still into all kinds of illegal activities around here. But he left enough in his journals at home to tie a lot of the loose ends together. I got to read some of the more enlightening entries. Like that he'd found out about my crime scene expert and the theory about a shooter being in Mandy's kitchen. He knew I would never stop. So he decided to use Audrey as his pawn, knowing how vulnerable she was at the end, with her illness. He's the one who put her up to the Gatlinburg visit, the abduction. He'd planned on framing me for her murder. It was all part of his plan to stop me once and for all. If he'd just killed me, shot me from a distance, he'd probably have gotten away with everything. But he wanted me to suffer. He wanted me humiliated. He'd planned to have me killed while in jail. If you hadn't helped me escape at the station, I'd definitely be dead right now. Thank you."

"You're very welcome. Did his journal say anything about how Audrey died? How he got her to do it?"

"Unfortunately, no. But the ME said she had high levels of painkillers in her system. Much higher than the recommended dose. It's likely that Wyatt had something to do with that, then somehow tricked her to pull the trigger."

"How sad."

"Very. She didn't deserve that." He was silent for a few minutes. "Something else Knoll told me. He got the final DNA comparisons back on Mandy DuBois's clothing from the lab I hired. It corroborated the story Olivia and Wyatt told. It was Olivia's blood, likely from the nosebleed Mandy caused when she punched her."

"It's a shame the clothes weren't tested when Landon was arrested."

"Actually, given the conspiracy in place, the results would have likely disappeared and wouldn't have made a difference in his trial. But at least having them now helps paint the full picture of what actually happened. Knoll said her family is deeply appreciative that we figured out who the killer was. They never believed Landon did it. Now they have some closure."

"Everywhere you go, people are better because of it."

He looked down at her. "I can name dozens of people who wouldn't agree with that sentiment."

"I can name dozens who would. And *my* dozens aren't families of criminals involved in corruption."

He laughed, then gently disentangled his arm from hers. "I'd better go. My team's probably at the airport getting antsy to get home to their loved ones. Private plane or not, they have a schedule to keep."

He jogged down the steps, then turned to look up at her. He opened his mouth several times to say something else, then seemed to think better of it. He finally just smiled and walked away. He'd left her, again. And this time, he wasn't coming back.

Chapter Twenty-Two

Mason pitched his phone onto his kitchen counter. Calling his parents had been a mistake, one he'd never make again. Even a month after Wyatt's death, they weren't willing to forgive him. The fact that Wyatt had hurt their daughter and caused the death of their oldest son, and that Mason had shot Wyatt to save Olivia's life, didn't seem to matter. There was too much water under the bridge. And there was no forgiveness in their hearts for their one remaining son. They continued to blame him for every bad thing that had happened.

He picked up the shot glass full of whiskey he'd just poured. It would be his first since leaving Beauchamp. But he sincerely doubted it would be his last. After all, he had an anniversary to mourn. It had been exactly one month since he lost the woman he'd realized far too late meant more to him than drawing his next breath.

He tossed the shot back, then crossed to the glass doors that opened onto his backyard. Only it wasn't really *his* yard today. It belonged to his team. As he did every holiday, he celebrated with them and their families one day early so he didn't interfere with their private gatherings. Thanksgiving was no different.

There were all kinds of games set up outside, from archery to cornhole, to a rowdy game of poker on the back deck. But with the sun going down, everyone was settling into chairs that had been arranged in a huge circle around the roaring firepit—much like the firepit back in Beauchamp. Only instead of talking about a murder investigation, they'd carry on the tradition of talking about what each of them was thankful for this year.

"You gonna stay in here the rest of the day and get drunk?"

Mason turned to see Bryson leaning against the kitchen island, arms crossed.

"Sounds like a good idea."

"It sounded like a good idea to me too, after being shot and relegated to a wheelchair. I'd probably still be in that chair if you hadn't refused to let me give up. You gave me hope again, the will to rejoin the world rather than spend the rest of my days sick and alone and feeling sorry for myself."

Mason turned back to the glass doors. "Our situations are different. Besides, Teagan is the one who gave you hope. I can't take that credit."

Bryson stopped beside him. "You're the reason I met Teagan, so it's basically the same. And your situation doesn't seem all that different to me. I'd given up. You've given up." He reached past Mason and slid open one of the glass doors, then paused. "I don't know whether or not you realize it, but Hannah looks at you the same way Teagan looks at me. Like she's discovered the missing half of her soul. That's rare, a precious gift to be treasured and cherished, not tossed aside when things get complicated. It all boils down to one question. Is she worth fighting for? If the answer is yes, then what the hell are you still doing here?" He left Mason standing there and joined the others around the fire pit.

Mason stared out the back door, Bryson's parting words replaying through his mind.

Is she worth fighting for?

He closed his eyes, remembering.

Hannah, sitting at her father's desk when Mason locked himself in the office at the police station while trying to escape. She was beautiful and poised, charming him with her saucy *Well, this is awkward* comment. Then later, surprising him when he found out she'd been pointing a gun at him beneath the desk. She was so brave, smart, unexpected. And such a warrior, never relenting in her fight to prove his innocence. Willing to sacrifice her own future to fight for what she felt was right.

Another memory. Hannah, throwing her expensive phone out the window without hesitation to keep the police from tracking their location.

Hannah, mowing down small trees and practically destroying her SUV without thinking twice about it just because she wanted to protect him.

Hannah, at the cottage, tears streaming down her face, telling him she was already half in love with him, and afraid that she wouldn't survive if she fell the rest of the way and he left her.

He braced himself against the doorframe, looking past the tables overflowing with food, the bows and arrows scattered in the grass, beanbags lying on the cornhole board—the trappings of people who cared deeply about one another, a family by choice if not by blood. He treasured each and every one of them. And yet he felt empty inside.

Is she worth fighting for?

He swore and grabbed a set of keys from a peg beside the door. Then he headed outside. When he reached the circle around the firepit, instead of taking the last remaining seat, he stopped in front of Bryson's chair. Everyone fell silent. Mason tossed the ring of keys to Bryson.

"What are these?"

"House keys. I need you to lock up after everyone leaves."

Bryson arched a brow. "Any particular reason?"

"You asked me a question earlier. The answer is *yes*, she's worth it." Mason glanced around the circle. "Happy Thanksgiving, everyone. If you'll excuse me, I have a plane to catch. Looks like I might be eating mudbugs for Thanksgiving."

The team cheered as he jogged toward the house.

Chapter Twenty-Three

"You're his *family*," Hannah snarled into the phone to Mason's father as she paced in the side yard past her parents' garage. "It's Thanksgiving, for crying out loud. Did it even occur to you to invite Mason? Does it bother you to think about your son in Gatlinburg, without any family, while you stuff your faces on food his money probably bought? You've banished him from your lives. Why? Because you care about what some silly neighbors think? Or that the family of one of the corrupt jerks he helped put in prison throws a few rolls of toilet paper on your house? Seriously? Do you realize how petty that sounds?"

"Now look here, young lady," he said.

"No, Mr. Ford. You look here. Mason is one of the most honest, decent men I've ever known. He has more integrity in one pinkie than your whole family combined. I asked you to call him, to try to repair some of the damage you've done over the years. To let the one son that you have left know he's worthy of your love, and that you're sorry. But you know what? Forget it. You don't deserve the wonderful son God gifted you with. Because you're too selfish and blind to even know what you threw away. Well, I'm not. I know what I lost. I just pray it's not too late to tell him I love him. He deserves to know there's at least one person in this world who truly, deeply cares about him."

She ended the call and shoved her phone in her pocket.

When she turned around to go back inside, she froze in shock. A very tall, extremely handsome man in a navy blue suit stood just a few feet away, his warm brown eyes locked on her.

"M-Mason?"

"Hello, Hannah. Were you talking to my family?"

Her face flushed hot with mortification. "Your father, actually. I'm so sorry. I swear I didn't plan on berating him or your family. But when I asked him to wish you a Happy Thanksgiving, and found out they weren't even talking to you anymore, I just lost it. I couldn't—"

"Don't apologize." He stepped close, making her belly do crazy things as she stared up at him. "I've made excuses for my family for so long that I couldn't even see them for who they really are. But my eyes are wide open now. Thanks to you. I'm moving on."

"Moving on?" Afraid to hope, she simply waited.

He threaded his fingers through hers. "I owe you an apology. You offered me your love, and I couldn't see past my bitterness and hatred of this place to accept that miraculous gift. It didn't take me long to realize the mistake I'd made. But it took me far too long to try to make things right."

"Mason, I—"

He pulled a phone out of his pocket. "I meant to give you this before I left and forgot."

She took the phone, her stomach dropping in disappointment. "You came here, on Thanksgiving Day, to replace my phone?"

"Well, that wasn't the only reason."

Hope flared inside her. But instead of kissing her or professing his love like she desperately wanted, he tugged her past the end of the garage, then motioned toward the driveway. Confused, she looked at the collection of cars belonging to her parents and sisters. But there was another car now. A shiny new blue Tucson with a big red bow on top.

She pressed her hand to her chest. "You didn't!"

"I did." He handed her a metal key ring with a fob attached. "It has all the goodies, just like you asked."

She shook her head, frantically holding the key fob out to him. "Mason, no. I was joking when I said you could buy me a new car. I never wanted your money."

He ignored the key. "Well you'll have to take my money anyway. It comes with me. Because I want you. Yesterday. Today. Tomorrow. In my life, with me. Always." He pressed a tender kiss against her lips. "I'm not asking you to marry me. Not yet. I'm thinking I'll take you on a few dates first." He winked, which had her whole body flushing with heat.

"I'm going to court you, Hannah Cantrell. I'm going to turn on the charm and wear you down until you can't live without me. Then I'll get on bended knee and pop the question. Consider yourself forewarned."

"Mason—"

"I was a fool to expect you to give up your family, your home. I realize that now. We can live here, in Beauchamp. I could buy the Fontenot estate, if you want. Or a town house in the historic district. Or we can build something brand-new. All that matters is that we're together."

"You…you would do that? Move here, to a place you hate? Just so you can be with me?"

"If that's what it takes to make you mine, I'll do that, and more. I'm in love with you, have been probably from the moment you pointed Wesley at me in your father's office. But until you taught me what real love was, I didn't recognize it. Now I do. Whatever you want, name it. If it's within my power, I'll make it yours. All I ask in return is that you give me a chance to show you that we really can have a future together."

She burst into tears.

His face fell. "Hannah?"

"Happy tears," she gasped between sobs. "Really happy tears."

His expression turned hopeful. "Then I'm not totally crazy here? To think we can make this work?"

She wiped her eyes, smearing makeup on her fingers. "After everything you've been through in this town, you're willing to stay here, for me…" She struggled for words. "You don't need to move back here, Mason. I'm willing to move to Gatlinburg."

He frowned. "That's not fair to you. What about your family?"

"Sarah and Mary have their own families in other towns. And my parents, as soon as Dad's fully recovered, are going on a whirlwind RV tour to work on their bucket list. There's nothing here for me anymore. But even if there was, I'd still be willing to move somewhere else. You aren't the only one who realized what a mistake they'd made over the past month. Being without you has been agony. I don't want to let one more day pass without you in my life. And you sure don't have to court me, although I think the idea is exquisitely romantic. I'm ready for that question, Mason. Ask me."

"I don't have a ring."

She tossed the metal key ring with the fob to him. "Yes. You do."

He threw his head back, laughing with such a joyful sound it brought more tears to her eyes. Still chuckling, he dropped to one knee on the driveway and held the key ring up in the air. "Hannah Cantrell. Will you please do me the honor of being my wife?"

"Yes! Yes! Yes!" She held out her left hand, grinning as he slid the key ring onto her finger.

He swooped her up against his chest and spun around in a circle, both of them laughing.

The sound of a door banging open and excited shrieking was their only warning before they were surrounded by the entire Landry clan, including two toddlers and a pair of barking retrievers.

Mason carefully set Hannah on her feet. The look of bewilderment and wariness on his face as he eyed her clapping, laughing, smiling parents, sisters, brothers-in-law, niece and nephew nearly broke her heart. He'd been treated so badly by his own family that he didn't seem to recognize the love and acceptance on each and every one of her family members' faces.

Her father, leaning on a cane, held out his hand. "Welcome to the family, son."

Mason's eyes widened. His Adam's apple bobbed in his throat before he took the offered hand and shook it. "Thank you, sir."

"Call me Dad," her father corrected.

He stared at him a long moment, as if struggling to speak. "Dad." His voice was raw and gritty.

Her mother shoved between them and slid her arms around Mason's waist. He hesitated, obviously not sure what to do.

"Hug me, son," her mother ordered. "The Landrys are huggers. And you're one of us now. You'll have to learn to hug every time we come to visit or go home. Heck, sometimes just because we enter a room."

He blinked several times, and Hannah realized he was fighting back tears. He put his arms around her mother, his breath coming out in a ragged exhale as he rested his cheek on the top of her head.

When he finally let go, her mother stepped back, her own eyes wet with tears. She cleared her throat, then motioned to the others. "Come on, everybody. The food's getting cold. Hannah, bring your young man inside, and let's get this holiday started."

"Yes, ma'am." Hannah held out her hand toward Mason as the rest of them hurried into the house. "Happy Thanksgiving, Mason."

He took her hand, his eyes full of wonder, no longer shadowed by the past. "Happy Thanksgiving, Hannah, my love. Now quit dawdling. Our family's waiting for us." He squeezed her hand and winked, his smile growing even brighter as they went into the house.

* * * * *

COMING SOON!

We really hope you enjoyed reading this book.
If you're looking for more romance, be sure to
head to the shops when new books are
available on

Thursday 10th June

To see which titles are coming soon, please visit
millsandboon.co.uk/nextmonth

LET'S TALK
Romance

For exclusive extracts, competitions
and special offers, find us online:

f facebook.com/millsandboon

🐦 @MillsandBoon

📷 @MillsandBoonUK

Get in touch on 01413 063232

For all the latest titles coming soon, visit

millsandboon.co.uk/nextmonth

MILLS & BOON

THE HEART OF ROMANCE

A ROMANCE FOR EVERY READER

MODERN — Prepare to be swept off your feet by sophisticated, sexy and seductive heroes, in some of the world's most glamourous and romantic locations, where power and passion collide.

HISTORICAL — Escape with historical heroes from time gone by. Whether your passion is for wicked Regency Rakes, muscled Vikings or rugged Highlanders, awaken the romance of the past.

MEDICAL — Set your pulse racing with dedicated, delectable doctors in the high-pressure world of medicine, where emotions run high and passion, comfort and love are the best medicine.

True Love — Celebrate true love with tender stories of heartfelt romance, from the rush of falling in love to the joy a new baby can bring, and a focus on the emotional heart of a relationship.

Desire — Indulge in secrets and scandal, intense drama and plenty of sizzling hot action with powerful and passionate heroes who have it all: wealth, status, good looks…everything but the right woman.

HEROES — Experience all the excitement of a gripping thriller, with an intense romance at its heart. Resourceful, true-to-life women and strong, fearless men face danger and desire - a killer combination!

To see which titles are coming soon, please visit

millsandboon.co.uk/nextmonth

MILLS & BOON
MEDICAL
Pulse-Racing Passion

Set your pulse racing with dedicated,
delectable doctors in the high-pressure
world of medicine, where emotions run
high and passion, comfort and love are the
best medicine.

Eight Medical stories published every month, find them all at

millsandboon.co.uk

MILLS & BOON
Desire

Indulge in secrets and scandal, intense drama and plenty of sizzling hot action with powerful and passionate heroes who have it all: wealth, status, good looks... everything but the right woman.